Douglas Ratner's work in healthcare transformation, *The Wealth from Health® Playbook: The Dramatic Path Forward in Healthcare Spawned by the Covid-19 Pandemic* was published in April, 2021. His Wealth from *Health Playbook* has garnered; The 2015 Gage Award from the America's Essential Hospitals, Hearst Health Award 2016, and The New Jersey Health Hero Award 2017.

Ratner is a retired New Jersey physician and Chair of Medicine at Jersey City Medical Center-RWJBarnabas Health (JCMC). He overlooks hospitals and enjoys life with his grandchildren, Salem and Mirah, his children, Jess and Dave, and his wonderful wife, Linda.

Dedicated to my wife, Linda, who, for 38 years, has been beside me during difficult and rewarding times, while serving as the anchor for our wonderful family.

Douglas Ratner MD

MARCHETTI'S INFERNO

AUSTIN MACAULEY PUBLISHERS™

LONDON • CAMBRIDGE • NEW YORK • SHARJAH

Ordering Information
Quantity sales: Special discounts are available on quantity purchases by corporations, associations, and others. For details, contact the publisher at the address below.

Publisher's Cataloging-in-Publication data
Ratner MD, Douglas
Marchetti's Inferno

ISBN 9781685628055 (Paperback)
ISBN 9781685628062 (ePub e-book)

Library of Congress Control Number: 2022922296

www.austinmacauley.com/us

First Published 2023
Austin Macauley Publishers LLC
40 Wall Street, 33rd Floor, Suite 3302
New York, NY 10005
USA

mail-usa@austinmacauley.com
+1 (646) 5125767

Many thanks to Karen Venable, Jill Welsh, and Vicki Hessel Werkley for their creative and meticulous developmental editing on this work.

I would also like to thank Susan Walsh, MD, whose abilities are only dwarfed by her modesty; and my esteemed assistant, Julie Zisa, who truly understands the meaning of deciphering a doctor's handwriting.

Lastly, to my wife and best friend, Linda, and to my beloved children, Jess and Dave, daughter-in-law, Krystal, and precious grandchildren, Salem and Mirah.

Table of Contents

Prologue

Dan Marchetti sat motionless in the bleakly lit courtroom while he watched his portly attorney raise another point of order. He squeezed his eyes shut, the voices now only a buzzing in his ears. He recalled the thunder of applause in his proudest moment: accepting his diploma as part of the graduating class of 2018 at Tufts Medical School. Hearing those words, 'Dr. Dante Michael Marchetti', he'd stood on the stage, clutching his parchment as the traditional academic hood, green for the field of medicine, was draped across his chest and over his shoulders…

"The Commonwealth of Pennsylvania," a booming voice broke through the buzz, "versus Dante Michael Marchetti."

Dan's eyes snapped open, as if surprised to see a courtroom instead of that distant auditorium. How was it that just one year later, he was here, on trial, indicted for willfully murdering his patients? He was a doctor, not a danger; it was his job to save people's lives, damn it. How could anyone think otherwise—that he'd willfully kill patients?

"I'm innocent, God damn it to hell!" he screamed at the top of his lungs.

Chapter One

"Almost midnight already," Dante Marchetti said to himself as he stole a glance at his new watch and made tracks for the on-call room to catch a little nap while he could. Admiring the bright-yellow face, light-blue trim, and black Velcro wristband, he discovered he'd neglected to remove the $12.99 price tag from his Amazon special. He could feel his face redden as he peeled off the tiny sticker and tucked it into one pocket of the spanking-new white coat he wore over his scrubs.

At twenty-eight, he was three years older than many of his fellow interns. Following college, he'd spent a few years traveling Europe, working as a waiter and an English teacher while experiencing the cultures of Italy, France, and Switzerland. After several months, boredom set in, so he decided to do something about it. Crashing the study materials, he aced the MCATS and bang, got accepted into a few medical schools: a feat that surprised him more than others.

Running, sports, and close attention to his diet, had kept his six-foot-one frame lean and toned, but he'd never thought of the face he saw in a mirror as handsome. There was no mistaking his Italian heritage—when, at twelve, he'd lamented his Marchetti nose, his mom had suggested he "think of it as 'definitive'." But those genetics also bestowed an easy tan, dark-brown eyes, and curly hair. And through the years, more than one girl had commented on his 'endearing grin' and kind eyes.

After hanging his white coat on the rack above his cot in the on-call room, Dan noticed, for the first time, the spaghetti stain on one pants leg of his light-blue scrubs. "Come on, man, what kind of shit is this?" he muttered under his breath. He wondered how many people had seen it—patients, his superiors, other medical colleagues? Stains, price tags left in place, what a fuckin' disaster. What's next? A booger hanging from his nose? What had Dr. Hugh Ballard, revered Chairman of Medicine and the Director of the Residency

14

Program, noticed? How could patients trust a doctor to manage life and death if he couldn't keep spaghetti sauce off his trousers?

Glancing around, he took in the pale-green walls and mismatched chairs, the dog-eared medical journals heaped in one corner, and empty Styrofoam containers crowding the battered nightstand mixed with the smell of days-old sweat. Not only did he not look the part, he didn't feel the part, which was much more worrisome. Furthermore, the vagaries of scheduling had dropped him directly into the risk-fraught world of the coronary care unit (CCU) for his first rotation.

His thoughts touched on the epic poem *Inferno* by his namesake, Dante Alighieri. With a little chill, he remembered the end of the lengthy cautionary inscription over Dante's gates of hell, *"Lasciate ogne Speranza voi ch'intrate...*Abandon all hope, Ye who enter here." Coronary care would be intense; he needed to be ready for anything at any time. As his CCU attending, Dr. Glenn Covington had said earlier during orientation, "Chest pain can come at all hours and with every complication you've studied."

He punched the lumpy pillow and tried to get comfortable on the narrow and flimsy hospital cot. Interns certainly deserved better than this excuse for a bed. Though he was only three and a half hours into his first official twelve-hour overnight shift, he'd clocked in an additional four hours at the beginning of the day. He had come early to walk through morning rounds, thinking it would give him a head start on figuring out how the unit worked for his 8:00 p.m. to 8:00 a.m. shift. When the intern assigned to the 8:00 a.m. shift, Diane Werner, had a last-minute childcare emergency that kept her from reporting before noon, Dan offered to stay. After bolting a burger and coffee in the cafeteria, he spent the rest of the day getting the 'lay of the land', as his pop would say, acquainting himself with the facility, the people who kept it functioning, and the technologies he'd be using.

Dan had met Diane months ago when they interviewed on the same day. They'd maintained a friendly, professional email contact since then. As a Deerwood, PA local and former Deerwood Community Hospital (DCH) employee, she'd advised him on a number of decisions, including which apartment complex to choose in his new town. A decade and a half older than the other new interns, she was a nurse here before deciding to attend medical school and become a physician.

Lying back on the cot now with his eyes closed, Dan still couldn't switch his mind into rest mode. Instead, it offered a procession of new faces, and he tried to remember the names that went with them all.

Dan liked nearly everyone he'd met so far and was glad his first month was with Dr. Covington, who was not only a top heart man, but also shared Dan's passion for baseball. Though now sixty-five, in his early years Covington had spent three seasons as a minor league utility infielder. His body might be thicker and slower moving, but his clear blue eyes missed no detail, and Dan found that the man was quick to assess a newbie's knowledge and skills.

Theodore 'Teddy' Nash, Dan's very first patient, was the sixty-three-year-old owner of a legendary East Coast dinner theater. He'd been admitted the previous day when he sustained a heart attack after completing only two minutes of a treadmill stress test designed to determine if his arteries were blocked.

Before entering Nash's room on rounds this morning, Covington had brought Dan up to speed on the case: the patient's condition had proven resistant to all medications that could slow his speedy and abnormal heart rate. Dan could see that if Nash went south on them again, drastic action may be necessary to save him.

Inside the room, Covington scarcely had time to introduce Dr. Marchetti as his new intern when the expression changed on Nash's affable face, and he whispered, "Doc, my heart's racing again, an' I'm having a little trou…ble… uh breath…ing."

Dan glanced at the monitor: SVT at 180 a minute and blood pressure dropped to 78 systolic.

"What do you want to do, Dr. Marchetti?" As Covington's eyes alternately fixed on the monitor, his fingers found the man's carotid artery.

Dan looked to the older man, searching for clues in the unreadable face, and said, "Gotta get that heart rate down."

Covington nodded. "How?"

"Well, since none of the meds have worked to date… maybe a diving reflex?"

Covington made a go-ahead gesture. Dan turned to the nurse standing behind them, Cheryl Herrera. "Ice, please. Quickly." As she rushed out, Dan grabbed the empty basin on Nash's bedside table. "You hang in there. We'll get you fixed up right away." He moved past Covington and hurried to the bathroom to half-fill the basin with cold water from the tap. Cheryl appeared at his side with a clean pitcher filled with ice that she added to Dan's basin until he said, "Enough. Thanks."

When he returned to the patient, Dan focused entirely upon Nash. "Okay, Ted. I need you to sit up on the edge of the bed for me." Nash did so, staring at the basin with some trepidation as he struggled to breathe. "This won't be much fun, but I'll explain later." Dan set the sloshing basin carefully on Nash's lap, out on his knees, and instructed, "Hold this." When his own hands were free, Dan reassuringly placed one on the man's upper back. "Now, I need you to trust me, okay? I want you to take a really deep breath, then put your face as far into the water as you can, and hold it there until I tap you. Understand?"

After glancing at Covington, Nash nodded, his gray eyes wide and round. Clutching the sides of the basin, he drew as deep a breath as possible and thrust his head into the water, flinching as some splashed out on legs barely covered by the thin hospital gown.

Dan kept an eye on the yellow face of his watch as the seconds ticked away. Only thirty of them, but it must've seemed like an eternity to the patient. Dan tapped his shoulder, and Teddy emerged, gasping for air with his white hair plastered to his skull and ice water dripping down his neck. The ever-efficient Cheryl handed Nash a towel and took away the basin.

"Good God, Doc!" Teddy whooped as Dan took his wrist and confirmed what he saw on the monitor: the pulse had dropped from 180 to 82. "Now tell me why I had to do *that*!"

"We call it the diving reflex," Dan explained. "When you plunge into cold water—the colder the better—the body shuts down certain responses and your heart rate lowers. How are you feeling?"

Still mopping his head and neck, Nash considered. "Hey, I guess it worked, didn't it? My heart feels normal, and I can breathe again. Some trick! Will it last?"

Covington spoke then, moving back to the bedside. "Maybe. It may just take care of things; it's more of a restart—like rebooting your computer." His eyes twinkled as he included Dan in his smiling gaze. "Better take care of yourself, Teddy, and keep your heart quiet. Don't make me send Dr. Marchetti back in with another bucket of ice water."

Remembering that now, lying in the on-call room hours later, Dan chuckled. He'd also done alright with the other patients they'd seen. Tricky as the CCU could be, they hadn't lost one. Patient Raymond Lawlor had given them a bit of a scare, but he, too, had come around. Not bad for his first day at work and only his sixth day in Pennsylvania.

In fact, he'd arrived in Deerwood late the night before orientation, extending his Florida vacation until the last possible moment. Dan hadn't had time to see more of the town than when he'd first interviewed six months ago.

The idea of practicing in a community hospital appealed to him more than some university program, as he assumed universities would be more impersonal. Yet, he didn't feel he was giving up much for the small-town atmosphere he sought. DCH, with the bottom four of its ten floors nestled into the hillside of a scenic river valley, had a sophisticated flair and a solid reputation to match. For a suburban facility with just 300 beds, it boasted state-of-the-art medical technology thanks to generous donations from wealthy patrons, such as the Candlebury Foundation, and a renowned teaching faculty. Both drew Dan to the family friendly community close to Pittsburgh.

It seemed he had only closed his eyes for a minute when the phone rang from the nightstand by his head. He flailed an arm toward it, bashing against the brown Formica surface, much-abused by countless groggy interns over the years.

"Dr. Marchetti," he mumbled into the receiver.

"It's Cheryl."

"Oh, hi. Thought you went home."

"Split shift. Not sure whether I should bother Dr. Covington with this question. Dr. Clay and Alex are tied up with Millie Sorensen."

"The post-op surgical repair in Room 4?" Dan felt himself swimming back to the surface. "Do they need me?"

"No, it's Mr. Lawlor—the acute anterior-wall M.I. He seems to be throwing some couplets despite the lidocaine drip. But BP is good; he's pain-free; the pulse is 80 and regular; and except for the extra beats, he's basically resting comfortably."

"Okay, be right there." Dan hung up the phone, making the old nightstand wobble, a perfect mirror of his own shaky level of confidence. Eager and anxious to answer the call, Dan decided not to bother with his coat for what was likely a brief foray. But walking down the hall, he regretted the choice when he remembered the spaghetti stain on his scrubs. Casually placing a hand to hide the spot, he contemplated his next move with Mr. Lawlor.

Undoubtedly, if the couplets were as real and as frequent as described, he'd have to up the lidocaine. But what if that wasn't the best—or the only—remedy?

He reminded himself he had a backup. The night shift's senior resident in charge, Dr. Clay Lebeau—a lanky, soft-spoken thirty-year-old from Louisiana—radiated quiet confidence, which sealed the deal on his nickname, Big Easy. At 11:30 p.m., he'd urged Dan: "Go get some rest. It's all quiet for now; Alex and I can handle this." Alex Cole, the other new intern on nights, had appeared confident, perhaps even a little cocky, as he waved goodnight.

Pressing the metal wall plate that opened the doors, Dan stepped into the spacious CCU. Individual patient rooms were arranged in a semicircular pattern, facing a central telemetry console with a monitor for each room. It was eerily quiet save for occasional beeping sounds from IVs demanding attention. A spotless white writing surface formed the physician's desk with matching chairs placed conveniently in the center gave the area the look of a TV studio's control room.

The place was quiet for now, between scenes like a Broadway stage before the curtain rose. He approached the central telemetry station. Unlike a play, it wasn't starlets who sat at the console desk, but two middle-aged CCU nurses, their graying hair clipped short in nearly identical, no-nonsense styles, watching his entrance in silence. Dan knew most of these nurses had been working in the CCU for ten years or more and were quick to pass judgment on any of the interns. He saw one of them give the other a look that clearly said, "This guy probably doesn't know his ass from his elbow."

Dan resisted the urge to glance down; hoping to God his hand was still obscuring the spaghetti stain. Nodding to them, he asked pleasantly, "How is everyone tonight? Is Mr. Lawlor still in Bed 2?"

Faint smirks appeared on their faces. "Yes, Doctor," they said in unison. Dan tried not to look like a deer caught in the headlights and turned toward Room 2. He saw that Room 4 was also lighted; the door was open with the curtain was drawn. Apparently, Clay and Alex were still dealing with their post-op patient.

Dan walked into Lawlor's room. Cheryl was already there, laughing with the patient as she adjusted the leads attached to his chest beneath his hospital gown. She looked up and gave him a welcoming smile and said: "You remember Dr. Marchetti from this morning, don't you? He's one of Dr. Covington's interns this month."

"Sure. How are ya tonight?" Lawlor appeared a lot better now than he had earlier in the day. The color in his face was no longer ashen, but soft pink and healthy looking. His hair had been neatly combed, and the sweet smell of aftershave permeated the room. "Don't you guys ever sleep?"

"Yeah, sometimes, but I thought I'd check on you before turning in. Any chest pain?"

"Nah, I'm fine," he replied good-naturedly. "Don't know why I'm even here instead of home in my own bed."

"Well, Mr. Lawlor—"

"It's Ray, remember?"

"Okay, Ray." The spasm in his neck muscles waned; his patient seemed so improved and in such superb spirits, Dan felt reassured. No mistakes and no surprises with this one; Lawlor could just remain stable and recover from his ordeal. "As we discussed earlier, your EKG shows evidence of a possible heart attack," Dan told him, "and we're waiting on the blood chemistries to confirm it. We're looking for cardiac enzymes. If the heart muscle undergoes cell death, which occurs in a heart attack, then these enzymes are released into the bloodstream."

"But they took my blood a long time ago."

"Chemistries usually take a few hours. In any event, everything is stable now, and you should do just fine."

"That's great news. When can I go home? My boys are quite worried."

"We'll take you up to the telemetry floor in a bit, and eventually you'll go home. Then, you'll undergo cardiac rehab—"

Dan was interrupted by an alarm on the telemetry unit above Lawlor's head. It showed the irregular, wavy pattern all-too-familiar from textbooks: ventricular tachycardia. Lawlor's eyes rolled back in his head, and his color instantly changed to a dusky blue.

"Oh, shit!" Dan cried. "Call a code!" But the CCU nurses, having seen the lethal rhythm on the monitor at the telemetry console, were already pushing a crash cart into the room. Someone had hit the code button, and Dan heard the hospital P.A. system blaring repeatedly: "Code 99, CCU-2; Code 99, CCU-2; Code 99—"

Be cool, Dan, he coached himself, *think clearly.* First, they had to restore blood pressure to a normal and efficient heart rhythm. The concept was standard medical practice. This patient, however, was real: Dan's first at-bat since coming up from the minors of medical school. Unfortunately, Covington wasn't at his elbow to bail him out if he threw to the wrong base.

"Paddles set at 200 joules, please!" As Dan waited the few seconds it took to charge the defibrillators, the code team came barreling in. Senior residents Clay Lebeau and Alex Cole followed with an anesthesiologist and a respiratory therapist hot on their heels. Dan offered the paddles to his senior resident, but Clay shook his head. "know what to do."

The paddles were charged, and as Dan leaned against the side of the bed to apply them to the patient's sternum and left side, Cheryl warned—firmly but not loudly—"Clear!" Dan quickly broke contact with the bed. *Jesus, what an asshole I am.* He saw a knowing smirk on one of the older nurses as she left to keep an eye on the central telemetry console. The other one, who was assisting Cheryl, hid her own smile.

"Clear!" Dan repeated. The paddles in place, he pushed the button and was momentarily awed by the sight of Lawlor's flaccid body springing to life: arms and legs jutting into the air as if they belonged to a marionette. The monitor showed a transient return to normal heart rhythm, but within a few moments, it was back to v-tach.

"Charge!" Dan's voice was lower, more determined, and surprisingly strong "Come on, people." The anesthesiologist-pushed a tube into Lawlor's airway, and the respiratory therapist, Vinny something or other, attached an Ambu bag and started squeezing oxygen into the patient.

Twice more, Dan defibrillated Lawlor. "One amp sodium bi-carb...one amp calcium chloride... Also, let's get some pressors ready." Dan saw Clay nod approval and, working quickly and efficiently, Cheryl and the other nurse administered the medicines.

"Code 99, CCU-4," the P.A. system blared suddenly, "Code 99, CCU-4!"

"Crap!" Clay said. "That's our Miz Millie. You've got this, Dan, Vinny. C'mon, Alex; I'll need you." The anesthesiologist didn't have to be told and quickly followed the other two from the room.

Good God, I'm on my own after all. Certainly, he had great support staff who anticipated his every need and order, but he was the one who needed to save this guy. Minutes dragged by as Dan alternated chest compressions with the defibrillation. Fatigue crept into his body, threatening to sap him.

Flexing arms that felt like jelly, he started yet another round of compressions, he glanced up at the clock: ten to one. "How long have we been working on him?"

"Forty-two minutes," Cheryl answered rather mechanically. "Doc…"

If Lawlor could be resuscitated successfully, it would have occurred by now. Dan stopped pushing on the man's chest and said firmly, "Enough."

One simple word but with so much impact. Dan shook his head against the slide of his thoughts into confusion and absurdity. Looking at the other faces before him, he saw various reactions to the situation: some sadness and resignation but mostly detachment. His own eyes suddenly glazed over with tears. It was only then he realized that his senior resident, Clay Lebeau, was standing close behind him. Clay reached over to give Dan's shoulder a comforting squeeze. "Go ahead," he said softly. "Call it."

"Time of death, 12:54 a.m.," Dan intoned. "Could someone please get me the patient's home phone number?"

He'd met Mrs. Lawlor earlier in the day when her husband was admitted. She clearly adored him, as did their two teenage sons, one of whom had Down Syndrome. It was obvious the boy hadn't understood the significance of his father lying in the hospital bed. "Come home," he'd said "and play baseball with me." Who would explain this to him—and how?

"Dan? Here's the number."

He thanked Cheryl and took the slip of paper.

Clay gave Dan's shoulder another supportive touch. "I gotta get back to my patient. I left Alex holding down the fort."

"How's she doing?" Cheryl asked.

"We got her back, and she's stabilized for now." The nurse nodded and Clay headed to Room 4.

Dan was unable to avoid a tiny twinge of envy for Alex Cole's first-code experience as he made his way out to the physicians' desk.

The veteran nurse watching the monitors avoided his eyes but were no longer smirking. No one wanted to see the interns fail. Look foolish, sure, but not lose a patient, especially not his first time out on the floor.

Following the formality, Dan called the patient's local family doctor first and left word with her service of Lawlor's passing. Then he punched in Mrs.

Lawlor's number. As the phone rang, his mind escaped to the last few weeks of his vacation: the fun of letting go after graduation; his first surfing lesson; volleyball and running on the beach; getting laid in that little cabana with a woman he barely knew.

"Hello?" Mrs. Lawlor's tired and frightened voice sounded as if she'd been crying. "Is this about my husband?"

"Yes. This is Dr. Marchetti. I'm so sorry…" He heard a long gasp and the sound of the phone dropping. Then there was silence. "Hello? Mrs. Lawlor?" No answer, although he knew the line was still open.

He waited, uncertain of what to do; a few moments later, someone picked up the receiver and anxiously said, "Hello?"

"Mrs. Lawlor?"

"This is her sister. The news is bad, isn't it?"

"Yes, I'm sorry," Dan told her. "Mr. Lawlor has just passed away. I'm so sorry." Like a dark wave, despair overwhelmed him and roiled in the pit of his stomach. There were questions he'd been instructed to ask, but they seemed so brutal. He swallowed to keep nausea at bay. "Do you wish to view the body before we send it down to the morgue?" Thank God there was no need to ask her about an autopsy.

"Oh, I'm not sure. Let me talk to her; we'll call back in a few minutes. Thank you for all that you tried to do." A little sob escaped. "I can't believe this. He was smiling and laughing when we left him tonight. Those poor dear boys—" Her voice trailed off.

"Once again, I'm so sorry." Dan winced, hearing the same empty phrase come out of his mouth.

"Yes, thank you," she said in a barely audible voice, followed by a final click on the other end of the line.

It was done. Dan rushed to the nearest bathroom and lost his dinner. Shakily, he rinsed his mouth and splashed water on his face. Leaning against the edge of the sink, he stared at himself in the bathroom mirror. His brown eyes had never looked so lost. "I'm not cut out for this shit," he told himself.

Dan's eyes closed tiredly, and he rested them a minute longer, then ran one hand through his unruly dark hair, preparing for his return to the CCU.

Clay and Alex joined Dan there to inform him that Millie Sorensen seemed out of danger now. With the unit quiet again, Clay suggested one of the two interns take advantage of the on-call room.

"Should be Alex's turn," Dan mumbled, though he wanted nothing more than to get out of there for a while.

"No way!" Alex exclaimed, his naturally pale face flushed, his tea-brown eyes alight. "This is the most exciting night of my life! I couldn't sleep a wink right now."

You've got to be fuckin' kidding me, Dan thought to himself.

"Go on, then, Dan," Clay insisted, so he gratefully escaped.

He slipped into the on-call room and closed the door on the rest of the hospital, the rest of the world. Collapsing on the cot, he tried to close his eyes and sleep, but he couldn't bear the movie replaying in his mind. Dan's eyes snapped open and saw his white coat, the emblem of all his medical achievement, mocking him from its hook. He tried to distract himself by studying every other detail of his claustrophobic surroundings, but hot tears rushed into his eyes and throat.

His pager beeped, and set to Voice, it continued: "Dr. Marchetti, CCU— stat! Dr. Marchetti, CCU—stat!"

Stat—from the Latin *statim*—means without delay, immediately. Sighing, Dan hauled himself to his feet, on the way to his next challenge, or maybe just the next circle of hell?

Chapter Two

"P-E-E-P, PEEP, oh how I get such a kick out of putting those letters together."
Positive End Expiratory Pressure, PEEP, Vinny loved the acronym. So
innocent sounding but alas, not so innocent indeed. Yes, by increasing its
number after adjusting a dial on the ventilator, the patient's ability to put
oxygen in his or her blood oftentimes improve, though going too high can
make the patient crash as well. That point of diminishing return was different
for each patient. Vinny knew this as he was a licensed respiratory therapist and
nevertheless, he would experiment to see at what level of pressure a patient's
vital signs would begin to deteriorate. Only then would he return the pressure
to its previous value, a form of Russian Roulette if you will, a game of sorts.
Great fun. Like running up to the edge of a cliff and suddenly stopping!

With his right hand on the ventilator dial, Orlander turned his left shoulder
ever so slightly so that he could observe his critically ill patient as he fiddled
with his settings. A fixture at Deerwood for more years than he cared to
remember, his job was to manage the ventilator. "Going to increase the PEEP
and see what gives. Going for a world record... 15, then 20 and..." Suddenly
the patient's blood pressure began to dip precipitously, 80 systolic,
70...60...Enough. With a quick turn of the knob, the PEEP was back to 8 and
moments later, blood pressure rebounded to 130 systolic. *DeNiro and Walken
in the Deer Hunter had their Russian Roulette game, Orlander had his own.*

Suddenly, Vinny recalled the time he brought a stray cat home only to
discover a few weeks later that she was pregnant. The litter was huge, twelve
adorable kittens, one cuter than the next.

"Can't keep 'em, you inconsiderate boy." With that, his father grabbed the
sizeable cardboard box that housed them and walked swiftly into the bathroom,
slamming the door behind him for privacy. Vinny then put his ear to the wood,
fearing the worst. Filling the sink with water, the older man proceeded to hold
each defenseless critter underneath until they drowned. Ten minutes later, he

emerged from the bathroom, shoved the box of dead kittens into his son's tremulous arms and barked, "Now dig a hole in the backyard and bury them and don't you dare cry."

"Did I just hear the alarm go off dude?" asked Stephen, the nurse taking care of Mr. Calhoun and four other ICU severely ill individuals. "Just finished suctioning him, heart rate always goes up then, nothing to worry about. Got to go to my next patient, see ya."

"Ok, take care," replied the unsuspecting RN. Vinny exited the room but couldn't help contemplating the fact that a hospital was such a perfect setting to observe the frailty of life on display. Excellent for experimentation.

Chapter Three

Switching to eight-to-eight day shifts for the last two weeks of his CCU rotation, Dan found that his body clock still had trouble adjusting. His tired eyes focused on the charts he held, Dan made notes about his newest patient, Martin Siegel, a slightly built man in his seventies.

The man's voice sounded frail and a little baffled. "Dolly and I hadn't been volleying long when I got this awful chest pain, which I thought was just indigestion."

"I told you it wasn't my blintzes, Marty…that you should call the doctor." Dolly Siegel winked at Dan before turning her attention back to her husband. "But do you listen? No! You wait till you have to be brought in by an ambulance."

Marty Siegel's hand lifted in a gesture of surrender. "Enough Dolly, not here, not now."

Clay Lebeau's notes in the chart spelled it out: anterior wall MI with pulmonary edema, meaning a heart attack with fluid filling the lungs. Assisted by nurse Cheryl Herrera, Dan examined Siegel, whose tanned body showed surprisingly little fat. Even clad in the flimsy Johnny coat, he looked distinguished: his full head of silver hair was expensively cut and his nails perfectly manicured. A CEO, Dan surmised, or a senior partner in a TV legal series. Now with a blood pressure of only 70 systolic, Siegel appeared ready to star in his own CCU drama: to exit the stage left.

Meanwhile, Dolly maintained her one-sided banter, "I told you, Marty. It was too soon for tennis after such bad flu."

"Flu?" Dan interrupted. "There was nothing about that in the chart."

Dolly shrugged. "We didn't think of it. That was almost two weeks ago, and he recovered."

Dan shot a significant glance to Cheryl, and without a word needed she went to page Covington.

As Dan quickly finished up his exam and notes, Cheryl returned, escorting in the Siegels' son, Benjamin, a fifty-something replica of his father.

"How bad is it, Doctor?"

"Your dad's condition is very serious," Dan told him, "but I believe we've intervened in time. We're fairly certain he's had a heart attack—his blood work will confirm that—but there's also a possibility he's contracted viral myocarditis, an inflammation of the heart muscle due to his recent flu." Ben Siegel's shoulders suddenly sagged, his brown eyes wide and frightened. "We'll need to work on your dad fast without interruption. I'll make sure you're updated when there's any news."

Ben took his mother by the shoulders. "Come on, Mom. I'll be here with you. Kathy should arrive any minute," he said while nodding to Dan. Cheryl showed them toward the waiting room.

A moment after they were gone, Covington sailed in and clapped Dan on the shoulder. "Okay, what've we got?"

"He's going to need an aortic balloon pump and an inotrope."

"Let's get him up to the cath lab immediately. He looks like he is going to crump."

Within moments, Mr. Siegel was on the move.

Covington pulled Dan aside. Though his eyes remained kindly, his tone became more professorial. "Well, I expect you to read up on tachycardias, the acute coronary syndrome, and balloon pumps. By the next shift, you should be able to answer any question that I throw at you—from any source. No one leaves my rotation without becoming an expert in bedside interventions and diagnosis. It'll get easier as you gain experience. Correcting a mistake always takes much longer than avoiding it in the first place."

"Yes, thank you, sir," Dan managed to say in a voice barely louder than the sudden rumble of his stomach.

While Covington left to speak with the family, Dan quickly attended to a ham and Swiss on rye, chasing it with green tea that was now room temperature. He was just wiping his mouth after the last sip when Marty Siegel's son headed his way. Dan rose and moved around the counter. "What's up?"

"Our whole family's so very grateful for what you've—" His voice cracked with emotion.

Dan gripped the older man's arm supportively. "You're very welcome. That's what we're here for."

When Ben found his voice again, he told Dan, "Y'know, I know your family. My kids were coached by your dad all the way through high school."

Ben grabbed Dan's hand in a forceful shake. Dan returned the warmth of the handshake, thinking how much he needed to feel something positive right now. Despite everyone's best efforts, the CCU had lost several patients in the past three weeks, though Ray Lawlor still haunted him the most.

****

An hour later, as he finished the last of his paperwork, he saw fellow first-year Brian Callahan approach, and Dan lifted a hand in greeting. Though Brian stood about the same height as Dan, he appeared ganglier. Still, he was handsome enough that the female nurses and house staff had voted him "Hottest New Intern." Aside from the guy's first-class looks and his almost nonstop joking, Dan considered him one of the brightest of their group.

"Hey, if you're lookin' for something to do, I heard a bunch of nurses and interns are meeting at Casey's for TGIF." He wore what Dan had come to think of as his 'mock-mournful' expression.

"You sound really bummed, Bri."

Big sigh. "I'm Irish, remember. You wanna take this shift after all so I can go to Casey's?"

Dan chuckled. "Sure, sounds like a great swap—" He gave his friend a gentle punch to the shoulder, adding, "Not!"

"If you change your mind, you know where to find me."

Dan considered Brian's parting prescription for a pleasant Friday night: beer and burgers. He was presentable enough after changing out of his scrubs and into jeans and a wild patterned red-and-yellow T-shirt with the word *Florida* worked into the design.

Other than Diane Werner, he hadn't yet worked with the other two female first-year interns, but he immensely respected what he'd seen at orientation and from making rounds with them. Patty Yates had amazing focus and a warm smile but hadn't yet, as far as Dan knew, cracked a single joke. The exotic-looking Willow Blackstone was half Cherokee and half Chinese and had come from California. She wielded plenty of wit but with a tendency to be acerbic and a bit militant. Maybe she'd chill out and relax more after she'd been at DCH a while longer.

The sun was setting as Dan nodded to the security guard and walked out the front doors. The sky, deep blue now, held a slice of rainbow low at the horizon: a typically gorgeous summer evening in Pennsylvania. Filling his lungs with the freshly washed air and hearing occasional dogs barking and a lawnmower idling, Dan felt suddenly invigorated and turned toward the pub.

The first year intern could feel a tingling sensation as he passed 150-year-old clapboard houses nestled in the quiet cul-de-sacs, very similar to the home he grew up in. Near the hospital, several city blocks had been razed to build apartment complexes, the state-of-the-art in 1990. A few of them, including his, were reserved at a lower cost for hospital staff. Many of Deerwood's physicians and other professionals lived in Lake Harbor Homes, a gated community on the other side of Candlebury Lake where posh new condos snuggled around its golf course and boat docks.

Passing the high school ball fields on the way to the bar, Dan reflected on his own family who still lived in their upstate New York farmhouse. Having a high school coach for a father hadn't been easy, even with all the extra training and mentoring.

Dan smiled, remembering that when anyone accused Sal of being too tough on his boys, he'd just say he didn't believe in giving kids a swelled head. His mom, Gloria Marchetti, was equally traditional in her warm, compassionate nature. The foundation of the Marchetti spirit was the rallying point for all their dreams and aspirations—as well as for their heartache.

Dan stared at an empty ball field, nostalgic for the passing of the days when all his younger self needed to think about was baseball and girls. He pulled his thoughts from the past and hurried forward.

It was dark by the time he reached Casey's, but the place was bright and noisy inside. Leaning on the bar were four men in high-end suits and accessories who looked somewhat out of place. Laughter seemed to overpower the music of a lone guitarist doing his thing in the far corner. A strong smell of scotch wafted his way. Herrera from the CCU stood at the bar picking up a beer and a dish of peanuts. She greeted him as he walked in. When he thanked her for the ham and Swiss, she said, "Sure. Glad you got to actually eat it. Oh, been meaning to ask: is that apartment at Woodside working out okay?"

"Yeah. You won't see it in *American Home,* but it's all I need. And only two blocks from the hospital."

Dan caught sight of Alex at a table off to the right with Diane Werner, Willow Blackstone, and Dave Levine, all huddled around a huge pitcher of beer. Alex grinned at him, held up an empty mug and waggled it invitingly. Dan touched Cheryl's arm, almost apologetically. "I'm gonna go say hello. Catch you later?"

"Sure thing," the nurse answered as she pivoted on her way to rejoin her friends.

As he headed toward his own group, Dan saw Willow rise and move toward him and hike her shoulder bag to its customary position. "Leaving so soon?" Dan asked, hoping he didn't sound too disappointed.

She grimaced, and Dan liked to think he heard the regret in her voice when she said, "'Fraid so. I'm on duty tonight." She displayed her nearly empty bottle of mineral water to show she hadn't been drinking alcohol. "Besides, I'm not used to this." Wrinkling her nose, she gestured at the noisy atmosphere. "In California, it is much more mellow."

"Smart," Dan said, resisting a smile. He'd only known her three weeks, but he couldn't count the number of times she'd compared her new home in Pennsylvania to her life in California—always unfavorably. He gestured toward the gang and the beer. "Maybe another time?"

The grimace gave way to a lovely smile, and she tossed her waist-length, black-as-could-be hair over her unencumbered shoulder. "Hope so!" It sounded quite genuine, at least he hoped it was. "Bye!"

He watched her go, then turned back toward the table.

"Hey, what took ya so long, asshole?" Alex called, pouring a pint for Dan. Apparently, he'd already had a few. Dave, quiet as always, nodded a greeting.

"Yeah," Alex added in a voice just above loud-enough, "this is *Deer*wood." Sliding Dan's beer over in front of him, Alex winked, as if urging Dan to appreciate this witticism.

The younger intern lived down the hall from Dan, and the two had quickly struck up a friendship, hanging out together as often as schedules permitted. Alex liked to talk about himself, especially his academic triumphs in medical school. He had a right to be proud. He'd attended New York City schools as a child, skipping a couple of grades along the way, and completed medical school in a three-year program to arrive at his internship year at the advanced age of barely twenty-three. Did he really think that little wisp of a mustache, two shades lighter than his bristle-cut red hair, would make his pudgy face look older?

"Drink up!" Alex insisted and gestured toward the cluster of video game machines. "Then I'll whip your ass at Golden Tee." This was Alex's public face, a demeanor others viewed as arrogant, but Dan had come to believe there existed a rather sweet guy underneath it all.

"Okay. You're on."

At the moment, no one else was paying attention. Rick and Dave had started discussing, with enthusiasm, rumors that District Attorney Bradden could become a candidate for the state attorney general, and Diane was disagreeing with them both. Dan felt a world away from local politics; it simply didn't interest him.

"Damn," he said good-naturedly and drained his glass. "I better go practice."

"Fat lotta good it'll do ya. I hold the record on that machine." Alex refilled Dan's glass and took a big gulp before leaving the table.

It wasn't until he'd stationed himself at the golf-themed machine that he glanced over to the corner table where Cheryl had joined three other young women. He recognized another CCU nurse and raised his glass to them. They returned the gesture and the last two, whose backs were to him, turned to look in his direction.

One caught his attention. A stunner in a tight green T-shirt, body-hugging dark jeans, and a mane of wild copper hair. She raised her glass to him and pushed back her stool.

He nodded to her and grinned, hoping to appear casual. Suddenly, he detected a whiff of a sultry, mysterious fragrance just before a low voice said, "Oh, too bad!"

Turning toward her, he caught from the corner of his eye the multicolored shapes on the screen blinking out. *Game over.* "Just not my day," he muttered.

She laughed softly. "The night is young."

She sat down on a chair she pulled from the closest table. In this light, he could see her hair was actually a rich auburn and the eyes, a smoky green. Dan took a deep breath. "I'm Dan Marchetti. I—"

"I know all about you," she interrupted, still smiling. "Real name Dante. First-year intern; graduate of Tufts; single; in the CCU this month, ICU next." She laughed, "I'm Nikki. Nikki Saxon, an RN in pediatrics."

"Oh. Right. Have you worked long at DCH?"

"Five years."

"So whatta y'think of the place?"

"It's top-notch with a great peds unit."

"Pretty lame talking about work, huh?"

"Wanna get some air?"

"Absolutely."

Dan enjoyed the view as he followed her out into the night, mesmerized by how her reddish hair brushed her back, halfway down to that tiny waist.

Outside, they filled their lungs with the cooling summer air, but the smoke and raucous music trailed them out through the open door. "Let's walk," Nikki said and started off briskly in the direction of the town's park. Dan followed and fell into step beside her, wondering how to start a conversation that might help him feel less foolish.

When they could no longer hear Casey's, Nikki slowed the pace and studied-Dan for a long moment. "Maybe that's' a little presumptuous of me, but you look a little glum."

Dan regarded her with surprise. "Tough first rotation. I've lost a few patients, and I guess these past three weeks have just given me a reality check."

"You'll get used to the work," she assured him. "It's natural to feel bewildered at first. But you find ways to make sense of things. And you have to remember: you can't save them all."

Dan gave a helpless shrug.

"Some are going to die," she interrupted, "no matter what we do." They walked in silence for the next few minutes.

"You live close by, right?" Nikki asked suddenly. "We could go listen to some music. You have some mellow stuff, right? Not that loud garbage at Casey's."

Dan grinned. "Sure." God, what tunes did he have on hand? Mellow? Well, not Pearl Jam then.

Smiling up at him, she took his arm. Her closeness, her fragrance took away his breath and any powers of speech he might've had left. He pointed out his street, and they walked the long block to his apartment building in a silence

33

that felt both comfortable enough to enjoy the fresh evening air, and yet electric with anticipation.

"Dahn-tay," she repeated his name, savoring the word, and he loved the way her mouth moved saying it. "That's a pretty intriguing name, Dante Marchetti."

Dan wanted to quip something clever, but nothing squeezed out past the alcohol in his throat. With a languid smile, she set her glass on the faux-cherry end table and slid closer, still facing him on the edge of the sofa. Her hands, bare of any rings, pale and beautifully formed yet surprisingly strong, reached first to grip his forearms, then his shoulders and up around the back of his neck.

Nikki's kiss was so hungry it startled the both of them. *No need to tell him just then that she was married even though a sham of a marriage as it were.*

Chapter Four

"Girl-y!" said a sudden, hollow, nasally voice rolling through the aisles of the Deerwood Pet & Feed Center.

Linda Ferrante dropped her selected items into her shopping basket, laughed, and left the Aquarium Section, moving around the corner into the next aisle. She grinned up into the gigantic birdcage and greeted the store mascot, "Hey there, Mack!" Fluffing his almost impossibly dazzling plumage—red, green, blue, and yellow—a big scarlet macaw hopped down to a tree branch perch closer to her and reached out one gnarled, taloned foot to grip the bars separating them.

How great to have a place where she could partake of a little critter therapy, petting and playing with small animals of varied species. The Deerwood Pet & Feed Center provided only the scents of fresh grain, naturally clean animals, and well-kept habitats. Imagine being lucky enough to work with animals all day. A far cry from the defense-attorney life she currently lived in which everyone is "innocent." which she knew was a crock.

Not that law had been her first choice for a vocation. As if to remind her of this imperfect fit, she suddenly found herself unable to ignore how her shoes were pinching her toes at the end of a long day and, sometimes, a very long week. Those three-inch Audley heels flattered her legs, but were a killer for her feet. It seemed every article of her clothing had its own complaint; especially the red Hugo Boss silk blouse, a gift from her estranged husband, Mike, which had never quite fit right. But it was the best complement she'd found for the subtle pinstriped navy suit that was almost required of her to wear at the office.

At the store's front counter, Darlene was chatting amiably, perhaps even flirting a bit, with a customer who'd been standing there when Linda first came in. She could tell by his purchases, still waiting to be rung up, that he must be a serious freshwater fish keeper.

Glancing toward Linda, Darlene acknowledged she had another customer waiting and reached for the fellow's items, saying brightly, "I better get these things rung up for you, Vinny."

"Take your time. No rush to get home. Not as if I have a hot meal waiting for me."

Linda noted that he was attractive if you liked tall Nordic-looking guys with buzz cuts. She preferred a more Mediterranean look, something that echoed her own dark hair, brown eyes, and skin that always appeared perfectly tanned. He made a better match for Darlene, who was also blond and blue eyed. "Excuse me, I couldn't help noticing that you collect all kinds of lizards, frogs, and of course exotic fish whenever I see you here. Where do you put them all?" Linda asked curiously.

Vinny looked behind him, not yet understanding that he, Vinny Orlander, was the target of this attractive woman's inquiry. "I'm sorry. Were you talking to me?"

Linda chuckled. "Yes, yes I am. I see you here all the time. I'm a critter person too."

"Well, I have a rather large turnover you see. Hard to keep many of them alive, they seem to attack each other a lot." *He knew that this was a lie but how could he admit that he 'experiments' with them.*

"Oh," Linda responded. *Strange answer.*

Vinny took his leave with a polite nod to Linda. When the women were sure he was gone, Linda grinned at the pet store owner. "He's cute, Darlene…" She let it trail off with the hint of a question.

Darlene dimpled and blushed. "He's sweet…and a marvelous customer. Something sad about him though, he's a little off, I'm afraid."

"How do you mean?"

"I asked him once when he came in dressed in Deerwood Community Hospital scrubs, what he did there?" She hesitated.

"And? What did he say?"

"He brought people back from the brink, from the cliff's edge." Darlene just shook her head, recalling his strange reply. "That is all he said and then left."

Darlene's face suddenly brightened, quickly changing the subject.

"Some girl-pals of mine are taking me to the play tomorrow night—you know, *Wait Until Dark*? Would you like to come?"

36

A little stab of pain poked Linda's heart. Of course, she'd seen the posters all over town. Why did the local Candlelight Players have to choose that particular script for their big, midsummer performance? Not only had she landed its starring role in her senior class play, but some years later, she'd also chosen it for her own community theater directorial debut back in Boston.

"How nice," she murmured. "Sounds like fun. Too much paperwork though."

Outside Linda considered: how bad could it really be to watch a little theater performance of *Wait Until Dark?* Splendid memories or a painful reminder of more carefree days? She paused a moment longer—key in hand, gazing up across the car's roof—and lifted her face to the late-afternoon sun. *Bringing people back from the brink? The cliff's edge? Strange.*

Chapter Five

Alex Cole struggled not to sound annoyed. "What time did Ballard's secretary say he'd be rounding this week?" He and Dave Levine were just two of the interns milling around the hallway outside the ICU, waiting for the Chairman of Medicine to arrive. Alex watched Dan Marchetti rush in. He made eye contact, waved, and started toward them. Then Diane Werner distracted Dan, and he stopped to talk to her, apparently forgetting all about his other friends. Oblivious to it all, Dave still stared off into space with that look people get when they're reviewing details they've memorized.

Alex scowled. Was everyone going to ignore him today? "What time?" he repeated, more sharply.

Dave blinked at him as if coming back to the planet, though he seemed to have absorbed the question by osmosis. "Rounding? Secretary said 10:00 a.m. sharp."

Alex's watch read 10:10 a.m. He snorted. "Ballard's never been on time yet."

Dave shrugged, at the same time stifling a yawn and drumming his fingers on the chart he held, a classic sign of too little sleep and too much coffee. "It'll be worth the wait, no matter what time he shows."

Alex had to agree. The Chief dropped pearls all the time. He can be a little long-winded sometimes, but he seems to know everything.

As if on cue, the elevator doors opened and Dr. Hugh Ballard stepped out. It was hard to imagine a chairman looking any more distinguished. A tall, solidly built man, Ballard's thick hair was as snowy white as his impeccably pressed coat. Just above the Chairman of Medicine name badge, his lapel pin, commemorating his designation as a Master in the American College of Physicians, gleamed like a little golden sun. From his left-hand coat pocket protruded the earpieces of his prized Littman stethoscope, and his hand went there often in an unconsciously protective gesture.

Bright-blue eyes peered at them all from behind wire-rimmed glasses, and he beamed as if nothing could please him more than to see these fine interns before him.

"Good morning! We'll be a little short today." Ballard winked. "Important meeting, I'm afraid." He genuinely made it sound as if he'd much rather be there with them. Alex saw some of those gathered relax a little as if relieved. Well, Ballard *did* have a penchant for delving quite deeply into the history of medicine while exploring cases. Personally, Alex enjoyed that, but it prolonged rounds that'd already started late. But if Ballard noticed it, he never let on, and it certainly didn't dissuade him. "Where shall we begin?"

Alex made sure he spoke first. "Right here in ICU: Arthur Kresky." He got a little thrill when Ballard looked directly at him. A golden chance to impress.

"You're up, Alex?"

"That I am, sir, that I am." Ballard smiled and nodded to begin.

The group assembled attentively around their chairman; he was 'the Man' and everyone knew it.

Alex had pretty much memorized the chart and began with confidence. "Sixty-two-year-old white male presented twenty-four hours ago with chest pressure with an acute inferior wall myocardial infarction. He's Q-ed out in two, three and AVF, received thrombolytics, beta-blockers." Though he stared at some invisible point above Alex's head, Ballard listened carefully, nodding and scratching the side of his right cheek, a gesture familiar to all who had ever watched him concentrate. "Did well until this morning," Alex continued. "However, he became tachypneic, cyanotic; PO_2 in the forties on 100 percent rebreather, intubated; lungs clear; chest x-ray essentially normal; no left-ventricular failure nor brady arrythmias."

Ballard dropped his gaze, and Alex found those clear, blue eyes riveted directly on him, but the chief said nothing. Alex soldiered on, desperately trying to read Ballard's face for a sign of approval. "VQ scan was a low probability for a pulmonary embolus." Alex stopped talking and shrugged his shoulders. The case remained a mystery.

"What's his blood pressure doing, Alex?"

"Sir, BP dropped to eighty systolic during the night. The night shift presumed it was a right ventricular infarct with right-sided failure. Neck veins were distended. They gave normal saline, and the pressure came up."

Ballard just shook his head. "Let's go examine the patient." He turned abruptly and led the way into Arthur Kresky's room. A thin, balding man lay unconscious, his breathing supported by a ventilator. Alex stated that Kresky was a carpenter with a three-decades-long smoking habit. The only sounds in the room were those of shuffling feet as the house staff crowded in and of the rhythmic sounds of the machine breathing for the patient.

Ballard pulled his stethoscope from his pocket and engaged it, while placing his right hand on Kresky's chest wall. The residents studied their chief's every move, from how he listened to the patient's lungs to his examination of nail beds, for any clue, any key that would unlock the diagnostic box of unknowns. Why was this patient finding it impossible to oxygenate his blood? All the obvious causes had been ruled out.

Ballard removed his stethoscope and returned it to his left coat pocket, signaling that he'd made his diagnosis. "Can only be one thing, ladies and gentlemen."

He looked again to Alex, eyebrows slightly raised in question. Alex glanced away from that blue stare. At least all the other faces around him were as blank as his own.

"Any other thoughts to help Alex out?" Ballard slowly surveyed the group. "Dan?"

Dan stood at attention. "A shunt, sir?" Dan whispered in a barely audible voice.

"Speak up, son, some of my senses are fading rapidly."

"A shunt."

Ballard listened, expressionless. "What kind?"

"Right to left, sir."

"Why?"

"Reverse flow through. Some kind of septal defect." Dan paused a split second, and Alex could see something flicker across his friend's face as the last piece fell into place. "Patent foramen ovale, to be sure."

Ballard was smiling now, pleased as any teacher with a quick pupil. "What test will we need to confirm the diagnosis, group?"

"A 2-D echo, sir," Alex blurted, anxious to regain lost ground.

"Plain 2-D?"

"I suppose."

Dan offered, "We can do an agitated saline test right before we shoot the echo. If we are correct, the bubbles will be seen crossing the foramen."

Alex squeezed his hands till he felt the nails bite into his palms, struggling to keep his face blank as the chief's eyes scanned the group. "Good…"

Ballard's beeper signaled, and he checked out the message. "That's my meeting, ladies and gentlemen. We'll pick up again next week. Alex, go ahead and schedule the procedures Dan suggested for Mr. Kresky."

As he exited, Ballard gave Marchetti a playful pat on the shoulder, in clear view of the entire group. If that bothered anyone else, Alex couldn't tell; nobody let it show, but certainly, he couldn't be the only one feeling envious. "He's always showing us up," Alex muttered to Dave. "Always scoring points at our expense."

Again, that baffled look on Dave's face. "Who?"

"Marchetti, who else?"

Dave returned to his charting. "He's smart; can he help that?"

"Smart, my ass," Alex bristled. "Lucky, that's what he is, with the cunning of a fox. Wait till he screws up."

Dave gazed at him as if he'd said blood was green. "But isn't he a friend—your neighbor? Don't you guys hang out?"

Snorting, Alex gestured. "Sure. He's always up for some free wine or beer. He acts so nice with everyone."

Dave just stared at him, and then Alex realized Diane Werner was also within earshot. He saw the two of them exchange a glance. "You'll see," Alex predicted. "Everyone's got a dark side. Marchetti's no different." He slapped the counter with the file he was holding and began to march off, aware they were still staring after him with looks of wonderment on their faces—but all the while insisting to himself that he really didn't care what they thought.

****

That evening, back home in his apartment at Woodside, Alex Cole focused on the tasks he needed to take care of before finally turning in for the night: Brush teeth, rinse and store contact lenses, charge his phone.

He sank down on his couch across from the big-screen TV and Bose sound system, but he ignored all that fancy equipment. In fact, he rarely used any of it except when he had visitors, which almost always meant his hall neighbor

Dan Marchetti. He had bought it from a friend-of-a-friend back home in New York, at far below market value. Alex was pretty sure it was hot, but he tried not to think about that. It served his purpose: elevating the status of his humble digs, furnished very similarly to Marchetti's. Made it look like he had a little money though he could get a nicer apartment if he chose to. After all, he was going to be a successful doctor in a few years. Might as well start acting the part.

That's why he leased the BMW. It was only a couple of years old, but it was in great shape. He loved honking his horn if he passed you on the street, often taking time to show off all of its bells and whistles. Dan knew the truth. Alex had spilled the beans one night while they were drinking together.

"You could get something cheaper," Dan had pointed out in that annoying know-it-all way of his. *Everything was always so easy for Marchetti.*

Just one more thing to check before sleep: the latest test results for all the patients he was following. Though pretty certain he was up-to-date on them all, he knew he wouldn't sleep unless he reviewed them one more time. After all, he would be responsible for seventeen patients on his next shift: his six plus Marchetti's and five from Werner. All these patients and their entire stories were in the electronic medical record (EMR) system. Alex shook his head in bewilderment as he set his things aside, wondering how in the world did the old-timers like Ballard keep track of all this stuff back in their day.

When he fell into bed exhausted, sleep still eluded him, and he couldn't keep from reflecting on the day's events. Foremost in his mind was Ballard's face when Marchetti came up with that diagnosis. Just thinking about it made his chest feel heavy with frustration.

Why such professional jealousy? Alex asked himself over and over again. Psychologists often claim that jealousy in general erupts from a crisis in trust, either of others or of oneself. Was it *projection* on my part, perhaps my own fear of what would happen if Ballard looked at him as the 'Man' and the pressure that would place on him? Or *protection* in that it is warning him that perhaps he wasn't up to the responsibility of internship. Lastly, *competition.* Was he not simply competing for the same admiration given to others? *Think you bastard!* Alex slapped the side of his head with his open palm.

Maybe all three though the latter explanation hits home. Hadn't he always felt that his father favored his oldest brother despite the fact that he, Alex, had accomplished so much more scholastically while John languished in a low level job and no real future to speak of? Yet, Dad always found it easier joking and hanging with his older brother while his stiffness and serious nature seemed to put up a wall. Here, Ballard was in fact a 'father figure' of sorts or the closest thing to it. Alex punched his pillow and forced his eyes closed, pledging to himself that the next virtuoso diagnosis would belong to him. Who cares why he felt the way he did?

Chapter Six

Vinny followed Alex Cole from the room of a fifty-three-year-old female patient, newly admitted with pulmonary complications of recent surgery. Anticipating there would be orders, Vinny took out one of the small cards he carried in his lab coat pocket and poised his pen over it.

"She'll need an IMV of 12 and a total volume of 700," Dr. Cole told him.

"Got it," Vinny answered, noting the numbers. The cards were a big help in recalling salient points from patients' charts. He kept hoping Dr. Cole, or anyone would notice how efficient he was and how meticulous. But no luck so far, and it certainly wasn't going to happen anytime soon.

"Cellophane, Mr. Cellophane; you can look right through me and never know my name." Vinny sang to himself, pen still poised ready for any further notes. They'd reached the physicians' desk, and Dr. Cole had already scribbled a quick progress note and order into the patient's chart. However, the chart underneath seemed to grab his attention, and he flipped it open. Vinny craned his neck to read the name: Kresky, Arthur. No one he knew about.

"Damnedest thing I ever saw," Cole muttered under his breath as if he'd forgotten Vinny was even there.

"What was?"

"Huh?" Cole said distantly, still staring at Kresky's chart.

"What was the damnedest thing?" Vinny's jaw clenched as he did his best to keep a pleasant tone.

"Oh." Alex Cole blinked as if breaking free of a trance. "The agitated saline test."

"Come again?"

"My patient Kresky has a patent foramen ovale—a hole between his right atrium and his left atrium. It could've been there since birth, but it never closed on its own as it should have." Vinny nodded, encouraging the intern to keep talking, including him in this discussion of a case.

"Up till now," Cole continued, "it'd posed no problem. But his heart attack led to failure on the right side of his heart; the pressure increased; and the blood reversed flow from the right atrium to the left, bypassing the lungs." He looked again at the chart, studying the numbers.

"The test agitated something?"

"Oh, yeah! We put some small air bubbles into his IV line and, with help from the echocardiogram, we watched them cross the atrium through the hole. Neat trick; diagnosis made." Cole's face broke into a huge smile.

"That was your idea—to do that test?" Vinny asked, wanting to congratulate him.

Immediately, though, Alex Cole's smile vanished behind a dark scowl.

Vinny was quick to say, "Sorry if I…" It wasn't a career-enhancing move to offend a doctor, even a first-year intern.

"No, it wasn't me. It was from Dan. He seems to figure out everything."

Vinny watched the man catch himself, perhaps remembering, as Vinny did, one of the first bits of hospital lore you learn: If someone passes gas on the tenth floor, within an instant, everyone on the first floor will know about it.

"I would give anything to know as much as you do," Vinny offered quite sincerely.

Still staring at Kresky's chart, Alex murmured, "Sometimes no matter how much you know, it just isn't enough."

Suddenly Alex looked up and addressed the forlorn respiratory therapist. "Hey, Vinny. Couldn't help overhearing your conversation earlier with Marchetti. Seemed disinterested in what you had to say my friend," Alex noted rather matter-of-factly.

"I'm used to it from all the doctors, seriously." Vinny seemed annoyed and edgy.

"Not from me, you don't sense this quality in me, do ya?"

"Not so much I guess. What is your point, Dr. Cole?"

"Marchetti's a grandstander, likes to shine the light on himself, especially to the top of the food chain, if you get my point?" Alex stared directly at the respiratory therapist, making him somewhat ill at ease.

"What are you getting at?"

"We should knock him down a peg or two, don't you agree?"

"All right. How so?"

"Not sure yet, not sure. Will get back to you my friend. Soon." The two exchanged emails before going their separate ways.

Chapter Seven

Ducking out from the morning's drizzle and through DCH's main entrance vestibule, Dan paused as the inner doors whispered shut behind him. He brushed away at his now-sodden scrubs and muttered, "Didn't look like it was comin' down that much."

Dan caught sight of his watch. "I better scoot. Gotta get into some dry scrubs."

As soon as he'd changed, Dan joined the first-, second-, and third-year residents on duty for morning rounds with the intensive care unit (ICU) attending physician, Dr. Neal Driscoll. At barely thirty-five, Driscoll's youthfulness was refreshing. He seemed especially energetic this morning, and Dan caught Diane Werner's eye with a wink.

The ICU, much like the neighboring CCU, featured a central station of desks beneath monitors and surrounded by the individual rooms. Here, though, they were arranged with surgical patients on one side and medical on the other. All were designated 'reverse-isolation' rooms, meaning their filtration units prevented dangerous infections from contaminating other patient rooms through the air exchange system. Each could be sealed with a door in case of extreme susceptibility or contagion, but usually, only the curtain was drawn for privacy, allowing patients to feel more connected and the nurses to better monitor those in their care.

Dan had found the ICU as daunting an assignment as the CCU but with more variety; any ICU must be prepared to treat a vast array of complex illnesses, always serious and frequently grave. Patients with these life-threatening conditions required additional nursing care and a higher staffing ratio than any of the other departments.

Medical interns faced enormous responsibilities in the ICU. In the weeks Dan had been in the unit he'd decided the most important keys were to hone in on every detail and reevaluate constantly. The patients' medical condition, or conditions, were likely to change from moment to moment.

Dan joined Diane at the consoles, where she looked up with a tired smile. "Maybe today will be a light one. Only six beds right now, and look, everything's pretty calm."

He grinned. "Trying to jinx us?" He sat down in front of the computer and began checking for his patients' most recent lab values. "But I hope you're right. We could use an easy day for a change."

"Diane?" Dan glanced over from his computer screen. "What made you leave nursing to go to med school? And with three kids, no less." Working with her in ICU had only deepened the respect Dan felt for Diane.

She chuckled. "You mean, what was I thinking? I'm not sure, except that I'd gotten so bored." She shook her head, staring into the distance as if into the past. "Not with the work itself, but more with the limitations of my role. A rude awakening…"

Before she could explain her rueful sigh, Dan's beeper sounded, and he heard, "Dr. Marchetti, Radiology—stat!" He rose quickly as it repeated. Diane's nod showed she'd heard the message. He gave her an apologetic wave and hurried down three floors.

He found his emergency occurring at the CAT scan.

An unconscious woman lay on the floor not the table. Radiologist Dr. Paolo Lescani hovered over her, sweat dripping from his brow, as he rapidly cursed under his breath, *"Porca miseria, putana vaca…"* He was an older fellow, Italian-born, short, and a little pudgy. Dan had had some fun practicing his Italian with him and talking every and anything baseball. A nice guy, but now beads of perspiration dotted his forehead's deep lines showed just how long it had been since he had managed this crashed patient.

"What happened?" Dan called, striding toward the tableau. He made sure his voice sounded much calmer and more confident than he felt. He could see the woman was breathing shallowly. Short and plump and in her mid-sixties, she had a face surprisingly similar to that of his mother but much more sallow.

"I don't know!" Lescani answered. "She just collapsed while getting on the table." Dan bent over her, found a strong carotid pulse, caught a whiff of her perfume—weirdly the same one his mother wore.

Motioning to a nearby life-pack cart equipped with a defibrillator and other items for use in these such emergencies, Lescani asked in a panicky voice, "Whatta we do? Zap her? Start pumping?"

Dan shook his head. Even in English, Lescani's Italian accent was so pronounced and familiar that reflexively, before he was even aware of it, Dan slipped into the Italian he'd heard spoken so frequently at home and during his travels in Europe. *"Per che cosa bisogna questa CAT scan?"* he asked. Why did she need a CAT scan?

Lescani continued the conversation in Italian, which seemed to calm him, and Dan found it easy enough to translate: "For a neurological evaluation. She's had two fainting spells. Her physician's looking for evidence of a stroke... he believes those episodes represent TIAs."

Dan nodded. *"Va bene."*

The patient's wristband read "Damen, Sarah," and she was now regaining consciousness and breathing normally. Two orderlies arrived with a gurney along with the nursing code team, respiratory tech, and one of the second-year residents. "She's got a pulse. We should get her up to ICU," Dan directed. Studying her more closely, he noted a bluish tint to her lips that was nearly obscured by her heavy makeup, a result of her blood's poor oxygen content. Her eyes now open and wide with alarm, she grabbed for the nearest hand—Dan's.

As she was being helped up from the floor and onto the gurney, he gave her a reassuring smile. "Ms. Damen? You've fainted, and as a precaution, we're going to take you to the ICU, where we'll try to figure out why this happened. You're going to be just fine."

Sarah didn't let go of Dan's hand or take her eyes away from his face as they moved into the waiting elevator. By now, Dan had seen a lot of scared people, but he found this woman's terrified face especially unsettling. "What are you feeling right now?"

"Dread," she instantly replied. When the elevator doors opened, Dan saw the senior resident, Jacqueline Norris, flanked by Wyndolyn Hibbert, the best charge nurse on the floor.

Jackie grabbed the chart and moved away to study it. The nurse, an ample-figured Jamaican woman who always wore bright pink, took the patient's other hand and patted it. "I'm Nurse Wynnie, Miz Damen." Her voice, some fifteen years removed from its origin was still melodiously accented and retained her homeland *patois*. Dan had noticed she proved to be soothing and motherly for a number of her charges. "Gotta bed ah ready f'ya, now."

The patient, though, refused to look away from his face or release his hand. "I'll be right there," Dan assured her, and, with a final squeeze of her hand, he freed his own and let the orderly guide the gurney where Wynnie indicated. Continuing to talk softly to the frightened woman, they steered her to the waiting elevator for the ride to the ICU.

Dan and Jackie took the stairs two at a time rushing to beat the elevator. Jackie managed to study Sarah Damen's chart on the move. Arriving to the central ICU area, Dan peered over her shoulder. "What's it say?"

Despite the run up the stairs, Jackie looked as crisp as usual, her waist-length, walnut-brown hair pinned back from her face, falling like a shining curtain straight down her back. The only third-year female resident, Jackie also possessed a keen wit and wry sense of humor. She was one of only two members of the hospital staff who were openly gay. "Dr. Bruno thought she'd had TIAs."

"Which Dr. Bruno?" The Bruno sisters, Josephine and Melissa, were in practice together.

"Josephine." Jackie's eyes crinkled with amusement. "You know, the smart one."

As Dan nodded his agreement, Wynnie returned. "She ah tucked in."

They headed for Sarah Damen's room. Dan approached the patient smiling. "How're you doing?" He picked up her hand again and held it between his own.

"Much better now," she responded. Her face looked very tired. "It's been a strange two days. Nothing like this has ever happened to me."

"First time in the hospital?"

"Other than giving birth, yes." She paused, the worry deepening on her face. "Has anyone contacted my husband?"

Jackie introduced herself and said, "We've already called him. I told him you'd fainted again and were being brought to the ICU. He said he'd be here as soon as he could." Jackie referred to the chart again. "I see here that you just returned from a trip to Virginia?"

"Yes, we were visiting my sister. Ten-hour drive. We got home late and then went right to bed. The next day, my right leg was all swollen, and I was in a great deal of pain."

Dan immediately glanced at Jackie. Their eyes locked for a long moment, and he could tell she suspected the same problem: blood clots in the legs from sitting for so long. Quickly going through the physical exam, they found the unwelcomed evidence.

"I feel a cord," Jackie said quietly as she palpated Sarah Damen's right calf. Though Dan knew the cord, a large blood clot, was a very dangerous discovery, he reassured Mrs. Damen yet again, and the two physicians hastily left the room to confer.

"Those fainting episodes weren't TIAs," muttered Dan. "They were friggin' pulmonary emboli." Parts of the clot, an embolus, had broken loose and traveled through the bloodstream to the lungs, where they formed a blockage that severely limited oxygenated blood reaching the heart. There was precious little time to waste. For pulmonary emboli to cause fainting episodes, either they were very large, or there were many, many small ones. In either case, the next one could quickly make Ed Damen a widower.

When Dan looked at Jackie to see what she wanted to do, she tilted her head in a *Go ahead* gesture. He signaled to Wynnie Hibbert, who came right over to listen for Dan's directions: "Heparin aggressive protocol, please, stat!"

He looked back at Jackie, who nodded assent. Heparin was one possible therapy at that point. It wouldn't dissolve the clot that was already in the leg—undoubtedly the source of her pulmonary emboli—but it could help to organize it. By clumping the cells more tightly, the clot could stick to an artery wall so new clots were less likely to break free and travel to places where they'd be even more dangerous.

"Spiral CAT scan?" Dan suggested.

Jackie nodded again. "Call Lescani and tell him Ms. D. is on the way back down." She moved away to give instructions for transport.

By the time he'd contacted Lescani, Sarah Damen was back on the gurney, IV started, oxygen flowing through the nasal cannula from the tank tethered to the gurney, and on her way back down to radiology. As Dan headed back for the stairs, a ward clerk approached him with Sarah Damen's lab work.

"Thanks." Dan said as he took the lab work and scanned the blood-gas result. "Oh, crap." The percent of oxygen was in the 70s instead of the 90s. He didn't want to think about the family doctor's incorrect diagnosis. No point fixing blame. However, now there was much work to be done and quickly. He hurried down the stairs, knowing Dr. Lescani would welcome the company, and he'd get a quick read of the scan.

Dan expected to see a more tranquil scene than the last time he entered Radiology, but the view was eerily similar. As the table came sliding out of the doughnut-shaped device at the completion of the scan, Sarah Damen was turning blue, her eyes bulged, and her neck veins looked ready to explode. Dan rushed to her, and Dr. Lescani joined him, whispering, *"Dio mio, Dio mio."*

"She's wiped out her entire left lung!" reported a technician monitoring the equipment.

Dan yelled, "Call a code—now!" To Lescani he said, "She must've thrown another damn embolus." He ripped away the woman's hospital gown to expose her blue-tinted life-less body. He began chest compressions while Lescani grabbed an Ambu bag from the life pack. The diminutive radiologist started pumping air into her lungs at the appropriate times. Dan turned to the life-pack monitor and attached the wires to Mrs. Damen. The respiratory tech joined them, ready to help as needed.

"V-tach," Dan announced. "Paddles, please; charge 200 joules. Clear.!" *Zap.* Her arms and legs flew skyward, the eerie sight too familiar to Dan by now after his stint in the CCU. "Sinus rhythm; steady pulse," he said. "All right, let's get her upstairs—stat."

As the three men got her transferred to the gurney and covered again, the tech, Vinny Orlander, took the Ambu bag from Lescani, saying, "I'll get that now."

"Gladly, my friend." At that moment, he felt Sarah Damen's fingernails clutch his right thigh, literally holding on for dear life. Her eyes registered pure terror, and she batted away the Ambu bag with her other hand, letting out a piercing shriek that filled the small room.

Mother of God, think fast and get moving. Dan, Vinny and the harried orderly left a relieved Lescani in radiology and hurried the gurney and life-pack equipment down the hall toward the elevators.

Reaching the elevators, Dan dismissed the orderly, "We can take it from here."

"No room anyway," Vinny noted as the two men squeezed in next to the gurney and the doors slid closed.

"Relax, now," Vinny soothed as he fitted the Ambu bag's little mask back over the patient's nose and mouth. "Let me help you breathe, okay?"

At that moment, Sarah Damen's hand seized Dan's leg with the same intensity as before, her nails digging deep through the thin cloth of his scrubs. And then just like that she lost consciousness; her viselike grip fell away, and her hand was completely limp.

"Shit. In the elevator, goddammit! V-tach." Dan maneuvered into position the best he could in the cramped space and charged the paddles. He pulled away the hospital gown to reveal her blue chest with its burn-mark evidence of the earlier life-saving assault. "Clear!" He zapped her, but this time her vital signs did not bounce back. In fact, the wavering line of v-tach smoothed out to flatline.

"CPR!" Dan declared. There was simply no room to apply firm enough pressure so he jumped onto the gurney, his legs straddling the abdomen of his patient.

"This is surreal," Vinny murmured, staring mesmerized at the woman, even as he automatically worked the Ambu bag in concert with the compressions.

The elevator doors finally opened, and there was Jackie with two nurses who grabbed the gurney and hauled it from the elevator car, through the ICU doors, and back into the room the patient had occupied earlier. Dan balanced himself for the ride, continuing to pump Sarah Damen's chest. Vinny kept pace, still trying to fill the woman's lungs with oxygen. The entire ICU nursing staff, ward clerks, and all physicians on hand gathered around Ms. Damen's room as Jackie moved to the head of the bed, calling for and placing the endotracheal tube that would allow Vinny to keep pushing oxygen into her stiffening lungs.

After thirty minutes of futility, Dan looked up and shook his head. "She's gone." He sighed and pulled the hospital gown back into place as Vinny removed the Ambu bag. "Time of death—"

A sudden commotion at the main ICU doors interrupted him. A ward clerk called out, "Mr. Damen, please wait here..."

"Where is she?" another voice screamed. "Where is she?" A figure barreled toward them, wild-eyed and disheveled, oblivious to his misbuttoned sports shirt and the arms trying to restrain him. He pushed past, shrieking, "Oh God!" as he hurled himself onto the gurney, knocking Dan aside, to lie next to his wife's motionless body. He began to kiss her face repeatedly as if this could

53

suddenly revive her. He fixed his anguished gaze on Dan. "What did you do to her?"

Dan straightened to stand beside the gurney and stared at the floor beneath him, counting the number of black and white tile squares, anything to distract himself. So many eyes! Were they wondering what it felt like to lose a patient and be blamed for it in the same moment? Only Vinny wasn't peering at him but stood, still clutching the now-useless Ambu bag, his pale-blue eyes fixed with rapt attention on the lifeless body.

"Sarah! Sarah!" Ed kept pleading. "Oh, God…bring her back—please!"

Dan closed his eyes to the scene. He motioned all the staff from the room except Wynnie, the charge nurse. Ed Damen deserved at least a moment with his wife. As he left the room, Dan noticed the entire ICU staff watching him.

Close behind him, attending Neal Driscoll was discussing pulmonary emboli, the streptokinase that had just been emergently started, and the details of Sarah Damen's case with the house staff still present.

"For God's sake! Would you please stop?" It was out of Dan's mouth before he could think to check it. Into the embarrassed silence, he added, "The woman just died. I just don't understand why immediately following her death you need to discuss the case so dispassionately, as if… as if that is the only thing that matters. She was a living, breathing human being!" His throat closed on the words. Dan rose to leave the unit, profoundly shaken. *Whatever possessed me to pick this fuckin' godforsaken profession?*

Before exiting through the now open electronic doors, he turned to Diane and blurted, "Shit, does it really ever get better? What the fuck!"

Strangely, he had propelled himself back in time to his middle school's 'Career Day'. Dan couldn't take his eyes off the antique Waltham pocket watch, now opened to reveal the time to Dr. McDermott, who appeared affable enough despite being rushed for time. His completely white handlebar moustache seemed to span the distance of his face, waxed and twirled at its ends. The houndstooth suit with matching vest completed the picture for Dan Marchetti, the school's special day the high point of the year for him. He believed he wanted to be a doctor and listening and observing this sartorially distinguished older man describe in such eloquent terms the life of a physician, made such a decision firm and resolute. *To know what he knows and to receive such admiration from everyone for such knowledge was an overwhelming concept for the eleven-year-old.*

Diane paused, glancing away from the computer screen where she'd been checking labs, and contemplated his question for a moment. "Yes," she said quietly, "...and no. You'll learn how to deal, Dan. You'll do it because you have to. You just cope. My money is on you," Diane concluded before returning her attention to the computer.

Unbidden, almost against his will, an image of Nikki Saxon invaded Dan's thoughts: her alabaster body draped across his old green sofa, wearing nothing except the sparkle of that sexy ankle bracelet. Her radiant smile and the way her shoulder length hair fell back from her shoulders as she reached up for him.

Dan squeezed his eyes shut, trying to banish that picture. Only a day later, he'd learned the truth. Back on duty in the CCU, he'd found himself alone with his best nurse-buddy, Cheryl, who had seemed to avoid his eyes all morning. She'd been at Casey's and saw him leave with Nikki. "I sure like your friend Nikki," he ventured.

"She's married but unhappily as rumors have it," Cheryl said flatly, meeting his eyes, at last, probably reading in them the shock he felt.

To her credit, Nikki hadn't pursued him or even offered her number, though it was clear she was interested. She'd left it all up to him. And as much as it pained him, he knew what he had to do. Now, weeks later, he called upon that strategy again: Ray Lawlor, Nikki Saxon, Sarah Damen. They were part of the past. He needed to find a way to move on.

A few days later, the morning dawned bright and clear, and Dan awoke to feel reborn in a way. He didn't have to go to the hospital, a rare free Sunday in his internship. Instead, he had the luxury of sleeping late and sauntering down to the corner 'Baglery' for two everything bagels just out of the oven, crisp and hot to the touch.

Pouring a third cup of coffee, he reflected that he could be using the time to clean his apartment. He'd been promising himself he'd do that as soon as he had a free morning.

Instead, he'd kicked all his dirty clothes onto the floor inside the closet and shut the door. All his unwashed dishes were at least rinsed and stacked in the sink, and no biology experiments were allowed to grow unchecked in either the kitchen or the bathroom.

Now, time for some fun! For weeks now, everyone had been looking forward to a softball game between available members of the house staff and the attendings from the hospital. It was scheduled for eleven at the park. Dan grabbed his mitt, his keys from the caduceus dish, and a fat, red apple to eat on the way. He stepped over the pile of throwaway medical journals strewn by his door, a reminder to gather them up and take them down to the recycling bin.

He didn't want to rush his walk on such a glorious morning. The recent drizzle had washed away all the dust beneath an incandescent blue sky, and the sun's rays were already strong enough to bring beads of perspiration down his forehead. Before long, Dan arrived at the softball field. The house staff versus the Attendings. No hierarchy now, an even playing field or perhaps favoring the younger guys.

Dan grinned at the anticipation in the air and took his assigned position in center field, tossing a few balls back and forth to loosen up his arm, much the same way he would do as a young ballplayer.

A vivid flashback to when he entered the batter's box with the bases loaded as the starting catcher for the Police Boys Club ten-year-old division's all-star game. Pretending to smooth out the hard clay in the batter's box with his cleats (the pros did this all of the time), Dan took a deep breath and exhaled, determined to swing at the first good pitch to hit. And swing he did, sending the high fastball into deep left center field where his speed afoot allowed him to easily coast into third base with a triple, scoring three runs. The bench erupted in joy, the coach clapped enthusiastically while Dan pretended not to notice.

However, inexplicably, during the next three times up at bat, Dan looked at a called third strike each time. Why? The truth of the matter. *He became paralyzed with the fear of failing. From that day forward, he swore never to let that happen again.*

Back to reality, Jackie's next pitch was perfect, but Dr. Lescani was ready. The radiologist, his comb-over secured beneath a Pirates cap, swung compactly and sent a screeching line drive toward the gap in left-center.

Dan, in motion as soon as he heard the sound of the bat hit the ball, raced toward that gap and easily managed to scoop the ball up into his glove. Immediately checking his lateral momentum, he planted his feet. From the corner of his eye, he could see Lescani rounding first base and loping confidently toward second. With one fluid motion, Dan positioned his front foot, cocked his right arm, and threw a bona fide missile toward second base. The softball traveled so fast and so accurately that the middle-aged radiologist was at least fifteen feet short of the bag when second baseman Dave Levine tagged him out.

For a brief moment, there was utter silence. It all happened so fast, players on both teams were still trying to take it in.

"Hey, Marchetti!" called Glenn Covington. "Never told me you had a goddamn rifle for an arm!" Dan just smiled. *Sport is such a metaphor for life. No matter the situation, there's always hope that the next thing will be better.*

When the ninth inning rolled around, the game was tied 6-6 as the attendings came up to bat for their last licks. With one out, they managed to get Emily Bosnan, the cardiothoracic surgeon, on second and the ICU's Neal Driscoll on third; Covington came up to bat. The one-time Tiger took strikes on the first two pitches before lacing into the third, sending a long fly ball to deep right-center field in a hit that must've carried at least three hundred feet. It was high enough to let Dan get underneath it, but it was also far enough to allow Driscoll on third time to tag up and score before Dan would be able to throw the ball back to the catcher. At least, that'd be the assumption of everybody but Dan.

Watching the ball hurtle toward his glove, Dan grinned. His throwing arm had always been a marvel; Pop had called it a bazooka. Dan fired toward home plate. That ball whistled back the entire 300 feet and smacked into the catcher's mitt just seconds ahead of Driscoll. Neal had actually slowed down, obviously incredulous that there was any play at all. Frank Ryan tagged him out followed by enthusiastic cheering from the house staff.

After the game, Covington seemed to hang back and was the last to approach Dan. "That's some arm you have, Marchetti!" Sincerity was written all over him.

"Thanks."

"Did you ever pitch for a semipro or maybe a college team?"

"Nah, never gave it much thought. By that time my focus was on my studies." He laughed. "I wasn't as smart as you—finding a way to have my cake and eat it too."

Covington nodded and smiled wistfully. "I still miss those days sometimes. Thanks for taking me back a bit." They slapped shoulders and went their separate ways.

Dan watched the others drifting away to their cars, heading to Casey's for the post-game brewskies. Tossing his mitt in the air as he began to jog after them, he imagined life as a professional athlete. Then again, saving lives just might beat out the perfect throw! What about losing lives? *Don't go there Dan!*

Chapter Eight

Eyes closed tightly, Linda Ferrante turned her face up into the full force of the shower spray. Pushing back her jet-black hair with both hands, she let the water wash any lingering traces of shampoo down her back only to swirl away into the tub drain. As she dried her body, Celine Dion's haunting 'My Heart Will Go On' came on the radio. Coupled with the sensual touch of the thick terry cloth as she rubbed the moisture from her skin, she drifted to lustful moments in her life. She imagined that the fingers now exploring herself were those of men she had known or simply met briefly. They all possessed sweet, kindly smiles and gentle natures, men who would welcome raising a family.

She longed for children but her ex did not, and Linda found nothing to love in his streak of professional ruthlessness. He was quick to point out deficiencies of peers, real or imagined, to his bosses or ridiculed them in public forums. His apparent inability to view anything from the perspective of the downtrodden or disadvantaged reminded her far too much of her father, though Mike had no reason to change his name to lessen the embarrassment of his Italian heritage. Let them all change their last names; she clung to Ferrante, one way of honoring her paternal grandparents, Rosealba and Giuseppe, who'd instilled in her, if not in their son, an enduring pride in their mutual heritage.

An active member of two amateur theater groups, she had sandwiched her law studies between rehearsals and directing. While she received rave reviews for her performances and innovative directorial work, she'd barely finished in the top half of her graduating law class, much to the chagrin of her parents.

She dropped out of her theater groups, declined all offers to participate in creative projects, and completely threw herself into law. Fifteen-hour days of study, often grabbing only four hours of sleep, only to go back at it again. She passed the bar exam on her first attempt. From there it'd been surprisingly easy to get hired at an outstanding, middle-of-the road firm. However, the entire matter represented a colossal error in judgement. For the most part, practicing law made her miserable. Linda touched the dark shadow beneath her right eye, a result of too little sleep. At least the theater had taught her how to handle that problem.

Transferring toasted bread to a plate, she sat on one of the stools at her counter bar and spread the first piece of toast with egg salad. As she happily munched and sipped her coffee, Linda gazed around at her little domain. Of course, it was tidy. Even before taking her shower, she'd tucked her bedding and swung the Murphy bed up into the wall, revealing the floor-to-ceiling mirror on its underside.

Considering all the big mirrors—out here and in the bathroom—Linda had decided shortly after moving in that this garage apartment hadn't been outfitted for anyone with body-image issues. Someone, undoubtedly her widowed, single-parent landlady, Beth Marshall, had done a fine job creating this homey rental space and making it a model of efficiency, comfort, and pleasing aesthetics.

The mirror hung over the headboard of the bed made the room look larger by amplifying the natural light from a picture window on the southern exposure, which offered a view across the grassy backyard to the woods in the distance. Two narrower windows had screens that opened to provide both a fire escape and access to Linda's two bird feeders: one for seed eaters on the left and another for hummingbirds on the right.

The hummingbird feeder outside her window was full of nectar and awaited the first ruby-throats of the day though she was struck by the irony. When she moved here, finally free to choose a pet for herself in her newfound independence, it was a larger dilemma than she'd imagined. Her work schedule kept her away from home for long hours, and that wasn't fair to a social creature like a dog—or a bird, for that matter. A cat needed less interaction, but she'd been reluctant to go that route because she couldn't forget Mike sneering in the back of her mind, "Well, now you're leaving me, I guess you can get yourself a cat to keep you company like all the other single women living alone in their little apartments." *Men were always humiliating her but not just men, really.* She recalled her peeking through the small opening in the curtain that separated the stage from the audience, Linda looked vainly for her parents. Her minor part in her school's 'One Flew Over the Cuckoo's Nest' theatrical production, would later serve as the reason for their not attending.

"We'll come when you land a good role. Besides, how much of you would we really see of you in this show? You can do it, landing the big one honey," they beseeched their crestfallen daughter. *They just didn't get it. The only reason she studied acting was to rival her brother for their attention.*

Noting the time with surprise, she hurried to wash up her breakfast dishes, forcing herself to leave them in the drainer rather than drying and putting them away. "No time for dawdling," she admonished aloud.

From her desk just inside the door she grabbed up her purse and briefcase. As she turned out the lights at the wall switch, she told the fish, "Bye, now. Have a fantastic day, everyone."

Two hours later, Linda shifted on the hard wooden chair. Beside her, her seventeen-year-old client was turned in his chair, talking in low tones with his parents, who sat just behind the courtroom railing. At least they were trying to keep the tones low, but the level was rising, and there were nasty undercurrents and insolence from young Cameron McClure layered over the exasperation and desperation from his parents. The only other people in the yawning courtroom were a bored-looking bailiff and a court recorder busily text-messaging someone and stifling giggles at the responses she received.

Linda suppressed her own yawn and groaned inwardly, picturing that morass of paperwork, neatly stacked but undisturbed for days now, waiting on her office desk. No doubt new files had been added in her absence. How would she ever advance in this career when her plate was constantly heaped with menial tasks that a paralegal would be tasked with doing? Noticing the bailiff moved to open the door to the judge's chambers, Linda turned to her client, signaling his immediate attention.

"What the fuck...?" Cameron stopped abruptly midsentence, turned away from his parents, and faced forward. Not only clean scrubbed and well pressed in his $1,000 suit, he now managed to look as contrite and angelic as she'd instructed.

He'd been caught at a 'huffing party' and in possession of alcohol and other controlled substances. He had a clean record otherwise, though Linda was convinced he'd only been lucky before now—or perhaps money had changed hands somewhere along the line.

At least he hadn't been behind the wheel of a car. With the current charges, Linda was confident she could get him off rather lightly. What a waste of her time.

"All rise," intoned the bailiff. "This proceeding is now in session. The honorable Andre LaCroix presiding."

As Linda and Cameron stood and straightened their clothing, Judge LaCroix swept into the room and took his place on the bench. An old-timer appointed a few decades earlier, he still showed class. Impeccably groomed and bright of eye, the judge's handsome face appeared much younger than his sixty-plus years.

Showing no shred of emotion, he gave his complete attention to Linda's case for Cameron's spotless record, his remorse, the strong support of his parents—whose standing in the community was impugned.

"Sixty days' probation," Judge LaCroix said at last. "And to be remanded to his parents' custody." He tapped his gavel to end the proceeding.

His parents laughed nervously and added their fervent thanks, though they were respectful enough to call her *Ms.* Ferrante.

Standing at the top of the courthouse's impressive granite staircase, she took a deep breath. Linda started down the long series of steps. She smiled, thinking of her affable red-tailed shark. Did fish ever get tired of the life they lived, trading their freedom in the wild for a safe, clean environment where every need was met for them? No adventure, no risk, no moments of elation from unexpected wins or yes, sadness from sudden disappointments. Such an existence had never held much of an appeal for Linda. Thoughts drifted back to her father. "Michael just received a patent for his three-dimensional board game he calls 'Imaginable'," beamed Tony Ferrante, staring at the MyUSPTO website. "He is only twelve, can you imagine? So smart…"

Linda smiled dutifully, cursing silently the fact that his IQ of 160 was no match for her pedestrian 130. The unmistakable thrilled faces her parents made when regaling their friends with stories of their son's achievements continued to haunt her. *She simply couldn't compete with him and even this job paled in comparison to his CEO position of a hundred-billion-dollar tech company.* But here she was, having sent another little creep back to his entitled life and heading out to her mountain of paperwork that seemed to grow higher the more successful she was. Yes, it had been one of those days.

Vinny Orlander was absolutely gobsmacked when his right wrist was abruptly seized by someone immediately behind him. Turning, Alex Cole stood there just smiling strangely, slowly releasing his grip.

"What are you up to with that ventilator pal?" Standing there with his arms folded, he awaited an answer to his rhetorical question.

Vinny didn't respond, knowing instinctively that when "one is in a hole, it is best to stop digging."

A memory of his father made its unfortunate presence. "Let me out. I'll behave myself. Please…" Vinny wailed, the locked front coat closet with the musty smell, shrouded in darkness, petrified the not yet seven-year-old. The elder Orlander simply ignored his young son's plaintive cry, his punishment for talking back to him. Besides, he had given him a choice between corporal punishment with his oversized belt buckle or a day spent commiserating with the winter outerwear. Vinny chose the latter and for good reason. The belt buckle and the bruises it inflicted one month before took weeks to heal, making every movement agonizing. At least, the closet's claustrophobic environment allowed for imagining all the ways he would get back at his enemies. *Father was off limits however.*

Alex's measured voice brought him back. "I get your little secret Vinny. Saw you playing that strange game the other day. I must assume you find it enjoyable, huh?"

" I…"

"Look, I am not going to report you." Gazing down at his patient, "these patients aren't going to make it anyway. No harm, no foul I suppose." Cole turned to walk out of the room, the ICU unusually quiet that afternoon for some reason. Looking back at the still startled therapist, "You owe me my friend. You owe me big time…"

Chapter Nine

"Have you ever placed a Sengstaken-Blakemore tube in a patient, Dan?"

"No, I haven't but I saw one placed as a medical student. A little tricky…" Dan remarked truthfully to the on-call gastroenterologist, Chris Kilmartin.

"Nothing to it. I'll talk you through it," Kilmartin responded rather matter-of-factly. The truth of the matter was that on this particular Sunday evening, he didn't much care to come in and thus interrupt his enjoyment of some movie Dan heard blaring in the background. Alex and he had tried everything to get his patient's variceal bleeding to stop and the 'SB' tube was one of those Hail Marys that sometimes manages to quell the hemorrhaging in the patient's esophagus, albeit straight from the Marques de Sade handbook. The varices, engorged blood vessels, hemorrhoids if you will in the food pipe, brought on by a lifetime of excessive drinking leading to cirrhosis of his liver.

Dan laid out the components of the apparatus on the adjustable nightstand at bedside, rubber tubing, two inflatable balloons and an attachment that hooked onto the facemask of a football helmet of all things, to keep it in place. Needless to say, the assemblage of items crude to say the least, developed in the 1950's but used only infrequently. The tubing when inserted down the throat to lie amongst the dilated blood vessels would then expand, hopefully exerting enough pressure to tamponade or stop the bleeding in its tracks. If it failed, the patient would continue to bleed and go into shock, a 'death spiral'.

"Let's do this!" Kilmartin implored over the telephone, his evening beginning to slip away. The patient, now slipping in and out of unconsciousness, offered no resistance, not a good sign.

Fuck it, just buying time after all. What was there to lose? Even so, he wished Kilmartin would drag his ass in to supervise. But after all, hadn't his mother prepared himself for difficult situations?

! The summer of his fourteenth birthday and his mother worried that he could get in trouble Dan supposed. She had simply taken it upon herself to

volunteer the boys at the local Cerebral Palsy Center. How could she do that without discussing with them beforehand?

After having received his assignment to assist the older than thirty-five group in the summer camp activities, Dan recalled his tortured walk to the solarium to greet his group members. Frightened beyond belief of what he would see, horribly crippled bodies and contorted faces, he took small steps as if delaying the inevitable would somehow relieve his mounting stress level.

After making a left turn into the sizeable room where sunshine bathed the dozen campers whose wheelchairs were arrayed like spokes of a bicycle wheel, Dan was introduced to the group by a gracious supervisor who looked to be his mother's age. "Everyone, let's welcome," taking a moment to gaze at his adhesive backed paper nametag on his New York Yankees tee shirt, "Dante Marchetti." What happened soon thereafter may have changed his career trajectory forever. Each camper either using their feet to propel them forward in their chair or were wheeled over to him by a volunteer in order to proffer him a welcoming handshake. From that moment on, Dan became stricken with such overwhelming affection for these physically challenged human beings that the experience ultimately convinced him to seek a career in Medicine. *Mother certainly knew what she was doing!*

The entire insertion of the 'SB' tube went smoothly enough he figured, even though when Dan looked down, the entire front of his scrubs was covered with blood. Films showed the tube in place however and when the balloons fully deployed, the bleeding appeared to stop within a few minutes.

"Doctor Kilmartin, I believe we are in business." Marchetti exhaled deeply, allowing himself a brief moment of satisfaction.

"Dr. Kilmartin, still there?" Dan checked his cell phone which had been put on speaker the entire time. Satisfied that his phone was still transmitting, he repeated,

"Dr. Kilmartin?"

"Yes, yes…great, great. Good work Marchetti, I'll make certain to let the Chief hear about this. Call me if you need me but he should do well." *Do well? Yeah but for how long?* The phone went dead.

****

"S-e-n-g-s-t-a-k-e-n B-l-a-k-e-m-o-r-e," Vinny typed the name of a piece of medical equipment on his computer, having just completed the cleaning up after dinner. It's description, diagram, and actual picture immediately appearing on his laptop. Marchetti had installed one of his patients that very day. *Fascinating contraption, looks like something straight out of the S&M toy list he orders from.* He read further.

"The Sengstaken-Blakemore tube is a red tube with three ports on one end and two balloons on the other. One balloon goes into your stomach and is filled with air using one port. The other balloon sits in the esophagus and is inflated with the second port. The third port, called the gastric suction port, suctions fluid and air out of your stomach.

However, what really piqued the resourceful Orlander was the cautionary note at the bottom of the page: Esophageal rupture is a deadly complication should the instructions not be correctly followed, that is, amount of air insufflated and/or adherence to strict guidelines pertaining to correct balloon placement."

Chapter Ten

Returning from a much-needed meal break, Dan found the hall outside the ICU's doors crowded with three generations of what was clearly a single family: two sets of grandparents, the parents, and a daughter in her early teens. Apparently, only a few were interested in the nearby lounge where they could sit comfortably; they were all silent and looked at him as if he had the information they were seeking. He greeted them with a nod and moved on through the doors, which swung shut behind him.

Jackie Norris looked up from the central physicians' desk.

"Wow!" Dan tried for a light tone. "I go away for just a little while and… What's up?"

"Interesting new case for our team. An eleven-year-old boy, Steven Bailey, with what looks like meningococcal meningitis. That's his family in the waiting room."

In the month he'd been assigned to ICU, this was the first time a child was admitted. Dan felt himself frown. "Who gave the clearance for a pediatric case? Whose service is he on?"

"It was Dr. Tischler but switched it to Dr. Haye after the ER tap. Paul's down in the micro-lab now gram-staining the spinal fluid. Oh, guess he's done." She gestured, and Dan turned to see another physician out in the hall, talking to the family: Dr. Paul Haye, Chief of Infectious Diseases at DCH.

A strange but not unfamiliar nervousness rose in Dan. He just had to admit it to himself: seriously ill pediatric patients made him hyperventilate. Losing them was the worst: looking down at a cherubic face, now expressionless. He'd had some experiences early on, and now he did his best to avoid all things pediatric. Most of the seriously ill kids were transferred directly to the Children's Hospital, but occasionally they ended up in the ICU for stabilization. Of course, he'd never shy away from any patient assigned to him, but maybe someone else could take Steven Bailey.

Dan watched Haye touch the father's arm out in the hall, then gesturing them all toward the waiting room lounge. When they were reluctantly on their way, Haye turned to enter the ICU, approaching with the chart in his hand. He spoke to both Jackie and Dan: "Meningococci confirmed. When you get a chance, go to the lab and look at the gram stain." He turned to Jackie, "Any change while I've been gone?"

She checked the appropriate monitor and shook her head.

To Dan, Haye elaborated, "At the last exam he was obtunded…completely out of it. I'm hoping the IV penicillin we started downstairs will kick in quickly; we put him on 2 million units every two hours." He handed the chart to Dan. "He's all yours. Go introduce yourself to the family. Remind them they'll all have to take prophylactic rifampin, and I'll get the orders rolling."

Numbly, Dan took the chart, watching the older man rush away to find the appropriate nurses. Dan glanced at Jackie, who shrugged before putting her attention on another one of the monitors.

Dan turned and made himself move toward the doors, out into the hall and around the corner into the floor's main waiting room: a spacious lounge shared, as needed, by the CCU and the ICU. It wasn't hard to find the Bailey family; they all sat in one corner as near as they could get to the doorway just in case … Leaping up from the cushy teal-colored furniture as soon as they saw him approaching, they all gathered before him, avid as baby birds waiting for a parent to deliver a fat worm.

Dan introduced himself and nodded to each as they offered their names, but all he retained were the parents' names, Nora and Nate, and the daughter's, Jessica.

"Dr. Haye told you it is, indeed, meningitis and that you'll be getting a medication to help protect you from getting it too?" At their nods, he continued, hoping he sounded reassuring even while being completely honest to the circumstances. "As you know, this can be an extremely serious illness, but we've started Steven on some heavy-duty medicine." Their eyes remained fixated on his every word. "This disease is especially contagious, so we need to isolate Steve to protect him and the other patients to prevent spread. Your visits with him will need to be limited, and it's probably best if it's just Mom and Dad." The four grandparents nodded their understanding. Dan looked at Jessica, who stood slumped and forlorn with both hands jammed in the pockets of her red windbreaker. "Young folks like you have to be particularly careful

68

not to get exposed, even after you get the preventive meds." She nodded and bit her lip against the tears.

Steven's parents gripped each other's hands and followed Dan back around the corner and through the ICU doors; their faces were haggard with worry, making them look older than the mid-thirties he judged them to be.

Just outside Steven Bailey's room, which was the closest to the entrance, stood a cabinet with drawers containing folded gowns and others containing holding masks and latex gloves.

Dan removed his stethoscope and put it in the top drawer, then demonstrated how to properly suit up as they all would have to do each time before entering Steve's room.

He left them under the watchful eye of Wyndolyn Hibbert, saying, "Nurse Wynnie will help you both. I'm gonna go on in and start my exam." He pulled his mask into place.

"Of course," Nora said. "Don't let us slow you down."

When the little room's door had swished shut behind him, Dan picked up the yellow plastic stethoscope on the bedside table and regarded his newest patient. Comatose, as Dr. Haye had said earlier. The boy was of average size for his eleven years and of a fair complexion beneath the heat of fever and the disease's characteristic rash. Wispy, pale-blond hair stuck out in all directions.

As if to prove this point, as soon as Dan started his exam, the boy's head began to roll back and forth, further disarraying his hair. As his limbs thrashed briefly under the covers, Steve mumbled incoherently and then came to rest again without ever opening his eyes.

Dan pulled aside the bedding and Johnny coat so he could see the entire length of the boy. The rash covered most of the frail and hairless form. Dan had somehow forgotten just how innocent a prepubescent body could look. Steven's parents were both in the room by now, and Dan watched their eyes widen above their masks as they saw how the rash had progressed. He let the hospital gown fall back across the boy's torso, leaving the legs exposed, and fished a pen from his pocket underneath his own gown. The Baileys watched, mesmerized, as he drew a box around one area of lesions on Steve's right thigh.

"This will help me gauge the progression or regression of the illness," he explained gently. "Over the next hours, we'll be able to count whether we have more or fewer spots in the box." The parents obviously heard him but didn't

69

look up. They fixed their stares on the patch of reddened blotches as if they would, at any moment, see them change before their eyes.

Dan checked the IV delivering high-dose penicillin into the boy's arm and felt powerless. It didn't help to have Nora Bailey ask, "What now?"

Dan stifled a sigh. "All we can do at the moment is support Steven's systems until the penicillin has time to wipe out the ...uh...bugs." What he didn't say out loud was that, unfortunately, those organisms had a head start. Only time would tell.

Again as if reading his mind, Nora said, "If only we'd brought him in as soon as he mentioned a headache and we noticed he was feverish." She was clearly the talker of the pair. Her husband stood just staring down at his son, who moved restlessly again and muttered unintelligible phrases.

Dan reached to squeeze Nora's shoulder comfortingly. "Kids get fevers. Kids have headaches. Their parents can't run them to the ER for every little thing."

Nora's eyes welled as she whispered, "Thank you, but I just wish—"

As he cleaned his hands, he saw Nurse Wynnie look his way, and he waved her over. He indicated the Bailey room with a nod of his head. "You'll keep a close eye on all of them, right?"

She smiled sympathetically. "No-o-o problem, Dr. Dan. Mebbe you tek some rest now, eh?"

"Not yet. Haven't checked on my others for a bit. Has Ms. Walsh's fever come down at all?" Wyndolyn nodded, and Dan felt a sigh of relief. Some positive news during all this.

"Good. Listen, the Bailey boy? Be sure to call me with any change whatsoever. No matter where I am, okay?"

This time she gave his shoulder a motherly pat. "All fruits ripe, Dr. Dan." He'd learned that meant: Everything's hunky-dory. "Me tink dat boy gwina be jus' fine."

"From your mouth to God's ear!" he said fervently and earned a radiant smile from her.

Some hours later, Dan's beeper dragged him from sleep: "Dr. Marchetti, ICU Medical—stat; ICU Medical—stat!" *So much for a quick catnap.* He'd spent most of the night tending to young Steven every half hour to monitor his urine output, listen to his heart and lungs, and check his rhythm and vital signs.

At times the boy was awake, but still incoherent and babbling nonsense; his fever hovered around 102° Fahrenheit.

Inside the ICU, Wynnie intercepted him before he got too near Steven's parents, who anxiously awaited him. "Blood pressuh tek a lit'le drop," she reported. "Sev'ty systolic. Urine ou'put drop ta 40 cc's last hour."

He gowned up quickly. Examining the unconscious boy and finding the blood pressure had dropped even further, Dan increased the normal saline running into his vein. Mentally, Dan made a quick review of all the pediatric dosages for medicines he had looked up in the call room that might be needed should the boy's heart rhythm deteriorate…or stop.

Dan degowned and went out to reassure the parents. At least he tried. They nodded that they understood, but as he massaged the sanitizing gel into his hands, he could see they were hovering near the edge.

"We're desperately trying, Doctor, not to lose it but frankly…" Steven's father's voice tailed off.

"Go on in," he urged them. "If you check that box I drew on his leg, you'll see there aren't quite as many spots in it—a terrific sign."

"Thank God. But he is not awake yet, correct?"

"That is correct." After a short silence, they gowned up.

Off to the side, a bit away from the ICU's main traffic patterns, Dan lowered himself wearily onto a handy reclining chair, pushing all the way back into the soft tan leather until the angle was comfortable enough to catch a nap. He closed his eyes. "Hey, Dante," a voice said. "Need coffee?"

His eyes snapped open. Nikki. How could she look so put together at this ungodly hour?

"I had to bring down some paperwork for Diane's new patient."

"From Peds?" Dan managed.

"Yeah. Twelve-year-old girl with asthma. Her appendix perforated, so now she's a surgical case with some complications, so you guys get her."

"She's Diane's?" At least he was talking now.

Nikki nodded and brushed a wave of auburn hair back from her face. "So, do you want some?" When he began to stammer in surprise, she laughed and clarified, "Coffee. The machine on this floor is broken. My shift's over, so I volunteered to make a run to the cafeteria. Maybe pick up some snacks."

"Oh, coffee. Sure. Thanks."

"Dash of cream and one sugar, if I remember correctly."

Dan felt his face flush at this reference to their one 'morning-after' breakfast nearly a month ago. "Yeah. Say, I'm sorry I never called you—"

She gestured dismissively. "S'okay. Cheryl told me she told you I was married. Sorry, I didn't tell you myself. If you'd known, nothing would've happened, right?"

When Dan nodded, Nikki smiled wistfully. "Well, sorry for the lack of honesty. Does it help that we are separated and heading for divorce?" Her smoky green eyes stared straight into his, unabashed. "I truly hope so." Then she turned away, calling back brightly, "I'll get that coffee now."

He watched her go. She was even trimmer than she'd been when he last saw her, and she moved so gracefully. How sexy she made a set of hospital-green scrubs look. *Well, there'll be no sleeping now*, Dan thought as he moved back toward Steven's room, gowned up, and went in.

Looking down, he suddenly saw his patient's body stiffen; the eyes were open but rolled back, the pupils hidden beneath the lids. Tonic-clonic seizure. "Wynnie!" he cried. "Dilantin, 6mgs per kg, he is 45 kilos—now!"

She whirled and rushed away to the med room. As his patient's muscles continued to contract violently and then relax only to contract again, Dan held Steven's head to one side. Glancing up to check on Wynnie's progress, he saw the horrified faces of the Bailey adults peering through the glass. They hastily moved aside as Nurse Wynnie raced back, suited up, and rushed into the room with the bag of fluid medication. She moved past Dan to the IV stand and expertly connected the bag to the IVAC machine that would administer the drug at the proper speed. Dilantin could lower a patient's blood pressure to critical levels if given too quickly. After just a few minutes, Dan felt the seizure activity lesson in the boy and then cease altogether.

At last, Dan emerged from the room, thankful that another potential disaster had been averted. "He's stopped seizing," Dan told the waiting Baileys. "Give me a minute?"

They nodded wordlessly, but their widened eyes fixed on him as if they'd never look away. Moving to the physicians' desk, he dropped his weary body into the chair and scribbled quick notes in his patient's chart before returning to the family. Dan led them all back into the lounge where they could sit comfortably, though not-one of them wanted to relax.

Feeling those seven pairs of eyes burrowing into him, he began, "We gave Steven a highly effective seizure medication, Dilantin, which should prevent further episodes. If they do reoccur, we have other medications at our disposal."

"What caused the seizure?" asked Nora Bailey.

"I'm pretty certain it was a result of the infection itself, though I've ordered some blood work to eliminate other causes."

She blurted, "Is…is there any chance he's…suffered any…brain damage?" She nervously ran her fingers through that wispy, pale-gold hair, unknowingly making it spike from her head almost like her son's. She was probably equally unaware her mascara was smeared behind the glasses she now wore, so her contacts could avoid rifampin staining.

Dan stiffened, his mouth suddenly dry. "Your question is one that I cannot answer right now. Could he…? Possibly. But did he? There's no way to know at this point," he answered as honestly as he could. "Let's say a prayer for him, shall we?"

She bit her lip but nodded, and he placed his hand on her shoulder, facing the entire family.

"You have my word that I won't keep anything from you." He hesitated, but then added, "I suppose it doesn't have to be said, but I want nothing more than to see that boy open his eyes and give each of you a big hug." He was surprised to hear how resolute his own voice. "Steven is always on my mind."

"Thank you." They all seemed to say it at once.

How he wanted to see this boy come around, live a full and normal life. Correction, he needed to see it.

"Sorry it took so long," someone said. *Nikki,* he thought. He struggled to bring the recliner to a more upright position and reached to take the Styrofoam cup she held in one hand. "Had to wait for a new pot so I could bring some that were a little fresher." He noticed a cafeteria cart across the room surrounded by eager staff and some of the Baileys, who were pouring cups from a restaurant-style pot and adding the cream or sugar she'd also provided. There seemed to be something else they were divvying up. "I waited for a little longer cuz I thought you guys might like some fresh pizza too."

The scent hit his nostrils then, and he was salivating before he even focused on the huge slice of pepperoni and mushroom on the paper plate she held out to him.

He set aside the coffee on the wide arm of the recliner. "Wow, thanks." He took a huge bite. "So delicious," he hummed.

"Careful," she warned.

When he'd munched enough to be able to speak, without breaking all the rules of etiquette, he said, "That was really great of you. Especially to hang around after since you were done for the day."

"Well," she said quietly, "there's not much for me to go home to these days."

Dan stopped chewing, almost choking on the bite he was swallowing.

Nikki picked up Dan's coffee and held it as she sat herself down on the recliner arm. She was very close to him, but gone was all the flirtation and coyness.

"My marriage is over, who knows about the future? But in the meantime, I hope we can be friends. You know, like you're friends with Cheryl and Diane. I promise not to involve you in anything about Matt, but most of us can use friends to talk to about the stuff we have to deal with in this job."

"Definitely," he said again.

"In fact, you look like you could use a listener tonight. I hear Steven seized while I was gone?"

"Yeah, but he's resting okay now." Dan set aside the empty paper plate and accepted the coffee from her, taking a long, satisfying drink.

"My senior elective in pediatrics in medical school. Pretty devastating. Interested?"

"Tell me."

Dan closed his eyes for a long moment, staring back into the past. Then he looked right into her eyes. "Worst night of my life. I lost two teenagers in a matter of hours. One from cystic fibrosis and the other from leukemia." She didn't speak, but her eyes never left his as she reached to squeeze his upper arm. It wasn't the touch or gaze of a lover but that of a friend.

He continued, "Of course, I remember the kids, but it's their parents' faces I can't get out of my mind. The images are etched indelibly: those haunted expressions as they listened to me answer questions about their children's deaths. I remember standing in an otherwise empty waiting room. Behind them, I can still see the wall clock marking midnight and rain sliding down the dark windowpane."

"Some of those images never do leave you," Nikki murmured. "Believe me, I know."

As he hesitated, she signaled him to go on. "Well, Adam had cystic fibrosis. More kids are surviving longer, and into adulthood these days. But Adam would never have made it as long as he did without the heroic efforts of his mother. Everything fell on her since his dad was an officer in a Navy submarine and away from home for extended periods of time—though he got leave to be there for Adam's last days. Anyway, I saw his mom each day, working with the nurses and taking on much of the treatment herself. Every single day, I watched her have to pummel her son's chest..." he paused, "...to clear secretions." He sighed. "There's a way mothers touch their children, embrace them. My own mom's like that, pure love, but Adam's mom..." his voice raspy, trailed off.

"Dylan's parents were special in the same way. He had acute myelogenous leukemia and was hospitalized the whole time I was in peds. Sometimes I'd see him running around the halls or the nurse's station like any other thirteen-year old. And then he'd quickly succumb to infection, spiking fevers suddenly to 105° and barely surviving to the next day." Nikki motioned him to continue. "Before he got sick he'd been a very active kid, especially interested in the outdoors and scouting. They made the most of every second they had when he wasn't in the hospital."

Nikki prompted, "So both Dylan and Adam died on the same night?"

"Yeah." Dan sighed again. "That was enough for me. Guess I thought I could spare myself that headache by not going into pediatrics." He studied her a moment as if her face could reveal a secret. "How do you do it? How do you face the reality that you could lose a kid at any moment?"

"Nurses like helping people get well. Me, I like helping the most helpless to feel better."

"But I can't imagine how many you have to watch who never get better. All those young lives cut short."

"It's hard," she conceded and gave a self-deprecating laugh. "I want to save them all. But I can't. And sooner or later, no matter what part of medicine you're in, everyone has to face the death of a person too young. It's inevitable. So you're actually ahead of the curve."

He grimaced at this distinction. "I guess. I just wish—"

Nikki covered his hand with her own. "Me too. We just have to do what we can for those we can help. And for every person, child or adult, it is important. Like every single grain of sand."

"Oh, like in Blake's poem?"

"Poem?"

"Never mind. I think I'm starting to lose it."

"Uh-huh, you're looking pretty tired. Coffee only works so long." She stood, reading the wall clock. "God, can it really be 3:00 a.m.? I better go. I'll let you get some sleep." Nikki pointed out, "Less noise in the on-call room."

"Maybe later. I wanna be right here if something else changes with Steve." He yawned, then blushed with embarrassment. "Sorry!"

"Take care, Dante. See you around."

He watched her cross to the ICU doors. *Just friends,* he reminded himself. Didn't mean he couldn't appreciate having another quality listener in his life. It was an hour later, but it seemed like seconds when he heard "Dr. Dan. Hey, Dr. Dan." Wynnie Hibbert's sweet intonations called him back to consciousness.

He mumbled something, and she said, "Is'a Steven Bailey."

Blinking, Dan gazed up at Wynnie standing over him. He pushed himself to a sitting position on the recliner and steeled himself for the answer to his next question: "What's up?"

"He's awek and talkin' bout breakfas'."

"Tremendous!" Dan was off in a flash toward the isolation room and gowned up in record time. Steven was sitting up in bed, rather glassy eyed and gloriously disheveled, but alive and awake and able to speak. "Nurse Wynnie said… Are you, Dr. Dan?"

"Yes, I am," he answered, sitting down on the edge of the bed. Dan placed his hands on the boy's shoulders. "Hey, buddy," Dan whispered around the sudden knot in his throat. "How are you feeling?"

"I'm hungry," the raspy voice began. Then another thought, "Is Mom here?"

"Yeah, champ, your whole family's here. I'll go get them, but first I need to check you out a little. Okay?"

Dan examined him thoroughly, as he had so many times through the night. Convinced that his young patient had indeed vastly improved, Dan said, "You're doing great, Steven. I'll get your parents."

Outside the room, after giving Wynnie orders for the boy's meal, Dan eagerly headed to the lounge where he found all the Baileys. A few were asleep in chairs or slumped against each other on the couches. Nora, of course, was awake, sitting sandwiched between her sleeping husband and daughter, both leaning heavily on her, and she spoke as soon as she saw Dan enter the room. "There's news?" Though her voice was low, everyone else was immediately awake, rising to approach him.

"Steven's awake and looking first-class. Asking for Rice Krispies, though I think that'll have to wait a bit."

The room erupted with laughter and joyful tears, each family member hugging the others as they released the tension that had mounted over the long hours of fear, hope, and despair. Wet-eyed Jessica came and touched his sleeve, shyly smiling up at him. "Thank you for saving my brother."

Then everyone was thanking him, shaking his hand, and slapping his back; he felt himself choke up and asked quickly, "Mom and Dad, want to go in and see Steven?"

This time it was Dad who spoke first, "Absolutely!" His wife had already hurried out to be with her son.

Still laughing and talking excitedly, they all followed Dan out into the hallway. "Only Mom and Dad in the room for now," he told them. "Grandparents can look in the door the way you have before."

"What about me?" Jessica, hands back in her jacket pockets, stood looking lost and lonely as the rest of her family surged through the ICU doors.

Dan leaned down closer to her height. "I'm sorry, but I think it's safer for you if you wait a few days."

She nodded her understanding, but tears came again to her eyes, and she chewed her lip. Casting a glance toward her elders, all busy inside trying to help Nora and Nate gown up, but getting in each other's way, Jessica drew something from her left-hand pocket and held it out to Dan. "Could you give this to Steve, please? Tell him I'm, really, really sorry I hid it?"

"Sure." Dan took the little stuffed bulldog and slipped it into his own pocket until he could find the proper moment alone with Steve. Dan winked at Jessica and grinned. "I'd be mortified to tell you how I tormented my little brother!"

She smiled with gratitude and headed resolutely back toward the lounge.

Dan turned and entered the ICU, watching the Baileys with pleasure. Steven would be around for a long time. Dan looked through the glass when Nora Bailey signaled for his attention. She came quickly to the door and signaled to her mom, who suddenly grabbed Dan and gave him a big hug.

77

"That's from all of us, Thank you, Doctor, so very much. From the bottom of all our hearts."

Tears began to run down Dan's cheeks, causing Nurse Winnie to say, "Here he go agin!" He quickly excused himself and hurried from the ICU into the nearest elevator. Once inside with the doors closed, he didn't push any buttons. He just let himself cry. He'd broken down the night Adam and Dylan died, but this was like no crying he'd ever done before. His weary body surged with supreme joy, screaming as loud as possible, "Yes, yes!" So loudly, in fact, he thought he had damaged his vocal cords. He'd saved lives before, but this was different, this was a child. He desperately needed to remember this feeling.

When he'd pulled himself together, Dan left the elevator and managed to slip unnoticed back to the consoles where he noted Steve's progress before slipping back down the hall to the on-call room where he hoped to catch up sleep before the next crisis.

****

Suddenly, he exited his bed as if an imaginary force hurled him toward his laptop. Alex sipped from his now lukewarm Coolata while booting up his laptop. Once his browser was available, he typed in 'Sentinel Events' which took him to the Joint Commission website, the body that oversees hospital accreditation. Sentinel events, defined as "patient safety event(s) that results in death, permanent harm… and the listing of hundreds of events hopefully to prevent these types of mishaps from occurring in the first place."

Just the ticket. He would copy the link and send to Orlander who with his fertile imagination, should find exactly what he needs. After all, any future sentinel events at Deerwood Community Hospital mirroring any of the numerous, albeit seemingly one-offs recounted on the site, could indicate precedents already established, should anyone check of course. Making the argument that such mishaps have occurred elsewhere. That is, unusual yes but unheard of, not true. Once he pressed 'send', Alex returned to the warmth of his bed, his much needed sleep now commencing within minutes.

Chapter Eleven

Cold fear curled all around fifteen-year-old Nikki, and she chewed the inside of her cheek to keep it at bay. "Let's not fight, Mom. Please just let me drive."

Frances—swaying slightly, car keys dangling from her fingers—tried to focus her vision on Nikki. "N't legal. Less go; we're late."

What should I do? Nikki wondered desperately. They simply couldn't miss this twice-postponed renewal interview with social services. Mr. Murphy, their caseworker, had bent over backward to accommodate them, but there were rules, and he couldn't break them. If we lose our benefits, how will Mom get her medicines? Frances depended on those now. Though appointments frequently had to be canceled or postponed, when-push-came-to-shove, Frances had always managed to drive where they needed to go, but Nikki knew that luck would fail one day. Unaware her daughter had been teaching herself to drive by taking the car to a nearby supermarket parking lot at dawn every Sunday morning, her mother never even knew she was gone. She slept like the dead and really late into the afternoons almost every day. It'd been a little scary at first, getting from the house to the relative safety of the parking lot, but Nikki had studied books about the mechanics of driving—thank goodness the Chevy was an automatic—and now, with practice, felt confident she could get them to their appointment more safely than her drug-muzzy mother.

Nikki had only just now confessed to her mom, who was so out-of-it she hadn't even gotten mad. "Did you have more than one pill this morning, Mom?"

Frances blinked. "Maybe." If so, it was accidental. Nikki knew, for all her faults, Mom didn't intentionally take too much. "I can drive, Nikki. The last thing we need's a ticket and you getting caught by the police."

I can think of worse things than that happening. She sighed. "Okay, Mom, but we gotta go now."

Mr. Murphy, who had everyone call him Mr. M., had warned them, "My hands are tied. If you want to keep your benefits, Nikki, you simply must get your mom to this meeting—and on time. My schedule is packed."

Looking away now from the car keys in Mom's hand, Nikki checked her watch. We'll probably be a few minutes late; let's hope he can still take us once we get there.

Normally Frances didn't drive too fast—and she was still only five miles above the speed limit—but when the light turned green ahead of them as they came to the corner of Pine and Wilson, Frances accelerated without paying attention to the cars that should be stopping for them. The red-light-running SUV slammed into the Chevy's passenger side and spun it across the intersection; the driver's side got T-boned by an oncoming bus.

It was weird, Nikki always thought, to remember so little about the crash itself. I'm sure there were horrible metal sounds, screaming, sirens, flashing lights. But those memories were no more vivid than some once-watched TV drama.

What she did remember was the hospital. She woke up—terrified and with both legs in casts—in the ICU at County Hospital. She tried not to cry, but she was so scared she couldn't even ask questions and find out what had happened. It helped some when the nurses arranged the curtain so she could see her comatose mother through the glass of the adjoining room.

Those nurses were like angels. Back then they still wore all white as they hovered around her with reassuring smiles and words. Not just the ICU nurses, but those in the pediatric ward where she was moved before too long. The doctors were another story. Brusque, patronizing when they told her anything at all. "You're a lucky girl," one remarked. "Broken legs and a bunch of cuts and scrapes? Could've been a lot worse."

Like Frances, who'd been crushed by the bus, with massive internal injuries and trauma to the brain. It was a very long time before she ever woke up. By that time, Nikki had been on the ward a whole week. At least once a day, a nurse brought her back down to ICU in a wheelchair. Nikki would sit a while, holding Frances's hand. The nurses encouraged Nikki to talk to her mom. Nurse Alice, Nikki's favorite, told her, "The comatose often can hear what we say to them," and "She still has a wonderful chance, and you can help her come back."

But when Nikki went to her mom's bedside and took up her hand, she experienced for the first time in her life that certainty of knowing a patient would not survive…perhaps not wanting to go on living. Nikki fought it and tried to get Frances to fight too. When left alone with her, Nikki would whisper, "Come on, Mom. You can do it, and we can get through all this together. I need you, Mom."

****

Dr. Cole's message confused him. Perhaps he needed to refresh his mind as to the word's exact definition. Vinny googled the word, 'precedent'. "An earlier event or action that is regarded as an example or guide to be considered in subsequent similar circumstances." Hmmm. *I get it now.* Medical mistakes like these happen all the time in hospitals in the United States. Just the price of doing business. Sometimes bad things happen and are intentional like the time he exacted revenge on his tormentors in seventh grade.

"Heh you, a real life bastard!" Vinny recalled his refusing to turn around to face his obnoxious classmate sitting directly behind him. Once some of the other eighth graders had discovered 'the truth', that Vinny's father never officially married his mother, the bullying had become unmerciful.

"Father's Day is a nonholiday for you. Is there such a holiday as A Bastard Son Day?" Vinny pretended not to hear, even as the trio behind his seat all laughed in unison. No matter, he had brought his baseball to school, now hidden in his locker. They will pay. Sure enough, once his last class of the day finished, he took his place behind a large Tulip tree in front of the school. Whack! All three boys lay on the ground writhing in pain, one in particular grabbing an injured arm that Vinny was certain he fractured. *No guilt at all. In fact, it felt good, real good.*

****

Dan couldn't escape the monumental dilemma staring him in the face. This forty-year-old man, Ian Forman, had just been admitted after incurring a sizeable pulmonary embolus, a clot to his lung. One not quite as large as Sarah Damen's but life threatening however. In attempting to determine where the clot broke off from, he discovered that at the site of a previously corrected atrial septal defect (a hole in the wall separating two chambers of the heart) that the cardiac surgeons repaired one year to that day, a large clot had formed. While it remained adherent to the wall, the turbulent blood flow in the heart that normally exists lead to the clot bouncing around as if it had a mind of its own. As if this wasn't dangerous enough, it took the shape of a large cherry with its stem intact. The stem was the bridge between the wall and the body of the clot itself.

"Ian," Dan began, "You have this rather large clot that has developed at the site where your hole in the heart was repaired. We have no choice but to try to dissolve it with a very strong medicine, a 'thrombolytic'. The surgeons do not feel that they can safely remove it in the operating room so this remains the best option." Dan waited to see if his patient comprehended the precarious situation he was describing to him. Left unsaid was the worry he maintained of the 'stem' so to speak dissolving first and releasing the 'cherry', the large clot to travel upstream to the lungs and most assuredly end in death. There was simply no way to predict how this would go while doing nothing was definitely not a viable option. Nevertheless, it was offered and quickly dismissed out of hand by Mr. Forman since a piece had already broken off to become a pulmonary embolus. The next partial clot could prove fatal. The entire clot, absolutely.

"Let's do it, Dr. Marchetti." And so the treatment started. Dan made certain he did not leave the ICU for too long, just in case. "Call me for anything, Missy, pulse Ox changes, tachycardia, chest pain…Now, it is just a waiting game."

"Will do, Dr. Marchetti." Missy was the quintessential intensive care nurse, professional, diligent, and above all, caring.

Chapter Twelve

"Sorry," Dan apologized, even before his yawn was finished. "Uh, you saw Dr. Freibolt a month ago for some problem?" He blinked three or four times, struggling to wake himself up. It was 2:00 a.m., and still, the emergency room was getting new patients.

"Yeah, Doc. He said I had a balloon or something that needed fixin' in my belly."

Cold water in the face couldn't have shocked Dan more awake or more quickly. This was no gomer. Sixty-seven-year-old Roscoe Delmar, unshaven and half-dressed in red sweatpants and what appeared to be his black-and-red plaid pajama top, was twisting and repositioning himself on the gurney, as if unable to find a comfortable position.

"What's bothering you right now?" Dan asked.

"Couldn't sleep tonight. Kept tossin' and turnin' in bed, the pain was too much."

"Where is the pain?" The man pointed to both the midline of his abdomen and to his mid-back. "I'm going to put my hand on your belly. Tell me if it hurts, okay?"

Delmar nodded, his eyes darting back and forth between Dan's hand and his face. "Yes! Right there!" His own face contorted in agony.

Dan immediately removed his hand, having recognized the pulsatile mass of a dissecting aortic aneurysm. Blood was now leaking into a previously weakened section of the body's main artery, filling and swelling it slowly but unequivocally like water into a balloon. "Sir, when you last saw Dr. Freibolt, what did he say he wanted to do about this balloon?"

Delmar flushed with embarrassment. "Oh, he wanted to operate, but I asked him if we could wait until after Labor Day. I have a big community barbecue planned." He managed a weak, but proud grin. "I'm the main cook and organizer."

"I see." Labor Day was still a distance away. He'll be lucky if he sees a sunrise, Dan thought as he checked the monitor. Blood pressure was 180/80. "I'll be right back." To the night nurse Sylvia Jenks he said, "Keep an eye on him. Especially his BP."

Dan headed directly to the main desk in the middle of the Emergency Room and, dialed the operator. "Hi, Dr. Marchetti here. Please get me Dr. Freibolt."

It took only seconds to reach the vascular surgeon, who answered groggily from his bed. "Freibolt."

"Dan Marchetti, the medical intern. Sorry to bother you, but I have one of your patients here in the ER—Roscoe Delmar. He appears to be dissecting."

"Shit, the stupid bastard. What's his BP?"

"It's 180 over 80."

"What time is it?" Freibolt asked, yawning.

"Just after 2:00 a.m."

"Okay. I'll come right in. Make sure you keep his blood pressure up."

Dan had barely hung up the receiver when he heard Sylvia call him from Delmar's room. He rushed back to find her in the process of increasing the saline fluid running into the patient's vein. Delmar had crumpled back on the gurney, eyes closed, moaning softly. "BP 60 systolic," Sylvia announced.

"Let's start a pressor, and get out the MAST trousers." Dan didn't have to tell her to hurry. Sylvia had the dark-brown rubberized device that might be able to save Delmar's life already at hand with its attached compressor within easy reach.

Dan helped her slide the rubber piece underneath their semi-lucid patient and wrapped it snugly up around Delmar's legs and lower torso like a pair of pants. It took a few minutes to work out the kinks in all the Velcro straps and to get the compressor insufflating air into the suit's inner lining. Delmar slipped closer to unconsciousness, mumbling incoherently, his blood pressure precariously low.

"Mr. Delmar," Sylvia called, enunciating slowly and clearly. "If you can hear me, we need to raise your blood pressure, and these inflatable pants will help us." No response. She met Dan's gaze with a grim look of her own; when she rechecked the patient's blood pressure a few moments later, she said, "Seventy palp."

He's toast, Dan thought, but aloud he said, "Let's up the dopamine." Either Delmar would get on top of it and stabilize enough for surgery—or he wouldn't. *The odds were seriously stacked against him.*

In the meantime, Vinny methodically prepared the aerosol treatment for his thirteen-year-old asthmatic patient in the Emergency Room's Bay #3, immediately to the left of Marchetti's patient. The traffic next door was continuous, the patient clearly in dire straits. It didn't take a MD to recognize the gravity of the situation. MAST trousers were a last ditch scenario. Vinny couldn't remember the last time, if at all, they were employed to save a patient. *Too bad Marchetti, can't win them all.*

Orlander finished administering to the boy and busied himself cleaning up the packaging materials left behind after having assembled the breathing treatment paraphernalia. However, his attention was now drawn to the hubbub next door to them.

"Blood pressure at 90 systolic, trousers seem to be keeping him from bottoming out," a nurse shouted out, moments before leaving the room to retrieve another bag of saline.

Vinny peaked through the break in the curtains separating the two patients' gurneys and noticed the room to be unoccupied for a brief moment. Leaning forward, he found that his hand could barely reach the valve on the trousers, enough to rotate the circular metal button-counter clockwise, enough to watch the rubber suit deflate precipitously. Peering at the luminescent pressure gauge, it began to register the pressure loss. Satisfied, Orlander immediately ducked back into his own bay.

"Feeling better Rick?" His asthmatic patient nodded, oblivious to anything other than his own comfort level.

Another night nurse, Gail Sanduski, appeared in the doorway. "Hate to break this to ya, but I've got a woman crowning in room nine, and the OB-GYN resident is tied up in labor and delivery. At least another fifteen minutes."

Sylvia asked, "You spoke to Dr. Pedersen yourself?"

"Well, Nikki Saxon called for me. She came down on a break to ask about my sister's wedding. Saw how tied up we all are and offered to help. She's trying to reach the attending now, I believe. She's already called in their obstetrician Dr. Majors."

Nikki? Now Dan noticed her sitting at the central station, talking into a phone.

Realizing he was the only physician present, he turned to his nurses. Gail Sanduski, a tall string bean of a woman in perfect contrast to Sylvia Jenks's two hundred fifty pounds stood staring. "Geez, a perfect fucking storm!" Alex finally got a dinner break, "both the attending and the OB resident are unavailable, I've got an aneurysm crumping, and now a woman's about to give birth!" Dan gulped air into his lungs. *I had only one delivery during my OB-GYN rotation in med school.*

Gail moved closer, touching his arm gently. "You're not alone here." Her brown eyes were so comfortingly calm, Dan could feel his anxiety begin to recede, but barely.

Sylvia looked up from the man in the inflated trousers and assured Dan, "I've got this, Doctor. I'll beep Dr. Cole back down here. And that baby won't wait."

"Too right," Gail said cheerfully, leading the way toward room nine. "It's her third, and it's coming pretty fast."

Just outside the room, Dan paused and confided to Gail, "I've only delivered one baby as a med student! And the attending was right there at the time."

She smiled and repeated an old med-school adage: "See one, do one, teach one."

Dan had to laugh, and that, too, helped relax him more as he entered the room and saw a good-looking African-American couple who appeared to be in their late thirties. The patient lay motionless for the moment, resting between contractions and seemingly relaxed and unworried. Her husband stood at her shoulder, clumsily patting her hand and appearing far more nervous. Dan made his voice sound easy and confident. "I'm Dr. Marchetti." He glanced at the chart Gail showed him. "Mr. and Mrs. Hamilton? Keesha and Louis? How ya guys doing tonight?"

She spoke right up. "Well, the third time around for us, but this baby seems impatient. And he's got a big head like his daddy's."

Lou Hamilton smiled weakly at the joke and kept patting his wife's hand as he asked, "Where's Dr. Majors?"

"She's on her way in, and the OB resident will be down shortly. He's delivering another baby upstairs."

By now, Dan was seated on a stool at the foot of the gurney, staring at the sheet draped over the woman's bent knees and down past her feet in the stirrups. He could tell by her change in breathing and the sudden tensing of her body that the next contractions were beginning.

Dan placed his hands on her bent knees, hesitating a moment as if hoping for further instructions or for that resident to arrive and take over. Lifting back the drape, he saw the top of the infant's head crowding the opening of the birth canal—a full head of damp, dark hair. At his side, Gail nudged him and he slid his hands into the gloves she held for him.

"Ahhh, the baby." Keesha panted, sounding remarkably calm.

"Push!" Dan urged, and Lou's and Gail's voices joined in, "Push, push, push."

Dan watched the crown of that head strain to push free, like a shoulder against a door not quite open enough. He opened his mouth to ask Gail for the Mayo scissors in case an episiotomy became necessary, but there was no need.

Suddenly the head popped through, followed by a whoosh of hot amniotic fluid, soaking Dan's scrubs all the way to his skin.

When Dan gently rotated the head so the shoulder could be present, the whole baby came shooting out like a wet and slippery seal pup, and Dan almost failed to catch it. For one harrowing heartbeat, he bobbled the child before gaining purchase. Staring down at the precious cargo he held, he watched the dark, wizened face screw up against the bright lights and erupt with a bellow.

Gail's voice murmured in his ear, "Nice catch, Dan." Then, to the parents, she announced, "It's a boy!"

"Lou Junior!" the dad said proudly. He and Keesha were gazing at each other with adoration, blissfully unaware of Dan's near-fumble and that it was Gail who guided Dan through the next steps. When he had the umbilical cord securely clamped, he asked if Lou wanted the honor of cutting it, but the man shook his head with a little shudder. Dan still gave him credit for being there at all. Not every husband could face the ordeal of labor and delivery, even one as relatively easy as this one.

Gail took the baby, who was still crying, from him and started cleaning the infant prior to the routine tests to make sure everything was okay.

"Tip-top lungs," Lou said with a huge grin.

"Amazing!" Keesha winked at Dan. "His daddy's big head and his big mouth!"

Dan laughed, but before he could respond, Sylvia Jenks's huge frame suddenly filled the doorway. "Room two's crashing, Doctor!" She was gone as quickly, back to Delmar's side.

"I'll handle this, Dan," Gail told him. Dan raced to Delmar's bed, but he could see it was already too late. The monitors were flatlined, and Sylvia looked up at him, shaking her head.

Delmar's face made a hideous sight, bluish and blotchy with the tongue half-severed. Dan had heard of that happening: a patient's teeth clamping down involuntarily during cardiac arrest. Delmar's mouth was a bloody mess, the partially torn tongue resting hideously on his chin.

"Jesus Christ!"

"You should go get cleaned up," Sylvia said softly.

Dan looked down at his drenched and stained clothing, now cold where it clung to his skin. He shivered. "Yeah, in a minute." He made himself look back at Delmar, wondering just how important that barbeque would seem to his family now. Aloud, he said, "Well, there wasn't much hope for him, even if the rubber pants had worked."

Sylvia frowned. "Yeah, about that. Weirdest thing. Those MAST trousers failed; deflated."

Dan stared at the nurse. "Come again?"

"I thought maybe the valve was broken or something, so I inflated it again, but I guess it was too late for Mr. Delmar."

Sudden exhaustion swamped Dan, and he found it hard to grasp this simple conversation. "It deflated?"

Sylvia nodded. "So far, it's stayed reinflated."

"But how could that happen?"

"I dunno. A slow leak, maybe? Valve malfunction?"

"Maybe. Better get it checked out by engineering. Were you in the room the whole time?"

"I was gone for a few minutes to get another saline bag to hang, and when I got back, I had to catch the phone. By the way, Freibolt's stuck on the turnpike. All lanes are closed for a jackknifed 18-wheeler." She gazed regretfully at Delmar in the now-useless pants. "Soon as I got back, I saw they were deflated. I went to get you, but you were really busy. So I came right back and pumped them up again."

"How long ago was that?"

"About fifteen minutes. And see? Still working."

"Doesn't make sense," he said, and Sylvia just shook her head in agreement.

But Dan couldn't let it go. Could the valve not have been closed correctly the first time? That could happen. Though it seemed unlikely with someone as capable and meticulous as Sylvia Jenks. Best not to mention that possibility. By now, Sylvia was leaning against the wall while dabbing at her eyes with a tissue. No need to add extra guilt or risk offending her by questioning her conscientiousness, especially as the guy really was a dead man walking as soon as his aneurysm had blown.

While they were entering a time of death in the records, a voice called from the doorway, "Hey, where's the mom to be?" Glancing over his shoulder, Dan saw the OB-GYN resident Gary Pedersen.

"Room 9, but you're too late. What took ya?"

Gary shrugged, looking as tired as Dan felt, but managed a philosophical grin. "Babies arrive when they're ready."

Dan turned to fully face the resident, indicating his wet scrubs. "Tell me about it."

Gary laughed. "Oh, man! I see you got baptized." He waved and moved off toward Room 9.

When Dan turned back to Delmar, Sylvia was removing the MAST trousers from the lifeless legs. "You losing your magic touch, Marchetti?" someone said behind him.

Alex, Dan's exhausted brain processed. He turned and stared at his friend, who was looking past him at the corpse of Roscoe Delmar. Strangely, a half-smile crooked the corner of Alex's mouth. "What?" Dan managed.

"Never mind." Alex Cole turned his attention to Sylvia. "Nurse, we need you for a new admit in respiratory failure. Room seven." She immediately left Delmar and bustled out.

Alex followed her, calling back over his shoulder, "Can't win 'em all, can we, Marchetti?" *Orlander had taken the bait.*

What's with Alex these days? Dan wondered. Much of the time he seemed his old self: knowledgeable and focused at work, friendly and talkative off the clock.

But that wasn't the same as it used to be either. Talking sports and women, music and movies was fine, but if the conversation turned to work or anything about medicine, the muscles in Alex's face would tense up and quiver while his arms remained folded, and his feet constantly shifted positions. Competitive? He'd always been that way if any other interns were around, but he used to let that fall away when they were alone.

Gail Sanduski poked her head in the door. "Thought you'd like to know. Little Lou Junior checked out just fine. They're all on their way up to Maternity. They wanted to thank you for everything you did." She studied him. "You really should get cleaned up, Dr. Marchetti." Gail winked. "Before yet another emergency rolls in."

Dan groaned, then yawned, the exhaustion returning in a rush. "Haven't tied up the Delmar case yet. Gotta make some calls."

Through the open door of room seven, he could see Alex and their attending, Mike Upton, working on the newest patient, a very-pale young man with an apparent gunshot wound in his side. Vinny Orlander was in there too with his lifesaving equipment.

With lead weights on his eyelids, Dan headed for the central station to leave Delmar's chart. The chairs were empty. *What a shit show. Sure a new life was ushered into this God forsaken world but one went out too!*

Chapter Thirteen

Dan stared intently at the screen as the tech performing the echocardiogram on Ian Forman passed the handheld instrument over the anxious patient's chest. For his part, Forman also turned his head to the screen though the images would not mean very much to him without explanation.

"Looks good everyone, clot is gone," the tech declared.

"You certain?" Dan inquired quickly.

Bringing up the image of the older test that showed the flopping object that even a lay person could deduce was not normal, the new one was clean.

"Not a trace, good work."

Dan placed his right hand on the patient's shoulder and could not hide his grin that stretched from ear to ear. *His patient would never know how close to losing his life he had come!*

****

Four weeks later, on the last shift of his ER rotation, Dan was ready to congratulate himself on making it through another high-energy, high-risk assignment. Walking back with a belly full of pot roast from the cafeteria, he checked his watch: 9:59 p.m. Ten hours and then a whole day to sleep before facing the trials and tribulations of Nine West. He had to smile. After the units and ER, the medical floors should be a piece of cake. Maybe after a while, he'd miss the drama of those intense rotations. After all, he'd learned so much each and every day. Reflecting back, he recognized there had been no other time during his ER stint that was quite as fraught as the "Delmar-Hamilton Night," as he called it. Like a famous prizefight: birth vs. death, calling it a draw. There'd been plenty of other interesting and challenging cases, the majority involving alcohol, drugs, violence, or motor vehicles—sometimes all of the above.

Tonight it seemed eerily quiet. Until a familiar raucous laugh caught his attention and he spotted Dr. Mike Upton, talking animatedly to one of the male nurses across the room. Upton, who had the bedside manner of an annoying frat boy who thought he was hotter, funnier, and smarter than his bros. Aspiring, it seemed, to offend everyone, he'd reached the age of forty-three without losing his taste for scatological and sexual humor, rude practical jokes, and a ready leer that he couldn't hide, even in the tiny cave formed by a thick black mustache and goatee. He had a cue-ball head, shaved and waxed until it shone, undoubtedly an attempt to hide a receding hairline and any gray beyond that. If he hadn't the uncanny ability to choose the quickest path to the right diagnosis in the midst of chaos, the staff would have long ago figured out a way to send him on his inappropriate way. In fact, the more chaotic the better, as if his neural pathways required disorder to fire.

"Yeah, got a live one for ya, Marchetti," Upton called loudly, waggling those x-rays at him now. With a grateful look, Hank Currie took the opportunity to escape, hurrying off toward the elevator with the single word, "Dinner," cast over his shoulder.

"Chest mass," Upton continued, almost as loudly as before, though Dan had nearly reached him. "Big one."

Dan cringed, wondering if the patient was close enough to hear. "I heard you." Keeping a respectful tone with this clown was never easy, but he was the attending on duty.

Laughing as if Dan were joking, Upton assured him, "No worries there. No-speak-a-de-English, y'know?" He held the chest x-rays up toward the light, ignoring the lit reading boxes. "Yep. Really big chest mass." He smirked as if enjoying a private joke at Dan's expense. "Came in with severe pleuritic chest pain."

Dan took the films from him and went to hang them on the reading box where he could see them better. "Could be mediastinal." The bright white area appeared to be in the center of the chest, between the lungs instead of inside either of them. "She a smoker?" Dan knew the patient was female because of the ample breast shadows on the films.

"Don't know," Mike answered with a shrug. "Probably."

Dan looked his way. "Don't know? Did you get a history?"

"Not that easy with the language barrier. Besides, I prefer to leave all the meticulous work to you young geniuses."

"Sure." Dan found it impossible to hide his annoyance. Upton was as lazy as they come. "I see the ER's just teeming with patients."

The attending grinned and answered, "Gotta go see a man about a horse." As Gail joined them, he gave her a broad wink. "A very large horse, if you know what I mean." Then he laughed heartily at his own joke and headed for the restrooms.

Dan shared a grimace with Gail. "God, I cannot stand that guy! My condolences on being stuck with him."

Gail's eyes twinkled as she handed him the new patient's chart and led the way toward the appropriate room. "Well, this time, he would've loved to stay longer with the patient. But *she* very clearly asked for a 'new doctor'."

Mystified, Dan entered the room, reading from the chart. "Hello, Ms....Elena Guillermo? I'm Dr. Marchetti and—" He glanced up, and the words tangled in his throat so nothing more could get out.

Sitting on the edge of the gurney glowered an absolutely stunning young woman of perhaps twenty-five. Above the very snug spandex pants in fire-engine red, even the unflattering lines of the incongruous blue Johnny coat couldn't hide the abundance of bosom hinted at on the x-rays. She looked anything but sick. Dan noted the shining black hair parted on the side that fell to her shoulders, the perfectly applied makeup, red polished nails, and the matching red-satin stiletto heels with a sexy ankle strap.

And her eyes! Huge and, in this light, so dark they appeared blacker than her hair, they smoldered now and greeted Dan with the challenge, even as she winced in sudden pain. "No Upton?" she demanded, breathing in short, shallow breaths.

"No Upton," Dan confirmed, smiling. Upton must have set a record pissing this looker off. Pointing to his name badge, he said, "New doctor. Dan Marchetti."

She nodded, seemed to relax a bit, but her eyes locked with his and Dan could tell the jury was still out on him.

"Ah!" The involuntary cry wrenched from her as she leaned farther forward, clutching the edges of the gurney with white-knuckled hands.

"Are you in a great deal of pain?" Dan asked, still making no move to touch her.

She tilted her head ever so slightly as if to indicate that she didn't understand. "I no speak," she managed to whisper between obviously painful breaths, "very well English."

"We need an interpreter," Gail commented. "But I think everyone's gone home. Even Alma Ramirez. She's a nurse on the ninth floor. She's from Argentina."

"Ah, *si! Argentina!*" exclaimed Elena, pointing excitedly to her chest and then holding her hand there, pressed against the pain.

Dan and Gail both nodded their understanding, but Gail told Dan, "I'm pretty sure Alma's on days right now. I'll make a call after you've done your exam."

Dan nodded, reading her loud-and-clear. He certainly didn't want to be left alone while examining an offended woman who didn't speak the language and had already had to demand a new doctor.

Dan held up his stethoscope. "I need to listen to your heart and lungs, Ms. Guillermo." She stared at him with suspicion. He put the earpieces in place and pressed the disk of the chest piece to his own upper body to demonstrate. Then he faced it toward her and asked, "Okay?" He pulled gently at the edge of the blue cloth and placed the chest piece just beneath it, saying, "I need to listen under here." Elena looked uncertain.

Her reluctance was clear, but she said, "Okay."

"Debajo," Gail said suddenly and shrugged at Dan's surprised look. "Below. Funny what words you pick up here and there."

"Debajo?" Elena repeated, looking at Dan, then Gail. "No Upton?"

"No Upton," Dan promised solemnly. He held his gaze steady on hers for the long moment those dark eyes probed him, hoping she could read his intent there.

Finally, with another wince of pain, she nodded assent. *"Debajo."*

With the greatest of care, Dan slowly and respectfully moved his hand and stethoscope chest piece beneath her clothing, first around her upper chest, then, very cautiously, beneath her left breast. She kept her eyes locked on his, and he sensed she was watching for the slightest hint his intentions were not entirely medical. Apparently, Dan was passing the test because, still watching him closely and continuing the deep inhalations and exhalations, Elena pushed herself completely upright, battling the increased discomfort. This lifted her heavy breasts and made it easier for Dan to hear her lungs and heart from below. When he removed the stethoscope's diaphragm and applied it to her back, she slumped a little forward again with obvious relief.

Dan moved back a step. He had heard a clear 'rub', a sound most likely of the mass coming in contact with the pleura that lined the chest cavity, covering the lungs. Such pressing together of tissues with every breath certainly explained the chest pain.

Her eyes sought his verdict.

"Do you smoke?" Dan asked, pretending to take a cigarette in and out of his mouth. She nodded yes, seeming somewhat embarrassed to admit it. He wasn't surprised, as he'd detected a faint odor of cigarette smoke, even though her hair was clean and her fingers showed no nicotine stains.

Chances were that the mass was cancer, yet she appeared so healthy. Slender without that too-thin look of so many girls today; clear, bright eyes and tawny skin that glowed with well-being. The chart revealed vital signs taken when she first came in. Pulse rate, BP, and temp were all slightly elevated, but easily explained by stress, anxiety, and anger over her first encounter with Upton. The pulse-ox reading showed the saturation of oxygen in her blood to be a little low, but she'd been breathing shallowly to lessen the pain. Dan was surprised that except for the pain, she seemed relatively healthy, something not well explained with a large cancerous mass.

He patted her shoulder gently. "Okay. I will be back soon." With two fingers pointed downward, he mimicked legs walking out to the main area and then back into the room. Understanding dawned in her eyes and she actually laughed, though that broke off quickly with the pain it caused. She nodded.

As Dan and Gail left the room, he told her, "See if you can find that interpreter, okay?"

"Sure." Gail's mouth quirked with a teasing smile; she kept her voice low. "You seem to be doing okay on your own, Dr. 'No Upton'." She moved away toward the phones.

Mike Upton himself was back at the lightbox, staring at Elena's chest x-rays. He looked up with great curiosity and a little smirk as Dan joined him. "Get that history you wanted?"

"Not too much; we need an interpreter. But we figured out that she does smoke. The exam didn't reveal anything except the rub you'd expect from that mass where it is." He pointed to it on the x-ray in front of him. "She seems completely healthy otherwise."

"Healthy? I'll say. Quite athletic, in fact." When Dan looked at him in complete bafflement, he asked, "You didn't find out? She's a stripper at the Kit Kat Lounge."

"A stripper. How do you know?"

"I never forget a, you know, face." His open palms were coming up to describe those breasts.

Dan looked away, back at the x-rays that revealed the truth within that ample bosom. "Think it's CA?"

Mercifully distracted, Upton glanced at the films again. "Possibly. Lung or maybe lymphoma."

Dan kept staring at one of the images; he couldn't seem to look away. Dan pulled the film free and took it around to the side of the unit, stepped on the foot pedal to activate the hot light, and held the film up to it. "What're you looking at, Dan?" Mike Upton came around to peer over his shoulder.

"Calcification, maybe. Or something. Geez, it looks like a tooth."

"A tooth?" Upton squinted at the image then clapped Dan on the shoulder. "Well, I'll give you it's an irregular calcification, not surprising for a large mass. But I don't see a tooth. Then again, you're the intern so you run it down to radiology and see who's down there to check it out."

Dan rubbed his eyes and ran a hand through his rumpled hair. He *was* tired. But it did look like a tooth.

"First, let's get some labs, blood gas, a bed upstairs, and some pain meds going." He sounded as if he were reading from a cookbook. "Write the orders, okay?" Upton yawned and stretched. "I'm heading for the on-call room before the universe realizes we got a practically empty ER here."

Dan offered, "How 'bout I get a CAT of her chest in the a.m.?"

"Yeah, superb idea."

Quickly, Dan wrote the orders, the first for Elena's pain meds, and both Gail and Hank came to take care of them. Gail confirmed she was still waiting for a call-back from any of the three people who might serve as an interpreter. Finished with his tasks, for now, Dan buzzed radiology.

"Dr. Schneiweiss," a voice answered.

"Oh, nice. Working late again, Pete? It's Dan Marchetti. Can I bring down some films to review with you?"

"Sure. Nothing to do but to go home and be with the family."

Dan took the stairs down to radiology and greeted the amiable tow-headed Pete, who'd recently earned the honor of DCH Employee with the Largest Nose.

"Patient came in with pleuritic chest pain; smoker; everything normal otherwise. In fact, the very picture of health." Dan handed Pete the films, and Pete—all business now—hung them and scrutinized each silently. Dan fidgeted. "Sorta looks like a lymphoma, but I thought I saw something else."

"Oh, you mean this tooth? You've got good eyes, Dan. Good instincts. So, what do you think that means?"

Dan searched his memory banks, remembering how certain crude tumors formed from rudimentary embryonic cell layers and sometimes included bits of hair, bone, fat, teeth. "It's a teratoma?"

Pete smiled at his approval. "Think so. Could still be a lymphoma—or even a malignant teratoma—but with her health so robust, I bet it's benign."

"Great."

"Either way, it'll have to come out. Better call Bosnan." Pete Schneiweiss checked his watch. "You can use my phone. I'm gonna head home." He sighed and gave Dan an ironic smile.

"Thanks for staying, Pete."

Schneiweiss shrugged into his windbreaker. "Thank *you* for bringing me something interesting to look at."

He found Elena sitting back comfortably on the bed, smiling and eating some lime Jell-O. The pain meds had obviously kicked in. She'd slipped out of her stilettos—which lay nearby on the floor—and now sat like some teenager with her bare feet up on the bed and those lovely red-clad legs unconcealed by the hospital gown. She'd been talking in Spanish to another young woman at her bedside, but as he entered, Elena gave him a huge smile, then pointed toward the other woman with her spoon. *"Mi prima, Doctor Marchetti."*

He looked to the other woman and held out his hand. "You're the interpreter? Nurse Alma Ramirez?"

She shook his hand, laughing. "Interpreter, yes. Nurse, no. I'm Elena's cousin Yolanda." She looked a few years older but was pretty and fit enough that Dan wondered if she practiced the same profession.

"Thanks for coming in, Yolanda. We can really use some help with translation."

"So I hear." Her dark eyes teased him, but gently.

"Please tell Elena that we've found what looks like a growth in her chest." Dan pointed to the area between Elena's breasts. "When she breathes, it rubs against her lungs and causes the pain." He waited for Yolanda to catch up with him.

He watched Elena's eyes get very serious and she set aside her Jell-O. Neither of the women were smiling now.

"What kind of growth?" Yolanda asked, even before Elena—her eyes suddenly fearful—could prompt her. "Cancer?"

"It may be, but we think that it's probably not a cancer."

Yolanda quickly conveyed this, and the fear eased a bit in Elena's eyes, which she kept riveted on him while she listened to the conversation. "We think it's a kind of benign tumor called a teratoma. This one's pretty unusual and seems to have a tooth in it."

"A tooth? She swallowed a tooth?"

"No, no, nothing like that. This type of tumor is very rudimentary." He paused, wondering just how much English Yolanda knew. When she nodded that she understood him, he went on. "They have pieces of tissue from different parts of the body inside. Not all would show up on an x-ray, but the tooth did."

Yolanda turned back to her cousin and translated this, then the words Elena spoke in response: "What now?"

"Surgery."

Yolanda interrupted, "Even if it's not cancer?"

"It still has to come out," Dan told her. "It's already causing her terrible pain and will continue to grow and interfere with her breathing." While Yolanda conveyed all this, Dan decided against telling them that, if the mass broke into the trachea, Elena could even cough up hair and fat and other tissues.

"Will there be a scar?" Yolanda asked.

Dan looked away from Elena's piercing gaze, at Yolanda. "Yes. The surgeon needs to make an incision through her breastbone." He traced the line down his own chest.

"No, no!" Elena wailed. "Dancer. No cut, no cut!"

"We have no choice," he told her, meeting her gaze steadily now. "I'm sorry." This she didn't seem to understand.

"She's a dancer," Yolanda repeated, giving her shoulders an unambiguous little shimmy.

"Yes, I know."

"She will not be able to make a living anymore." Yolanda's eyes implored him to amend this course of action. Tears gathered in Yolanda's eyes. "Her family in Argentina depends on her."

"I'm sorry." Dan looked first at Yolanda, then at Elena, addressing her directly. "You must have the surgery to stop the pain. The growth will keep getting bigger." When Yolanda had translated this and Elena's expression remained unpersuaded, he continued, "You won't be able to dance if you can't breathe." Now, as Yolanda's voice explained his words, tears filled Elena's eyes as well.

Dan reached out to comfort his patient by holding her hand. "I'm so very sorry." Elena immediately brought his hand to her lips and kissed it, holding his gaze with what he read as gratitude and high regard.

And just like that, Dan felt his body become aroused. Funny, all the time he was examining her magnificent breasts, he'd felt completely professional. Yet now it was undone by this woman's appreciation. Feeling the rush of color to his face, he gently freed his hand and used it to pat her shoulder awkwardly, answering her soft, '*Muchas gracias*' with, "You're welcome, Elena."

Gail came in to say, "They've got a room ready for her upstairs, Dr. Marchetti."

At the end of a rapid exchange in Spanish, Yolanda turned to Dan and said, "Elena wants to know if this is really weird…if she's a…how you say…freak or something?"

"It's very unusual," Dan said to them, "but not in a bad way." As Yolanda conveyed this, a thought came to Dan, and he couldn't resist. "Tell her she's an exotic dancer with an exotic tumor!"

It pleased him to see Elena laugh again.

Chapter Fourteen

"You work in the Respiratory Therapy Department at Deerwood, right?" Diane inquired of one of the men unloading the fresh lobsters trucked in from Maine that summer morning. This day, Sunday, was slated to be an event for the ages, hosted by the Werner family, replete with a deeply dug pit heated by hot coals and covered by seaweed. Underneath, a cornucopia of delicious corn on the cobb, the aforementioned lobsters, whole chickens, and potatoes. The entertainment, two country western bands and a dance floor.

"Correct, I'm Vinny Orlander, a RT at Deerwood, Dr. Werner. Trying to make some additional money, that's all."

"Great. I get it," Diane smiled brightly, peeling off to help with the table arrangements.

So this is how the wealthy people live. Huge home, multiple acres of expensive real estate, two adorable blonde haired children, three annoying shih tzus barking constantly at him.

"Orlander, bring the crates close to that pit at the edge of the property over there," pointed the transportation manager for Diane's husband, the owner of a large trucking company that his father had built over many decades. Only to die suddenly of a massive stroke five years ago, leaving the running of his huge enterprise to his only child. Craig Werner was an interesting type, a foul tempered, elitist who couldn't relate to his wife's fellow interns and their life devoid of money and expensive toys. Much more in tune with the country club set.

Vinny positioned the dolly and managed to load more crates than most, his strength an asset he leveraged to his benefit. One of the younger dogs continued to growl and nip at one of his hairless legs, exposed when he chose cargo shorts on that steamy day.

"Get the fuck away from me you little shit," he muttered under his breath. Unfortunately, his canine 'friend' didn't understand or just chose to ignore him. *They have two others, they won't miss this one.*

Nikki and Dan were the first to arrive, an hour early, after mis-remembering the start time.

"This is some shindig Dan. Not one but two country bands, a dance floor, the property is magnificently laid out, the gardens..." Nikki gushed.

"I know, a far cry from the house staff parties we have planned." Dan just shook his head and laughed.

"You mean the toga party where you took a sheet off your bed, wrapped it around you and threw some chips and beer out for everyone?"

"I know, didn't get to bed until 5AM the next day. Question, where are the eats? Did you see anything?"

A few hours later, the backyard was full of over 100 guests. "Come to think about it, no I haven't except for a few bowls of peanuts, dips, and crackers."

Moments later however, Diane announced to her many friends which included many hospital attendings, and the entire house staff.

"Now, to uncover the pit." With that, she pointed to the men peeling back the coverings of a dirt pit, approximately ten feet by fifteen, and at least a foot and a half deep.

"By the way, has anyone seen a shih tzu with a rather difficult disposition running around? The other two are in the house." Diane laughed at her inquiry. Nobody responded however. "Oh well, she'll turn up yet." With a wave of her hand, Diane returned to the house to retrieve some bottles of red wine for the bar, now tended by Vinny.

In the meantime, a few of the workers continued to uncover the pit, the cooked seafood, chickens, potatoes and corn suddenly making their appearance, steam jetting into the air right above them. Spontaneous applause rang out along with screeches of delight after the sizeable crowd now encircling the feast realized the smorgasbord of fantastic eats that awaited them.

Suddenly, Dave's girlfriend stationed at the far end of the pit yelled, "Oh my God!" before turning her head away. Dan gazed at the area of concern, at first believing the whitish object represented a chicken that perhaps hadn't received enough heat from the burning coals but on closer inspection, was the dead carcass of the missing dog.

"Must of gone in after the food and succumbed to the heat," a surgeon Dan recognized from the vascular service, commented.

Vinny just smiled ever so slightly from behind the portable bar.

Chapter Fifteen

Dan waited anxiously for the conference to begin, know that his esophageal varices case was to be dissected. Abraham Tucker's quote, "forewarned is forearmed," would precisely fit the moment.

"Dr. Marchetti, the autopsy showed that the patient's esophagus was split open by a Sengstaken-Blakemore tube that had migrated a fairly substantial distance from your original placement, this according to your notes. Additionally," the pathologist now glancing at his notes, "the balloon pressures both exceeded the recommended maximum 15mmHg, one was 27, the other 25. Consequently, such pressures undoubtedly damaged the walls of the esophagus and split it like one of those Chinese paper lanterns."

Dan's arms seemed to go limp, this last minute Morbidity and Mortality (M&M) meeting and findings, shaking him to the core. Just then the damaged structure excised from the corpse appeared on the computer screen, the macerated cylindrical structure a hideous site indeed.

Dan sat staring at the macabre image, damage he apparently rendered with his fucked up placement of that outdated Machiavellian monstrosity. The M&M meeting, convened monthly to discuss mishaps and medical errors needs to be renamed the 'Maul and Mutilate' conference. The fifty or so attendees began to file out, some shaking their heads in disbelief, having never seen such an occurrence, ever. *How did this happen? He was certain his landmarks had been correct and that the SB tube had been adequately secured, or at least he believed so. Had his overwhelming fatigue contributed to such a debacle? A Libby Zion disaster?*

Chapter Sixteen

Linda Ferrante grimaced and took another sip of coffee, trying to fill her nostrils with its pungent aroma. She'd managed to limit her time at the courthouse defending punks to only a few quick cases. Instead, today she was hunkered down with extra paperwork and research for Connor, Bryson, and Sherman, using her considerable writing skills to move along several important cases and putting her in charge of the paralegals and office interns.

While she enjoyed the enthusiasm of her staff, much of the tasks were mind-numbingly boring, and they also kept her cooped up all day with the malodorous Kip Carpenter. An exemplary employee, he was a nice enough man, a shy and skinny forty-year-old with a touch of gray at his temples. From the beginning, Linda's acute sense of smell had been affronted by his habitual bad breath, but for the last few weeks, he'd been suffering from some terrible allergy that clogged his sinuses, so that he not only was constantly sniffling but was also forced to breathe through his mouth.

Linda set aside her now-empty mug and reshuffled the papers she'd been perusing, then clipped them together and placed them in her outbox. Behind her, Kip sniffled, then released a long, gusty sigh, no doubt expelling yet another tide of fetid breath. She was just wondering if the new Evergreen Spice scent she'd seen in the store might be more effective than this Heavenly Gardenia air freshener she had plugged in when her phone rang. Startled, she grabbed for it as guiltily as if she'd been caught in some underhanded plot against a colleague. *Guilt overtook her and she hung up the telephone.*

That night, Dan turned in early but not too long after, Dan awoke suddenly and screamed loudly, the power of his voice echoing throughout his apartment. The sparse furnishings unable to dampen the noise level. His tee shirt was drenched as was his mop of hair, partially plastered to the front of his skull. The nightmare still so fresh, so absolutely frightening. A Sengstaken-Blakemore tube had been ripped from his throat, balloons deployed, the tubing a bloody mess. Torrents of blood poured from his mouth, threatening to drench his entire bed and rug. Laughing in a chair enjoying it all was none one other than Alex Cole, his mercurial and 'loyal' friend.

Dreaming about such an event was not surprising, in and of itself, since the debacle so recent with his patient. Gnawing at his gut however was the presence in his subconscious of his neighbor and fellow intern, Alex Cole. In reality, Cole wasn't really a good friend, too self-absorbed, too obsessed with being noticed. Dan simply needed to face the facts about him. But there was something else. Alex seemed to derive some pleasure in the cascade of events that had befallen Dan. Whereas others rallied around him, knowing the tremendous anguish he was feeling, Alex remained aloof, detached. Could he actually be reveling in his agony? Dan just shook his head in disbelief. Very fucked up. *Go back to sleep, your thoughts are getting exceedingly dark. Can't go there now.*

Chapter Seventeen

"Hullo?" She winced; too late to answer properly with: "Ms. Ferrante. How may I help you?" A crisp female voice commanded, "Please hold for District Attorney Bradden," and was gone before Linda could reply. *I hope he doesn't inquire as to what lead to her hanging up the phone the previous time.* A long moment of dead air followed, then a *click* and his resonant voice, sounding very cordial: "Ms. Ferrante...Linda? I hope you'll remember our meeting at that Bar Association mixer recently."

"Of course. How are you?" she said, unable to keep the curiosity out of her reply.

"Fine, fine." He chuckled. "I must say you made quite an impression on me."

Linda swallowed nervously. That hadn't been the first time they'd met, but he probably didn't remember those earlier encounters because she'd maintained such a low profile. The last time they encountered each other, he'd interrupted her conversation with a small group of other defense lawyers. Already annoyed at his interruption, she didn't stop to think whether it might be wise to correct the D.A. She just did: courteously, but in such succinct detail that it was clearly irrefutable. He'd laughed and saluted her with his wineglass and then asked her name and which firm she worked for.

Before Linda could think of anything to say, Bradden went on, still sounding amused. "You really piqued my interest, so I've been checking you out. Besides all the knowledgeable folks at C, B & S, I talked to the firm you worked for in New York. Quite impressive work there. Everyone spoke very highly of you. And, as it happens, I'm well acquainted with Mike Lowengaard."

It hadn't seemed to matter that she remained silent; he just kept talking while she desperately wondered what this was about and what Mike had to do with this call.

"I didn't realize you'd done so much prosecutorial work—and with such commendable results. It seems one of Deerwood's brightest lights is hiding under a bushel basket."

She had to say something. "Uh, well, thanks?"

"So I think it's time you came out to shine. May I take you to lunch next week?" But as she tried to find an appropriately polite way to decline, he added, "I'd like to offer you a job."

Shocked, Linda's first thought was, *No thanks.* The idea of working in the D.A.'s office held very little charm, especially under the authority of an arrogant political carnivore like Scott Bradden, but behind her, Linda could hear Kip Carpenter begin one of his unrestrained sneezing fits. "What kind of a job?" she managed to ask in a low voice.

"As an Assistant D.A., naturally. I can't guarantee a sizable bump over your current salary but the position is a bona fide resume builder. Let's meet so I can give you more details and answer all your questions. Shall we say, next Wednesday, noon at The Arms?"

The hotel offered palate-pleasing food worthy of an award-winning restaurant with a superb lunch menu from the grill. She pictured herself savoring a delectable meal in one of those cavernous booths, sitting across from the District Attorney, a man any woman would admit was "easy on the eyes," as Nonna used to say of her favorite movie actors. Realizing lunch didn't mean she had to accept the job, she agreed, "Okay, Mr. Bradden."

"It's Scott to you, Linda, whether you come to work here or not. Now, I just realized I'm about to be late for a meeting, so I'll let you go. See you at noon on Wednesday; bring your appetite." He clicked off before she could utter another word. Linda set down the receiver and stared at it and wondered why he had reached out to her. Was he was looking to improve the agency's gender balance? Maybe he wanted a New York touch? There'd been a lot of speculation around the firm's watercooler lately, especially when the state's Republican Party had endorsed Bradden as their candidate for Attorney General. He had the cunning yet implacable demeanor they needed, the courtroom savvy, and the lust for power. Maybe in addition to money, he was also shopping for an attractive, younger professional woman to smile for the cameras. Acceptable arm candy for a political run with a New York, politically correct gender hire and maybe some photo ops. Linda bit back a sudden chuckle. *This should be interesting.* Yes, she should think this over very carefully. Go have a nice lunch and listen to what Scott Bradden had to offer. She respected her bosses, but maybe it was time for a change.

Chapter Eighteen

Dan gulped his fourth coffee that morning, his body rebelling against his having been awake for what felt like eternity without a minute of sleep. Another hour or so and he would be allowed to go home but hell, all that caffeine…

"Vinny, can you bring me the EKG machine outside the door please?" Dan asked rather groggily, his voice now reflecting the strange combination of his bone weariness mixed with the equivalent of a few 5 hour energy drinks. The effect, bizarre, somewhere between Robin Williams doing standup and an MMA fighter getting the shit being pummeled out of him.

"This shouldn't be too hard to accomplish," Vinny muttered to himself. He would offer to place the leads as the EKG techs were nowhere in sight, quietly reminding himself to place the EKG's precordial leads greater than two centimeters above their correct placement and the others left and below the designated areas. This would guarantee an erroneous interpretation if Marchetti didn't notice first and correct them. He folded and stuffed his 'cheat' sheet, prepared days before in case the occasion arose, into his oversized pockets which afforded him so much room to hide the objects of his trade. Prefilled syringes, medical vials, and the like.

Orlander pushed the EKG machine, housed behind an open hallway closet door, and quickly bent back and forth movement to the machine's delicate lead wires so as to possibly facilitate interpretation abnormalities. That and lead placement irregularities (he would perform the placement) should undoubtedly cause Marchetti to overreact and believe the heart muscle was in trouble. He would then act accordingly. *This is really fun, certainly adds a level of intrigue to my humdrum day and clever as all get out.*

"Tell me again about your chest pain, Mrs. Flores."

"Hurts when I take a deep breath," she managed to speak in an interrupted fashion, cautiously inhaling each time, the discomfort so severe. Dan had concluded from his exam that the pain was more than likely not coming from ischemia, insufficient blood flow to her coronary arteries. Perhaps pleurisy, an inflammation of the coverings of the lungs, the pleura.

Still she sported a big-time smoking history and high blood pressure, surefire cardiac risk factors he should not ignore. Dan looked around, wondering where Vinny was with the EKG machine he requested.

"Vinny, you there." Suddenly, the taciturn respiratory therapist appeared, pulling the cart behind him, brushing the opened door as he entered.

"Be careful with that bud, thought you skipped town on me," Dan whispered good-naturedly to the enigmatic respiratory therapist. Wasting no time, Vinny placed the leads on the 60 year old woman, who had been admitted with an infected gallbladder.

"Thank you. I could use the help."

"Please stay as still as possible," Vinny advised. Before long, the EKG began to print. Dan recalled that her admission EKG had showed signs of a thickened wall of her left ventricle, a result of her longstanding hypertension, but nothing otherwise alarming. That was then but not now.

"Is something wrong, Dr. Marchetti?" Dan stared at the recording being run, his consternation now visible on his boyish-looking face. *ST depressions, 4 millimeters throughout all the leads.* Dan's gaze quickly descended to his patient lying in the hospital bed, his quizzical expression now alarming Mrs. Jackson.

"Well, there are some changes here and I believe it prudent to transfer you to the Coronary Care Unit or at least the telemetry unit to be on the safe side."

"Am I having a heart attack?"

Dan reached for her now tremulous right hand and held it between his own. "I don't know as of yet but I am going to order new medicines and check some lab work right away. No matter what, you are in exactly the right place."

"I came in with a gallbladder attack and now my heart is causing trouble?" Just then she yelped at another spasm of pain, sounding ironically like a cat howling at the moon.

Chapter Nineteen

Dan entered room 915 and introduced himself to the couple awaiting him. Joseph Bonfiglio, the patient, looked to be in his mid-thirties, and, though he gave Dan a ready smile, the man seemed too pale for his Italian heritage and embarrassed by the sagging on the left side of his face.

Bell's palsy, Dan thought. "So, Mr. Bonfiglio—"He broke off abruptly and laughed at the grimace he saw. "Ah, Joseph…?"

The grin was back; he was the kind of guy Dan liked right away. "I'm Joe. Not even my mother calls me Joseph anymore. And this is my wife, Sue."

Having already shaken the hand Joe offered, Dan turned to do the same with a cute brunette with worried eyes and a slight bulge in her yellow maternity T-shirt proclaiming *Yes, I am!* over an arrow pointing down.

"Hey, Doc, okay if I call you…" he read the name tag as if making sure he'd heard right, "Dante?"

"Make that Dan, and we're in business."

Both Joe and Sue laughed. The way their heads tilted unconsciously toward each other hinted they'd been laughing together for many years despite their youth.

"We are so anxious to get some answers as to why my husband feels so poorly."

"I understand. So, Joe, how have you been feeling?"

Joe gave a little nod as if making up his mind about something. "I like you and feel I can trust you. A firm handshake; not afraid to laugh or be called by your first name—and a fellow *paisan* to boot." Suddenly, Joe's face took on a serious expression. "I'm gonna level with you, Dan. Not so cracking lately. Always been healthy as a horse; I eat right and keep fit. Painting houses is strenuous work, y' know. My little business has really taken off with all the renovations in this area. But now I'm feelin' tired all the time. I had to hire extra college kids to help out this summer." He paused to swallow, the effort

111

clearly uncomfortable. "My throat's been sore for more than a week. And now this." He pointed to the left side of his face with a sheepish, lopsided grin. "Damnedest thing."

"Well, let me check you out, okay?" Dan proceeded to get Joe's history and complete the physical exam. Joe, indeed, had a facial nerve paralysis, extreme pallor, and yellow-pinpoint Roth spots in his eye grounds—all ominous signs. Dan saw something else in those eyes, a certain look. *He suspects that he is seriously ill.*

*"Beep, beep, beep...*Dr. Marchetti, call hematology lab 3455...3455."

"One minute, Joe." He gestured toward the bedside table. "Mind if I use your phone?" He winked. "Local call."

"No problem, but leave a quarter." Joe turned his attention to his wife, patting her hand reassuringly as they started talking about visiting hours and when the rest of the family might arrive.

Dan dialed, and the phone rang once before the tech down in the lab got on, sounding urgent: "Dan, your man's got leukemia or something. White count is 180,000, and the smear is full of blasts."

Dan recognized the voice. With a name like Isaak Zoller and the initials I.Z., it was easy to see why everyone called him Izzy. The private joke among the house staff, who referred to him as the 'extra resident' because he so enjoyed participating in the diagnostic process, was asking, "Izzy a doctor yet?"

"What else do you have for me?"

"Bonfiglio's hematocrit is 22, the blast forms—looks like myeloblasts. Platelets are 22,000."

Shit, AML! Dan could feel his entire body stiffen as he tried not to look at Joe. Fortunately, Joe didn't know the call concerned his tests, and in case he suspected, Dan wasn't ready for him to know the gravity of the news. He managed a light tone. "Thanks, Izzy. You're the greatest. A true member of the hall of fame of lab techs."

Izzy laughed out loud. "Fuck you, Marchetti. You with him now?"

Forcing a chuckle, Dan answered, "That's correct."

"G'luck with that."

They both hung up, and Dan turned to his patient. "Joe, I'll be back later to see you after we have some more lab results. Okay?"

"Sure." Joe pushed back his covers. "I'll just take this opportunity to hit the john." He struggled awkwardly to his feet, wrestling to keep the flimsy hospital gown protecting his dignity. "Damn. Hate these things." Joe started for the bathroom, clutching the gown behind him to hide his bare buttocks, but still exposing far too much of his well-muscled legs. Add to that those little, DCH-issued terrycloth slipper socks with nonskid soles, Joe offered a poignant glimpse of "patienthood."

"Oh, by the way," Joe's nurse, Mandy, interjected, "you have visitors: your mother and your kids." She glanced at Dan to include him in her next question. "Should I send them in?"

"Not right now I'm afraid. We will need to consider taking precautions concerning microorganisms, 'bugs' I mean that could be brought in from outside. I'll catch up with you a shortly. I need to make some calls and alternative arrangements," Dan told him, and Joe nodded as he slipped into the bathroom and closed the door.

Mandy shared a look with Dan. He could tell she'd guessed the seriousness of Joe's illness. She went to straighten Joe's bedclothes and check the level of ice water in the pitcher. Dan followed Sue out into the hall and waved as she left him, on her way toward a cluster of figures not far down the corridor. Dan had a quick view of a woman in her forties shepherding three little girls, one who looked to be around six and the others, clearly identical twins, probably three years younger—all with round faces amid mops of wildly tousled black hair.

Would Joe live to see them grown? The labs were consistent with acute myelogenous leukemia, and the Bell's palsy almost certainly indicated central nervous system involvement. He could be gone before his fourth child even arrived.

The real prospect of that gave Dan a gnawing sensation in the gut as he moved to the nurse's desk and flopped down into the chair. "Oh brother."

Dan knew that Joe's attending always consulted the oncology attending, Dr. Cyrus Klonter who though smart as hell, remained harder to read as a person. His wispy blond hair and mustache seemed perfectly matched to his reticent and self-effacing manner.

While Dan left a message with Klonter's service, he wondered how Joe would respond to such news. The strong desire to be 1,000 miles away on some Caribbean beach started to surge up in him, partly fueled by how much he identified with the laid-back *paisan*, but someone else's emergency interrupted.

"*Beep, beep, beep*...Dr. Marchetti, Room 902, stat...902, stat!"

Dan leaped up and rushed down the long hall. He didn't recall any patient of his yet in that room. He clenched his jaws hard, pushing the thought of Joe and his family to the back of his mind.

Luckily, the new patient just required some oxygen and reassurance and Dan next looked in on Elena Guillermo who was two days post-op in the next room. He found her doing very well, and Dr. Bosnan expressed great pleasure at how smoothly the surgery had gone as well as the news that the tumor was benign. "We sent it down to pathology for a frozen section," she told Dan. "No malignancy. You might want to go down there and take a look at it. Not every day you see a teratoma—much less one with both a tooth and hair."

By the time he returned to Joe's bedside that evening, he had become militantly optimistic about the young family man's chances, not based on fact but fervent hope. Meanwhile, Cyrus Klonter told Joe he had leukemia: cancer. The reserved oncologist said the usual things about grave illness and unknown outcomes. They talked about the treatment that was needed to bring him into remission and that he needed to stay in the hospital a while.

Joe and Sue sat sitting side by side and listened without interruption. When prompted, they nodded, but Dan was sure they weren't taking it all in just yet. He saw the blankness of their faces, eyes that seemed focused inward on the turmoil of their own thoughts, and how they grasped each other's hands so tightly the fingers started turning blue from lack of circulation. When asked if they had any questions, they both shook their heads.

Still, he thought that the Bonfiglios would eventually start to ask some of the questions—especially after the news had sunk in a little. but Joe and Sue just stared at each other.

That evening, Dan headed home by walking out of his way to enter the park, needing some time to process what his family had in common with the Bonfiglio clan. Even though he was healthy, he knew that some young doctors identified too closely and imagined themselves contracting the disease. Dan needed to steal himself from that trap. So he headed for a favorite spot, a lakeside bench in a little stand of weeping willows. Since it was hidden from view until he was nearly upon it, he didn't see till the last moment that it was already occupied. Starting to walk past, he recognized the long auburn hair and the slender figure dressed in jeans and a dark-green shirt. She looked up as his sneakers crunched toward her over the scattered leaves. Nikki Saxon.

Her face brightened. "Hi, Dante!" She'd been sitting in the middle of the bench, not inviting a casual passerby to join her, but now, she scooted over and left him plenty of room to sit. He did, lowering himself with a little groan at the way his body felt after too many nights on the creaking on-call cots.

Nikki laughed. "Sounding old, Dr. Marchetti!"

He laughed and stretched. He turned to face her, and for the first time, he noticed that her eyes were a little red and puffy as if she'd been crying. Her whole face looked tired. He'd gotten a bit used to that look. Everyone who pulled long hours and worked variable shifts, especially those who dealt daily with misery, had the same look.

Nikki was thin. He realized she was wearing the same outfit as when he first met her: black jeans and that long-sleeve polo shirt in Deerwood High green. Those garments had been deliciously snug three months ago, but now they fit her more loosely. Not at all unattractive, just different. Maybe more was going on in her life than just the stresses of work.

The sudden honking of Canadian geese winging southward pulled Nikki's gaze to the sunset sky.

"I love this spot," Nikki murmured, still gazing at the view.

Dan turned his face to the beauty of the dying day, the way red and gold light rippled across the water toward them just before the sun sank out of view, beyond the trees on the lake's opposite shore. "Yeah," he said, "me too." She looked at him with those sad eyes, a shade darker green in the dimming light, and he felt suddenly as awkward and stirred as the first moment he met her. Remembering their pledge to stay friends, he put on another voice, imitating a lounge lizard with a worn-out pickup line: "You come here often?"

She didn't laugh, but she did smile, taking most of the sadness from her eyes. "Mainly when I need to think."

But the suddenly stiffening breeze ruffled her reddish hair, pushed long strands across her face. She shivered and rubbed her sleeves to warm her arms inside. "Ooooh! Time to go, I guess."

He hopped up. "Yeah. It'll be dark soon. Thanks for sharing the spot for a little while."

She rose and began to move in the opposite direction. "Any time."

He gave her a little wave and started to turn away, but her voice called after him, "Dante!" He spun around at the intensity in it.

But she didn't say more. After a moment, she just sighed and shook her head with a little hollow laugh. "Nothing, really. It was nice seeing you again."

Keeping it light, he doffed and flourished an invisible hat, bowing over it. "The pleasure was all mine."

They both laughed and waved, then went on their way, as if this had only been a chance meeting of two friendly colleagues—as it should be. Dan wanted desperately to look back and watch her go, but he didn't.

Chapter Twenty

"Oh forgot the chart," the orderly spoke out loud to no one in particular. However, Orlander overheard the lament hidden from view inside a doorway ten feet away.

Finally, satisfied he was alone with the patient, he entered the hallway. The patient's gurney had been pushed to the side, abutting the wall after the orderly realized that he had left Mrs. Simpson's chart in the CAT Scanning Room. Orlander eyed the heparin drip hanging from the IV pole, its rate of infusion carefully programmed to deliver the potent anticoagulant at a carefully configured dose, in order to 'thin' her blood appropriately. Reaching for the IVAC's programmable device, he began to increase the amount delivered in order to cause massive bleeding in this Marchetti patient, the wayward respiratory therapist suddenly froze.

"What are you doing?" yelled Lloyd Smith, a recently hired Deerwood employee, who had returned unexpectedly thanks to the Radiology tech who had discovered the patient's chart and had run to meet him in the hallway.

"I…I uh, I heard the beeper going off and wanted to see what was up with it, no biggie." Orlander's face began to flush, shifting his weight from one foot to the other nervously.

"Bullshit, you were adjusting the infusion yourself, I saw it. What the fuck…" The burly orderly abruptly pushed the Nordic looking Orlander away from the IVAC.

"Going to report this shit when I return Mrs. Simpson to her bed upstairs. Are you crazy?"

Thump. The needle entered the side of the man's neck, its full contents now discharged into the fleshy area, the muscle paralyzing agent instantly began coursing through the unsuspecting orderly's body.

Vinny immediately dragged the now motionless man's body through sliding doors that exited onto the loading platform, a usual beehive of activity in this bustling hospital where everything from medical supplies to baby formula were unloaded. Not at that moment. Vinny had peaked through the small windows on the doors, fortuitously for him he saw no activity and dragged the now cyanotic looking orderly with his bulging eyes and board-like body until he reached a small alcove where the large Oxygen and Nitrous Oxide tanks were stored. Laying Lloyd down next to one of the clearly labeled Nitrous tanks, he immediately placed a venti-mask over his victim's face and carefully attached a rather long stretch of plastic tubing from the mask to a valve on top. Once he was satisfied with the connection, he turned on the Nitrous gas to its maximum flow rate. *Vinny remained quite certain that when the body was ultimately discovered, everyone would conclude that Lloyd 'accidentally overdosed' in his quest to get 'high' on laughing gas. End of story.*

Chapter Twenty-One

"Dr. Dan!" Elena Guillermo beamed as soon as she saw him enter her room.

"Hi, Elena, Yolanda." Dan nodded, smiling, to his patient and then to her cousin. The two were gathering Elena's belongings, including items supplied by the hospital—basin, toothbrush and the like—so she could be discharged from DCH.

"Ready to go home?" Dan asked, unable to think of anything more inspired.

"Yes!" Elena said before Yolanda could try to translate. "Home!"

As if she could read his thoughts, Elena pointed toward her chest and said excitedly, "I ...got ...job!"

"Hey, cool!" Dan felt flush with surprise, embarrassment, and confusion. He was afraid to try to ask what, but she was eager to tell him and turned to Yolanda with a gesture for her to take over.

"Yes," Yolanda confirmed. "Alma's uncle manages a ballroom dancing school. As soon as 'Lena's healed, she goes to work as an assistant instructor. That was the work we both did at home in Argentina," Yolanda told him with a gently chiding tone. "We know how to do all those 'real' dances, you know. 'Lena is a hometown champion in tango. In Argentina, we do *real* tango."

Dan could feel himself blushing. How unfair of him not to see these women as more than the role they were forced to play here. He tried to dig himself out. "Will you be working there too?"

Yolanda laughed and tossed her head in a mockingly flirtatious way. "Oh, no. I can still make much more money at the Kit Kat."

Dan laughed with her, hoping his color would soon return to normal. "Dr. Bosnan gave you Elena's discharge orders?" Still smiling, Yolanda pulled the folded pink sheets from her pocket and waggled them. "And she explained everything, so you're both clear on how to care for the incision and when to come for follow-up and everything?" At her nod, he said regretfully, "Then I guess it's time to say good-bye."

Elena understood enough of that, gave Dan another little hug while slipping a small piece of paper into his hand as she turned and sat down in the wheelchair.

Dan was left alone in the room studying the little piece paper, a small business card. Ciervo School of Dance, it read with an address on Main Street, a phone number, and a little silhouette of tango dancers. He turned it over and found a cell phone number written with beautiful precision in blue ink.

It was easy to imagine holding her, even lusting after her, but could he imagine falling in love with her and making a life together? Was she looking to settle down maybe with a rich American doctor as a fast-track to citizenship? *No, not Elena.* His folks might think that, but Dan found it hard to believe …

"What now?" he murmured, he imagined seeing Elena's beautiful face again and her smoldering eyes just before they parted earlier today. "What's my next move?"

No tango lessons, that's for sure, but maybe an easier, gentler form of dancing. He pictured her in his arms, slow dancing in an otherwise empty room, their bodies in full contact. Dan drifted off into a dream that did not end with dancing, where she was healthy and athletic, and the scar on her bare chest was hardly noticeable at all.

Shaking his head to clear it of all thoughts that seemed wildly inappropriate in a sterile hospital room, Dan walked down to the cafeteria. His appetite was soon ruined by another too dry, too salty cafeteria tuna casserole congealing on his plate. With his paperwork miraculously all finished, and all the rest of the house staff busy with their own duties, meals or naps, Dan opted to pay a surprise visit to one of his favorite patients, Joe Bonfiglio.

Dan knocked lightly on the closed door of the private room where Joe had been moved before beginning his seven days of intensive chemotherapy. "Room service?" Joe's voice came faintly through the door.

"Yeah," Dan said as he entered. "You ordered the pineapple-anchovy pizza?" Joe tried to give him a big grin but he looked a little green around the gills. "Sorry, Joe. That was dumb."

Joe, as usual, was forgiving. "Well, kinda hoped you'd be delivering beer. Not much appetite for food these days. In fact," he said as he swept a hand toward-Luigi's pizza box on his bedside table, "I have more pizza than I can face. Help yourself; no sense it going to waste."

Just seeing Luigi's box could make Dan salivate. He opened the lid and stared down at a whole pie missing only one piece. "Wow, thanks," Dan said, "my favorite: the works!"

Joe smiled like a proud father who'd brought home the bacon for a ravenous son. "For a minute there, I thought you were here to stick more needles into my back."

"Nah," Dan told him between bites. "I'm true to my word."

Joe watched as Dan finished the second slice of pizza. "I'm always glad to see you, Dan, but I can't relax till you tell me if there's some reason for this visit. Maybe my bone marrow results came back?"

"No!" Dan responded so suddenly he actually launched a small piece of mushroom with the word. He picked it off his sleeve and grabbed a napkin from the handy stack by the box. "Probably tomorrow for those bone-marrow labs. But now, no ulterior motive, Joe. Just thought I'd come to see how you were doing."

Joe relaxed with a little sigh of relief. "I'm okay, I guess. Considering, y' know?"

While Dan packed away a third fat slice of Luigi's best, they talked football, local news, and family—including the Halloween costumes Sue was making for their girls: a fairy princess, a cheerleader, and a doctor. "That one's for you," Joe told him. "My Josie, she's the oldest and really focused on medical stuff right now. Says she 'wants to be like Dr. Dan and help sick people get better'."

Dan felt a blush rising. "I'm flattered."

"Hey, in the meantime, a game of hearts?" his raspy voice seemed to plead.

"Sure." Dan closed the pizza box and set it on the foot of the bed. He moved the bedside table to a more convenient alignment and cleared away everything except the old deck of Bicycle playing cards.

"Deal!" Joe commanded, "and prepare to lose big-time," desperately trying to sound upbeat but not all that successful.

They played for half an hour, paying little attention to who had accumulated the most points. Dan thought maybe finally Joe was ready to ask those big questions everyone had been avoiding, but he didn't. He just yakked and joshed and laughed, slapping his cards down as if he had nothing more important to care about. Then he began to wilt visibly.

"I've worn you out," Dan said at the end of the last hand, rising to clear everything away.

"Only way you can win," Joe mumbled, sinking back into his bed and closing his eyes. "Thanks for the company."

"Sure." Dan pulled up the covers and dimmed the light.

Without opening his eyes, Joe whispered, "Hey, take the rest of that pizza with you. Finish it or share it..." before sliding into sleep. *How many more pizzas would this man be enjoying? Not many.*

Chapter Twenty-Two

Just inside the door of his studio apartment, respiratory therapist Vinny Orlander shrugged out of his white lab coat. Letting out a big sigh, he tossed it over the back of the one comfortable chair, which served as a catchall, the only place in his life where he allowed clutter.

He straightened his new cargo shirt, a bit rumpled from a long shift inside the lab coat. Good to know this cotton-blend khaki would soon release any wrinkles, and each deep pocket had a satisfying button-down flap.

Tall and blond as his Norse ancestors, Derek Vincent Orlander preferred to wear his hair in a crewcut, and he'd long ago given up trying to cultivate a convincing crop of facial hair.

His ice-blue eyes looked to the wall clock, a cheap model, generic except for the letters: L-E-V-A-Q-U-I-N spelled out in the background, a gift from one of the many pharmaceutical reps roaming the hospital and cafeteria hallways. Vinny had no problem accepting freebies, and he'd never have to buy a notepad or a pen as long as he lived. Each of these trinkets required little more than five minutes of attention to a drug rep, usually a sensational-looking saleslady. Vinny wasn't the real target; the doctors were. He was just being used to get to them. It was a game and everyone played. *Turnabout is fair play. After all, he mattered also.*

He looked away from the clock to his compact efficiency kitchen thinking that he should be hungry for lunch, but the food could wait. There was something far more interesting on his mind. He reached into the right inner pocket and pulled out an ampule filled with a clear liquid and couldn't help smiling. It'd been too easy to lift the vecuronium bromide from the ICU's medication cabinet and stash it in that handy pocket. No one thought twice about seeing Vinny around the meds. He was an intrinsic part of DCH's interior landscape: fresh linens and intravenous tubing, bedpans and gurneys, Johnny coats, and Vinny Orlander.

Lots of people might take comfort in blending in so well, and he certainly used it to his advantage when it suited him. No one ever appeared to notice him, a far too familiar experience. Nothing he ever did in his whole life had satisfied his parents, or even half as persuasive as his big sister, Astrid. He could feel his muscles begin to tighten, the anger burning a hole in his gut.

He took a deep breath, his attention going to the huge freshwater fish tank across from his couch. The mock-leather futon also unfolded to serve as a bed. He'd spent countless hours lying there and staring into that entrancing underwater world, just watching those colorful swordtails and tetras and barbs swim in and out of the environment he'd created for them.

"Hi, guys," he said, moving over to peer into the immaculate water. "I'm home." He'd swear they all got more animated when seeing him; they raced through the hand-crafted tunnels and rock arches he'd constructed, painted, and placed strategically.

He gazed with pride upon his most innovative feature: an up-sloping hill of adobe-colored boulders that rose well above the surface at one end of the fifty-gallon tank. The above-water area covered about a third of the tank's length; the natural hollows formed containers for tiny terrarium plants.

Vinny's attention returned to the water as two green tiger barbs, Chuckles and Phynn, played hide-and-seek in the honeycomb of the pale-blue ceramic mesh. Vinny tapped the glass with the vecuronium vial. "Don't give me that. I fed you before I left last night. And don't worry, I won't forget to get some more supplies today. Don't I always take excellent care of you?" A movement on the rocks and under a leafy plant caught Vinny's eye. "There you are," he said. The red-eyed tree frog probably thought it couldn't be seen, hidden as it was. Vinny had brought it home several days ago, but never given it a name.

Vinny set the vecuronium on the futon, reached quickly into the tank and managed to catch the frog without too much effort. "Gotcha." Gingerly petting the creature's head, he said, "Bet you'd like to stretch your legs a little, wouldn't you?" and set it down on the spotless hardwood floor.

The tiny frog hopped several feet away, but finding it wasn't pursued, it stopped and looked back at its keeper.

"Stretch your legs," Vinny chuckled, unbuttoning the top pocket of his shirt. He drew out a plastic syringe and a needle, removing both from their packaging and assembling them. He picked up the ampule of vecuronium and deftly flicked its top with his right middle finger. With his left thumb, he snapped the tip of the vial. Concentrating on the syringe in his right hand, he prided himself on a new trick he'd learned: pulling out the plunger one-handed. This drew into the syringe a little air, which he could then inject into the ampoule before withdrawing its contents. He set aside the empty vial and regarded the loaded syringe with satisfaction.

With one long stride, Vinny stooped to pluck the frog up off the floor. Without hesitation, he plunged the needle into its belly and injected a tiny drop of the drug. Placing the startled amphibian back on the floor, he capped the syringe and placed it on the laminate counter before him.

At first, the frog hopped straight ahead as if to get as much distance as possible from its unpredictable owner. But then it veered to the left and then to the right. Vinny waited, his eyes narrowing for the effect he was expecting. The frog's four limbs suddenly shot out straight from its body and froze; the eyes, too, were frozen, wide open in terror, but with no hint of movement. Fascinated, Vinny repeated again, very softly, "Stretch your legs."

He'd seen the effects of this drug, a powerful paralytic, on humans, rather dramatic. The induced paralysis allowed the ventilator to do its thing without any interference from the patient's bodily responses. In time, a human patient would be 'reversed' and allowed to breathe naturally. No such luck for the frog or orderlies. Within moments, Vinny knew, it would cease to breathe and die. Vinny sat down next to it on the floor and stroked it gently with one finger. "I think I'll call you Stretch. You like that name?"

Riveting his gaze on the frog, he wondered if he'd be able to tell the exact moment that death claimed it. A strange tingling thrill rippled through Vinny, arousing him in a way that brought on another memory. Once, while engaging in sex, he'd lost control and nearly strangled a girl until her well-placed kick brought him back to reality. That'd been close, and, though he'd apologized repeatedly and professed tremendous remorse, he hadn't been completely sincere.

As the frog gave up its last gasp, Vinny moved to the syringe, wrapped it in a piece of foil, and placed it on the top shelf of his apartment sized refrigerator. "Sorry Stretch, never really got to know you." This time he really had time to enjoy the whole spectacle. *A sadistic personality was once considered a mental illness but hell, he preferred to consider it more a lifestyle choice.*

What he needed tonight was a girl. He immediately thought of Trudy, a member of the DCH housekeeping staff. She'd come in handy more than once. She was sweet, but homely and shy, and it was clear she comforted her loneliness with food. Still, she kept a tidy house and was always clean, always willing. Also on the plus side, she liked having rough sex. Never pushed him away or grabbed at his hands. Or she tolerated it without complaint, so what was the difference?

Chapter Twenty-Three

Joe Bonfiglio didn't look sterling, but he definitely looked better than he had over the past three weeks. Though dressed in his street clothes, he laid back on his bed. "Need to conserve my energy for the trip home." Propped up against the pillows with his eyes closed, he seemed frail compared to the day he was admitted nearly a month ago. Dan could see loose wisps of hair on the pillow.

"Hey, bud," Dan said quietly, and those brown eyes opened.

"Hey." The face managed a smile, but it almost seemed too great an effort.

Ultimately, the cancer had fought back. In the first week's chemotherapy, the drugs killed the cancer cells, and unfortunately, many newly forming healthy cells. They noticed also that those dying cells had poured toxins into Joe's blood, making him even sicker. Sure, he was somewhat better now, well enough to go home, but the posttreatment news delivered by Klonter this morning was devastating.

"The latest tests on your bone marrow," Klonter had said, his eyes on the papers he was consulting, "show no appreciable clearing of the cancer cells."

Dan saw Sue beside Joe's bed, clutching her husband's hand so tightly. "You want your man home, don't you?" he asked rhetorically. Sue bit her lip and teared up, but neither spoke.

Klonter gave a little cough, still not making eye contact. "We'll go ahead and discharge you today as planned. I'd like you to go home and discuss the options. Then come back next week and tell me how you'd like to proceed."

"Options?" Joe managed.

"You can continue to fight it with chemotherapy. We have a couple of different drug protocols you could try. Basically, cycles of five days of treatment followed by three weeks off."

"For how long?" Sue asked, unconsciously stroking her rounded belly with her free hand.

127

Klonter shrugged. "Until remission or a clear indication the body is nonresponsive."

Joe stared at Klonter, who still avoided his gaze. "Or?"

"Or you can remain at home on palliative care or in hospice."

"Throw in the towel, is that what you are saying?" Sue gave a little gasp and began to cry, but quietly.

"I'm sorry it's not better news," Klonter told them, his sincerity almost painful to see. "But nobody is throwing in the towel."

Knowing the stress of these last weeks had led to some worries in Sue's pregnancy; she'd opted early on to have an amniocentesis, which, thankfully, had come back normal, and had revealed the fourth Bonfiglio child would be their first son.

"No bona fide Italian boy," Joe murmured, "should grow up without ever seeing his father." Dan offered a sympathetic grin, having no alternative to offer. However, Joe had an idea and ventured hesitantly, "What about, you know, weed?"

"No problem. We can do that. I'll be back with the prescription and a list of places to fill it."

"Then I think I'd better get Joe outta here," Sue's voice said suddenly with forced levity from behind them.

With effort, Joe slid off the bed and stood gingerly, steadied by Dan's firm support on his arm. "It's about time. I've got a big night ahead of me. Hope you bought lots of candy; I'm gonna give every kid a double handful."

Dan embraced the sick man, warmly but gently, aware of the frailty of Joe's once-robust body. "You take care now." Dan managed to make it sound light. "You guys keep in touch; let me know when you'll be here in the building, okay?"

Amid the good-byes and the arrival of Nurse Gallagher with the wheelchair, Dan slipped out of the room and down the hall in the opposite direction the Bonfiglios would take.

Out of sight, he took a moment to pause and collect himself at one of the huge glass windows along the corridor.

Leaning his hands on the sill and staring out, he realized he was looking down at the lovely green peace of Woodlawn Cemetery, not the best town planning board move, he thought. Bowed forward till his forehead rested against the cool comfort of the glass, he noticed the long strands of dark hair on his sleeve. *Joe's hair.* He closed his eyes so that he didn't have to see it, but he didn't brush it away either.

Chapter Twenty-Four

Fourteen-year-old Nikki, her insides a roiling sea of pain and anxiety, despair, and disgust, felt the waves of anger rise. Hands on her hips, she surveyed the wreckage of the room—a tiny combined kitchen-dining-living area—surrounding her. Smashed coffee table, two broken lamps, ripped-down curtains, a litter of mismatched silverware and crockery, papers scattered everywhere—most crumpled or torn. She also noticed that spaghetti stain on the wall. Most of the pasta had slid down onto the shattered plate on the floor below. *But all that red sauce?* Nikki sighed. *I'll never get it outta that old wallpaper.*

Just thinking of the tasks ahead exhausted her. She had homework and a geometry test tomorrow, but the mess had to be cleaned up first.

Once, only once, had she tried to intervene and pull Tony off her mom, pounding him with her small twelve-year-old fists and yelling for him to stop. He'd turned on her and punched her so hard in the face that she actually bounced off the wall before hitting the floor. Tony then turned to Mom and growled, "That better never happen again, Frances. Do you hear me? I gave that little bitch life, and I can take it away. Don't think I won't." He swung back to glower down at Linda again and repeat, "Don't think I won't."

Later, her mom was adamant, "Promise me, Nikki. Promise me you won't ever do that again. Don't get in his way; don't try to stop him; don't try to protect me—though that was wonderfully brave of you, sweetheart. Bad as things may seem, he can make them worse. Believe me, nothing would hurt me more than if he really harms you. Promise me."

And two years later, it was much the same, only worse, because now Nikki felt so alone. She stared at her mother, who sat slumped in a splintered chair, gazing out the window as if there were something to see out there besides the stains on the stucco wall of the next apartment building. Frances had pulled a thin cotton robe—ripped at the shoulder—over her nakedness but seemed to have no thought beyond that. Surely she felt the bruise coming up on her cheekbone or the splinter of glass embedded in an ooze of blood on one barefoot. Yet she appeared oblivious to it all.

Nikki wondered, *How can she just give up?* Hands on her hips, there in the wreckage, Nikki addressed her mother: "Don't guess you're gonna help me at all?" Perhaps Frances didn't hear her, or maybe her ears were still ringing from Tony's fists, but she made no attempt to answer. With a grunt of disgust, Nikki began putting the room in order. If only life could be put in order this way. *I am not going to live like this for the rest of my life!*

Nikki shoved her cart forward, despite her tear-blurred vision brought on by her trip down memory lane, crashing into another cart. "Oh!" she cried, blinking furiously. "I'm so sorry." Her eyes came clear, and her voice froze in her throat.

"No biggie," said Dan Marchetti, grinning apologetically as he maneuvered his cart out of her path. "Wasn't watching where I was going." He glanced away, perhaps to ignore her wet eyes, and waved a hand at the array of laundry detergents. "So many! All claiming to be the best. Any recommendations?"

Quickly dabbing away the rest of her tears with one sleeve, Nikki mumbled. "Sorry. Allergies." Then she leaned in to pick a box from the shelf. "I like this kind." She handed it to him for review. "Works fine; smells awesome; softens in the wash, and it's economical."

Barely glancing at it, he plopped it into his cart. "Works for me. Thanks." He looked directly into her eyes. "Great to see you outside DCH. I see we're on the same wavelength today." He grinned.

Then she noticed he, too, had chosen apples, bananas, seven-grain bread, salami, provolone, and a similar variety of canned goods—only opting for Cocoa Krispies instead of shredded wheat. "Not very inspiring, huh?"

"Well," he laughed, "when you're cooking for one, it's hard to get too inspired."

"Yeah, same here." She watched that thought sink in, saw the spark of curiosity in his gorgeous brown eyes as he tilted his head in polite inquiry. She took a deep breath. "I left my husband last month and filed for divorce."

He shifted his weight, and she liked the expression in his eyes as he said, "I guess I should say I'm sorry."

She shrugged. "No need. It's just over."

Nikki decided to change the subject. "So what's for dinner at your house tonight? None of that stuff, I hope."

Sheepishly, he confessed, "I've gotten pretty fond of a particular frozen meatloaf; it's delish hot, and leftovers make great sandwiches. Just haven't picked that up yet." After an awkward silence, he said, "Well, I'll see you at work…and remember, I'm here if you need that friend."

She nodded and thought she saw more interest in his eyes than friendship. Maybe after the divorce was final? She could only hope as she pushed her cart forward. He let her move by him to take the lead. In the narrow aisle, her arm brushed his, raising every hair on her skin with the energy of that touch, and she could tell he felt it too.

Chapter Twenty-Five

Not bad for a government office, thought Assistant District Attorney Linda Ferrante as she surveyed her new domain with satisfaction. The huge oak desk dominated an acre of thick burgundy carpet.

Towering bookcases covered three of her walls that were filled near capacity by leather volumes, many gleaming with gold embossing. However, it was the fourth wall, at a perfect 90° angle to her desk, that Linda adored the most about the room: it featured a huge plate glass window looking out onto a wooded cove on the edge of Lake Candlebury. Weeping willows brushed the manicured lawn; deer sometimes came to drink at the edge of the pond, where there was, at all times, some gathering of ducks swimming, feeding, or playing in the placid waters. Worlds away from her childhood and that cramped cubbyhole she'd shared with Kip Carpenter. Linda grimaced. It hadn't been as easy as she thought to leave Glickman, Glickman & Berkowitz, however. Change can be hard.

Certainly making up her mind to accept Scott Bradden's offer had come easily. Even before she'd finished her meal with him there at the Deerwood Arms, she knew she would accept. She wasn't fooled by his impeccable manners and solicitous behavior, she knew he was still the same ruthless jerk beneath it all.

So she'd left Bradden with a cool, "Let me think on it a while, Scott," and he didn't even urge her not to wait too long, as she'd thought he would. However, when she finally did accept and gave her boss the notice, it wasn't easy to see the depth of disappointment in Sam Glickman's eyes.

"I understand," he'd told her. "Your talents are being wasted at our firm. We just can't offer you anything more right now." He'd been so helpful not asking for a full thirty days because Bradden wanted her to begin by the first week in November. Sam had assured her, "If you ever want to come back, there'll be a place as if you'd never left."

Now, four days later, on the Friday of her first week in the new job, Linda was glad the transition had been as easy as it had. She stared out her big window at a pair of ducks swimming a bit away from the little flock on the pond, nibbling affectionately at each other's necks.

She moved back to sit behind her desk in that oh-so-comfy, ergonomically correct chair and filled her nostrils with the fragrance of eucalyptus. Reaching for the next file on the top of the stack, Linda realized she was actually looking forward to this new life and the challenges ahead of her.

Chapter Twenty-Six

Dan just stared at the pediatric nurse from the doorway. Finished with his shift, he had decided to peek in on his newfound friend, Nikki Saxon, before heading on home.

"Sweetie, here is your medication, down the hatch. You will feel better soon." The patient looked to be about six or so, pale and thin, but sporting a big smile.

"You want to hear a secret Jessica?" The child shook her head affirmatively.

"When I was your age, my mother had to put my medicine in ice cream because the liquid was so bad tasting. Not like today where it is so delicious." They both laughed together.

She is so wonderful with children, so kind, reassuring. Images of her silken hair and her radiant smile flashed before his eyes more and more each day.

Just at that moment, sensing she had a visitor, Nikki turned around to see Dan leaning against the doorway, his arms folded and a large Cheshire grin adorning his face.

"I see we have a visitor Jess," she observed.

Approaching the two, Dan bent over to place his hands on his thighs, their eyes now at the same level.

"Hi Jess, I'm Doctor Dan. How are you sweetie?"

The child suddenly got frightened and hugged Nikki ferociously.

"He is a nice man darling." Nikki gave Dan a knowing glance, "He is not here to examine you sweetie. Just to say hello." *The mere sight of a doctor these days meant more painful tests and scary needles.*

"Try to go to sleep honey."

Jessica finally relinquished her grasp and seemed to settle in after Nikki lowered the shades.

After exiting the room, Dan became overcome and embraced the slender woman avidly, her response equally lovingly.

"I will be finished soon. Meet you at your place?"

"I would like that." They both kissed, looking both ways beforehand, knowing such actions verboten in a hospital setting. *It felt good to break the rules just then.*

Before long, they were caressing each other's bodies in Dan's unmade bed while kissing intensely and lustfully.

For both, the excitement of the moment was so energizing, a break from the vagaries of the day and the emptiness that can rob an individual of strength and resolve.

****

Now, three weeks into his November rotation, Dan was never sure who'd be in his care when he returned after a day off. The east wing of the eighth floor, classified as the 'Step-down Unit', was populated by patients who no longer needed to be in ICU, but still required more assiduous care and monitoring than in a regular hospital room. "Did the fall from tree come around?" Dan asked.

"Mr. Odom?" Dave yawned again. "Yeah, he regained consciousness yesterday. Already moved upstairs to...uh, let's see...Nine East. Seems just fine."

"Glad to hear it. So who're you leaving me?"

Dave brought him up-to-date, but on the last chart, Dave frowned and tapped it with his fingernails, seeming annoyed.

"What?" Dan asked, craning his neck to better see the name: Salter, Jane. Without reading the notes, he remembered a forty-two-year-old white female with a pancreatitis that resulted in acute respiratory distress syndrome. Dan nodded. "Pancreatitis and ARDS. She's getting worse?"

"Not really, but not getting any better either. However, that's not the problem." Dan waited, eyebrows lifted, and Dave continued, "It's her damn husband—he's just flipping out. He's calling me every hour for an update on her condition."

136

"Every hour? That's a bit much."

"No kidding, and now he's started appearing out of nowhere whenever I go out in the hall, all angst-ridden with his inane, 'How's she doin', Doc?'" Dave made him sound like white trash. "Hell, yesterday he practically followed me to the crapper."

"People can get crazy. A real 'doorknobs' kinda night, huh?"

Dave laughed at the reference to a shared observation: old-fashioned doorknobs tended to make everything look distorted. "Worse than that! It was a 'Kontiki birds' kind of night."

Dan chuckled. "Now *that* sounds serious—if I knew what it meant!"

"Ever been to Disney World?"

"Yeah. In fact, just before I started here at DCH."

"I was pretty young the first time I saw the Tiki show, and it really creeped me out!"

"In the Tiki-Tiki-Tiki-Tiki Tiki room," chanted Dan, "All the birds sing words and the flowers croon—"

"Yeah, but it's been the whole night here for some reason! Mrs. Bilenko, the 300-pounder in 842, just suddenly woke up after a three days in a coma just as Nurse Earl was doing a blood draw. The woman sat straight up, hauled off, and slugged him with her other arm. Poor Earl smacked back against the bedside table and sent everything clattering to the floor. She yelled, 'Stop doing that!' and then lost consciousness again and fell back in the bed."

Dan pictured the scene with the wiry little male nurse reeling from the attack, but then he asked quickly, "Is she okay? Earl okay?"

Dave nodded. "She's awake again now, resting quietly and *very* apologetic. Earl's fine, but he's sporting a black eye and embellishing the tale every time he tells it. You'll get your turn, I'm sure."

Dave checked his watch. "Time to go. But I wanna look in on Jane Salter one more time before I leave her to you."

"I'll go with you." Dan took the patient's chart and scanned it as they headed for Room 850.

Just as they passed the Eighth Floor waiting room, Jane Salter's husband popped out, calling, "Hey, Dave, hang on a minute!" Dan felt Dave bracing beside him. Salter—a thin man of maybe forty-five with a ruddy complexion— wore tight jeans, cowboy boots, and a Western shirt with the top four buttons open to reveal curly, gray chest hair and a large medallion.

Salter seemed quite relaxed and sauntered up to clasp Dave's arm as if they'd been friends for years. "So, Doc; how is she?"

Dave hesitated a moment, "Well, Mr. Salter…"

"Now, you're s'posed to call me Terry, remember?"

"Well, uh, Terry," Dave continued, "she's holding her own. As I told you earlier, it'll be a day-to-day thing, and—"

"Yeah, that's what I expected," Salter interrupted, "so I'm prepared for the long haul." Looking beyond Salter, Dan could see into the waiting room, which had undergone a transformation. A cot was set up in one corner, its covers rumpled and strewn with magazines. On the windowsill, a portable television flashed a series of channels at the touch of a woman wearing a snug sweater and one-size-too-small jeans above high heels. Her head of platinum-blond curls looked familiar. Having located *Wheel of Fortune,* she turned around, and Dan recognized the attractive, fortyish face of Eleanor Gordon, wife of patient Rodney Gordon, who currently lay comatose after suffering a large bleed within his malignant brain tumor. She gave Dan a wan, self-conscious smile as their eyes met.

About half the seats in the waiting room were occupied by family members of other patients, all registering varying degrees of annoyance. "You wanna turn the volume down please?"

Dan turned back to what Dave was saying to Salter: "I'm going off duty now, and your wife will be under the care of my colleague, Dr. Marchetti, here."

Salter turned his attention and a cheerful grin to Dan. "Hey, glad to meet you." He leaned to read the ID badge, "Dante!" He winked. "You don't mind me calling you by your first name, do you?"

"Not at all," Dan replied, still marveling at the unusual scene in the waiting room. "We're about to go look in on your wife. We'll let you know right away if there's any change, okay?"

Salter's curly head had swiveled back toward the waiting room. "Sure, sure."

Giving a jaunty wave of his hand, he pivoted on one boot heel and returned to the group in the waiting room.

Dan and Dave just stared at each other for a long moment before turning to continue down the hall toward Jane Salter's room.

In a low voice, Dan began to complain, "I find that guy really irritating, man."

"No shit." Dave moaned, punching Dan in the arm before they began to go their separate ways. Suddenly, he turned to face his friend again. "Did you hear about the guy they found dead on the loading platform today who apparently was tapping into the Nitrous?" Dave inquired, a disturbed look on his handsome face.

"I sure did. Pretty fucked up. Heard he was found with the ventimask on his face and tubing that connected directly to the metal canister. Pretty obvious," Dan remarked rather matter-of-factly.

"Too obvious if you ask me," Dave responded, now looking in Dan's direction.

"Well, I spoke to one of the technicians who said the tank was still completely full. Strange."

Late in the afternoon, as Dan started to walk briskly past the waiting room lounge and hoped to avoid being accosted yet again by Terry Salter, he paused midstride, struck by a very different scene. The TV was turned off, and the room was almost empty. Only Terry Salter and Eleanor Gordon remained, laughing as they played cards on one of the end tables and obviously flirting with each other! Hurrying on, Dan grimaced. Repulsed, he flopped into a chair at the empty physicians' desk.

*"Beep, beep, beep…*Dr. Marchetti, Room 833, stat…833, stat!"

Recognizing the room number of a "bad lunger," Dan leaped up and hurried down the hall. By the bed he found the pulmonary medicine fellow, George Anastos, listening to the lungs of a middle-aged, cyanotic-looking man.

"Get respiratory therapy, stat!" George barked and, to Nurse Coral Parker, "Sixty milligrams IV Solumedrol, stat!"

Dan quickly placed the call, then went to his newest patient, who was gasping for air. Using his own stethoscope to listen to the fellow's lungs, Dan commented, "He's not moving any air."

George leaned over his patient. "Mr. Monroe, how're you doing?"

"Not so good." The voice was barely audible, and he was looking bluer by the minute. "Please help me. I—" He fell back on the bed unconscious, and his electrocardiographic monitor revealed a dangerous slowing of heart rate. Dan could tell he was about to stop breathing.

"Need to intubate," George said. "Want the practice?"

"Yes!" Dan stepped close and eagerly took the laryngoscope Coral placed in his right hand.

"I'll push the atropine," George told him.

A ward clerk came in, handed George a copy of the patient's arterial blood gas numbers. "Shit," the resident muttered. "Big-league acidosis." He looked at Dan. "You recognize this guy?"

"No. Should I?"

"Charlie Monroe. Used to manage the Pittsburgh Pirates. Retired five years ago, but does some scouting now."

Dan nodded. "Yep! Didn't recognize him."

As he turned away to write orders that would return Monroe to an unconscious state, George shook his head. "People just don't look like themselves when they're blue."

Monroe squeezed Dan's hand while tears appeared at the corner of his eyes. Suddenly, he took his right hand and patted the area over his heart. *Coach was telling him how thankful he was for his caring.*

****

Hours later while at bedside, Vinny recalled that the highest PEEP any Deerwood Community Hospital patient could tolerate was Mr. Jordan Weiskopf, a torr of 29, who presently held the Orlander 'PEEP-ON' record. Now for Mrs. Salter. Vinny stuck his head out from the ICU room to see if anyone was coming. Secure in the knowledge that such chicanery was hidden from any prying eyes, he twisted the dial to approximate 20 torr. This time however, he would not wait to reverse it as there would be no reprieve in this 'NEW PEEP-ON' as he exited the ICU to round on his other patients. Now he was playing for keeps.

Chapter Twenty-Seven

Dan found himself ensconced in front of the computer the next day, checking labs. He noticed Nurse Coral approaching. "Hi, Dan." Pursing her lips, she shook her head. "Have ya seen 'Salter's Saloon' yet?"

"Salter's Saloon?" he repeated blankly.

She didn't stop, obviously on her way to administer some meds. "That's what the staff's calling the waiting room lounge now."

With a little shock, Dan realized he'd never once seen Salter at his wife's bedside. Always in the lounge. If Terry Salter was so committed that he was setting aside his job and sleeping at the hospital, surely he could visit her occasionally. *Strange.*

By now, Nikki had completed her shift and had waited until he completed his work before joining him to walk to the poorly lit parking lot together.

"Listen, we'll sorta have to sneak past the waiting lounge, or we may get tied up for a while. Most of Mr. Salter's audience has gone home; and apparently he gets especially clingy around that time, according to Dave."

He quickly filled her in on the man's holding court in "Salter's Saloon," and about the fellow's flirtation with Eleanor Gordon, whose own husband had had to be resuscitated earlier that very day. Nikki frowned and followed him quietly down the hall.

As they neared the lounge, Dan noted that it appeared empty. Oddly, the lights and TV were off, and there were no sounds of voices or laughter. However, there were other sounds, soft and furtive, and Dan realized that the lights should always be on and the room open for the relatives of the seriously ill. It took a moment for Dan's eyes to adjust to the dimness, but the big window on the far wall let in a lot of light from the nearly full moon beyond. Nikki gave a sharp intake of breath beside him.

The two cots had been shoved together, and beneath a thin hospital blanket, two entwined figures moved in an unmistakable rhythm. Nor was it difficult to recognize the two curly heads—one graying, one platinum— as Terry Salter and Eleanor Gordon. Both of their spouses lay just doors away, barely clinging to their lives—and losing ground.

"*Beep, beep, beep*…Dr. Marchetti, Room 833, stat…833, stat!"

Dan said, "Shit! That's Monroe."

****

The next day, upon returning to the hospital for his next shift, Dan learned that Jane Salter had died the same night as Rodney Gordon. In fact, only about an hour after he went off-duty. No more peering at that anguished, tortured face unable to scream at that bastard of a husband. He'd known that Jane was unlikely to recover, and now she wasn't suffering anymore. But, unexpectedly, there was a bit of an uproar about the case.

Somehow Jane Salter's positive end expiratory pressure (PEEP) had been dialed up to twenty, when he knew it was no more than five the night he'd left. With her PEEP set so high, her blood pressure had dropped to a dangerously low and ultimately a fatal level.

Naturally, Nurse Earl had been blamed at first, but he'd just about come unglued with outrage when accused of such carelessness. While anyone could make a mistake—even capable employees could drop the ball—it was hard to believe that of Earl.

However, who else? Alex or Dave? Unlikely, but then everyone was tired and stressed, and causing someone's death—especially through carelessness— is every doctor's nightmare. *Mishaps with medical equipment seemed to be occurring with regularity. Strange. Unavoidable?*

Then a new rumor surfaced that was based on the fact that Rodney Gordon had died less than two hours earlier and the antics in Salter's Saloon. Maybe one, or both, of the spouses had just hurried things along? Maybe they'd conspired together? *Hard to believe, but stranger things have happened in Kontiki land.*

Dan returned home looking completely refreshed in his favorite old jeans and a blue fleece pullover. When their relationship had quickly morphed into a decidedly romantic one, Dan summoned his courage and asked Nikki to move in with him. *Wasn't this exactly what he'd been hoping for: amazing sex and companionship with someone who understood the stresses of his life?*

Nikki provided all that and more. Beautiful, smart, funny and a great cook to boot. Though sometimes he wondered if she wasn't trying too hard to be casual, making sure that he didn't dump her like her soon to be ex-husband. Yes, *asking her to move in with him seemed to him to be the right move at this point in his life.*

Setting the finished bread cubes aside, Nikki started chopping celery. He came up behind her, taking her around the waist, and kissed the back of her neck. "I must be the luckiest guy in all of Deerwood. Maybe all of Pennsylvania. Bumping into you that night was kismet."

Tears stung in her eyes; she was glad he couldn't see them. How had this happened so quickly? Divine intervention? After her lawyer confirmed serving the papers to Matt, she had headed out for a quick celebratory drink. It was where Dan found Nikki quietly sobbing into her vodka and soda as sorrow at the end of her marriage overwhelmed the joy of starting a new life. Comforting her as a friend quickly relighted their passion. Three weeks later, rather than signing her new lease, she joined him in his one-bedroom apartment. Happiness finally seemed possible. Afraid that talking about it could somehow make it all go away, Nikki changed the subject. "Busy day?"

He leaned against the counter and tucked into the stew, savoring a hefty spoonful before answering. "Well, there's still a lot of hoopla about the Salter/Gordon deaths."

"Oh?" She'd gone back to her chopping so she wouldn't have to keep looking at him.

"Yeah, there were so many of us around, and they can't pinpoint when Jane Salter's PEEP was changed. All of us saying, 'I know it was right when I last saw it.' Remember, I checked to make sure it wasn't above five?" He shrugged and swallowed another bite of stew. "Most people seem to blame Earl, but I believe him. He's Mr. Obsessive. Anyway, lots of us were on Eight East that night: Earl and Coral; Dave and Alex and me; Vinny Orlander. Not to mention the straying spouses."

"Think they did it?"

Shrugging again, Dan opened the refrigerator and refilled his bowl with more stew. "Sorta doubt it. They were pretty tied up in the lounge. Earl saw them before we did, and they were found lying asleep together when Jane was discovered dead. Doesn't seem like they'd have time to pull that off." Turning back to lean against the counter, he arched his eyebrows at her in a comical expression. "Unless, of course, they hired a hitman."

The oven timer dinged, and Nikki grabbed the hot pads to pull out the pan of dressing when Dan opened the door for her. She set the pan on top of the stove and then covered it loosely with aluminum foil. "This should be fine out here overnight," she told him. It was already nearing midnight. "I have to get up at five to put the turkey in the oven. Then there'll be some room in the fridge."

He nodded. "So what will you need me to do tomorrow?"

"Set the table. Mash the potatoes. Help me get the stuffing heated and ready for the table. Then carve the turkey."

He nodded again. "And you're sure you still want company tomorrow?"

"God, yes! I love Thanksgiving."

He pulled her into his arms and murmured, "You've had a hard day, and we've got a big one ahead of us tomorrow. Let's get some rest, Nikki."

Minutes later, they spooned comfortably together. After kissing her ear and whispering, "I think I am falling in love with you, Nikki," he promptly fell asleep. She, utterly exhausted in body, mind, and spirit, slipped from beneath the burden of all her worries and drifted off, safe and comforted—for now, at least—in Dante's arms with a smile of joy affixed to her pixie face. *At least for now. She simply didn't trust happiness.*

Chapter Twenty-Eight

The floor team, including Dan, formed a rapt semicircle before Dr. Felton Garfield, the seventy-year-old Chief of Neurology. He, too, was listening as the intern Dr. Selma Braunstein presented an especially mysterious new admission from the previous evening. Garfield peered through his half-moon reading glasses and focused on the patient chart opened to the lab results. His hair, or rather what remained of it, was combed straight back like a symphony conductor's, and he seemed to cultivate that sense of drama in every movement. His immaculately groomed beard was more gray than white, and, though his fingers showed the unkind touch of arthritis, Garfield loved to twirl bits of that facial hair while he listened intently to presented cases. Today he was wearing another one of his 'December ties'; this one diagonally striped red and green and tacked with a tiny golden Christmas tree.

Dan could see, like the venerated Chairman of Medicine, Hugh Ballard, this man clearly enjoyed his exalted status as the doctor other physicians sought out for curbside consults.

"Thirty-six-year-old white male," Selma had begun a little shakily. The house staff looked at each other. "Presented with right arm and leg weakness hours after complaining of a migraine headache." Selma paused to run a hand through her short, reddish-brown hair and chewed her lip.

Garfield looked up from the chart, now removing his glasses and taking the end of one earpiece in his teeth. He waited.

Selma shifted uncomfortably and continued, "Physical exam essentially unremarkable, except for a dense hemiparesis of his right upper and lower extremity. Some conflicting sensory changes that appear to come and go with downgoing plantars and equivocal position sense on the right. Labs are within normal limits, as was the cranial CT scan, which was negative for a bleed. He's on narcotics for pain but with only moderate relief, and there's no change in his paresis since admission."

"Interesting. Any previous history of this?"

Selma nodded. "Three or four times this year, he says but no primary care physician we could call."

"Really." Garfield said it without any inflection at all. "Let's go pay Mr. ah—" he said as he quickly squinted at the name on the chart, "Mr. Jeffrey Winters a visit, shall we?"

Garfield's entourage divided like the Red Sea, allowing him to enter the room first and amble toward the bed, while the rest of them crowded in after him with Selma in the lead.

The patient was clean-shaven with tousled hair and looked up suddenly, blinking. "Wha—?" He struggled to sit more upright.

"It's okay, Jeff," Selma assured him. "This is our Chairman of Neurology, Dr. Garfield."

Winters's gaze swept over all their faces twice, his nervousness more apparent to everyone in the room and increasing by the minute.

Garfield, too, apparently sensing the man's anxiety, sat on the bedside chair so he wouldn't be looming. "Hey, Jeff, how are you today?"

Winters squirmed, his whole right arm hanging limp, his eyes riveted on the elderly physician's hands as if he feared his wallet would be lifted. In a comforting gesture, Garfield leaned to take that limp hand in his own and pat it encouragingly.

"All right, I guess," Winters ventured at last. Then, gaining confidence, he continued, "That is, considering I can't move my right side, and this migraine's about to blow open my head."

"Yes, yes, I understand." Garfield rose and bent to speak to Winters in a low voice still audible to the group. "Can you indulge an old doctor for one moment while I examine you?" He winked. "These youngsters think I can still teach them a thing or two."

Jeff smiled, "Sure, Doc. Don't expect too much." Garfield nodded.

"Mr. Winters, please lie flat on your back, if you will." The patient obliged, and Garfield moved the bedding out of his way. "Now, please try to lift your right leg an inch off the bed."

"I can't, Doc. It's paralyzed from the migraine."

"Humor me, please."

The patient tried to comply. The residents watched their mentor slide one arthritic hand under Winters's functioning limb until it was resting beneath it, palm up, while Winters struggled mightily to raise the paralyzed one, but to no avail.

"Damn. Migraines do this all the time to me," Winters complained. Relaxing his body totally, his face registering complete disgust at his futile effort.

Pulling his hand from beneath Winters' legs, Garfield stood up to his full height and spoke with unexpected briskness. "Well, then!" His voice had lost all the softness. "Whenever you're ready, Mr. Winters, you are free to walk out." With that, the chief turned toward the residents, signaling an end to the bedside visit.

"Wha—at?" Jeff Winters was the only person to say it aloud, but everyone in the house staff looked as completely baffled as he felt.

The residents again opened a path as the Chief of Neurology strode out, leaving the patient with his mouth agape. Glancing between the two, the young doctors quickly moved to follow their mentor from the room.

Out in the open area, Garfield turned to face them and declared in a voice that meant to be heard by the patient, "He is a fake, doctors, and how do I know this?"

They all glanced at one another, still disconcerted by the abrupt about-face. No one seemed brave enough to venture a guess.

"A textbook neuro exam, that's how." He paused for effect and lowered his voice. "Jeff's supposedly strong leg never tensed while he tried to lift the one that was purportedly paralyzed, which is the complete opposite of what you should find. With a truly paralyzed limb, the patient always struggles to lift that limb by desperately contracting the muscles on the good side."

Still no one spoke; they let their nods and eyebrows express their sudden understanding and chagrin that they'd not foreseen the answer.

"Furthermore," Garfield continued, "his bad hand was anything but paralyzed while I held it as he was distracted by my exam."

Dan glanced back into Winters' room and saw the patient scurrying around and gathering his belongings, while his Johnny coat flapped open around his bare buttocks.

"He's on the move," Dan offered to anyone within earshot. "Completely recovered and not even trying to hide it."

"We must have compassion for the opiate addicted," Garfield told them. "But that doesn't mean we can afford to let them scam us while stealing our

147

time, treatment, and resources from those who legitimately need them." He twirled some beard hairs in anticipation. "Now! Next patient?"

Just then his neurology rounds were interrupted by the head of the Biomedical Engineering Department at Deerwood Community Hospital who passed by and motioned for his attention just then.

"About the EKG which you personally ran on your patient the other day, Medical Record number 11653." Dan immediately knew he was referring to Mrs. Jackson as all EKGs are usually performed by the technicians in that same department. Her EKG was the exception.

"During a routine maintenance check, the machine had proven to be defective. The abnormalities he noted were most likely due to a faulty lead wire which an astute EKG tech had noticed after the same abnormality began appearing on all her patients, even routine preop ones. Also, I asked one of the cardiologists who passed by and he commented that the lead placements could have affected the reading as well." The Deerwood engineer just shrugged his shoulders. Bottom line, his patient did not suffer a cardiac event at all making his treatment course problematic, perhaps even dangerous. *What the hell! Shouldn't he have figured this out himself?*

"Marchetti, I trust you will be joining us sometime soon?" Garfield inquired sarcastically. Dan quickly regained his composure though he needed to sort out these mounting number of strange events that were casting a pall upon his newfound confidence level.

Chapter Twenty-Nine

Eyes riveted on the monitor screen before him, Vinny Orlander absorbed the information offered by the lighted symbols, illuminated dials, and, most significant of all, the numbers. Blessed numbers: so pure and factual and unrelenting.

Filled with a great sense of peace and purpose, Vinny copied the appropriate numbers onto his clipboard. Beautiful numbers. So perfectly formed and exquisitely legible. The only time he ever got even second-hand praise from his mother was when she chastised his almost-perfect sister over the fact that Vincent's letters were proper and right.

"She never could match my precise figures," Vinny whispered with a tiny smile of satisfaction. He quickly looked around to see if anyone had heard, but he was still alone, except for the sleeping patient attached to the ventilator, Charlie Monroe.

The numbers told Vinny that the coach should be able to come off the machine soon, a surprise considering the damage he had done from all those years of smoking; not that anyone ever asked his opinion. As he continued his careful notations, he couldn't help reflecting for the thousandth time on the injustice of his position: he could furnish information meticulous in both form and accuracy, but was he allowed to inscribe those numbers directly on a patient's chart? Oh, no, he had to write them on some silly sheet of paper and let a *doctor* enter those same numbers into the real chart.

Glancing up from his clipboard, Vinny saw Dan Marchetti enter the room and nod in greeting. Only once had Vinny caught an error, and Dan had immediately thanked him. Perhaps not with the grudging attitude that often 'rewarded' his diligence and discretion, but he was still an entitled resident…as were they all.

At Charlie Monroe's bedside, Dan looked down at the patient, then glanced to the ventilator's monitor, but Vinny spoke up, keeping his voice low to avoid waking the patient: "His numbers are looking promising, Dr. Marchetti. He can probably come off the machine today, don't you think?"

Marchetti took the clipboard Vinny handed him and the patient chart with the last set of numbers, comparing them. "You may be right. These stats do seem promising."

Very quietly, and turning so his lips couldn't be seen from the bed, Vinny mouthed, "You're surprised that he made it through this last time?"

Just as covertly, Dan whispered, "Yes. I've been surprised every time. But he's a tough old bird."

Vinny raised his eyebrows in surprise and to change his expression. He laughed off-handedly and shrugged. "This time of year, a 'tough old bird' reminds me of my *bestemor*—my grandmother." Dan laughed. "Yeah, the old 'pretending-for-the-relatives' thing!"

Chuckling, Dan nodded. *"Bestemor?* Is that Norwegian?"

"Ja! Snakker du norsk?"

"No, but I spent some years traveling in Scandinavia and picked up a few words here and there. You called your mother Mamma. Isn't that Swedish?"

Vinny's laugh came out like a little bark of surprise. "Yeah. My mother insisted we call her that instead of the Norwegian…"

"Mor?"

"That's right! Not the usual words to pick up."

Dan shrugged. "I like languages. Is your mom Swedish?"

"Part. Using Mamma instead of *mor* was really because the word *mord* means homicide or maybe murderess, and she didn't want to be called anything that sounded so similar." Vinny, who'd avoided learning any more of his ancestral tongue than absolutely forced to, reflected that if there was a word for "murderess of the spirit," that would really fit her. By now, Dan seemed preoccupied with other matters. *Just pretending to make conversation with me, that's all that was after all.*

Chapter Thirty

When Dan arrived at DCH early the next morning, Greg Vanderbosk seemed to be watching for him. The security guard's blue eyes were characteristically serious.

"What's new with that future president Ivy Vanderbosk?"

Greg beamed. "Nine months old and she's already saying da!"

"Wow! That's one smart kid."

Two minutes later, Dan walked out of the elevator on the seventh floor and headed for the physician's desk. Theo looked up as Dan asked, "What's new here?"

Theo grimaced. "You're not gonna like it." He handed the chart he'd been holding to Dan. "Leo Ackerlynn threw a clot, and it went to his brainstem."

Clots weren't unexpected when a patient had to lie in bed so long, but blood flow would, typically, carry one into the right side of the heart and then upward through the pulmonary valve and artery that went into the lungs, where it could be dealt with as a pulmonary embolism. Unfortunately, not with Leo's uncorrected tetralogy of Fallot. The narrowed valve and restricted right ventricle had slowed the pulse of blood and pushed the clot through the septal defect in-between the two ventricles. Once on the left side, the clot was pumped out through the aorta with the oxygenated blood. Out into the body and, in Leo's case, up to the base of the brain, thereby causing a massive stroke.

"God," Dan said quietly. "No improvement?"

"'Fraid not. Looking more and more like locked-in syndrome."

Awake, aware, but completely unable to move or communicate and unlikely to change. The term 'brain-dead' came to mind, but that wasn't right. When people were truly brain-dead, meaning in a persistent vegetative state, the lower part of the brain still operated. It kept them alive and allowed them to move, except that the upper brain was so damaged it could no longer function or have any hope of recovery. The mind was simply gone.

However, in the case of locked-in syndrome, all indications were that the upper brain remained quite functional, but the damaged brain stem prevented practically all voluntary muscle movements.

"What about his eyes?" Dan asked, knowing that locked-ins usually can blink at least one eye voluntarily.

Theo sighed. "He blinks, but we can't tell yet if it's purposeful. And, of course, his wife is convinced he's communicating clearly, that he'll be coming back from the stroke, and we're just giving up on him."

"I guess that wasn't too hard to predict." Dan looked back to the chart, wondering about Leo's treatment to prevent more clots, since there was no thought of trying to close the septal defect. But the CT scan had detected a small bleed at the stroke site, so anticoagulants were out.

"Yeah, he's on the surgery schedule for an IVC filter later today and, if he hasn't started to recover, and still can't swallow, they'll do a PEG at the same time."

Dan nodded. With one of those nifty umbrella-like filters inserted and deployed within his inferior vena cava, Leo could be protected from further clots traveling upward toward his heart from the lower half of his body.

Meanwhile, unable to swallow, the patient needed to have nutrition delivered into his stomach if he had a hope of surviving.

"You've told the patient and his wife what's planned?"

Theo glanced away. "Uh, no. Sorry. Driscoll and I consulted and decided to give it some time to see if both the procedures would be necessary."

"You mean you guys left it to Covington and me not only to inform the patient, but also to his oh-so-affable wife?"

"Uh, I'm 'fraid so. Sorry."

Dan punched his friend's arm gently. "Thanks."

He chuckled. "In fact, I feel confident you can handle this one on your own."

Dan nodded. After a few more moments exchanging ideas with Covington who happened by, Dan went first to check on Leo and was relieved to find the patient, at least for the moment, alone.

"Hi, Leo. It's Dr. Dan Marchetti." He took the man's limp hand and squeezed it gently not knowing whether those half-opened eyes were seeing him. "Leo, I know you can hear me but cannot communicate presently. You have had a stroke, and we are fervently still hoping that the stroke can resolve to some degree with function returning. There is no way to know to what degree this can happen at this point." Dan paused. "Did they set up a blink code with you, Leo? Once for yes; twice for no?" No apparent purposeful eyelid movement at all. *Is he trying to convey something?*

Dan patted his hand. "Remember. Once for yes; twice for no. I'm going to give you a little look over, okay?"

Still no blink. But, as he did his physical exam, Dan saw some blinking resume, although randomly, but not in response to a question, such as, "Are you in any pain?"

Finished with the exam, Dan ended his notes with 'no definitive response via blinking' and moved to stand where he could directly peer into those vacant brown eyes, his face no more than six inches from his own.

"Leo, we are placing an IVC filter—by way of the femoral, a large vein in your thigh—that would help catch other clots from below the heart, where they are more likely to form. They will not be able to travel any further. For the feeding tube, a scope will be filtered through your mouth to confirm the anatomy of your stomach and choose the site for the placement of the feeding tube. Then a small incision will be made on your belly, and the feeding tube placed to deliver nutrition."

Dan saw no change of expression in Leo's eyes as he talked, though the eyelids closed and opened more than once to refresh the still surfaces of the eyeballs. "Do you understand what I've been telling you, Leo?" He blinked. "Hey! Were you answering me?" Leo's eyes closed once, then again.

"Of course he is answering you." Gwen's sharp tone startled Dan as she pushed past him and went to stand on the other side of the bed, taking up Leo's other hand. "It's okay, sweetheart; you're just taking your time, and don't worry about making mistakes. Do you want to try again now?" Leo's eyes closed and remained so. "That's it; just rest." Gwen looked up accusingly at Dan. "What were you telling him?"

"I was outlining the two procedures planned for later today: one to prevent more clots from reaching the heart and one to make it possible to feed Leo if he remains unable to swallow."

"Now tell me," she demanded. When he'd described the inferior vena cava filter and its placement, Gwen questioned why they had to cut into his leg vein and then push something all the way up to a place just below his heart, but perhaps she realized this might bother Leo, so she interrupted herself. "He'll be sedated, right?" Even as Dan nodded, she went on to the second procedure. "I assume you'll want to install a feeding tube if he can't swallow?" Again, he barely had time to nod before she pushed on: "If it's a PEG tube, you don't have to explain. We've been feeding Esther that way all her life." Esther, their youngest child, had been born with severe anomalies, not the least of them, pharyngeal atresia.

Of course. Pharyngeal atresia. Esther's constricted throat could probably swallow small amounts of liquid, but real nutrition in volume would need to be delivered a different way. "Yes," Dan said. "A PEG."

Gwen leveled a challenging look at Dan, motioning him to follow her out the door. "I've been on the Internet this morning researching locked-in syndrome. Those doctors Driscoll and Epplewhite said a lot about how short the survival rate is and other negative stuff. But I found other information. Are you acquainted with a fascinating book called *The Diving Bell and the Butterfly?*"

Before he could reply, she forged on. "It was published in France in 1997, written by Jean-Dominique Bauby, the editor of a famous French magazine. He ended up with locked-in syndrome, and he dictated the book by blinking his left eye for each letter of each word."

Dan remembered. He had read it in college. It took Bauby two years to write it, and he died of pneumonia two days after it was published. "Yes, communication can be possible with purposeful blinking and a clear code. Furthermore, scientists are working on new technologies that interface the brain directly with a computer. Even if it's not immediate, Leo will get better and be able to communicate. You'll see." With that, she put her focus on her husband.

Dan sat down at the physician's desk, reaching for another chart. He gazed, unseeing, at the new chart, unable to set aside the Ackerlynn family.

Bauby's book had described it as a vivid combination of a lifetime's relived memories blended with observations and descriptions of life all within that very narrow isolation of his present existence plus exuberant flights of imagination and whimsy.

What of Leo Ackerlynn? Dan wondered. How will he cope with perhaps years trapped within his own diving bell of isolation? And does he have it in him to find the beauty and liberation of thought—the butterfly of imagination—to help him survive it all without madness? And if not being able to communicate drove someone mad, how would we ever know? Lastly, if one truly wanted their life terminated, how would they ever communicate such a thought? *The truth is that every young doc imagines such a fate, whether it this nightmare or another possibly awaiting them and it is terrifying!*

Chapter Thirty-One

That evening Dan needed to get his mind right. "You know, I feel like I don't really know much about you." Dan looked up from his Scrabble letters, now peering across the kitchen table at his roommate just then.

"Really?" Nikki tilted her head ever so slightly.

"What would you like to know Sir?" Nikki's attention now returning to her own sizeable collection of vowels and multiple 'Rs'. "OH My God, I have the worst letters." Shifting in her chair ever so slightly but trying to act matter-of-factly nevertheless. Her book was better left unopened.

"Your childhood, your parents, whether you have brothers and sisters, friends, you know, favorite foods, musical tastes, bad habits, the usual stuff."

Nikki girded herself, bit her lip and became suddenly aware of a nervous facial twitch that always reared its ugly head when uncomfortable.

"Well," she began, careful not to make eye contact. Dante was perceptive if not really sharp. "Grew up in a small town in Wisconsin, blue collar to the core, uneventful childhood, no brothers and sisters, few friends, very shy, a loving mother, distant father, love chicken and fresh vegetables, a devout reader of literary fiction, have a habit of not closing cabinet doors, and am a sucker for interns with curly dark hair and brilliant minds." *Mostly lies but I dare not tell him the truth.* After all, why would someone so accomplished want to be with someone so damaged. You see Dan, my 'father' verbally and physically abused my mother and I, we lived on food stamps. I never ever invited anyone home for fear of them witnessing the horror show that was my life and oh yeah, I have real trust issues.

"L-I-E-D," Dan blurted out.

"What do you mean?" Nikki responded defensively.

"Whoa, my word, a double word, only 15 shitty points I'm afraid." Dan placed his letters on the board, charting his points, before looking up quizzically.

"Why the reaction Nik?"

"Oh, I'm sorry, thought you were commenting on my description."

"Why would I do that?" He paused a moment to study her pained expression. "You seem suddenly agitated."

"I'm tired, Dante. Do you mind if I turn in early? We can leave the game as is and resume tomorrow evening. Ok?"

"Sure thing. Good night." Something seemed off.

Chapter Thirty-Two

Alex Cole thought, as he rapped a familiar cadence on Dan Marchetti's apartment door, the worst month of his entire life was finally over.

Dan opened the door almost immediately, and Alex greeted him with a grin, "Am I that predictable nowadays?" as he entered the room.

Dan shrugged, closing the door. "We're both off today. You probably saw Nikki's car leaving."

Dan tilted his head. "Hey, how 'bout a Yogurt Sunrise smoothie?"

Alex flopped dejectedly on the old green sofa. "Oh, I don't know."

Not dissuaded, Dan moved to the kitchen and started pulling ingredients from the refrigerator. "You been eating at all? You're looking kinda thin and pasty, man. Are you getting any sleep?" There were other sounds now of liquids being poured.

"Bad dreams."

"I hear that. A month in the ICU or ER or CCU can be rough. I don't know how the nurses survive day in, day out. At least we get to change rotations."

"They don't have the same responsibility as docs if things go wrong."

The blender whirred, making conversation impossible for several long moments. Then Dan countered, "Yeah, but we come in and handle the crises, and then we're gone except to check on people. But the nurses deal with the moment-to-moment care...having to watch patients suffer and listen to them moaning and crying in fear and pain."

Alex took the tall, frosty glass. "Are you trying to make a point about nurses and stress?"

Dan's eyebrows lifted, as if inviting comment. He sank into the beanbag chair across from Alex, lifted his glass in salute and drank deeply.

They sipped the smoothies in a long, companionable silence, then set the empty glasses aside.

Dan studied him. "So, Alex, what else is going on?"

He couldn't answer at first. Finally, he managed to say, "It's been one shit storm of a month."

"I'm having trouble concentrating. I've made some stupid mistakes—not big ones —and, thank God, someone's always had my back. So in addition to my personal life sucking, I'm not even a passable doctor anymore."

Dan nodded. "Hey, we all feel like that, and you've had some rough cases. I heard about that ruptured triple A you guys lost. Tough one."

Yeah, having an abdominal aortic aneurysm take out a twenty-nine-year-old was hard to deal with. "It wasn't just him. You hear about the Neurofibromatosis patient?"

Dan's eyes narrowed with interest. "No! I have yet to see one in the flesh— oh, wrong phrase!" He grimaced, then waited to hear more details.

"Barely more than a teen; twenty last month. Jimmy Kittle. He did look a lot like the classic 'Elephant Man'."

Tumors forming anywhere nerves were present, both internally and externally. Where most visible, these presented as large lumps and bulges, primarily just under the skin, which had to stretch to cover them, horribly disfiguring. While the famous real-life Elephant Man had a different diagnosis, his look was very close to the deformities of neurofibromatosis.

"You will probably never see such a patient again," Dan conjectured.

Alex drew a deep breath through clenched teeth. Dan could afford to sit there and take a clinical interest since he didn't have to watch the kid die, Alex reflected, but maybe talking about it would help to exorcise its memories. "Extensive tumors covering his whole head and neck...only one eye; some brownish spots on the skin; the bowed legs, much of the bones of his scalp tumorous."

"Why was he in ICU?"

"He wasn't. I was just taking my break, and a code was called in Radiology, so I went to help. They were trying to do a CT scan to assess damage from a fall he'd taken, in which he'd lost consciousness, and it was obvious he had an intracerebral bleed." Alex swallowed. "God, I could see his head growing while we stood there."

"Who was on duty?"

"No neurosurgeon in the house. They put in a call to Dr. Choi, but he wasn't available. Braunstein was the attending on hand, but she was giving me a chance to step in and learn something." Alex looked past Dan, back into memory. "I stared down into that one fixed and dilated pupil; a nurse called a 60-systolic BP, and I remember saying, 'We've gotta drain that.' When Selma nodded, I asked for normal saline, wide open and a 14-gauge Jelco. Trying to find the best spot, I palpated that mass of tumors on his temple. It felt like an old tire covered with huge, rubbery bubbles. My whole index finger sank all the way into the tissues." He looked down at his hands, clenching each other now, and shivered. "I froze—just stood there, watching the bleed swell his head like the goddamned Hindenburg."

Alex found he couldn't go on. After a minute, Dan prompted gently, "His skull was that soft?"

Alex looked directly into Dan's compassionate eyes. "It turned out he didn't have any bone at all on that part of his cranium. That's why a fairly minor fall resulted in such severe bleeding."

Dan nodded. "So what'd you do?"

"Courageous me said, 'Dr. Choi should be here any second.' But Selma said, 'No time.' Took the needle from me and inserted it right into the side of Jimmy's head. Blood just gushed out and sprayed all over her: white coat, sleeves, skirt, stockings; some splashed on me, but not as much."

"Mother of God. He didn't have a chance, did he?"

Alex shook his head. "It was clear by that time, but there was no DNR; his mom had brought him in and asked for us to do whatever we could for him. Selma looked at me and said, 'Someone has to go talk to his mother'."

Dan gave a sympathetic wince. "And how was that—talking to the mom?"

"Not as bad as I thought it'd be." She was ready, I think, for the worst news. She was obviously praying when I found her. I introduced myself and brought her up to speed, making sure I was very clear that draining the bleed was only a temporary measure, and there was quite likely permanent brain damage. She just nodded and said, "He's always been such a loving son. We knew his life was precarious, especially with no protection for his brain on that one side, but we wanted him to have a normal life. So we protected him—and taught him to protect himself—as best we could and gave the rest to God, you know?"

"I had to nod even though I couldn't imagine what that life would be like. Like, I don't mean to be cruel but he so monstrous looking that even I found myself diverting my eyes."

Alex's voice choked off a moment, and he swallowed hard. "Fuckin' coward I am, I went to the bathroom and bawled my eyes out. Then went straight back to the ICU and acted like nothing had happened."

Dan gestured. "It's not like I've never cried after a tough case. Bad diseases kill wonderful people. Kids too. I keep hearing how we have to get used to it if we're gonna be docs."

Dan sat up straight on the beanbag, leaned earnestly forward. "Hey, man, I mean it. We all feel that way some days, lotsa days!"

"Who are you kidding Dan? Every second, I feel sure I'm gonna wimp out or screw up. But you, everyone bows at your feet... you're eating it up."

Dan regarded him with concern, choosing to ignore the unkind and very untrue words. "Hell, Alex, your confidence is shot right now...these are really horrible cases. It's April now, which means new rotations for both of us. Leaving the ICU and ER behind! Where'll you be?"

"Geriatrics." Alex looked up to see if he could detect any chink in Dan's armor. None that he could tell.

"We're gonna lose some no matter where we are. Give yourself a break, man."

The truth was, Alex seemed to be battling his own inner demons. Besides, being a cheerleader when you have your own set of foul ups was at best, tiresome.

Chapter Thirty-Three

Monday came with the first truly spring-like weather of the season. Taking his coffee cup to a cafeteria table that held a discarded *Deerwood Times,* Dan sat and managed, one-handed, to uncover the Sports section's headline: PIRATES LOSE BUT PHENOM IS BORN.

The article was about Trey Hartmann, the Pirates' new hotshot from the Midwest. Yesterday, apparently, he'd pitched a total of seven scoreless innings. The Brewers scored the two winning runs in the last inning off a Pirates reliever. Trey'd been sensational, however, allowing only four hits and striking out seven.

Checking his watch, Dan rose, gulping the rest of his coffee. He was hoping to stop in to see Joe, who'd been admitted to oncology last night. He wanted to get in the visit before he was due to see patients at the eye clinic.

Dan grimaced now as he arrived at the hospital and headed down to Four West. Even knowing this day was coming made it no less hard to say good-bye to a friend. He greeted the nurses at their station and told them he wanted to check on his former patient.

Dan studied Cyrus Klonter's notes. Pneumonia. The lab values showed Joe's white-cell count was off the wall, and his leukemia was running completely unchecked now, uncheckable. Joe'd had some time on the outside with his family, but precious little of it. Barely more than five months.

Walking into the room, Dan was immediately struck by the change in Joe's appearance just since last month when he had greeted the arrival of Joey Jr.

The whole family was there with him. His mom was keeping an eye on the three solemn-faced girls as they colored pictures on individual clipboards while Sue sat close to the bed, holding little Joey where Joe could have him rest next to him in the crook of his arm.

Mustering what cheer he could, Dan greeted his former patient. "Joe, how are you my friend?"

"Fine, fine," Joe managed unconvincingly. Dan greeted Joe's mom and wife, then found a grin for the kids, all of whom wore jeans and black baseball caps turned backward. "Hi, guys," he said and playfully righted the hat of the oldest child, JoAnn, so that the gold-colored Pirates logo faced forward. "No wonder they haven't won a game yet!"

He could tell by JoAnn's eyes that she knew he was kidding, but, unsmiling, she countered, "Not my cap's fault. They pulled Trey Hartmann too soon."

The adults laughed at the refreshing spirit of this bright seven-year-old.

"Would you like a minute with Joe? I think he'd enjoy a chat with a grown-up male. I know he was hoping you'd come by."

Dan could see the strain on her face. "Sure," Dan said, reassured now his intrusion was welcome.

Sue rose with her cargo and glanced at her mother-in-law. "I'll take Joey to the changing station in the ladies room."

Joe's mom rose, too, and said to the girls, "I'm ready for a little break. Anybody else want a donut with sprinkles?"

Alone now with the patient, Dan sat beside the bed and put his hand on Joe's. He looked so pale, so gaunt. At the corner of his mouth, active herpes lesions added further insult to illness.

"That's one beautiful family you've got there, Joe."

"I know. I'm a lucky guy." His voice broke on the last word, and he looked away, blinking hard. "It's just so hard to believe, Dan. Six months ago, I was in the picture of health, on top of the world, and now..." He swallowed. "I just hate leaving Sue with all of this."

"She's got your mom."

"Thank God for that. I know I don't have much time now, Dan, and I want you to know I hope to go out as easily as possible for everybody's sake. Sue and I thought about it and talked it over and told Doctor Klonter. The DNR is on my chart. When the time comes, I just want to go. Last thing my family needs is having people pounding on my chest, stabbing me with needles, hooking me up to machines, y'know?"

"I absolutely do." Dan cleared his throat. "Listen, man. I'm so glad to have gotten to know you and your wonderful family."

Joe nodded, his eyes filling again. "I'm ready to go, Dan, but I just can't seem to get past how goddam unfair this is to them. To Sue, my little girls, and my son." With that, he began to sob.

Dan rose from the chair and sat beside him on the bed, embracing that frail body in the thin hospital gown, feeling every bone of his ribcage. The crestfallen intern held Joe in his arms, rocking a little as his own eyes filled and overflowed as he wept for this man. For the whole family who loved him and would miss him terribly.

When Sue returned with the family, Dan made his way out quietly, wondering if Joe would be there when next he had a moment to visit with him. Wiping his eyes, he took a minute on the stairwell to prepare himself for moving out of the world of visitor and back into the role of doctor. He would never see Joe Bonfiglio alive again.

"You okay Alex? You look so sad." Nikki commented while she fumbled with her keys for the front door to the apartment building. Meanwhile, Alex had exited his car with some groceries in hand and remained waiting patiently behind her. After all, only laundry and apartment cleaning awaited him on his off day.

"You're perceptive Nikki. I do get pretty down from time to time. Must be the fact that we get up in the dark and get home in the dark." He shrugged his shoulders, his portly frame accentuated even further by his bulky two-toned down jacket, a George Costanza special.

"Would you like to talk some? Been told that I am a good listener."

"Maybe later, thanks, you're very kind." With that, Cole made a beeline to his apartment across the hall, making certain to smile at his neighbor before closing his door. *Marchetti is so fuckin' lucky to have someone like that, God damn it. Women don't bother to give him a second look. Maybe I should take her up on her offer...*

"Nikki, I think I would like to talk," Alex spoke softly as he exited his apartment and knocked on her door.

"Great, great, can I get you something to drink?" she offered after having shed her coat and turned up the thermostat some.

"A diet soda?"

"I can do that. Be right back."

Before long, Alex was facing Nikki who had made herself comfortable on their beat up sofa, legs curled up underneath her while the troubled intern sat in a new darkly stained rocking chair to her right, a gift from Dan's brother on his birthday.

"So what is going on Alex. Your body language tells me that you are troubled. Am I correct?"

"Troubled? Why should I be? Doing fantastic so far in the residency, getting kudos here and there, just tired, real tired."

"Really, is that why you came over here, to tell me everything is copacetic, even great? I don't think so."

Alex bit his lip and took a sip of his drink. "Well, having some serious doubts about how I am doing. Been the one shining light in our family, two brothers who are fuckups, one is gay and morbidly obese and the other a meth head."

"The shining light, huh?"

"You could say that."

"Well, I too came from a 'dysfunctional' family as well. Don't you like our euphemisms for when we really mean fucked-up?" Nikki shook her head in disgust.

"Really. Had you figured for just the opposite. You compensate well I suppose."

"We survive, my good friend, we survive. Enough about me. Why are you so hard on yourself?"

"Great question. Maybe, just maybe…" Alex stiffened. *I can't honestly tell Nikki how God damned jealous I am of her boyfriend. How Dan represented all that he wished for himself, a quiet dignity with no boasting, no drama, just comfortable in his own skin.*

"Nikki," Alex quickly changed the subject, "Too bad there are no others like you around here. You are so easy to talk to."

Nikki blushed at the compliment. *If he only knew how close to the edge she lived. One disaster away from losing it.*

One A.M.…Alex just stared at the ceiling in his bedroom, unable to read, sleep, or even stream some movie or Tik Tok sensation. Thoughts kept coming back to his conversation, albeit brief, with Nikki Saxon. *There was some connection he felt and wondered if it had been experienced on her end. Maybe, just maybe she was reaching out to him. After all, two birds of a feather…that damn Marchetti.*

Chapter Thirty-Four

Dan hurried into the hospital's warmth, lifting a hand in greeting to the two security guards conversing there in the lobby. Greg, his favorite, appeared to be off today. After quickly shedding and stowing his outerwear in his locker, Dan zipped to the cafeteria to pick up a bowl of watery oatmeal with a scoop of granola, and some fresh blueberries floating on top. He wolfed it down on his way to the ICU.

As he reached the area outside the doors to the unit, Dan found a crowd of people spilling out from the designated waiting lounge. Normally, people are there because of a patient in the ER or ICU. The lounge always seemed reserved as families looked concerned, perhaps terrified, and tended to speak in low, serious tones. But these were young people, looking to be in their twenties, and they were swapping tales in animated voices and with raucous laughter, about someone named Rory. A miasma of cigarette smoke and alcohol fumes hung all about them, as if every pore were outgassing last night's partying. Everyone he could see had on at least one piece of green clothing. The most solemn, a willowy girl of perhaps twenty-one, was brushing back her green hair while nervously chewing her lip as she tried to laugh at the conversation. The majority of the other heads were varying shades of reddish brown.

One of those heads, this one with disheveled shoulder-length fiery red hair, turned to reveal a puffy male face flushed around the bloodshot eyes. Focused now on Dan, the fellow moved unsteadily toward him, calling, "Hey! You my brutha's new docta?"

Embarrassed to be caught off guard while emptying his oatmeal bowl, Dan answered quite honestly, "I don't know yet. I just got called in. If you'd all like to take a seat in the lounge, I'll find out and come tell you what's going on. Patient's name?"

"Rory Maguire!" said another voice, softer but firm, as a woman in her forties pushed past the hulking figure to smile anxiously at Dan. "I'm Erin Maguire, Rory's mother—and Shane's." The resemblance was unmistakable.

Dan quickly introduced himself, repeated his pledge to return with information, and exited into the sanctuary of the ICU. Brian Callahan appeared from Room Four and gave Dan an overworked expression. "Looks like you caught my 3-17 Bullet after all."

Dan followed Brian back into the room, surprised to see Cheryl Herrera, the nurse from his first rotation in CCU. They nodded to each other, but his attention went immediately to Neal Driscoll, the attending, who greeted him with, "Oh, smashing, you're here." Dan loved his British word choices. "Thanks for coming in for Alex. I'll leave Mr. Maguire to you. I'm needed for a bleeding ulcer in Room Eleven. I'll let Brian fill you in on the case if he doesn't mind hanging around a little longer?"

Even before Driscoll was gone, Brian began: "Rory Maguire, twenty-five-year-old white male, arrived in the ER at 3:00 a.m."

Dan stared down at the unconscious patient, whose breathing was currently supported by a ventilator. His extreme pallor made his freckles stand out even more on his fair skin. His hair, the same flaming red of his mom and brother, was unruly and long, though cut shorter than Shane's.

Brian's voice held a note of sad vindication. "Not too hard to guess this all started as a St. Patrick's Day party at Casey's Pub. Anyway, after a drinking contest, Rory and Shane got in a fight over a girl named Bridget. Maybe you saw her out there: green hair and a really short skirt?" Dan nodded. "His brother Shane tried to leave the party with Bridget. This genius here ran after them to the parking lot and decided to stop them by leaping up onto the windshield of Shane's car. Shane slammed on the brakes, and Rory was thrown off, ending up under the wheels. *My God!* Kicker is, Dan, that Shane panicked, thinking the wheels were still *on* Rory, and threw it into reverse to back up *over* him at a different angle."

As Cheryl prepared to replace the patient's urinary catheter, Dan picked up the chart and scanned the list of injuries as Brian continued, "It was touch-and-go in the ER, but we've stabilized enough for surgery. Lung damage, kidney damage, broken ribs, pelvic fracture, shattered ankles, and early ARDS. The worst damage was to the spleen and liver. You'll see they did the best they could under the circumstances," Brian was saying. "Removed the spleen, but the liver was just torn and oozing blood."

As Cheryl pulled back the patient's hospital gown and began to thread the catheter into Rory's penis, Dan stepped over and peeled back the huge, white bandage pad taped on the man's abdomen. Startled, he found the wound still open, giving full visibility to a dusky-looking liver tissue that was tourniqueted with big rubber bands—like toy airplanes looked when he was a kid—wrapped around a clamp several times. *Gruesome.*

"Lacerated and macerated," Brian said. "Miracle they got that bleeding stopped. They didn't suture him up so they could keep that gizmo in place and have instant access if the bleeding started again. You guys'll need to keep an eye on it."

Both Cheryl and Dan nodded. Amazed at the ingenious contraption, he remarked, "MacGyver lives. Anything else?"

Brian shook his head. "Dismal lab values, but you've got the chart. I don't envy you dealing with his family. That brother was pretty sharp with me. Gotta feel guilty as hell, y'know. Plus you don't have the buffer of being Irish."

Dan gave him a grim nod. "You go on. Thanks for staying to fill me in. Better take the back elevator and avoid that crew out there. They're my responsibility now."

Turning to his patient's empty urine drainage bag, Dan could see that though the catheter was properly placed, no urine had yet moved into the tubing.

"Damn, not good at all. Guess his kidneys are shot, ATN," he whispered to himself. Dan quickly perused the 'dismal' lab values Brian had mentioned. Muscle enzymes were also high. Low blood volume. Clotting parameters askew. Not to mention shock, the shredded liver, and lungs so bad that he had to be ventilated. The guy was a train wreck and younger than Dan. *He doesn't have a chance for survival.*

Pulling his stethoscope from his neck, Dan listened to Rory's lungs. "No breath sounds on the right side," Dan told the attentive Cheryl. "Let's get some chest films, stat." She nodded and went off to make the call. Dan suspected the right lung had collapsed under the onslaught of his conditions, and he would need a chest tube. The ventilator, which would help keep him oxygenating as his acute respiratory distress syndrome, ARDS, required high machine pressures to force oxygen into his ravaged lung tissues as body fluids seeped into the air spaces. But shock and the very use of high pressure could have caused a lung to collapse, a medical Catch 22.

By the time Dan had finished the rest of his exam, with nothing looking remotely hopeful, Cheryl was back, and he asked her to put a clean bandage over the open abdominal incision while he went out to update the Maguire family.

It was Erin Maguire who saw Dan first and moved toward him. "Let's sit down over here." He directed her to the two chairs a little way down the hallway outside the sliding doors. They sat and Shane came to stand next to his mom, towering over her, but with one huge hand reassuringly on her shoulder. Green-haired Bridget didn't join them but had edged within earshot. Shane cleared his throat to speak, but Erin Maguire signaled for him to wait, and she asked, "How's my boy doing, Doctor?" She managed a tremulous smile. "He's better now, right?"

Dan took a deep breath and looked directly into her green eyes. "I'm sorry, but Rory's condition could not be more dire." Somehow she kept that smile pasted on her face but she seemed to stare right through him as if she hadn't heard or couldn't really comprehend that news. When Shane made a sound of exasperation, or maybe skepticism, Dan continued before the brother could speak, "All of his systems are shutting down: kidneys, liver, lungs. He has broken bones and undoubtedly some nerve damage. His injuries are quite extensive and life-threatening."

Shane growled something profane, but Dan avoided eye contact, thinking what he would never say aloud. *You killed your brother, man—and for what? Winning the favors of a girl with a short skirt and green hair?* Behind him, he heard the girl sob and then continue crying more softly.

Erin's demeanor couldn't mask her fear and worry, but her voice came firmer now. "Rory's in God's hands. He'll pull through."

"Hell, yes!" Shane blustered. "He's a tough Irish Finn. Takes more'n that to kill a Maguire."

Erin patted Shane's hand on her shoulder, but kept her gaze on Dan, who tried again to prepare them for what had to be the inevitable.

"Mrs. Maguire, Rory is gravely ill. Though we're doing everything that can possibly be done for him, you need to understand that his kidneys aren't functioning; his liver may not even be salvageable; and he might have a collapsed—"

"Code 99! Code 99—ICU!" echoed suddenly throughout the hospital corridors, just as his own beeper went off: *Beep, beep, beep.* "Dr. Marchetti, ICU Medical—stat; ICU Medical—stat!"

Dan leapt up, excused himself, and hurried back to the unit. Brushing through the doors, he saw a radiology tech with some portable equipment, looking lost. The fellow motioned Dan toward Rory Maguire's room. Just ahead of him, Sondra wheeled the crash cart in next to the bed. Cheryl was already there, checking vitals, and Vinny Orlander stood beside the ventilator ready to help. Dan's eyes caught the monitor, which indicated a marked bradycardia, a perilously slow heart rhythm.

"BP 60; pulse 35," Cheryl called.

"Increase his fluids." The blood pressure responded accordingly.

Dan mused on the ethical issues of saving a life. *Maguire hasn't got a hope of survival, but he is so young.* Only a matter of time before he succumbs; in fact, his body was already trying to die.

It was one kind of irony for Dan to snatch a man back from sudden, certain death, only to preserve him for a torturous certain death. Even more ironic that Rory would've died not from his medical condition, nor from the multitude of grave internal injuries, but possibly because of the treatment itself: mechanical ventilators, without which the patient wouldn't survive.

Did it really make any sense to save him? Not acting had been unthinkable without a Do Not Resuscitate order on the chart. Watching Cheryl carefully tape in place the improvised chest tube, Dan said, "We should probably get a DNR from the family before we have another crisis."

Cheryl looked up at him with her mouth in a grim line. "Yeah? The best of luck with that."

As if this discussion had somehow penetrated to the patient, Rory began to stir. His eyes opened then widened in confusion? Fear? No wonder: waking up with a big tube down your throat and some contraption stabbed into your chest. Cheryl had already moved to the pole with its hanging bag of medications, including a sedative that was clearly no longer sufficient. Her eyes turned to Dan for direction.

"Two more milligrams Ativan, IV," Putting his attention on the patient, he picked up the nearest hand as it began to wave around. "Take it easy, Rory," Dan told him. "You've had an accident, and you're in the hospital." Maguire was trying to speak, grunting nasally with rising panic. "You won't be able to talk right now, because of the equipment helping you breathe." Hard to believe someone so badly injured could still fight for his life.

The vocalization stopped, but his body started to thrash on the bed. Dan held onto the hand reassuringly as Cheryl soothed in her best voice, tones of both nurse and mother, "Just try to relax, honey. We're taking care of you." Rory's eyes focused on her. Right about then, the Ativan took hold, and he slid back into blissful unconsciousness.

"What the fuck ya doin' t'm' brutha?"

Dan glanced over his shoulder, startled to see the reincarnation of a wild Irish warrior. Looking past the bulk of Shane Maguire, he saw Sondra on the intercom as she called security: "Code Blue to ICU! Code Blue to ICU!"

Oblivious to that, Shane continued, "An' what the *fuck* is that in his belly an' sticking outta his chest?"

Dan moved closer. "We had to correct a collapsed lung." Though aware Cheryl was now safer behind him, Dan's changing position was meant to mask the gruesome condition of his brother's body and the various contraptions piercing it from Shane's view. "He's stable right now, but—"

Shane's face contorted with surging terror, guilt, and despair. His huge fists balled threateningly, and his whiskeyed breath swept over Dan as Shane bellowed, "You butchers're killin' 'im!" Swinging his arm wildly and unexpectedly, his fist smashed into Dan's left cheekbone with a sickening *thwup.*

Flashes of light amidst the pain. *Shoulda ducked* was Dan's last thought as he toppled over backward, unable to stop his fall. Despite his flailing arms, he felt his head hit the linoleum covered floor and bounce, but then he was aware of nothing at all. *You can't make this shit up!*

Chapter Thirty-Five

Dan studied his reflection in the bathroom mirror. His short-stack pancake-sized shiner, once angry purple and red now, a week later, had faded to a queasy yellowish green. Similarly, the matching point-of-impact bruise on his left jaw followed suit. He touched that gently. At least x-rays had shown the hairline fracture of his jawbone would heal on its own without surgery, and he'd gotten lucky on the concussion too.

"Beneficial that head of thick, curly hair," Nikki'd teased. "Great way to cushion a fall."

Though he remembered his head hitting the floor, Dan had to admit that not much else was clear. His vague memories included lying on a gurney in the ICU with Neal Driscoll and the nurses hovering over him to check his vitals. Beyond them, that Viking Vinny Orlander was sitting atop a prone-but-still-bellowing Shane Maguire while the Mack-truck security guard, Burt Pollard, snapped handcuffs onto Shane's wrists. As Burt and Vinny pulled Shane to his feet and hustled him toward the exit, his mother Erin followed, wringing her hands and crying, "Calm down, boyo; you're in enough trouble!"

After tests, x-rays, and a brain scan to diagnose the severity of Dan's head trauma, there was no question that he was going home. "You've still got a week's vacation coming," Ballard had said. "Take it and make sure you report back to the ER if you have any worrisome symptoms. I wouldn't even let you go home if you didn't have one of our best nurses promising to watch you like a hawk."

Nikki drove very carefully to avoid jostling Dan and then helped him from the car and steadied him all the way up the stairs and to the apartment door. The floor felt like it was coming up to meet him, and the room was spinning like a top; Dan was glad for the assistance.

The bed turned down for him and some sleep sweats laid out ready. She helped him trade clothing and tumble into that cozy refuge.

Nothing like having a nurse to take care of you, Dan remembered thinking before collapsing into sleep. Buoyed by her new feeling of well-being and her delight in having him home with her, Nikki cooked delicious soups and soft stews, fruit puddings, and other delights that were easy on his healing jaw. It'd been a week of nurturing and cuddling that moved their bond into new territory, but Dan found he wasn't quite up for sex yet. Snuggling had to do.

And sleep. All those wonderful extra hours.

Now, leaving the bathroom to dress for work, Dan noted that the weather didn't seem to know it was nearly spring. Deeply cold with snow and ice pellets in the wind, but no accumulation to make the bleakness pretty. Tomorrow, March 26 already, rain and drizzle were predicted with the snow and ice.

When he'd bundled up and had his car keys handy, he slipped out of the apartment and hurried downstairs. It took a while to warm up the engine of the Accord, but he was soon on his way. It felt strange to drive such a short distance, but he needed to be careful for a few more days until he was feeling himself again.

Dan's thoughts turned to Alex, whom he saw in his rearview mirror as he pulled out.

"How are things?" he inquired through a partially opened passenger side window.

"Oh the usual. Managing complex patients, formulating differential diagnoses for shit. Being utterly and unfairly rejected by the woman I love and wanted to care for, with, apparently, no hope of getting back together. 'Other than that, how was the play, Mrs. Lincoln?'" Dan burst out laughing at his friend's delivery, instantly wishing he could take it back. Alex's smirk told the whole story. "You find this whole thing funny, Dan?"

"Not at all, Alex, I'm sorry."

"See ya."

Turning off his motor in the DCH parking structure, Dan shivered slightly. The trauma of being assaulted had faded, but he really didn't want to be anywhere he'd have to overhear any details about how the Rory Maguire case wound down.

Early in his imposed "vacation," Dan had made it clear to his coworkers that he just wanted to forget the whole Maguire clan. No, he wasn't suing them; they had enough hardship.

Now, as he arrived in the ER, he was warmly greeted by nurse Gail Sanduski, who handed him a chart. "Hope you're ready to hit the ground running. We're swamped."

Dan headed for Bed One.

"Will need the telecommunicator for Stan," Dan requested of Mary, the clinic director. Stan, short for Stanislaw, was completely deaf since childhood as a result of meningitis and had spent his entire childhood and adolescence bouncing from one state facility to another.

"I already anticipated this Dr. Marchetti," Mary quickly responded, handing Dan the iPad.

"Good morning, I'm Dr. Dan Marchetti, thanks so much for your help." The affable, somewhat portly woman who looked to be in her fifties, greeted him. "Glad to help."

Dan held up the screen to his patient. "Stan, a pleasure to see you again. How are you feeling?"

Stan peered anxiously at the woman who 'signed' the physician's words. At once, the affable man smiled broadly and signed back. "Doing well Sir. How are you?"

As Dan went about his physical exam, he became suddenly and inexplicably overwhelmed. The bizarre events of the past few months had finally penetrated to his very core and extracted the proverbial 'pound of flesh'. Cradling this grown man's head against his chest, he began to cry openly.

"Doctor, are you okay?" the voice from the iPad inquired.

Stan's eyes darted from the translator to Dan, deciding to return the hug in any event, smiling even more widely, if that was possible.

"Yes, of course, I apologize, just that this marvelous man has just given me a much needed kick in the rear. He just radiates such pure joy despite having received some really tough breaks. Hard to explain…"

"You don't have to. Why do you think I do this work. It is certainly not for the money." She smirked and shook her head. *How joyful this man appeared to be! Learn from him Marchetti.*

Chapter Thirty-Six

Dan wolfed down a ham sandwich as he drove to PNC Park—the Pirates' home field on the bank of the Allegheny River. Upon arrival, he had no trouble finding the gates of the players' parking lot. He pulled up next to the kiosk and fished out his driver's license, handing it to the attendant.

"Member of the press, sir?" the young man asked pleasantly as he scanned his list of people who could be admitted.

"No, just a friend of Charlie Monroe. He invited me."

"Oh, Coach Monroe!" The grin was quick and obviously genuine. "He's quite a character. Place wouldn't be the same without him. Ah, here it is: Dr. Dante Marchetti." He looked up from the sheet of paper. "You a real doctor?"

Dan smiled and nodded. He was used to the question, but always wondered if they thought he was too young or maybe looked more like he taught history, than he spent much of his time pounding on chests and palpating bellies.

Perhaps the fellow sensed this. "I mean, are you the doc who pulled Coach through?"

"One of many."

"Well, we're all grateful. Thanks." He leaned inside his kiosk to find the right gate pass, then handed it to Dan. "Park anywhere, and show this to the heavyset guy at the players' entrance. Enjoy yourself."

Dan parked and grabbed his duffel on the passenger seat. He was already dressed comfortably in grey sweatpants and a light blue hospital shirt, but he expected to get pretty sweaty and wanted dry clothes to change into afterward. He nervously tweaked the brim of the black Pirates cap Pop had given him.

The guy at the entrance checked Dan's pass and gave him brief, clear, easy directions to the locker room, then told Dan, "I'll call Charlie and let him know you're headed there."

Dan made his way through the quiet corridors of the five-year-old stadium that'd been built on the footprint of the imploded Three Rivers Stadium.

Soon, up ahead, he could see Charlie Monroe peering around the partially open locker room door. He still looked frail, leaning against the door for support. Dan noted the coach's dusky color. Little gasps accompanied his words: "Hey, Doc! Been waitin'."

The old man reached to embrace him then. "Great to see you, Dan!" Despite the body's frailty, Charlie's grip was surprisingly strong…for a moment at least.

"Gotta tell you, I'm thrilled to be here."

"Glad," Charlie puffed. "You… deserve…some fun."

Dan's resolve crumbled. "You feeling okay, Charlie? Breathing okay?"

Monroe jerked a thumb over his shoulder. "As long as my O_2 is in here. Come meet the guys. Told 'em all aboutcha." This sent a ripple of nerves through Dan, as he wondered just what the old coach had said to the players. Inside the door was parked a gleaming, red-and-silver power chair—boldly emblazoned with the word "Scalawag." In a basket between two saddlebags, Dan saw a compact portable oxygen tank in its cylindrical carry-bag with a padded shoulder strap. Charlie went to his scooter, but didn't sit down or even drape the tubing of the nasal cannula around his face. He just held the tiny twin nozzles against his nostrils and, eyes closed in relief, and breathed in the flow.

The men were ribbing each other and predicting how the warmup—and later game—would go. They'd lost their first home game against the Dodgers, but squeaked by them 7-6 last night; they sounded pretty confident about winning tonight's game.

Dan recognized the close-cropped red hair above a smiling face full of freckles. Trey Hartmann!

"Hey, thanks. It's an honor to meet you, Trey."

The kid was young enough and still new enough to it all that he blushed. "I don't have to call you Dr. Marchetti, do I?"

"No, no. Dan will do just fine." Liking him right away, Dan was surprised at the young rookie's physical presence. He looked more like he belonged in the NFL than major league baseball. His shoulders and chest were so heavily muscled that Dan had no problem guessing he must spend countless hours in the weight room. *These guys are some of the best athletes in the world.*

Charlie stepped over and clapped Trey on the shoulder. "It's easier to ride my scooter the long way around. Take care of my doc here, okay?"

"Sure!" Trey actually seemed enthused.

Charlie surveyed Dan's outfit. "He's got a cap. Rustle up some shoes for him. I'll meet you guys on the field."

A moment after the old coach left, Dan could hear the motor of the mobility chair around the corner.

"What shoe size, Dan?" Trey asked, walking to his locker.

"Ten."

"Well, I'm a 10½. Close enough." He held out a pair of shoes. "Here. Use these spares."

Dan thanked him, took the footwear and sat down on a bench, setting his duffel on the next seat. By now, the last of the players were leaving, headed for the field. Quickly, Dan exchanged his shoes for Trey's, thankful that he was wearing thick socks.

When Dan stood up, ready to go, but unsure on what to do about his duffel, Trey pointed to it and said, "You can leave that anywhere. It'll be safe."

"I feel like I have been dropped into a fantasy world where I find myself walking out onto a major league field wearing the shoes of the league's hottest rising star." They laughed. Butterflies rippled through him all over again. What if he screwed up? Really bad? Then again, the humiliation would be a small price to pay for an experience he'd be telling his grandkids about.

Trey grabbed some equipment, flipped a glove to Dan, and back-pedaled some distance away, before he tossed a ball to him. By the time a space of seventy feet had opened between them, Dan had caught the ball and smacked it back to Trey.

The new hope of the Pirates grinned, but cautioned, "Take it easy, Dan. Otherwise, your arm'll be super sore tonight—and worse tomorrow!"

Dan easily caught the soft tosses and returned them, still incredulous that he was there at all; much less working with Trey Hartmann. Watching Trey watch *him*, Dan couldn't help but wonder what Trey thought of him and how dorky he must look with his face lit up like a kid's at Christmas.

"You've played ball before?" Trey called.

"Some. My dad's a high school coach."

Tossing another soft one back, he marveled again at the fluid motions of this professional athlete born to the role, and destined for greatness. The rookie sensation, brought up from the minors after only two years, during which he'd led Triple A in wins and earned-run average, was now being hailed as another Nolan Ryan. His fastball had been clocked at ninety-eight miles an hour. It had so much movement that TV cameramen often chose to follow struck-out batters as they returned to their dugouts shaking their heads in disbelief. According to Nikki, the Pirates were hoping Trey could be the base of their rebuilding program, but he couldn't do it alone, or overnight. After last night's win, the team was still only standing at 2-7.

And he was sure management was delighted to have a good-hearted, good-natured, down-to-earth Nebraska farm boy. Trey Hartmann came straight from central casting.

"Let me see you come over the top more, Dan."

He nodded at Trey's instructions and began throwing with more of an overhand motion. This seemed to cause less strain on his arm, while adding more control. Too cool.

After a few minutes, Trey tossed the ball and glove to one of the eager batboys. "Let's do some running," he called, waving for Dan to follow.

Taking laps on the eighteen-foot-wide warning track along the outfield fence, Dan saw Charlie Monroe zipping around the field in his Scalawag, monitoring other players engaged in various forms of exercise. Another coach was working the fielders by hitting 'fungoes' to them with a longer and thinner fungo bat.

Dan put his attention back on his laps: running side-by-side with Trey, not competing, just taut muscles propelling them with efficiency and grace. The joy of it flooded Dan, even as the sweat began to bead and trickle and flow. The hospital shirt clung to his chest and back, but the breeze cooled the dampness. He reveled in the mindless movement of his muscles, so different than the way his body moved between the drama and tedium of his hospital work. *God, I love this!*

As Dan accompanied the scooter back toward home plate, he saw another of the kids who helped with equipment, a tow-headed lad of perhaps thirteen, dash out to hand Trey a mitt, then hurry back to help wherever he could. Trey donned and flexed the southpaw glove, then chose a ball from the tall bin on his side of the screen. "Batter up!" someone yelled.

"You go on to the batting cage," Charlie told Dan. "I gotta go sort something out." He whipped the Scalawag around and zoomed off toward two players who'd been practicing together, but now appeared to be growing increasingly argumentative.

When he reached home plate, Dan went to stand behind it, outside the steel-mesh batting cage.

As Dan watched, Trey's first batter, outfielder Ricky Mossberg, stepped up and took his stance for the first pitch.

Unhurried, Trey began his windup. His pitching style reminded Dan of the great Jim Palmer, the Baltimore Orioles' ace for many years. Same motion and a great assortment of pitches: hard fastballs, sliders, and change ups. *Maybe Trey will end up doing underwear ads, too,* Dan chuckled to himself as he breathed in the heady air of a professional ball team.

Dan recognized the Pirates' pitching coach, William—'call me Dex, not Willie'—Dexter, studying Trey from the sidelines. "Two more batters," Dex called out to Trey. "Then we'll give someone else a shot." With his thick white mane and deeply tanned face, Dex typified the image of the ex-major leaguer, addicted to the game of baseball, using his teaching skills in order to stay connected to the game.

Shortstop Randy Percado stepped up next and fouled off two pitches and singled on most of the others.

Dex called to Trey, "One more pitch, Hartmann."

"Nice heater, rook. I'm sure glad you're on our side!" They high-fived each other and went their own ways: the shortstop to the outfield, and Trey dropped to the grass behind the mound to do his customary hundred sit-ups.

Still leaning comfortably with his arms resting on the metal crossbar of the batting cage, Dan wondered with interest, who would be next up? He could watch this for hours.

"Hey, Marchetti!" Dex shouted. "You're up!"

Holy shit! Dan snapped upright, suddenly sweating again.

And there was Charlie, grinning like a kid behind his O₂ cannula. "Yeah, hustle it! An' try t'keep from throwin' into the stands—those balls aren't cheap, y'know."

Heart pounding, Dan reached out to take the mitt the tow-headed bat boy had to run up to offer, and wondered what the hell had he gotten himself into. This was real baseball, and these were the pros. These were men who didn't have time for amateur hour. What would Pop be thinking if he was watching him now. Proud? Or just waiting to throw an arm around his shoulder and tell him that failing at this level was okay too, as they walked out together.

He'd forced his legs into motion so they'd take him, despite his hesitation, out to the mound. Ahead of him, two more bat boys were wheeling the L-screen around to accommodate his right-arm pitching, instead of Trey's left. Beyond them, Trey paused at the top of one of his sit-ups to grin encouragingly. "Hey, just relax. You'll do fine."

"Oh shit!" Dan mumbled, turning to position himself on the rubber. He still couldn't bear to look up at the batting cage yet. He heard Dex call for Odell Shaw to bat.

"Do your thing, Dan!" Charlie urged. "But no spitters or knuckles, now—hear?"

Dan stood holding the ball, head down, trying desperately to control the trembling in his hands. The blob of gum in his mouth had lost every vestige of spearmint and seemed to only be making his mouth drier. Still, he couldn't seem to make himself move.

All of PNC Park seemed to ripple with tension. No wonder. Two-and-seven wasn't an illustrious showing for the season so far. This team had a lot of work to do, and he was holding up the train.

Steeling himself to begin his windup, he lifted his eyes, ready to confront his opponent, the pitcher-now-batter Odell Shaw, and had to blink at the unexpected sight. The player was garbed from mask to shins in a catcher's protective gear.

Dan felt his mouth fall open, and Charlie guffawed, slapping the handlebars of his Scalawag. Other players laughed too, good-naturedly of course, inviting Dan into the joke. He managed a smile and tweaked the brim of his Pirates cap to salute Monroe. Dan could feel his muscles release throughout his own body. Maybe he could best serve the team as comic relief, as if being a high school phenom was too many years ago.

Dan drew a deep breath, squared his shoulders with home plate, and began his windup. Even as the ball left his fingers, he winced, fearing the worst. The ball smacked the dirt at least two feet in front of home plate, and the batter had to jump to avoid being struck by the bounce. Dan peered into the catcher awaiting a new ball, refusing to take his eyes off home plate. Perhaps fearful he wouldn't be able to locate it again.

Humiliation swept through Dan like a tide and, unfortunately, made him try to correct the situation by immediately throwing another pitch. This one sailed over Shaw's head by almost a yard. Could he make a bigger ass of himself? He expected catcalls and laughter, but the players remained silent, probably as embarrassed for him as he was for himself, he thought.

"Settle down, Doc," Dex yelled, but not unkindly. "Don't aim. Just throw it!"

If only it were that simple, but then again, what kind of fool wouldn't listen to a professional pitching coach? Dan released a great sigh and followed Dex's advice.

That next pitch was perfect: over the middle of the plate with surprising velocity. The batter swung and fouled it off. Again and again now, Dan delivered the balls, each successive one crossing the plate with significant zip and movement. The batter soon shed the once-humorous protective gear, acknowledging the legitimacy of Dan's throwing arm, and was now earnestly dug in at the plate, awaiting each pitch with a face that showed deep concentration.

By the time Dex called for the next batter to succeed Shaw, many other players had gathered around the batting cage, and Dan liked to think they wore admiring expressions.

"You got a real gun there, Doc." Dan thanked him and moved on. Hoping to slip out without disturbing or delaying the practice further, Dan raised a hand to all the nearby players and said, "Thanks, guys!" To Dex, he said, "Please pass along my gratitude to all the other guys too, okay?"

Dan lifted the bottom of his shirt and mopped the perspiration from his face to hide the sudden embarrassing flush.

"Got something for you." Charlie turned to pull a black cap from one of the cart's saddlebags and hand it to Dan. "You earned this today."

Dan took it and saw it was much like the one he'd returned to his damp head, except it had a red underbill. Charlie flicked that with his fingernail. "Pirates were the first team ever to have that. We only wear these with the home team alternate uniform. This cap's special, from 2001 when we opened PNC Park; looking forward to our 'New Era in Baseball'. It's historic."

"Hey, thank you so much. Won't put it on till I shower. But I can't thank you enough for all of this, Charlie." He leaned down to embrace the old man noting how frail he was beneath his Pirates windbreaker.

The coach seemed choked up too, and started rummaging in his saddlebag again. "Here're your tickets. Two for Tuesday night, May 9, right?"

"Oh, yeah."

"And there are a coupla passes so you can come see us before the game."

"Wow. Thanks a million. Being here has made my week, my year. My dad's not gonna believe it!"

"Fine, fine," Charlie interrupted, blinking rapidly and seeming eager to end the long good-bye. "You better get on now." With that, he zoomed off to chastise some player he'd seen not giving a full effort.

"Take care of yourself!" Dan called after him, and the coach waved back over his shoulder.

When freshly showered and dressed in the warm-up suit he'd brought in his duffel, Dan sat in the otherwise-empty PNC locker room, pulling on clean socks and then his Nikes. Lacing up his own shoes, he observed, "Now back to my real life."

Speaking of which, he leaned down to lift the loaner pair, wondering what exactly to do with them. Didn't seem considerate to just leave them there on the floor like cast-offs. He noticed the door of Trey's locker was slightly ajar. He'd stick them in there, and to leave a thank you note for the young southpaw.

He found a pen in the outer pocket of his duffel, but no paper—except the holder for the tickets Charlie had given him, and was in no way going to use that. Glancing around, he saw a clean paper towel on another bench and quickly dashed his message:

Dear Trey, Thanks so much for the loan of your shoes and showing me such an awesome time. Great meeting you. Best of luck for a terrific season! Dan.

After tucking the note into the laces of one shoe, Dan opened the locker door even wider to place the pair inside.

Maybe it was best to just close the door and leave the shoes as originally planned, but already in those moments of deciding, the mass had begun to shift so the door now couldn't close more than half way.

Dan tried to reshuffle the mess, which only made it accelerate its slow-motion avalanche toward the floor. Embarrassed, Dan dropped into a squat, his hands trying to thwart the tide failing.

Dan couldn't help it; his attention snapped to the pale blue business card paperclipped to a yellow physician's referral form. Huskers Ophthalmology Partners, announced the blue card, Catherine G. Becerra, MD, eye physician and surgeon. The address noted a town in Nebraska Dan had never heard of before. The referral was to a neurologist in that same town, recommending an MRI of the optic nerves.

Dan froze, unable to look away and, for a long moment, unable to even think. Then he felt that eerie ripple of déjà vu. In the clinic, it had been young mother, Rita Rice, getting this referral. Could Trey be headed for MS?

"Dan?" a voice called as someone approached from the dugout. Trey's voice. "Y'still here? Wanted to run in an' say good-bye."

Dan didn't move. No sense trying to hide what had happened. Trey came into view with that signature grin of his, though his expression fell into almost-comical bafflement. Dan started apologizing, trying to explain about the shoes and the locker hinges.

Trey's eyes were riveted on what Dan held: the blue card clipped to the yellow paper. The grin vanished, and his fair complexion blanched, accentuating every freckle on his chiseled face.

"I wasn't trying to pry," Dan insisted, lifting the card he held. "It just caught my eye."

Trey glanced around as if making sure they were still alone. "You're a doctor," he said, coming to sit across from Dan, both men straddling the bench in front of the locker. "Can I speak in confidence?"

"Absolutely."

Trey took the paper, set it aside on the bench seat, but still didn't speak. Instead, he began to help Dan try to get his mess layered back into the locker. Dan worked in silence, grinding his jaws together to keep from asking questions. Together they managed to get the locker contents stabilized and the door completely closed. Like an old man, devoid of the boundless energy that had seemed to radiate from him, Trey removed the referral sheet from the seat before lowering himself to sit again.

As Dan took the seat beside him, Trey stared down at the referral. "Wondered where this got to." He tried, unsuccessfully, to chuckle. "I'm not the tidiest person in the world." He sighed. "Guess I'm glad it was you who found it instead of someone else." He still looked pale, and his hands trembled.

"Are you okay?" Dan asked.

Trey nodded, still looking at the paper instead of Dan. "While I was home off-season, I started having trouble with my right eye. Things got blurry all of a sudden, and it hurt something awful. Scared the shit outta me, so I went to my hometown doctor, the one who delivered me. He sent me to this ophthalmologist, and she said it was optic something—inflammation of the nerve."

"Neuritis," Dan supplied quietly.

"Yeah, something like that." Trey went on, "Said I should see this neurologist, get an MRI, because in healthy people my age, this is often an early sign of multiple sclerosis." He couldn't seem to get the word out and settled for, "MS."

Off-season was months ago, yet Trey still had the referral, Dan thought but said, "What'd the nerve doc say?"

Trey really avoided eye contact now as he admitted, "I never made an appointment."

"You still have symptoms? Blurred vision or eye pain?" Dan kept his voice calm and low while wondering how in the world he was managing to play ball—and so well.

"Not really. Seems to have cleared up." He looked at Dan with hopeful, but anxious, eyes. "So I guess it's not serious after all. Right?"

"Maybe," Dan answered. "I hope so. Glad to hear the eye's better, but I gotta tell you, I think you should still follow up."

"Why, if everything's fine? Why risk the media finding out about it now and be on their radar for the season?"

Trey gazed dejectedly at the floor. "If it is MS, I don't want to know." He coughed nervously.

"If I can't see and can't run, my career is over before it really gets started."

Picking up on this, Dan asked, "You're having difficulty running? Or any other symptoms with your arms or legs?"

"No, but that's what'll happen to me eventually, right?"

"Trey, you're putting the cart before the horse. First thing is to rule out everything else. And even if the eye symptoms are related to MS, it could be years before there are any other readily observable signs. Besides, there are several different types—all quite variable. MS wouldn't necessarily stop your career, especially not right away. The important thing is to find out what's going on so you can take care of yourself." Trey made a face like that of a little kid tired of being lectured but Dan went on, "Bottom line: ignoring it, whatever it is, won't make it just go away."

Trey sighed. "I know."

"Have you talked to the team doctor yet?"

"God, no. He's best buds with one of the owners, and I just don't trust him not to out me. Y'know, if the guys upstairs find out, they might not want to take a chance on me."

They both rose. "Charlie says you have tickets for the May 9 game. Maybe we could get together for a coupla brews around then." Trey offered.

"I'd like that." They shook hands, and the gesture turned into a back-slapping hug. Dan hefted the duffel strap over his shoulder and snugged his new, red-underbilled Pirates cap onto his still-damp hair. Maybe the talk had helped, or maybe not, but Dan felt he had taken it as far as he could for today.

They parted, and Dan hurried out. It was a hard drive home. At first, he couldn't stop thinking about Trey. Was it his imagination? Or did everyone around him seem ill? Punching the passenger seat with his fist, Dan forced himself to focus on something else.

Dan jerked his thoughts back to the joy of playing ball and the life of those men with whom he'd just shared the day, imagining again what it would feel like making a living playing a game. How different that was from the working lives of his peers toiling in the day-to-day anguish that existed inside any hospital. He wondered, not for the first time, if he was really up to it all.

Chapter Thirty-Seven

At Scott Bradden's wide gesture toward the settee across from his desk, Linda Ferrante sat down, crossed her long legs comfortably, and smoothed her cerise wool skirt. She watched him study her shapely legs, his mild interest an amused blessing rather than an offense, as he lowered his well-tailored self into a leather receptacle that was more of a throne than any mere chair. It was a stand-out piece of furniture; even in this room richly upholstered in deep chocolate brown, with tons of gold and brass accents.

His eyes came up to meet hers. He skipped any greetings, asked if she was finding her position as an Assistant District Attorney interesting and noted, "I'm sure it's an adjustment from what's primarily a defense firm."

Tapping manicured fingertips on the lone olive-green folder lying atop his desk, he let his gaze pin her in place. "I have a special case I'd like to entrust to you. It's rather delicate," he continued. "It may be nothing at all. But then again—"

Suddenly he grinned. "Yes, I think you're just the person for this little project." Still he didn't open the folder, though his fingers caressed it. "I believe we may have a serial killer at Deerwood Community Hospital."

That made her blink. "At DCH?"

He seemed pleased he'd startled her. "Yes. A series of suspicious deaths going back some four months or longer."

"What do you mean by suspicious? People die in hospitals all the time."

"Granted. And, admittedly, people in dire circumstances, seemingly hopeless. That's what makes it look like a mercy killer may be at work."

"One of the staff, then? Any particular floor or department?"

"No, spread out. ER, ICU, coronary care, medical floor…"

"Anyone look like a suspect?"

"Well, the hospital's Care Review Committee found no negligence on the part of any healthcare professional. But who knows how much of that's just corporate CYA? Received a few credible, albeit anonymous tips but specific and sophisticated. That is how it came to my attention."

"Sophisticated? How so?"

"Well, I can't stand here and tell you I understand the medical aspects thoroughly but…" Just then, he turned to retrieve a document from on top of his desk.

"A valve released prematurely on M-A-S-T trousers, an unauthorized dial change on a ventilator, a Sengstaken-Blakemore tube migration, whatever that is, and a doctored EKG machine lead wire. Three deaths and one near miss."

"Well, one thing is for certain. Our tipster is a health care professional, either a nurse, physician, or other highly knowledgeable individual. The person(s) are medically sophisticated."

Linda was well aware of Bradden's connections with several staff members of the *Deerwood Times,* both editors and reporters. It allowed tips to flow freely in both directions: he'd get early warning of any possible intriguing cases, and also, by leaking details of ongoing cases, could 'massage' publicity and public opinion for the department's benefit—and his own.

"I decided to look into it," Bradden continued. "But under-the-radar for now. I've put a private detective on it, Stacy Conover, a guy I've used on several other matters of discretion and he's compiled a database for which people's schedules overlapped with the suspicious deaths." Bradden glanced away from her eyes. "I'd like for you to go meet with him at his office and see if you can put a solid case together on someone."

So he wants the meetings away from his office. Linda wondered if he had chosen her as the most expendable should this case blow up the wrong way. Bradden handed the chart to her, but motioned to her to read it later, elsewhere.

"Are the police looking into this?" she asked, slipping the file into her brimming briefcase.

"'Looked' is the operative word. They concluded that no evidence pointed to any nefarious or illegal activity. Frankly, the acts can be particularly nuanced ones that your average detective would not truly comprehend. Or these may just be matters of malpractice, in which case, of course, we'll let the families deal with it. But there's a chance we may have to stop a killer."

A coup for his political resume came immediately to mind, but Linda quickly chided herself. Her assessment of his motive might be spot-on, and it was always the right course to stop a killer. But a mercy killer? As an animal lover, she'd often been struck by the reality that one of the most caring and humane things a pet owner could do was end the terminal suffering of a beloved companion. Human beings, though, were another matter, but in many cases, the dilemmas might parallel quite closely.

"How do you want me to proceed?" she asked.

His gaze swung back to her. "Go meet with Conover; find out what he's learned and see what still needs to be sought out. Keep me informed and keep it low-profile. I don't want to stir up a hornet's nest over at DCH unless, and until, we have a clearer picture of what's actually happening—and who's culpable." He handed her a business card from Conover Investigations. His eyes held hers. "Just remember, you've got my back on this."

"Of course."

Outside Bradden's office, she glanced at the business card, and realized she knew the name Stacy Conover. She remembered how, shortly after she moved to town, a series of news stories hit big in the *Deerwood Times*. The case ended with a terrific coup for DA Bradden: the conviction of a local school superintendent as an Internet stalker. However, before the man finally confessed, there'd been a firestorm of controversy and public hysteria. Although it turned out the only young woman involved was a twentysomething instructional aide he'd dated in secret, the early investigation and speculation in the media had parents nearly rioting at a school board meeting; in terror for the safety of their children.

Stacy Conover had been the investigator cited in the news. Recalling the few times she'd saw Conover actually interviewed on TV newscasts, Linda pictured a rumpled Columbo look-alike, disheveled hair, five o'clock shadow, stained lapels and all, perpetually chewing a toothpick as he answered questions in a gravelly tone, often punctuated with the type of throat clearing grunts that bespoke years of tobacco misuse.

Linda shuttered when thinking about herself, obsessive about how her clothes were arranged in her closet or the magazines on her coffee table were stacked chronologically. She was a little less than thrilled at the thought of meeting the 'great' man in person though she remained curious as to what he may have uncovered.

Chapter Thirty-Eight

Growling under his breath, Vinny Orlander slammed his arms through first one sleeve and then the other of his down parka and headed for the hospital exit that would take him to the parking garage. Climbing into his maroon Hyundai, he grabbed the steering wheel with such force that for a second, it seemed he would crush the faux-leather wrapping into the plastic itself. Slamming into drive, he steered out onto Deerwood Blvd, seething about the most recent exchange regarding the Myra Cleary case. Her daughter, Julia Cleary had gone postal after her mother's death and had everyone on edge, but as always, any 'mistake' with a vent patient was always the fault of the respiratory tech until proven otherwise. Those fuckers! He'd already been to the Care Review Committee twice, and all staff, including him, had been cleared. So why did he just spend another hour and half with the Chief of ICU and that twit Jacobs, having to answer inane questions like: "And can you explain again how you set the ventilator based on the last written orders?"

If Jacobs weren't his immediate supervisor, and therefore the guy who did his evaluations, he'd of knocked him down right there and shot him up with a bit of nasty paralyzing drugs. Watching for the terror in his eyes, all the while unable to cry out for help. Then what fun, watching him gasp his last breath while waiting for Vinny to do something, anything.

Turning on the street that would take him to his apartment much quicker than his usual more sedate drive, Vinny realized he didn't want to go home. Not even the prospect of his usual de-stressor, lying on the futon and watching his fish in their huge tank, would prove enough to soothe him today.

Thoughts drifted toward Dr. Cole's heads up to study the 'Sentinel Events' exhaustive list of hospital fuckups. So many examples of mistakes made that cost people their lives! *A treasure trove. Yes, a real treasure trove.*

He drove right past his apartment building, not paying much attention to his route or any of the views. Instead, his mind was back on the Cleary controversy. Three weeks had gone by, and still the DCH grapevine was abuzz with conjecture and gossip. Some even speculated about whether a vent-killer was on the loose at DCH.

Still other people were asking questions about that case and other ones. Relatives of patients, two plainclothes police detectives, some local reporters, and that scruffy guy hanging out in the cafeteria. Vinny had seen him several times at different tables and various times on weekdays and weekends. Always seemingly minding his own business and writing in a notebook as if oblivious to all around him. But Vinny knew better. Clearly the guy was snooping around and spent much of his time just listening for tidbits, idle chatter. A lot of grapevine news was disseminated in the cafeteria, and though the man looked familiar, Vinny didn't place him until something about the ever-present toothpick clicked. He was that private dick guy from the school case not that long ago.

Vinny took his presence to mean that it was more than Cleary's case being looked at by the cops; making sense out of the other big topic for Ye Olde Rumor Mill: the recent spate of suspicious 'misfortunes'. Should he be worried?

Alone in the car, Vinny's lips quirked in a tiny smile as he wondered what secrets might be revealed…even about such stalwart guys like Dan Marchetti. Thinking of Marchetti, Vinny felt some of his anger return. Not even a heartfelt thank you when he'd driven him home after getting clocked by that Irish guy, and his hot girlfriend had all but pushed him out of the apartment lest he get any of his germs in their little love nest.

Vinny suddenly realized he was headed directly for the Pet Center and took a deep breath. Why not? It was a place he always felt safe, happy, relaxed. If there weren't a lot of customers, maybe Darlene would feel like talking to him.

He parked in front of the store, pleased to see the other parking spaces were empty.

Inside, he found Darlene alone—or at least with no other customers. The place was alive with the gentle sounds of happy birds, and on her shoulder perched Mack, the scarlet macaw.

At the tinkle of the bell above the door, Darlene glanced his way and gave him a radiant smile. Fit and supple in her snug jeans and red-plaid flannel shirt, she wore her golden hair swept back into a ponytail with a fringe of bangs across her forehead.

"Hey, Vinny!" she exclaimed. Her eyes were smiling, too, a color he always thought of as "sunshine blue."

"Hi, Darlene." On her shoulder, Mack raised and opened his wings and croaked, "Com-pany!" Vinny reached over to chuff the parrot's neck feathers. "I trust a satisfactory afternoon, Mr. Mack, how's it goin'?"

"So!" Darlene twinkled. "What can I do you for?"

His thoughts quickly went from Mack to Darlene. Knowing that she was not likely to be interested in a guy like him, he had to think fast. He had already brought supplies just a few days ago.

"Uh, I decided I might want to get a Siamese fighting fish after all. You were going to tell me what you thought last time I was here, but we got interrupted."

"Ah! What is it about these fish and good-looking men?" Her eyes sparkled. "Beautiful but dangerous. What I always say is that Siamese fighting fish can't play well in the sandbox. They are always looking to attack before they are attacked. To kill or be killed. That's why it's best they have their own tank, especially for the males. Putting two together means only one survives, the bravest and strongest I'm sure. There are some smaller fish species that seem to be able to coexist with the fighters, but I always wonder if the little fish end up living in fear. Always being afraid doesn't sound like a great life to me. Anyway, come look at the new shipment I told you about."

She led the way to the back of the store, Mack clinging to her shoulder, waving his wings and bobbing his head to show off as he passed the cages of his feathered kindred, chortling, "Walkin' here!"

Vinny was stunned. He had never heard her talk so long and that line about good-looking had to be a come-on. He hurried down the aisle, practicing his 'beautiful woman and dangerous men' line in his head. But before he got the words out, Vinny was struck still at the fairy world of color and movement in front of him. Dozens of small bowls, each containing a single fish, shone with colors that ranged from flame orange to metallic blue. Flowing tails seemed to fill the tanks, some single, some double, some arranged like violent halos as they circled back around the heads. They were magnificent.

Darlene laughed. "I knew you'd love them. I've been waiting for a chance to sell you one of these beauties."

Twenty minutes later, Vinny had chosen two males; a magenta wonder, that despite its small size seemed to own the space in its transport bag, and a sleeker blue-green mix with strangely hypnotic bulging eyes and red tinged lips.

As he followed her back toward the front counter, where she had quickly added two individual aquarium bowls specially designed with small filtration units, Vinny snapped out of his fish reverie. He quickly ran through options for getting back to the 'handsome men' space but as always, the smarter half of his brain told him again that first-rate women were not for the likes of him. A sudden image flashed in memory: the bullfrog stretched frozen and breathing his last after Vinny had paralyzed him. Explaining that little part of his life to someone like Darlene was so unlikely that Vinny snorted. Darlene looked up quizzically.

"Just thinking of something funny," Vinny explained. "Really, it was nothing."

For a moment, he thought she looked disappointed. Maybe there was a chance that she'd understand. But before he could gather his thoughts, *Ta-twingle!* The bell over the door sounded as two preteen boys rushed in, shaking drizzle from their hoodies followed by the harried mother of one of the preteens.

Mack squawked and flapped up from Darlene's shoulder to perch on the highest shelf behind her, then warned, "Look out!"

"Hey, did the new snakes come in?" one boy asked excitedly.

Darlene nodded, her attention momentarily on the intruders. "Yes, Kyle. They're back in the reptile nook." The boys were already on their noisy way up the aisle, ignoring the 'Be careful and don't run' injunction from the mom, clearly mere background noise to the pair. Darlene's blue eyes swung back to Vinny with a child-tolerant smile.

But in that moment when her focus had wavered, so had his courage. He was already hefting his unexpected purchase and turning for the door. "Thanks, Darlene. Gotta go! Have a nice weekend."

"Will do," her voice said behind him, and he could swear it sounded wistful. "You too."

Chapter Thirty-Nine

It wasn't easy to ignore her surroundings. The windowless office, small because the building was constructed back in the '50s, now seemed almost claustrophobic. It was overwhelmed by its floor-to-ceiling shelves stuffed with thick books, folders, and storage boxes, all sprouting untidy tufts of paper documents. Linda sensed decades worth of tobacco smoke permeating every surface, despite the fact that nothing related to smoking was in evidence.

Stacy Conover was still standing, though Linda was now seated, offered, "Coffee? There's a machine at the end of the hall. I'd be glad to get some for you." That toothpick seemed to cling magically to one corner of his mouth as he spoke.

She slipped out of her coat sleeves and smiled. "No, but thank you."

She studied him. He was younger than she expected him to be from the remembered TV appearances and closer to her age than to Bradden's. Linda knew from the quick internet research she'd done that he was divorced and had a preteen son in New Jersey. His business was modest but solvent, his work considered reliable and thorough among the lawyers at the office.

Conover shuffled through the sliding heaps of folders on his desk and pulled out an olive green one that matched the one she'd brought with her. Pursing his mouth in a way that made the toothpick dance, he launched into the topic at hand. "Bradden tells me you'll be my contact and conduit to his office." She nodded. And he explained the premise about a mercy killer at the hospital?

"Yes he did. But…"

"Terrific!" From his opened folder he pulled a packet of stapled pages and handed it across to her. "Your copies." As Linda perused the spreadsheet, surprisingly comprehensive and well labeled, Conover explained, "I've been compiling facts about the house staff and other medical personnel—you know, med techs, respiratory therapists, phlebotomists, physical therapists, and so forth HR said were signed in on the days of the questionable deaths. As you can see, I've also included other patients assigned to the doctors, room numbers...that sort of thing."

Linda skimmed the sheets, impressed despite her initial appraisal, with the complexity and organized forethought of the work. She wondered how he had been able to get information so quickly, given the laws regarding confidentiality at a hospital, but decided not to ask.

It did help explain why Bradden wanted to be at arm's length until there was solid evidence. "And you found what?"

When she looked up, he was watching her and worrying that damn toothpick to death. "I ran a macro to see which employee names matched with any patient deaths at DCH over the last ten months. Those considered suspicious or unexpected are designated in red ink." Some were also marked with asterisks, but she didn't interrupt his monologue. "As you can imagine, nurses' names came up frequently—especially in the special care units. But when you compute the actual suspicious deaths, they tended to be attached to the same people who rotated in their assignments or worked throughout the hospital. I came up with three names linked in some way, even if only possible proximity, to each of several suspicious deaths."

As she listened, Linda continued to study his spreadsheet. When he stopped talking, she repeated, "And?" before looking up.

Conover handed her another sheet of paper: pale green and with only three columns: Patients; House Staff; Ancillary Personnel.

"Respiratory Therapist, Derek Vincent Orlander," Conover said as he slid another sheet to her. This one is an employee profile from the DCH internal website, including a color photo. Linda recognized him right away as the fish guy, Vinny.

"Alexander Samuel Cole, MD," Conover continued passing the next sheet. "First-year intern. And finally, Dante Michael Marchetti, MD, also a first-year intern."

As the last profile passed into her hands, Linda stared at the photo of that charismatic guy she had noticed during her Saturdays volunteering at DCH. Linda would bet a month's pay that he couldn't be involved, but then scolded herself for thinking more like a civilian than a lawyer. "What do we know about these gentlemen beyond what I can read here?"

"I listened quite diligently around DCH. Orlander's been there a long time. He's considered quite good at what he does, but doesn't seem to have any real friends there. People tend to overlook him, though God knows, that'd be difficult to do—he's built like a fuckin' Viking! Oh, sorry for the language."

She looked up and saw him watching her as if to gauge her response and sensitivities. She gave him the tiniest of nods. "And professionally?"

He grinned, deftly moving his toothpick to the opposite side of his lip. "For the most part excellent evaluations, although a coupla reprimands for overstepping occasionally when he changed ventilator settings because a doctor couldn't be located quickly enough. Each of those citations also included a note that his action had been exactly what the doctor would've ordered, and, in one case, was lifesaving. Yet, most of these suspicious cases have run the gamut, and there's no concrete evidence that Orlander was responsible, even by accident. On duty, yes. Present in the vicinity, likely. More than that, inconclusive. Also, could they all just represent medical errors and nothing more?"

Linda pulled up the second sheet. "Cole?"

"Also acceptable evaluations though," Conover took that moment to refer to his notes, "displays a false bravado quite often that hopefully will not impede his progress." Looking up from his notes, "and, apparently, an acceptable new doctor though wound a little too tightly for some. Anotherwords, youngest of this year's intern class, it sounds like he came in pretty cocky and obnoxious, but he seems to have grown on folks." The toothpick twirled as Conover ground it between his teeth. "Now here's the interesting thing: about two weeks ago, a RN, Julia Cleary, had a mother incur a bad fall and ended up in a terrible condition where, if she survived her other injuries, she'd have to be on a ventilator for the rest of her life. Most of the staff, I surmise, felt the kindest solution was to let Joanne Cleary go rather than force her to stay alive with a machine breathing for her while the family finances were sucked down the drain."

"She had a Do Not Resuscitate?"

"No. For religious reasons, it seems, the daughter refused that option. Then when her mom died on her own, there were questions about the ventilator setting, and Julia accused Cole of 'pulling the plug'. I hear the mom had sort of been in the way of a full adult relationship between the two if you catch my drift as the two had been dating. Officially, Cole was quickly cleared at DCH, but Julia dumped him rather viciously in front of their colleagues, and she is still out on a long-term leave of absence. Cole's taking the whole thing very hard."

"Was Cole Mrs. Cleary's doctor?"

"Not at the time of her death, but he looked in on her often in the ICU. He'd admitted and treated her in the ER, but the ICU resident at the time of her death was actually this other fellow, Dante Marchetti."

Linda thumbed to the last profile and studied the photo. Those beautiful brown eyes, full of intelligence and a touch of humor, seemed to stare back directly into her own with such openness that she, again, found it hard to believe he could commit even the crime of jaywalking.

"Marchetti's the oldest of the intern crop," Conover had been saying, "because he spent some time traveling and living in Europe, primarily in Italy. He's gotten glowing evaluations, seems to be the star of the class, but also a favorite on a personal level. Kind, understanding, good-natured, fun. Male staff admire him. Female staff all seem to have a crush on him, even the married ones, but they all know that he's committed to a live-in relationship with a DCH nurse, Nikki Saxon."

Linda nodded. Conover forged on. "Again, here's where it gets interesting. The two of them live in the same apartment building as Cole, who is described as one of Marchetti's closest male friends, and the two nurses, Saxon and Cleary, are also best friends."

Linda gave him a little smile. "Here, I thought TV medical dramas were complicated."

The detective leaned back in his chair, clasped his hands behind his head, and stared up at the ceiling pensively. "Yeah. Just imagine what a pressure-cooker of a life it must be working in a hospital. All these personalities and crises and life-or-death responsibilities, interrelated and often conflicting. Everybody stressed out, exhausted. What a stew. Gotta love the possibilities though!"

She kept her tone neutral. "So what're the suspicions related to this Marchetti?"

He continued to lounge, rocking a bit. "I assume you are privy to some rather interesting whistleblower information your office received concerning suspicious 'sentinel' events I believe they are called. They which were subsequently looked at by their M&M conferences and deemed unintentional mistakes from which to learn from."

"M and M, like the candy?"

"No, the letters 'M' and 'M'. Morbidity and mortality, meaning the suffering from the disease or death itself. They usually are also reviewed at the Clinical Review Committee at DCH, where those cases who die unexpectedly or have some unexplained complication get reviewed by the hospital head honchos. The process is still ongoing."

Linda sighed. "I've got to get up to speed. First up, I need to learn more about these procedures before I can formulate enough intelligent questions to proceed further."

He sat forward, leaned his arms on the desk, teeth grinding the toothpick. "We should cast a wider net and look at more cases. We also have to note the possibility that these aren't necessarily the work of a single person. Heck, Cole and Marchetti are colleagues."

"What if there's nothing there at all? I'm afraid the whole thing still sounds rather tenuous to me."

Conover actually reached up and removed the toothpick from his mouth and pointed the chewed end toward her. "Look, your boss seems to think there's something to find. I don't make the evidence. I just report what I find. That's it."

Conover took the toothpick and stared at its now splintered end. "Two years ago I quit with the cigars," he told her affably. "Got damn tired of the Columbo jokes, but I had a little health scare too. These have gotten me through in case you are a smoker also."

She smiled briefly at him. "I'm not. Whatever it takes, eh?" She tucked all the new material into the pockets of the folder in her lap and then into her briefcase. "I'll relay all this information to Bradden, and I'll get back to you if he has any comment at this point." She slipped back into her coat and then rose. "I'm sure you'll let me know as soon as you have anything to add."

The toothpick was back in place as he stood up. "Yep, I'll keep you informed."

She offered her hand, returning his firm grip, and hurried toward the exit, remembering that she had been doing some research and wanted to ask Darlene's opinion about a commercial bird blend that was supposed to draw more songbirds to her feeder. Also, she needed her opinion on whether she thought a nesting box might be an interesting addition to her backyard this spring. Linda had no need to think about her route, as her red Prius seemed to know the way to the Pet Center. Instead, her thoughts remained tangled in the conversation of the last half hour. She kept seeing the face of Dante Marchetti. Remarkable that he was on the list, but she knew that he deserved as much honest scrutiny as the other two.

Shaking thoughts of killers and victims from her head, Linda parked in front of the center and approached the shop's doorway, looking forward to seeing Darlene and the stress relief she could always depend on when interacting with Mack the macaw and the other animals.

Just then, the door opened with its familiar jingling bells, and a departing customer exited toward her. She found herself looking directly at the name badge of the man she now knew as Derek Vincent Orlander, another suspect in the DCH mystery. She glanced at his face, but he barely seemed to notice her, gazing forward and hurrying as if eager to get his purchase home...or perhaps fleeing an uncomfortable situation.

She avoided the temptation to look after him and caught the door before it closed. Inside, Mack joyfully screeched, "Hel-lo!" Darlene, a little sad faced, glanced Linda's way and then brightened visibly.

"Hey, Linda," Darlene called. "What's new?"

He just walked out that door. You should ask him.

Chapter Forty

Trey sat on his terrace and stared directly at the traffic below him rushing through downtown Pittsburgh. Everyone scurrying to their next business appointment, restaurant date, racquetball game, or what have you. So determined to get to their destinations; though staying put in his own place on a rare day off from a 162 game schedule suited him just fine. Today he was going to go downstairs, buy a paper, and head over to a diner to have breakfast with Dan Marchetti. Dan was on vacation from his residency, and the two had arranged to meet many weeks earlier. Trey splashed some water on his face, brushed his teeth, and placed his pale-blue Rowdie the Bear mascot baseball hat on his head backward. The team had been the Indianapolis Indians, a Triple-A affiliate. His green cargo pants, flip flops, and white T-shirt completed the look, and before long, he had taken the elevator, stopped at the newsstand, and entered the diner across the street.

As soon as he had been seated, a heavily made-up waitress, with Nicorette gum in her mouth and a pencil behind her ear, approached his booth. "What can I get you, honey?"

"Coffee for now, expecting someone to join me."

"Sure thing. Say, you're that baseball pitcher, right?"

"I am. Nice to meet you," he stole a glance at her name tag, "Sharon. How are you today?"

Just then, Trey felt a tap on his shoulder and quickly turned to notice Dan behind him. "Heh bud. Sharon, this is my friend Dan." They both smiled.

"You a ball player too?" Sharon inquired.

"Nah, I wish," Dan responded, deftly maneuvering into the booth opposite his friend.

The men gave their orders: eggs over easy, bacon and home fries, and a short stack of pancakes.

"You guys are hungry. Be back soon, I'll leave this carafe of coffee on the table."

"Dan, you wish you were a ball player instead of a doc?"

"You can't be serious, Trey. Of course. You get to play a game we both love and get paid for it. Besides, everyone recognizes you, idolizes you in fact. Doctoring can really get to you and the hours…"

"From where I stand, that's nonsense," Trey interrupted, "the pressure to excel in the big leagues is over the top. Especially when you know there are dozens upon dozens of talented athletes in the minors ready to take your place." Trey took a slug of his coffee before continuing. "Yet there are a lot of similarities between the game of baseball and medicine."

"How so?"

"Well, both rely on a team effort as well as the skill of an individual."

"True, true."

"The mechanics of a pitcher in getting a batter to make an out, the ability of a catcher to call the right pitches, blocking balls in the dirt, the quickness of an infielder charging a ball, an outfielder making a running catch." He continued with this line of reasoning.

"However, a big difference. The skill of an individual clinician is in making the correct diagnosis. However, the older a physician becomes, the more their expertise is sought after, while a ballplayer will probably notice a drop in their physical talents at the ripe old age of thirty-five or so."

Dan nodded. "You're on a roll."

"In baseball, we have generalists, utility players, and specialists, the so-called five-tool player who excels at fielding, running, hitting for average and for power, throwing and catching."

"Both are situational and dynamic," Dan offered while smiling broadly.

"The truth is, Dan, I envy you the knowledge you will have your whole life. Our careers are usually fleeting, and for every Derek Jeter who played twenty years, the average major leaguer's career is less than six years. And for pitchers, arm troubles are the rule, not the exception, unfortunately."

"Understood. So Trey, what did Dr. Choi have to say about your illness?"

"He seemed a bit optimistic, though you know docs always hedge their bets and said we'd know more after we see how I respond to the meds. And I told the team doc about the MS diagnosis."

"Bully for you, Trey. Reaction?"

"Oh, she was great. Very supportive, although ownership may not be so understanding. No long-term contracts in my future I guess."

"You are getting ahead of yourself. Besides, these guys get insurance for such things I believe. But what are Choi's recommendations?"

"He has suggested a number of treatment options and stressed the need to be followed closely with MRIs and exams." Trey just shook his head and ran his hands through his blonde mop of hair.

"You don't seem surprised." Dan leaned forward.

"Have you seen the list of side effects? Unreal."

"I know, I know. But my money is on you, it really is. You are one tough dude," Dan countered.

"To get to where you are today, it takes a very special person with an inner strength that knows no limits. No question about it."

"Actually, I think the disease has already begun to effect my pitching."

"In what way?"

"Subtle things like how I push off the mound. My grip on the ball. Even my pitching coach made a comment, though he knows nothing of my diagnosis, for now anyway. That's gonna change."

"It will be a relief for you ultimately." Dan smiled broadly, so sure of what he was saying. "You know, interns are always afraid that we will be discovered to be frauds and not up to the task of doing our jobs. In fact," Dan paused to down a piece of crispy bacon, "we always think we are going to screw up and forget to do something, something really important until it's too late."

"Sorry, but that is really comforting to hear for some strange reason." They both laughed at the incongruity.

"While I am on the subject, I have to laugh. Got a call from a collection agency the other day." Dan smirked. "Can you believe it? Like I'm a deadbeat or something."

"Do you need some money?" Trey asked sincerely.

"No, not that bad. You see, I along with most medical school students, owe one quarter of the Gross National Product in school loans. My medical school loaned me $1,500—which is virtually chump change compared to the hundreds of thousands I owe to all the banks who issued me student loan. Anyway, those bastards sent me to collection in the middle of my internship. All the others don't bother you when you are in training and defer paying the loans back until the three years are over."

"What the fuck?"

"You had to hear this guy. He spoke with a Southern drawl and essentially threatened me with all kinds of legal action unless I paid the loan back in full now." Dan made an incredulous look while extending both his arms out and palms up.

"What did you say?"

"'Excuse me, I am eating my dinner, do you mind?' To which he informed me that he would call me back in an hour."

"Did he?" Trey asked, intrigued by the story at this point.

"Oh yes. Exactly one hour later. He started by sarcastically asking me if I had finished my dinner yet. I then told him to fuck off and hung up. Don't let anyone fool you, owing hundreds of thousands of dollars is a pretty daunting and discouraging hill to climb." Suddenly Dan felt guilty. "But it pales in comparison to other things."

"You know, it is so refreshing to hear another guy talk so openly about his problems."

"Guys in baseball don't do this?"

"Not really. They are afraid that if they reveal any weakness, someone will use it to their advantage somehow." Trey shrugged his shoulders and began to gorge himself with pancakes and syrup, followed by a healthy forkful of his eggs.

"God, I love this stuff." *Dan wondered if it really was any different in the world of medicine. Probably not.*

Chapter Forty-One

Dan awoke from his afternoon nap slowly, blinking in the changed light and half expecting to see outfield grass and the crowd-packed stands beyond, so real had his dream seemed. Yawning, he sat up and checked his watch: 5:50 p.m. In a muddle of thoughts, he realized he should have started the coals long ago and wondered, *Where the hell is Alex?*

Perhaps Alex, too, had fallen victim to some well-needed intern sleep. Dan yawned again. Given the time, the smart thing would be to wake him up and ask whether he wanted to eat broiler steak right away or wait for the grill.

Shoeless, he padded down the hall, knocked on the door, and waited, listening for a call from inside. None came. He knocked again, a little louder. "Alex?" Still no response. He tried the door in case Alex had left it unlocked for him as he often did. Locked. Maybe he'd rested, then gone out? Maybe went to get some ice cream or something to go along with dinner?

Dan went down to the far end of the hall where he could peer down into the parking lot. Alex's 'beamer' was in his space.

Frowning, Dan headed back to Alex's door. Both his knock and voice were louder this time: "Alex!" Nothing. Unease curled in Dan's belly. "You awake? Come on, buddy—open up!"

Could he be sick or something? Dan's brain flooded with flashes from the past weeks of Alex's life: the distractedness and slippage of work ethic; the inability to concentrate on everyday life, even with a job as important as being a doctor.

Adding to that mess was the most recent image from this morning: Alex slumped against the hospital bed, completely immobilized, as his patient slipped away. This was a guy who had always aimed for success and strove to be the best. How might such perceived failures impact a person like Alex?

Cold sweat popped out on Dan's brow; dread ran through him like sickness. "Alex!" he bellowed, pounding on the door. "Open up!" He kept pounding and yelling, but no answer. Several doors opened along the hall, but when his neighbors realized it was him, most of them quickly retreated, apparently glad to let someone else deal with whatever-it-was.

Only the nearest neighbor, Mitch Smolinsky, asked, "Sure he's in there?" He sounded slightly annoyed. By the look of him—Pirates T-shirt and gym shorts, frosty beer bottle in hand—he must be trying to kick back after a hard day wrestling refrigerators.

"He may be sick," was all Dan could think to say.

"Don't you have a key?"

"Dammit! Yeah. Thanks!" Dan sprinted for his apartment and the key resting in the caduceus candy dish.

Alex's door opened easily, and Dan entered, finding only silence. He grimaced, nose twitching at the garbage-scented stuffiness. Leaving the door open, he called out, but heard nothing. The place was a mess, as if inhabited by a person who'd ceased to care. Dan found the bathroom empty and, glancing into the bedroom, saw only the rumpled covers of a bed that needed changing weeks ago. The whole room smelled worse than the others—like a rank laundry hamper. Dan grimaced again and backed away.

Where is he? Dan looked around the living room for some clue, perhaps a note, but found nothing of that sort, just overdue bills and scattered IRS forms littering the table. Then in the kitchenette, beyond the sink full of decay-encrusted dishes, on the counter amidst all the clutter, he saw the uncapped sample pill bottles—all for Ativan and all empty.

Shit! Panic clutched Dan. "Al-lex!" Dan rushed back to the bedroom and around the bed to the other side. And there lay Alex Cole, face down.

Oh my God! Oh my God! Instinct took over, and Dan dropped to the carpet beside the prone figure, turned him over. Pale though bluish, sweaty, but breathing...barely. Pulse thready. *If he loses it, he's going to need CPR—and quick.* Turning and shouting for help, Dan felt again for a pulse. None.

Breaths first. At the hospital, there was always a handy Ambu bag, or at least a mask for protection. As Dan tilted Alex's head to the proper position, pinching the nostrils shut and sealing his mouth over Alex's, he was thinking that he'd been taught not to do it this way these days, but his mask was in his antique doctor's bag in the trunk of his car. By then he'd seen the first breath inflate Alex's chest, and now heard it whisper out of the mouth against his listening ear. No obstruction to his lungs. He quickly added a second breath, then began chest compressions.

Working his way through the first set of thirty, his mind sought a way to phone 911 without leaving his patient—who could die if he stopped CPR. Working in the hospital where help was always just a step away, he had forgotten the first step in an emergency…calling 911. Having left the apartment without his cell phone, he frantically glanced around and patted Alex's pockets.

"Hel-l-lp!" he yelled, drawing the word out, hoping it would carry better. "Somebody! Please help me!" Time for two more breaths, then back to compressions and yelling.

"Dan?" a voice called tentatively though the still open apartment door. "Dan? You in there?"

"Yes! Bedroom! Hurry!"

Mitch Smolinsky sauntered in with that beer bottle in his hand. "What's happen—" As soon as he moved close enough to see Alex collapsed beneath Dan's hands pressing the chest, Mitch's mouth fell open. "What the fuck—?"

Dan's doctor voice—calm, firm, confident—came from his body, which felt none of those things. "Listen carefully. Overdose. Call 911 for an ambulance."

His neighbor continued to just stare mutely, looking a little wobbly on his feet.

"Now, Mitch!"

Chapter Forty-Two

Linda Ferrante took an eager bite of her cheese sandwich. Pepper jack on sprouted whole wheat and just the right balance of Tex-Mex tomato sauce. She felt herself relaxing against the wooden slats of the park bench as she closed her eyes, chewing with unhurried pleasure.

Whump! Something heavy landed on the park bench that backed against hers. Linda's eyes snapped open, but she made no indication that she'd noticed the interruption, as Conover settled himself. Amid grunting and snuffling suitable for a bear, came the rattling of a brown-paper bag and then the lighter weight wrapping of a sandwich.

Finally, the voice behind her—even before the mouth was completely cleared—said quietly, "Sorry. Just had to get some food in me first. No breakfast, y'know."

Back to back, any casual passer-by would judge them as strangers merely sharing a location without interaction. As on their two prior meetings, neither would speak if anyone else was in view. It was silly, Linda conceded to herself, so cloak-and-dagger, but far preferable than revisiting his cascade of an office or any other indoor space Conover might have suggested. Especially after Bradden went out of his way to say, "Your meetings and conversations with Conover? Keep them as brief and private as possible."

Linda heard soft swearing behind her and a sound that could be paper napkin scrubbing spilled sauce from a trench coat. She finished her lunch, however her patience had worn thin, and checking her watch, she asked, "Do you have something to report?"

The scrubbing sound continued for a bit, perhaps an effective cover, as Conover replied, "My New York contacts turned up nothin' usable on Alex Cole... You know, he tried to off himself recently. Unsuccessfully I might add."

"I had heard that."

"As for Marchetti, nada, niente, zilch."

Linda frowned as she contemplated his findings or non-findings as it were.

"Yes, though I still contend that we have the wrong guy in Marchetti. Cole is an enigma to me however. A suicidal gesture probably doesn't fit the profile for Cole to be a mercy killer or does it? Perhaps the guilt…"

By the sounds, Conover was back at his sandwich, but he managed a muffled response: "True, unless he felt unable to cover his tracks, and felt vulnerable."

Conover snorted. "Cole could have been in it alone and become overwhelmed by guilt, but Marchetti got there too soon. Or maybe they're in it together, some kind of sick partnership, and Marchetti decided he couldn't trust Cole now that his little heart had been broken, so he waited just long enough for his 'partner' to tragically succumb. That nosy neighbor showing up might have screwed up Marchetti's plan."

"Really?"

"You gotta think of everything in this business no matter where it leads. And remember, bottom line is that they're docs, which means they have the knowledge and access."

Eyes focused on the lakeshore, Linda noticed something that must have startled the ducks, as the parents were quickly escorting their babies to safety. She pulled an apple from her insulated lunch bag. "Okay, but where's the logic in all of this? Have you found anything in their backgrounds that makes you think they're killers, mercy or otherwise? Partners or not?" She bit into the apple and chewed thoughtfully.

"It's like I been telling you. Finding the threads that connect these deaths to those guys just starts the process. Now I gotta understand them, get into their heads. And I certainly haven't eliminated Marchetti as a suspect in his own right. Even though his superiors and colleagues have a better opinion of him than of Cole, 'nice guys' sometimes turn out to be murderers too." He paused to allow his words to percolate.

"And how about this one: what if Cole decided to take an extra step to expedite a future mother-in-law's demise, but asked his buddy to look the other way—or even participate just this one time? And if not the first time, if Cole and Marchetti were already a 'mercy team', the Cleary death would have been the easiest with the most benefits. Fact is though, these killers usually always act alone."

Linda sighed and swallowed bits of suddenly tasteless apple. She knew she had to work harder to keep an open mind. Conover might be crude, but if something funny was going on at DCH, it had to be stopped.

"Where does this leave us?"

"I'm planning to take a harder look at Marchetti, especially since he had direct links to each patient. Yep. It's time we officially checked that intern out, too." He belched, but quietly as if behind his hand. Noisily, he crumpled his paper refuse. "So I'll double down on Marchetti and that other guy with access, Orlander. He's definitely an odd duck. Other than that, I guess we'll just have to wait and see if the really suspicious deaths will stop now that Cole is temporarily sidelined, recovering from his overdose." He hoisted himself from the bench with another belch. "Or if they continue without him."

No need to answer or say they'd email each other when the next meeting. She couldn't actually hear his footfalls recede any more than she'd heard him arrive; the word 'gumshoe' came to mind, but Linda knew he was gone.

Gone, too, was her appetite. She tossed away the rest of her apple, delighting two squirrels that must've been watching her hopefully. Despite this unusually warm and sunny early March afternoon, Linda felt the shiver all the way down her spine.

Chapter Forty-Three

As for Dan, his first year of internship would finish at the end of June. Then what? A second year of residency at DCH or transfer elsewhere? *Or would he be out of medicine entirely*? Where had that thought come from?

With increasing frequency, he began to daydream about baseball. The trajectory of his throws from the outfield, the smell of the freshly cut grass. These flights of fancy had a way of creeping back in while he was unsuccessfully trying to staunch the arterial flow of yet another teenage boy acting out some *Jackass* movie stunt. Or covering the face of yet another patient who didn't make it despite his skill and efforts.

"Hey, guys. Let's fold our tents. Lucky none of us have to work in the morning." He reached for the check on the little black tray where their waiter had left it an hour ago, but, yawning, Trey brushed Dan's hand aside. "My treat, remember? I'm making the big bucks."

Clutching the bill, he rose and led the way toward the cashier at the front of the restaurant. Walking behind him, Dan immediately noticed that the ballplayer's steps were more tentative than before—despite the floor-hugging tread of his shoes—and at one point, Trey brushed the wall on one side. Too subtle for a casual observer, but as a physician, Dan found it striking, as if Trey had trouble judging any sort of distance or coordinating his movements. In fact, his last four starts were poor ones, each necessitating removal early in the games in favor of a long reliever. This after having started the season in great form and winning his first five decisions handily; his fastball clocked at 100 mph.

Outside the trattoria, Nikki slipped her hand into Dan's as the three walked in silence to the little parking area where they'd left their cars. Only two other vehicles remained, both in the spaces marked 'Reserved' near the back door of the eatery.

Dan squeezed Nikki's hand before releasing it, then smoothly angled himself between Trey and the door of his car. Noting the surprise in his friend's eyes, and, though the three of them were obviously alone, still he kept his voice low as he asked Trey, "So how long has your vision been blurry again?" It was the old trick of doctors, lawyers, and even detectives: state the suspicion as fact, making it harder for the suspect to evaded the question with a simple *yes* or *no* answer. Better still, more information often got disclosed in the process.

"I—uh—" Trey stammered; his look of astonishment began to tighten, as if he would deny everything. But then he released his breath in a huge, gusting sigh and shrugged in surrender. "A coupla days."

"How're your legs?" Dan asked.

"Guess I overdid my wind sprints tonight—" He'd blurted this out before realizing how much he was revealing.

Dan pressed on. "It's been, what? Two months or so since your appointment with the eye doctor?"

After a long moment, Trey nodded.

Dan kept his voice warm and friendly, but there could be no mistaking the determination in it. "That's it, Trey. You must follow up that neuro consult now. Two acute attacks in such a short time, plus new symptoms? That's serious."

Nikki grasped Trey's arm and wouldn't let him look away from her gaze as she told him, "Listen to Dante. He knows what he's talking about. You can't fool around with MS.

Come stay with us tonight. We'll bring out our air bed and a sleeping bag. Done deal." Trey started trying to decline, but she wouldn't hear of it. Maybe she could also sense Dan's fear their friend wouldn't keep, or even make, an appointment without Dan getting him there personally.

"Come on, man," Dan said gently, "you're outnumbered."

Trey flapped his arms helplessly and tried to grin, but in the lights from the buildings, Dan could see tears in his eyes. "Two against one. No fair." He gestured to his car. "What about—"

Nikki spoke right up. "I'll drive Dante's car, and he can drive for you."

That's what Trey chose to do.

Once home, though the hour was late, both men were too wired to turn in.

"*Call of Duty* and *Fortnite* are the greatest; I cannot stop this addiction…" Dan confessed to his equally engaged adversary.

"I know, Brian (Brian Walker-utility infielder) and I play this on the road all the time. He kicks my ass plenty." Trey reached over for some pretzels and a sip of his diet Coke.

"Heh, do you like all the travelling, or does it get old?" Dan asked,

"At first, it was cool but then it becomes repetitive to the point you wish you could just snap your fingers and you would be immediately transported to your hotel room and not have to pack your bags, board one more plane, check into one more hotel room, and eat one more restaurant meal, yada, yada, yada."

"You poor baby, listen to you." Dan interrupted his game by pretending to wipe away crocodile tears.

"I know. I'm such an asshole, complaining. Actually, in the pros, there are so many people who do most of the grunt work for you. Not like in the minors where everything is done on the cheap." Trey winced conjuring up the image of the endless, interminably long bus rides, discount lodging, and the small food allowances.

"But you know, as much as the life in the minors can really suck, you make really close friends and the…what is the word I'm looking for?"

"Camaraderie?"

"Yeah, camaraderie. Everyone is at the same level, and no one has any money, but that doesn't matter. It works and when you get called up, everyone's so happy for you and simply hopes you don't forget them."

"I get it. Not that different in a residency program really." Dan suddenly remembered something he read.

"Trey, didn't Michael Jordan, when he was trying to make it in professional baseball, feel so sorry for his fellow minor leaguers that he purchased a deluxe bus with all the bells and whistles to ride in instead of the crappy one they were using?"

"I think you are correct. That guy has more money than…"

"I know."

"Been thinking Dan. Is it too late for me to consider medicine as a career?" Trey inquired earnestly.

"Really? Another Doc Medich?"

"Who is that?"

Facing Trey, Dan responded, "He was a pitcher for the Yankees and Pirates who was also an orthopedic resident and then an attending. Combined both careers, amazing feat. What was your major in college?"

"Biology. Thought I would teach high school if baseball didn't work out. Never crossed my mind that I would get MS."

"Nobody plans on these things happening. It is doable, Trey. You will have to take the MCATS and all, but you can do it. You know, it never dawned on me that a professional ballplayer would envy what I do. The idea that you could change careers is inspiring. *Eleanor Roosevelt once said, 'Great minds discuss ideas; average minds discuss events; small minds discuss people'.*"

Chapter Forty-Four

The whole thing had started a few minutes ago, when Cindy rushed back from her break to whisper excitedly, "There's a celebrity down in the Pavilion!"

Russ looked up from his paperwork with only mild interest. "Oh, yeah? Who?"

Russ is a likeable enough guy, Vinny thought, standing unnoticed, nearby. Vinny's opinion of Cindy fell far short of that; he found her lazy and careless—a bad match for this postsurgical ward. He'd learned the hard way that she was also a tease sexually and a mean gossiper.

That essence animated her now as she leaned in and revealed in a low voice, "Trey Hartmann!" Call the HIPPA police.

Russ's face showed his surprise and, now, genuine interest. "The hot new Pirates' southpaw?"

A third nurse moved closer. "Oooh! I'll say he's hot!" Joyce was older than Cindy, but always eager to talk about what she called 'eye candy' among the patients, visitors, and staff. "I don't know, but red hair and freckles really do it for me." It was at that moment she'd noticed Vinny standing there in his wallpaper mode, hoping to remain undetected.

Perhaps embarrassed by what she realized he'd overheard, Joyce put on her best supervisor face and said coolly, "Thanks, Vinny, but we don't need you anymore right now. Take a break—I'll page you when 816's treatment is finished."

Dismissed, he'd shuffled off as if it didn't matter, but now, stooped behind the cart, he listened for more details.

Still keeping her voice low and conspiratorial, Cindy was just saying, "Yeah, I saw him at the outpatient desk, with that, you know, stunned look?" Russ and Joyce nodded; all hospital personnel knew that stunned look of the newly diagnosed. "He was with Dan Marchetti, who was asking for admission paperwork to be filled out."

"For what kind of treatment?" Russ asked.

"Dunno," Cindy admitted.

"God," Joyce said. "Y'don't think he has cancer, do you?"

The three just looked at each other in consternation. Vinny massaged his back where it was protesting his position and decided to move on. He slipped silently away. Knowing he had time before he'd be paged to pack up the equipment, he headed toward the fourth floor curious to see how the star pitcher and star intern had crossed paths, and whether there was any role for a star respiratory tech.

Chapter Forty-Five

The young pitcher was already slumped on the edge of the recliner, looking at the floor instead of at Dan or the nurse who was taking and recording Trey's vitals. "Just relax," Dan was telling Trey. "Lie back and put your arm here on the rest."

Woodenly, the patient obeyed as if all protest had been drained from him. Dan continued a light, distracting bit of conversation, while Nancy expertly prepped Trey's arm and inserted the intravenous port that could be left in place until the IV treatments were completed. Trey didn't watch the insertion and gave no indication that he'd felt it or that he'd heard Dan's words.

Nancy told Dan, "I'll go get the Solumedrol Dr. Choi ordered." When he nodded, she patted Trey's shoulder. "I'll be right back, Mr. Hartmann."

Ignoring Trey's mood and behavior, Dan stood beside the chair and said, "Thought I'd sit and talk a while, if that's okay with you?"

"Whatever."

"I know you are feeling like nothing will get better, right now," Dan said as he watched the Solumedrol slowly flow into Trey's vein. "Trey, you have to stop feeling sorry for yourself. I can take you upstairs and point out a dozen patients who would gladly switch places with you. You're strong and you can fight this."

Before Trey could respond, Dan's beeper went off. He checked it for the extension trying to contact him. "'Scuse me a second," he told Trey and went over to the house phone to be connected. After he'd said, "Marchetti here," he listened, then promised, "I'll be right there."

Hanging up, he went back to Trey but didn't sit. "Gotta go. They need me in the ER. Pileup on the interstate, and we're getting a bunch of incoming. You ready?"

Trey nodded, actually looking more relaxed. "Sure. I signed. Start the medicine then go be a doctor. Dan, I hear you. Won't give you any more trouble."

"All right then," Dan quickly attached the infusion. "I'll be back as soon as I can. And don't forget you're coming home with me after this."

"Sure," Trey repeated. "Thanks for the reality check, I think."

"Can't help it," Dan said, failing to mask the emotion in his voice. He reached to squeeze the other man's shoulder. Rushing out, he stopped to let Nancy know he had started the drip and watched as she noted the time. "I'll be back as soon as I can."

Vinny peered at the label on the small bottle he had placed on his cart. *Potassium chloride*, a great drug for euthanizing an animal or a human being for that matter. Though veterinarians prefer Pentobarbital but residue would be found in a patient's system. "Can't have that now, can we?" Vinny whispered to himself. "No potassium is always present in the body so excess amount would be deemed secondary to a system like the kidney malfunctioning and so forth. Furthermore, when potassium reaches the heart, it disrupts the delicate balance of sodium and potassium ions that keep the heart beating. Consequently, the patient's heart would begin beating irregularly and then presto, stop! One problem however, it causes pain when entering a vein. Hell, it would be all over before his screams would be evaluated. Keep it simple young man," he admonished himself.

Orlander slowly ambled over to his patient, not wishing to call attention to himself. Trey was listening to music on his Sony headphones.

"Excuse me," Vinny spoke softly, trying not to alert any staff member to his presence but standing in front of the big league ballplayer who lifted his headphone from his ears.

"Yes?"

"Excuse me Mr. Hartmann, can I trouble you for your autograph? Big fan." So much for anonymity Trey thought.

"Sure thing."

"To my good friend and ardent Pirate fan, keep believing!" Orlander unabashedly prompted him.

Vinny handed the star pitcher a piece of progress note paper and a pen which Trey hurriedly accepted, anxious to return to his music and solitude. He made certain to pull his golf hat down even further on his forehead. Meanwhile,

Vinny removed the capless syringe of potassium chloride, injected it in the IV's port quickly and returned the now empty syringe to his pocket, the obliging pitcher completely unaware.

"Thanks a lot," Vinny responded to the kind gesture and immediately made tracks for the exit.

Once in the hallway, Hartman's loud exhortation for help could be heard, followed by silence immediately afterward.

Chapter Forty-Six

Linda Ferrante kicked off her pumps and settled into her chair for her favorite evening entertainment: watching the deer family materialize, like ghosts, from the dusk shadows across the meadow below. As she raised her wineglass to her lips, anticipating that first glorious sip of Lambrusco, her cell phone rang. She groaned when realizing it was still in her purse by the door.

Defiantly, she let the damn thing ring and savored the light sparkle of the red wine's progress across her tongue and the after-hints of fruit and flowers, before she rose and went to pull the phone from its handy purse pocket. She checked the display as it rang for the fifth or sixth time. *Bradden.* Ready to complain that she was barely home from the office, the DA's voice immediately barked, "Local news. Right now. My office tomorrow—6:00 a.m. sharp!" He hung up before she could say a word.

She padded back across the room in her stocking feet and dropped back into the chair. Trading her cell for the TV remote on the end table, she clicked on the set.

"And now for that breaking news report we promised." The local sportscaster, mic in hand, stood in front of Deerwood Community Hospital. Across the bottom of the screen scrolled: SUDDEN DEATH OF PITCHER SHOCKS PIRATES. "An official spokesperson for Deerwood Community Hospital has just confirmed rumors that Pirates rookie phenom, Trey Hartmann, died suddenly this afternoon, apparently of cardiac arrest, while undergoing treatment at one of DCH's outpatient clinics. Citing privacy laws, our source declined to disclose the condition for which Hartmann was being treated, but stated that the death was unexpected; full resuscitation efforts were initiated immediately but to no avail. Further, the spokesperson revealed that the cause of Hartmann's cardiac arrest is still unclear, pending the results of an autopsy, but assured us that the hospital will investigate the circumstances fully."

No wonder Bradden's wetting his pants, Linda thought as she continued to listen in disbelief. Another suspicious death at DCH—this time a local celebrity.

The scene on the TV had changed: The station's other sportscaster was now speaking live from the field at PNC Park. "Shock waves have quickly rolled through the Pirates organization, where players, coaches, and trainers alike denied knowledge of any illness." Stepping to the side, he included another young man in a two-shot. "This is Hartmann's fellow pitcher, Odell Shaw. What can you tell us, Odell?" He tilted the mic toward the stunned African American ballplayer.

"I still can't believe it. Trey was younger'n me…strong and fast. He took care of himself. He was a great guy," Shaw's voice broke on the last word. "Everybody loved him."

With a compassionate, "Thank you," the reporter stepped away to a one-shot. "Most of the team is away from PNC Park today, since there's no game tonight, but a few people gave us statements. Batting coach William Dexter seemed mystified by the events of the day, saying, 'Hartmann was the picture of health and at the top of his form. It's a devastating loss, not only for our team, but for all of baseball and everyone who knew him.'"

The Pirates had never been Linda's team. She'd grown up a loyal Yankees fan like her grandpa, but, since moving so close to Pittsburgh and needing to function among her primarily male colleagues, she'd stayed informed about baseball in general and the Pirates in particular.

The newscaster continued his coverage by reporting that Hartmann's parents were being flown in at the club owner's expense on his private jet. "Retired manager, Charlie Monroe, now the team's senior scout who had discovered Hartmann and had become a mentor, said on behalf of the club, 'The Pirates will assist Trey's family with whatever arrangements they desire, whatever they need. It's the least we can do, as Trey is—was—a part of the Pirates family. For right now, we ask that the media give the Hartmanns some space and privacy during this difficult time.'

"Monroe also told us the team had considered canceling its home game here tomorrow against the Florida Marlins, but decided to play in Hartmann's honor with Odell Shaw pitching."

Linda's cell rang again, and she wasn't at all surprised to read the display: Conover.

"Ferrante," she answered.

"I'm sure you've heard the news. Just wanted you to know things are heating up. I moved a few rocks at the hospital, and all kinds of things crawled out. For one thing, I found out that, although Hartmann was pronounced dead in the ER when they couldn't get his heart started, he actually died in the infusion clinic, where people get drugs for stuff like chemotherapy. Patients don't usually cardiac arrest there, so that's suspicious."

"I see."

"Our young Dr. Marchetti's fingerprints are all over this. Maybe quite literally. For one thing, apparently, he had administered whatever drug was being infused, and are you ready for this? Hartmann wasn't even his patient!"

It was still hard to see the guy as a serial killer, but things were stacking up against him. She just wished Conover didn't sound like he relished this so much.

Unfazed by her silence, the detective finished the one-sided conversation with, "I know what you're thinking: no solid evidence yet, but there will be. And knowing Bradden, he'll probably want to see you early tomorrow. Now you have something to tell him. Don't worry, I'm sure I'll have plenty more to share and will be in touch as soon as I do." For the second time in an hour, a caller hung up without waiting for a reply from her.

She slowly set aside the phone and turned back to the TV screen. The news report had become a biographical sketch of Trey Hartmann's short life, snapshots and home movies of him growing up in rural Nebraska, followed by still photos and news footage of his rise to fame.

Realizing just how young he had been and how unfair life could be, Linda felt a tightness in her throat. She clicked off the set, picked up her wine glass, and settled back in her chair. Looking out the big window, she turned for the solace of her deer. But they were gone.

****

Trey is dead? Dan ran both hands through his thick, curly hair, now particularly unruly, a result of learning that Trey passed away soon after receiving his infusion. What the fuck! Suddenly the distraught intern kicked the nightstand so ferociously, the cheap laminated wood shattering in pieces, leaving a large gash in the wall, exposing the sheetrock below it. Old

Styrofoam coffee cups filled with just enough leftover coffee now staining the carpet in multiple spots and dripping down disgustingly from the pale green walls. Curdled milk completing the perfectly symmetrical 'coffee blot', a Rorschach test of sorts. Dan stared at it for a moment, convincing himself that it represented exactly what was coursing through his mind, his world that had become a *cauldron of despair and nightmarish outcomes.*

Chapter Forty-Seven

Ferrante dialed the number for the JCAHO Sentinel Event Department, "Linda Ferrante, Assistant Prosecutor here in…"

"Please choose from the following menu…"

It took a seemingly endless number of handoffs before her determined effort to speak to a bona fide conversant human being.

"Can I help you, Ms. Ferrante?"

"Yes, my department is investigating a number of medical 'errors', which we will label for the time being here at Deerwood Community Hospital."

"Before you proceed any further, we are not allowed to release any information unless ordered by the courts as such action would surely lead to a drastic reduction in reporting of such sentinel events…"

"I understand, I understand. I actually am calling to educate myself as I am learning about this side of hospital reporting for the first time. Please bear with me…"

"Not a problem."

"I see from your website a list of the 10 most commonly reported events, 80% occurring in the hospital itself, nationwide."

"That is correct."

"Falls, medication errors and so forth. Wrong side surgery?"

"Yes, unfortunately it still happens."

"Events like MAST trouser malfunction, ventilator setting errors, a …now I'm reading from my list, a Sengs… taken-Blakemore tube causing an esophageal rupture…a malfunctioning EKG…"

"That's some list counselor," she paused, "all of these events in one hospital?"

"Yes, one hospital and all within a short period of time."

"How short of a period?"

"Less than a year for certain. I would need to check the exact dates."

"There is a real problem there perhaps. Now, we know that sentinel events are still grossly underreported but this pattern needs to be explored further in my humble opinion."

Just what I thought.

"Scott, I scoured the internet to try to understand the history of these 'Medical Serial Killers' or so-called 'Angels of Mercy'. Interesting findings," Linda occasionally glancing at her notes.

"Go on, I'm listening." Stealing a peek at his watch, he appeared to be ready to bolt.

"Many go undetected for years before being found out. They of course can flourish because of the level of trust their patients hold for them, mostly nurses by the way, 86%, while some expand their victim pool from terminal patients to simply ill ones. Italian nurse Daniela Poggiali took pictures of herself next to the deceased bodies and shared them on social media." Linda hesitated, her voice beginning to crack, "Genene Jones, a pediatric nurse, killed four children. Now most work alone though four nurses in Vienna worked together and enjoyed pouring water down patient's throats after pinching their noses."

"Unbelievable. This is very interesting but how does this inform about our cases here?" Bradden's annoyance beginning to show.

"Common characteristics include attention seeking behavior, strange behavior when a patient dies, frequent changes in hospital working locations or hospitals themselves, and a disciplinary record. Also, many frequently have a substance abuse problem, state oftentimes that the patient was a 'burden to take care of', a tendency to 'predict' when a patient will die, and a history of difficult personal relationships."

"And, and…"

"I made a chart and assigned one point for each. Orlander with 5 points, Cole with 3 points, and Marchetti with zero points." Ferrante stared intently at her boss.

"Leave the chart, I'll look at it when I get back. Have a meeting with the State Republican Party people." With that, he grabbed his jacket and raced out the door. Before exiting, he looked back and remarked, "Our fellow just maybe broke the mold."

Chapter Forty-Eight

Exhilarated by the deep breaths swelling his lungs, the beads of sweat gathering momentum on his face and torso, and the slap of his Nikes on the path paralleling the shore of Candlebury Lake, Dan ran.

Lack of physical exercise certainly hadn't helped lighten the heaviness of his mood over the last few weeks. *Trey's death, the other unexplained equipment failures. Madness.* It would've been challenging enough to cope with the loss of a patient. But when his efforts probably hastened the bad outcome and furthermore, his main support system, Nikki, seemed to be pulling away when he needed her the most. Was he imagining this? w Entertaining his worst fears, she held him accountable.

They'd spent a quiet Sunday with the phone turned to voicemail. It wasn't much of a day for gardening. Yesterday's drizzle had returned intermittently with distant curls of thunder, and the temperature never went much above 60°, but Nikki had insisted, citing forecasts for continued rain. Shrugging into her waterproof windbreaker and holding Dan's out to him, she'd predicted, "This may be our best chance." He knew she wasn't only talking about the weather but also about the uncertainty of what the next days would bring.

Together, and mostly in silence after Nikki turned on her favorite Fugees CD, they worked in concert to secure the redwood flower boxes around the rim of the balcony railing. After filling them with the potting soil she mixed, they got all the individual plants settled into their new homes, each where she thought best maximized their visual impact.

When they'd finished and were enjoying the colorful new panorama from the shelter of the living room, Dan found himself physically tired, but somehow soothed. "There is something relaxing about working with your hands in the dirt. Guess that's why they call it getting grounded," he whispered to himself. *Nikki's silence seemed to speak volumes.*

Chapter Forty-Nine

Today, another day on a medicine floor promised more of the same; keeping track of several patients who'd been sick enough to need a hospital stay, but no one ready to crash and burn or even take a turn for the worse.

He had bypassed his usual scrubs for pressed khakis and a favorite light blue shirt given the lower risk of a body fluid spill while on the wards. Leaving his Nikes out to air, he laced up his second-best sneakers and slipped on the last fresh lab coat in his closet. He pinned on his DCH badge and pocketed his wallet and keys. On his way out, when he stopped to grab an apple, he took a moment to scrawl *C U 2nite!*

Dan glanced at his watch and decided to catch Greg later. He had just enough time to check on some lab results before rounding. Besides, Dave Levine, in his effort to cheer Dan up, had promised to make a Starbucks run before the shift.

Dan hurried off to the medicine floor, where he greeted his colleagues. Third-year resident Jackie Norris, stood yawning and complaining about an all-nighter. Patty Yates was logged in at one of the computers. Nurse Cheryl Herrera, on loan this week from the CCU, waved as the phone began to ring and she picked it up.

"Where's Dave?" Dan asked. "He's bringing Starbucks, right? He promised to treat me to an espresso macchiato, whatever that is."

Jackie yawned again, her eyelids threatening to drop the last fraction of an inch. "I just need *coffee*—hot and black."

Cheryl put down the phone. "That was Dave. There's some kind of tie-up at Starbucks, but he'll be here soon."

They took a moment to speculate about what kind of emergency could tie up a Starbucks—a barista meltdown? Running out of stir sticks? A whipped cream riot? Dan slid into the seat in front of one of the other computer terminals, eager to check the lab results on his patient Clark Resko, who was battling an infection resulting from wound neglect. Yesterday's labs showed he was responding to the antibiotic coverage, which took into account both his penicillin allergy and his compromised immune system thanks to his diabetes. Dan hoped to see evidence of more improvement now.

"Hey, Patty," Dan said after a minute. "You been having any trouble with your computer? I can't log on."

Patty shook her head, eyes still riveted on her own screen's information. "No trouble at all."

"Weird," Dan said, searching the countertop for a staff directory so he could find the help-desk extension.

His beeper went off to indicate a text, so he had to look to read it. Surprised, but pleased, he told the others, "Hunh. I'm being called to Ballard's office. Be back when he's done with me."

Cheryl, rising to answer a patient's blinking call button, twinkled up at Dan, "Oh, yeah, sure. Dr. Marchetti's in trouble again!"

The three women laughed as Jackie made a shooing motion at him. "Don't keep the Chairman of Medicine waiting. We'll soldier on without you."

As Dan hurried for the elevator, he heard Patty's response to Jackie: "Pretty soon you and I'll be rounding alone." She called after him, "Hey, Dan—you're remembering our trade? You've got my shift tomorrow?"

"You bet!" he called from inside the elevator as the doors were closing. Alone in the car, he tweaked his clothing, though nothing had yet gotten out of place; the creases were still fresh in the khakis. He was glad he had dressed professionally today even if there was no tie. Watching the floors tick by, he speculated on the upcoming meeting. Dan had rarely been called to the chairman's office, a spacious kingdom the staff joked was big enough for large-scale sleepovers or for more formal circumstances. Was this possibly about next year's rotations?

Dan approached Dr. Ballard's office bathed in the glow of how much promise and potential he hoped these icons saw in him, determined to do his best and not disappoint.

At the imposing desk outside a closed door, Dan stopped and grinned at the secretary stationed there. "Good morning, Peggy."

He'd expected her characteristic smile and greeting, but she seemed nervous and distracted today, her eyes averted above a mumbled, "Mornin'," as she set aside the papers she was shuffling and buzzed her boss. "Dr.

Marchetti is here, sir." Listening for a response through her headset, Peggy picked up the papers to shuffle and then nodded at Dan. "Go in, please." All without eye contact.

Puzzled, but realizing everyone could have a bad day, Dan moved to the door emblazoned with Ballard's name and title, pausing to knock politely just the same.

Hearing the chairman's deep, familiar voice, "Yes, come in," Dan opened the door and entered. An unsmiling Dr. Hugh Ballard stood, impeccable as always, behind his desk at the far side of the room. "Come in, Dr. Marchetti." Dan's heart began to pound. He had been 'Dan' to the Chair for quite a while. Something was terribly wrong. "Sit down."

Dan, his attention now riveted on the bespeckled physician, let the door swing shut behind him, and moved toward the chair the man had indicated. As he crossed about a mile of plush carpeting, Dan quickly went through his last couple of weeks. There must have been a patient complaint? Or maybe one from the nurses? Maybe Clark Resko? Even though he had been frustrated at the guy's lack of cooperation he thought he had stayed relatively courteous...only calling him a fuckin' idiot in his head.

When Dan got to his destination, he didn't sit right away. The Chairman of Medicine was still standing, looking taller and straighter than he ever had before. For a moment, Dan thought he'd seen Ballard's gaze dart past him and deliver an expression that seemed to say, *Remember, I'm in charge here.*

But almost as quickly, the gaze came back to Dan, the expression softening. Folding himself into his own chair, Ballard gestured again with his open palm. "Sit down, Dan." Feeling more confused by the moment, Dan complied. "I'm sorry, but I need to ask you to hand over any and all hospital property in your possession, including your identification badge and keys, your pager, and your employee parking access card."

What the hell? He twisted around to see where the Chairman had glanced earlier and was stunned to see two uniformed policemen standing at ease in a part of the office that'd been obscured by the door as he entered.

Dan froze, stared at the badges, the belt-clipped handcuffs, and the holstered guns. Incredibly, he could still find his voice: "Dr. Ballard—what's going on?"

"Dan—" Hearing the Chairman speak his name, made Dan turn back to his mentor. Though the Chairman's tone was as professional as always, Dan could sense the reluctance and compassion underlying the rather formal words of protocol.

"Under the circumstances, as Chairman of Medicine and Director of your Residency Program, I have no choice but to immediately suspend your employment at this hospital, pending resolution of this matter."

"What 'matter'?" he echoed. "Dr. Ballard, I don't understand."

The chairman, his usually affable face, twisted by a pained expression, simply looked at the officers as if to communicate to Dan, *This part's out of my hands.* He came to his feet and gently said, "I'll need those items now."

Somehow, Dan realized that he had to cooperate and let it all get sorted out later. He began emptying his pockets as instructed onto Ballard's desk. He separated his two keyrings, then returned his own and his wallet to his pants pockets.

"Rest assured," Ballard was saying, "the department will make arrangements to deliver any personal items that may still be in your staff locker." Dan nodded as if he understood what was happening, and, as he reluctantly removed his ID badge from the front of his lab coat, Ballard spoke again. "I'll need your white coat as well."

Not that! Dan thought. After only a moment's hesitation, he slipped it off, feeling strangely like a defrocked priest. Mechanically, he folded it, placed it on the desk beside the other items stripped from him. He felt all eyes in the room on him, and, though he stood still clad in his khakis and favorite blue shirt, he felt naked.

The policemen came up beside him. "I'm Officer Emmett," said the taller, balding one.

"Officer Dransfield," supplied the other. "Deerwood Police Department."

"Officers, please," Dan implored. "What's this about?"

Neither answered the question right away. "Step this way, sir." The one named Emmett indicated a path around Dan's chair and toward the office wall. "Turn and put your hands against the wall."

As soon as Dan complied, Dransfield began to pat him down. Though both men had behaved professionally and courteously, Dan could remember no experience quite this bizarre, humiliating, or unsettling. His mind was suddenly numb.

He didn't bother trying to ask any questions aloud again. Like a robot, he submitted to all the instructions, which ended with, "Put your hands behind your back." Then he felt the cool metal click close around his wrists. Handcuffs.

"Dante Marchetti," intoned Officer Emmett, "We're placing you under arrest in connection with the homicide deaths of Trey Hartmann and Matthew Saxon and criminally negligent homicide deaths of…"

Dan's mind froze as if it needed a 'reboot'. *Am I really hearing this correctly?*

"You have the right to remain silent," Emmett began. Dan listened numbly to the rest of his Miranda rights being read, responding, as prompted, that he understood. *Say something, you twit!*

As the officers nudged him toward the door, Dr. Ballard's authoritative voice made them pause a moment. "I'll remind you gentlemen that this is a functioning hospital and a community comprised of thousands of employees, patients, and visitors. I respectfully request, for the well-being of all, including Dr. Marchetti, that you escort him from the premises with as little disruption as possible."

One, or both, of the policemen answered Ballard in a short, courteous exchange, but all Dan could think about was the prospect of being perp walked through that DCH community of his friends, colleagues and superiors. Then the chairman's voice cut through the buzz in Dan's head, calling his name.

When Dan looked back at the white-haired man standing again behind his desk, Ballard said, "Dan, I wish you well."

Dan got the impression the next words were not just for his benefit, but for the other two men: "And I want you to know that this will be cleared up, I'm sure!"

Such a wave of gratitude swept through Dan that tears filled his eyes. He wanted desperately to thank the Chairman, but nothing could squeeze past the knot in his throat. All he could do was return that steady gaze of those clear blue eyes and give a little nod before he was maneuvered out through the office door.

He caught a glimpse of Peggy, her eyes big as saucers before she averted them, and then he was hustled down the hallway toward the main lobby. The usual hubbub of the hospital seemed especially intense. Dan felt that he was the center of the tumult; in fact all eyes were staring at him, every whispered conversation about him. He heard more than one surprised voice call his name, but even if he'd been allowed, he was incapable of answering.

He managed not to focus on any of the startled faces that flowed around and past him, until he met the eyes of Greg Vanderbosk at the front door security desk. "This is a big mistake," he whispered embarrassingly as he passed the security guard. Greg's expression wore a combination of bewilderment and impending disgust. Or so Dan surmised.

The officers hurried him through the first set of glass doors that were sliding open. They crossed the vestibule, stepped through the outer doors into the sunlight and into another ring of hell.

A noisy mob of people pressed toward him, forming a semicircle at the hospital entrance. Still-cameras clicked and whirred; shouldered video cameras stared at him like baleful cyclops; fists reached toward him, brandishing microphones. Someone demanded, "Is that him? Is that the suspect?" even as another voice gave the call letters of the local TV station, followed by, "This is Carolyn Regis, reporting live from outside Deerwood Community Hospital—"

How in the world did the media know about this? He wondered dispassionately, as if this was a scene from a TV crime show and not, horribly, his real life.

"That's gotta be him, Dante Marchetti." The speaker managed to mangle the pronunciation of both names.

"Sir," called the woman from WDWD, "just a brief statement, please. Did you kill Trey Hartmann and Matthew Saxon? Can you tell us why you killed them both? How are you related to the victims? What about the others?"

All the while, the police officers were moving him into and through the crowd, making it near impossible for him to separate the shouted queries. A gaggle of voices all began shouting at once: "Why'd you do it, Marchetti?"

"Hey Marchetti—over here! You trying to skunk the Pirates?"

"Is it true Matthew Saxon was the husband of your lover?"

Dan finished the 'perp walk' and reached the waiting car, where Emmett went around to the driver's side and Dransfield bent to open the back door. It gave Dan a moment to look over his shoulder and catch Dave with the tray of Starbucks coffee occupying both hands.

"Leave him the fuck alone!" bellowed Dave, who'd leapt close to push the cameraman back. The tray tilted and Starbucks splashed all over.

Dan didn't see what happened next because that's when Officer Dransfield admonished, "Watch your head," and firmly pushed him down and into the back seat of the patrol car.

****

Alex took pains to make certain no one could see the two together should the authorities attempt to connect then. The only person in that section of the ER was a deaf man he had observed signing with his hands a few minutes back to a hospital worker.

Apparently, though she meant well, her signing was rusty and when she asked the patient to write down his thoughts, he indicated that he had never learned to read or write. Stan, Marchetti's patient, just smiled at the men who acted as if he didn't exist.

"You did good Vinny with your efforts to discredit Dr. Dan Marchetti. Marchetti's sterling reputation has been harmed and is in trouble to be certain. Let's keep up the pressure."

Unbeknownst to the men, Stan could certainly lip read fairly well. He frowned and shook his head to and fro and though he hadn't the slightest idea as to what these men were talking about, words like 'harm' and 'trouble' he knew to be a problem for his kind doctor. What did these men mean by those words? He continued to observe their faces even if it was impolite.

Chapter Fifty

"Mr. Derek Vincent Orlander, my name is Linda Ferrante, and I'm from the prosecutor's office. May I come in?"

"I suppose so, but what have I done?" Vinny asked defensively. "By the way, everyone calls me Vinny."

"Okay, Vinny. I am looking into some recent suspicious events at Deerwood Community Hospital. May I come in?"

"Oh? I sup…pose so," he answered hesitantly. Vinny immediately turned off the television and motioned Ferrante to a chair while he sat at the edge of his sofa.

"How can I help you?"

"Okay, are you familiar with a patient named Roscoe Delmar who presented with a—" she paused to look at her yellow legal pad, "a 'dissecting abdominal aneurysm' while still in the Emergency Room only a few months ago?"

"I do remember the case vividly. He didn't make it."

"No, he didn't. What was your involvement, if any, in that case?" She already knew he had been present in his capacity of a respiratory therapist because the chart had a note written by him regarding the ventilator settings he had been instructed to carry out. It was always smart to see if the individual being questioned knowingly lies with opening questions.

"Well, I recall the patient had managed to sever his tongue when he went into shock and his teeth essentially guillotined the lower portion. You don't forget those kind of things, at least I don't. The doctor had to intubate the patient through his nasal passageways, which was technically much more difficult even for a trained anesthesiologist."

"Who was in the ER bay with you at the time?"

"Dr. Marchetti, a nurse named… I believe Felicia Gonzalez, and myself. The anesthesiologist had left immediately after intubating the patient. But I also went next door to treat an asthmatic, a teenager. Can't remember his name though."

"Okay. Now, I understand Dr. Marchetti had employed the use of a rather unusual intervention to buy time for the vascular surgeon who was en route?" Again she referred to her notes: "MAST trousers they are called."

"I don't recall that. 'MAST trousers' you say?" Vinny shook his head to indicate he had no knowledge of this.

"Well, I am no doctor, but I understand from my research that they are pneumatic anti-shock trousers, which once the patient's lower limbs are placed inside, air is injected. The results are an immediate increase in blood pressure. Interestingly, it was used extensively in Vietnam according to my reading."

"I wouldn't know." Vinny shrugged his shoulders and smiled meekly. "Really? MAST trousers? Perhaps you forgot that you included it in your notes that day," Linda stated matter-of-factly.

"Oh I did? Can't recall."

"By any chance, did you witness anyone releasing the valve on the trousers?"

"There was a valve?" he asked innocently.

"Yes, that is how the trousers stay inflated," she answered, trying hard not to demonstrate her annoyance with what began to appear to be insincere replies.

"Mr. Orlander, let me switch gears here for a moment if I may. You participated in the ventilator adjustments for a patient named Myra Cleary. Does her case ring a bell?" Linda asked directly.

"Honestly, I have had so many patients that I cannot remember each one individually. Should I? Was there a problem?" he asked rather warily.

"Well, this patient had advanced lung issues, 'COPD' the chart says. She passed away as well."

"Excuse me, Ms. Ferrante. I don't feel comfortable with this questioning at all. Should I have a lawyer present?"

"Why, Mr. Orlander? If you have done nothing wrong that—"

Suddenly, his memory kicked in. "That was the case with the ventilator settings on parameters that didn't jive with the records. Correct?"

"It was. Do you know anything about this inconsistency?"

"You mean the changed settings?"

"That's right."

233

"Not at all. Our Director asked us all that question, and my answer remains the same. I did not know anything about changed settings. Now, I believe I have answered enough of your questions. That's it." With that, Vinny opened the door to his apartment and motioned for the prosecutor to leave.

"Thank you. One last thing. Do you happen to know anything about the Pavulon vials missing from the anesthesiology carts? Ten in all."

"Why don't you try the lost and found department at DCH ?" Vinny smirked. Linda just smiled and exited the apartment. *This guy is hiding plenty. He would be mistaken to take me lightly.*

Chapter Fifty-One

Ballard just stared at the open folder of Deerwood patients with poor clinical outcomes of the past many months, listed in chronologic order. The cases slated to be reviewed again by the Peer Review Committee that week, one of many committees he chaired. What he read alarmed the sagacious physician because of their strange nature. "Sloppy ventilator management, a ruptured esophagus from a Sengstaken Blakemore device poorly positioned and calibrated, EKG that had been misinterpreted, and MAST Trousers whose release valve had been activated and left to deflate. As if this was not enough, an unexplained cardiac arrythmia in a Multiple Sclerosis patient receiving a steroid infusion. In all my years..." he whispered out loud. The last one, a cardiac arrythmia from steroids? Unheard of! Suddenly his administrative secretary quietly appeared after knocking softly on his open door with no response.

"Mr. Orlander here to see you Doctor." Ballard still deep in thought, didn't respond.

"Doctor Ballard?" Amanda raised her voice a little louder, aware that her boss was becoming even more alarmingly hard of hearing, dragging his feet in getting his hearing aids adjusted for his additional hearing loss. Entering on cue, Vinny stood there, wearing his blue jacket with the words, 'Department of Respiratory Therapy' in script embroidered on the front along with a striped tie for the occasion.

Ballard suddenly looked up from the disturbing report, "Oh yes, come in son, take a seat," pointing to one of the two chairs in front of his desk.

"How can I help you Mr. Orlander?"

"Well Sir, I work in the Pulmonary Department as a respiratory therapist for the past few years, seven to be exact."

"Yes, yes, I have seen you around the hospital."

"Well, I am not an overly sensitive guy but… but I feel that one of your interns seems to ignore many of my suggestions regarding ventilator management, especially when it comes to understanding the danger of increasing PEEP beyond physiologic levels."

"Who are you referring to young man?" Ballard looked puzzled.

"Marchetti, Sir, Dr. Dante Marchetti."

"Dan?"

"He is one of our brightest interns. Do you have any specifics regarding this alleged deficiency?"

"Well, Sir, I do. The Salter case. We had difficulty oxygenating the poor woman and Dr. Marchetti turned the dial up real high without charting it, to see how she would do. Unfortunately, he got called away and forgot to reverse the change once she decompensated."

"That doesn't sound like him at all." Ballard looked at Orlander, his eyes registering his incredulity.

Ballard frowned. "You are the one who filed the complaint I imagine?" With that, he pointed at the folder on his desk.

"I felt it my duty to do so with so much attention given these days to preventing patient harm and medical mistakes."

"Of course, you did the right thing." Just then, Dr. Siegler, a General Surgeon, popped his shaved head into the doorway, the sides of the doorframe supporting his ample weight while he leaned forward. "Sorry to disturb, about your patient, JS, do you have a minute to discuss? Just finished operating on her."

"Sure thing." Turning to Orlander, "Will You excuse me?" Without waiting for a response, the Chief joined the surgeon outside the door.

Without missing a beat, Vinny took out his phone and began taking pictures of the papers Ballard had pointed to on his desk. Needed to know more about what is being noticed and written about these mistakes.

Once completed, Vinny exited the room and mouthed to the Chief of Medicine that his beeper had gone off. Ballard acknowledged that he understood and interrupting Siegler, "Thank you for coming in. I will address the issue."

"Thank you doctor." Orlander calmly departed, anxious to look at his camera's images right away.

Chapter Fifty-Two

Linda Ferrante sipped the hot black coffee and grimaced, not at the taste because the Kona had been perfectly brewed in Scott Bradden's Jura, but at the spectacle she was being forced to witness. There, on the huge plasma screen in the DA's home office, she watched Dr. Dante Marchetti being hustled out of DCH toward a waiting police vehicle amid a frenzy of press attention. Another young doctor, trying to juggle a tray of Starbucks as he leapt to defend his colleague, was bungling both efforts.

She cringed as the situation escalated: dismayed shouts from reporters and camera crew suddenly splattered with hot coffee, whipped cream, and sprinkles were countered by angry words and gestures of the drenched physician clearly trying to defend his friend.

Bradden, however, actually guffawed, and Stacy Conover, who lounged in the comfy chair near hers, chuckled around the toothpick clinging to his lip as he opined: "Always thought those froufrou drinks should have stronger lids!"

Meanwhile, as most attention focused on the sidewalk scuffle, the patrol car slipped away from the curb, bearing the arrested Dr. Marchetti.

The news segment ended in a series of broadcaster questions—among them: "Who *is* this Dr. Dante Marchetti?"; "Can it be that one of Deerwood's newest and most talented physician is a murderer?"; and "Has the DA's office found any links to several other suspicious patient deaths at DCH?" A viewer might easily be left with a solid impression that the intern was guilty of at least two murders and that the DA had airtight cases. That wasn't even close to the truth, despite what the DA might hope.

"Nice!" Bradden crowed. Leaning back in his executive desk chair, he used a remote to click off the TV and face his minions. "Very nice indeed!"

Conover lifted his coffee mug, saluting his employer. "Great work."

"You're awfully quiet, Linda."

Her eyes snapped to her boss. Vaguely conscious of how the two men had been congratulating themselves on their investigation, she pointed out, "This could've been done more discreetly—just in case the man's innocent." Bradden and Conover both snorted at the word *innocent,* and she felt the stubbornness flowing up through her, straightening her spine. "Well, the case appears pretty thin from where I sit."

Big snort from the detective. "Marchetti's been on my list from the beginning—at least for the deaths recorded since he started working here. Remember, I'm not convinced there's only one culprit. That Orlander has been at DCH a long time. Maybe *he* brought the new doctor into the mercy business until Marchetti branched out on his own."

"If we squeeze Marchetti…" Bradden started to say.

"Maybe he'll squeal on an accomplice." Conover finished.

Linda could tell her boss didn't like being interrupted by the detective, but he donned his politician's smile. "Precisely. And lucky for us, the Hartmann death is high-profile enough to draw the notice this case needs, uh, deserves."

She leaned back in her chair, hiding behind the huge coffee mug she'd been given. It was difficult to stomach how delighted Bradden was at the thought of trying and winning this case; which could propel him to Harrisburg. As she sorted her own thoughts, she stayed peripherally aware of the men's conversation but heard nothing new in their listing of facts. Most came from Conover's interviews and investigation, some came from her own research, though Bradden had heard them all from her in their weekly meetings.

Certainly, they all knew by now that Trey Hartmann had been murdered. The introduction of potassium chloride to his drug infusion had clearly been intentional, especially since the IV rate had been changed from what'd been entered on the chart. Unfortunately, Marchetti's fingerprints were on that IV equipment, making that the closest thing they had to solid evidence, even though he had readily admitted to the DCH committee that he had started the infusion.

True, Marchetti had been alone with Hartmann when the infusion began and a while longer before being called to the ER for the car crash patients. So he'd been present in the ER when the young pitcher's death was officially called, according to several sources questioned. Whatever tainting of the Solumedrol occurred in the infusion room or less likely, central supply.

On the other hand, Vincent Orlander had been there in the infusion clinic when the code was called. He even offered up no official reason to explain his presence there except his curiosity to see the celebrity there. Furthermore, he had accompanied the patient all the way to the Emergency Room oxygenating him until the final pronouncement. Orlander smelled to high hell but Ferrante needed more.

Savoring the last of her coffee in tiny sips, she tried to play devil's advocate and make the case for Marchetti: opportunity, means, and motive. Without question, as a doctor and a DCH employee, he'd had means and opportunity to commit murder. But what could possibly motivate that murder? It didn't make sense to her.

When Linda set her empty mug down, it made such a resounding *thunk* that the two men paused in their spate of self-congratulation and looked at her. "What about the motive?" she asked in the momentary silence. "I thought this investigation was about finding a mercy killer."

"Yes," Bradden said, "and all that still stands. According to our psych consultant, sometimes serial killers change their focus or *modus operandi* to fit the situa—"

Barking out laughter, Conover interrupted Bradden yet again. "Like I said, our boy is branching out." Taking the toothpick from his mouth, he used it to emphasize his points. "See, I think these two murders have to do with sex."

"What?" Linda couldn't have been more startled.

"Think about it: the second vic, Matthew Saxon, is still married to the woman who cohabits with Marchetti, Nicole Saxon, a nurse from the hospital. Matt Saxon was insanely jealous of the good doctor according to a number of confidantes and that the still married couple fought about her relationship with our young doctor."

"Matt Saxon is dead?" Bradden inquired.

"Autopsy pending. Even money he was victimized by Marchetti."

"Well, how does Hartmann fit into that?"

Bradden leaned forward on the desk blotter, his eyes avid as he asked Conover, "You have some new information?"

Finishing his coffee, the detective grinned. "Scuttlebutt around the hospital. Just gathered the last few days." He set his empty mug next to Linda's on the little table.

"Apparently, Marchetti got real friendly with some of the Pirates team, especially this Trey Hartmann kid. Marchetti and Ms. Saxon attended a game back in May and Hartmann took them out to dinner afterward; another time he stayed overnight. Who knows what the three of them got into?"

Linda's breath sucked in as a little gasp of surprise.

Conover gave Bradden a broad wink. "The nurse looks plenty fetching to me. A mighty attractive woman and a professional ballplayer with matinee-idol looks. Anything could have happened."

She slowed her breath, willing relaxation onto her face and body. "Is that all?"

Conover gave her a lazy grin. "According to the nurse who set up the infusion, Hartmann was s'posed to stay overnight again on the day he died. Maybe Marchetti thought the kid was moving in on his woman." The detective twirled the toothpick with his tongue. "In fact, two of our witnesses, a pair of physical therapists, heard Marchetti arguing with Hartmann in a hospital courtyard just before that fatal infusion."

"Arguing about what?" Linda asked.

"About proceeding. Well, they couldn't hear all of the actual words, but the tone was unmistakable."

Frowning, she shook her head. "I don't buy it. I don't like this a bit. Circumstantial at best."

Bradden's palm slapped down on his blotter. "Too bad. Because it's still your case, and you'll be my second at trial. I'm sure you can find a way to introduce the idea he's been under suspicion for unexplained the deaths at the hospital, even if the judge rules on their inadmissibility. Y'don't think the case is strong enough? Then make it that way. I want you to put this Marchetti away—or better, put him on death row. We can't have our doctors running around killing their patients, sports celebrities, or even jealous husbands, now can we?"

Linda, hearing the makings of a stump speech in his words, opened her mouth for rebuttal, but Bradden came to his feet and signaled an end to the meeting. As his guests rose, too, he came around his desk to pump Conover's hand and thank him for all his efforts. "Keep up the superb fuckin' work. I'll see you back at the office, Linda." He checked his Rolex. "There's a lot of work to do."

240

Drawing, not for the first time in this job, on her training as an actress, "Right, see you there." With a cheerful nod toward the men, she shouldered her purse and headed for the door. Out in the parking lot, she squeezed the life out of her key fob and tried to unclench her jaws. Clearly Bradden planned for her to do all the dirty work, eviscerating that young intern and taking the credit if she managed to pull it off.

Not that she wanted to. Somehow, she just couldn't believe that man could be a killer. The Trey Hartmann connection made sure there would be tabloids salivating even more. *And much worse, she firmly believed that a killer was still out there. Indeed.*

Chapter Fifty-Three

Vinny sat there in the office he shared with the other respiratory therapists. Constant complaining that he merited his own office always fell on deaf ears. His mouth hung somewhat agape as he viewed Ballard's peer review papers from his phone. The list of cases came as no surprise to him, simply pro forma, but it was Ballard's notes on the side that contributed to his present angst. "A saboteur in our midst?" Holy fuck! Should have checked out the Sentinel event section on the JCHAO website you ol' bastard. *These things can happen.*

"Too damn smart for his own good!" Orlander uttered through gritted teeth. Had he contacted anyone yet about his thoughts? Maybe not, it looked as if he was in the middle of penning another note when I interrupted him. "Looking again at the incomplete sentence, I need to contact..." Nothing else.

Ballard has got to be stopped!

While running on the treadmill at the local YMCA, Nikki experienced a gnawing at her insides when recalling the conversations she and Dan had on many occasions as to how futile many of the cases had been on the medical floors and the concept of "death with dignity." Did he act on this belief by expediting their demise? She shook her head violently to clear her head and took that moment to engage her bike and begin a hellacious workout. *Can't do this.*

"You look like you have the weight of the world on your shoulders," an older woman commented on the bike next to her, taking her towel to wipe the sweat from her face.

"Oh, I always look like that," Nikki answered her quickly, not wishing to engage a stranger with such private thoughts.

While wiping down her bike with a cleaning agent that she grabbed from a hook on the wall along with a few paper towels, the woman opined, "I know this is none of my business, but in the past, I always noticed the joy you exuded when exercising, a freedom of spirit. But today, it is so different. Take it from someone who has been around the block more times than I care to admit. Life is still to be treasured. Each day is to be treasured. Enjoy." With that, she turned and headed for the locker room.

Nikki just sat there motionless for a moment, then followed her out.

Chapter Fifty-Four

Vinny Orlander arrived early for the 4:00 p.m. meeting. That way he could hide himself in a shadowed corner of the spacious room, where a quirk in the architecture formed a little alcove beyond the draperies. He couldn't suppress a tiny smile of pride. No one knew all the nooks and crannies at DCH better than he did. Because, of course, he hadn't been invited to this meeting. His smile slid into a scowl. This one was for the elite—the doctors—and would be led by the Chairman of Medicine, Dr. Hugh Ballard.

As usual, Vinny found satisfaction and amusement in how a person as big as a Viking could disappear in plain sight if he was still for long enough. From this vantage point, he could see the place begin to fill up fast. The arrivals weren't limited to the invited physicians who happened to be on the schedule. The email memo for the house staff had attracted even those who were off-duty; nearly all the interns had showed up and most of the residents plus more attendings than one would expect. Then again, everyone cared about Dan Marchetti. They wanted to know what exactly had happened to him and what was *going* to happen to him. Even those who did not know him directly, found it a bit exciting to be in the middle of their very own *Law and Order* episode.

An agitated buzz crowded the room, the voices of people eager for solid information and anxious about what they might learn. But the moment Chairman Ballard entered, all conversation ceased, and everyone standing, sat.

Ballard, rubber soles whispering across the carpet in the silence, walked to the lecturers' desk at the front of the room but didn't sit behind it. Instead of putting it between himself and his audience, he stood in front of it, leaning back and folding his arms across his chest. Vinny thought he looked tired, especially those blue eyes peering over the wire-rim spectacles as everyone gathered.

"Well," Ballard said into the expectant hush, "I have some tough news to report. Dan Marchetti has been accused of serious crimes that were allegedly committed, I repeat *allegedly* committed while employed at this hospital. He was arrested by the police and suspended by the hospital. I felt that I needed to bring this information to your attention formally and allow for questions. Remember, please, this is a hospital and no place for idle chatter or gossip that I have heard filling the halls since his arrest. Disciplinary action will be taken should you be guilty of said conduct. Thank you."

Gone was that ever-present signature smile, now replaced by a serious, gloomy demeanor. Vinny had seen that smile many times while working at DCH, although it was never aimed at a mere respiratory therapist like himself.

"Incidentally," Ballard continued, "I'm sure our Dr. Marchetti will be pleased to know he has so many people concerned about him as I am. And everyone is assumed innocent until proven guilty in a court of law.

"As for the charges," he continued, "I'm praying that they're completely without merit. In my judgment, Dan Marchetti is not only an exemplary physician, but also a fine human being. I believe in his innocence, and I stand behind him 100%." The audience responded with some applause and cheers.

After the room had quieted down some, Willow Blackstone interrupted with a passionate, "But does anyone know what's going on? Can he get an outstanding lawyer?"

Dave Levine raised his hand, and Ballard nodded to him. "I called Nikki just an hour ago," Dave told the gathering. "She's been in touch with Dan's brother, who said the family would cover any costs. Nikki has connections with the Glickman firm, and she's retained their best defense attorney."

When expressions of relief had swelled and subsided around him, Dave answered a question from Diane Werner. "Nikki said Dan was arraigned within a few hours of his arrest, but no bail was allowed due to his being charged with capital crimes. However, the lawyer says he can petition for bail at Dan's preliminary hearing set for Tuesday morning—"

"That's three more days and four nights in jail!" exclaimed Theo Epplewhite.

After the groans and expressions of outrage and worry subsided, Dave picked up the thread, saying, "According to a trial layer friend, chances for bail are better if there's a show of support from people who know Dan."

"We can sure make that happen," Diane proclaimed and other voices agreed. "Should we call Nik to find out the best way to proceed?"

Dave shook his head. "She's asking for us not to call her right now. She has a lot to deal with, and also needs to rest. She will post email updates. We can take it from there."

Seemingly satisfied with this, the house staff turned its attention back to the Chairman. Vinny made a note to himself to find out the exact time of the arraignment.

"Thanks, Dave," Ballard said. "I'm glad someone has current info." He paused for a moment to survey the faces focused on him.

"Now we need to talk about the craziness that's probably coming our way. I know many of you were questioned by the police, the Care Review Committee, or both, last month after Trey Hartmann's death. Law enforcement personnel will undoubtedly be questioning you soon about Dan, the daily routines here at DCH, and so forth. Just be truthful and stick to the facts. It's possible they'll ask you about other employees here who might be capable of euthanizing patients. Do not, I repeat, do not, offer up theories, conjectures, and the like. Are we clear?"

Everyone in the room nodded, and many voices offered an emphatic "Yes."

In his corner, Vinny also nodded but with a smirk, knowing well enough that the theories and conjectures were already flying fast and furiously up and down the DCH grapevine. The Chairman could mandate all he liked, but nothing would stop a good scandal from rocketing through the floors.

Ballard sighed. "We can only guess the level of media and tabloid scrutiny that is about to descend on us. Should you be approached by reporters for your comments, refer all of them to our public media team. If you see any strangers in the patient areas without a visitor tag, tell them to return to the lobby, and call security. Don't let yourself get pulled into a bad situation. We've instructed the guards to make more frequent rounds, and you all know the code for security if needed."

Vinny chuckled. The media had already located the gathering spots outside the hospital grounds; there was jockeying among many of the staff for face time, or being the designated 'confidential source'. He expected that even some of the doctors might get involved once a few more days had passed.

Dave Levine ducked his head to avoid the chairman's gaze, remembering that he was already notorious for the Starbucks escapade running on the newsfeed throughout the day.

"Understandably," Ballard continued, "emotions are high just now. But, no matter how we may be tempted to react, we must remember our responsibility to this place, our colleagues, and above all, our patients. Likewise, it serves no one, you, the hospital, or Dan for us to try his case in the public eye. Let's allow the judicial system to do its job."

Ballard stood up from his perch on the desk edge. The movement was slow, hinting at the toll of a long and stressful day. Then he straightened to his full height, and some of the weariness dropped away. "We'll get through this," he assured them all. "If you need someone to talk to, my door is always open as are those of the counselors here at Deerwood. Talking helps. In fact, is there anything anyone wants to say now?"

"The whole thing just makes me feel really vulnerable," blurted Brian Callahan. "That you can be the kind of doctor Dan is and get accused of such horrible stuff."

As Vinny waited for the meeting to be over and the room to empty so he could leave, but the house staff talked on for a time, airing anxieties, and attempting to reassure themselves and each other. Vinny watched with interest, realizing the more experienced doctors had hung back, even though those senior residents and attendings must have trepidations of their own, allowing the interns to open up first, then doing their best to console and guide.

After being still for quite a long time, he flexed and relaxed some of his muscles, a tactic he'd perfected through years of covert action, and felt extremely grateful he clocked out before coming to this meeting.

They left the room, some with arms around each other, all vowing to be there for Dan and for one another.

At last Vinny was able to make his escape and head for his own staff meeting. Reflecting on the interns' camaraderie with a twinge of envy, he prepared for the larger meeting where he was sure most of the questions would be directed at job security and overtime pay if this arrest began to impact the hospital operations. He felt like he was leaving the mountaintop to return to the valley dwellers…again.

****

Before too much time had passed, Vinny had printed out the floor's patient listing, scanning the right column for Ballard's patients. To locate him, he would start from the highest floor and work his way down until he sighted the unsuspecting physician. *Think of something, some place to catch him alone.* He remembered something an elderly patient with COPD once told him when explaining his two pack a day smoking history. A survivor of the infamous Auschwitz-Birkenau concentration camp when he was a teenager, finally ending up as a patient on a Tuberculosis ward in London, England after the war. Working at the same hospital as an orderly was a former Nazi guard at the camp, known for his particularly sadistic treatment of the prisoners. Also identifying the former SS officer were two other terribly malnourished patients who had survived, barely, none of the three weighing more than 100 pounds each when liberated by the Allied soldiers. No matter. They followed him into a bathroom and the three managed to turn the unsuspecting man upside down and drown the bastard in one of the toilet bowls. Their actions were never prosecuted though they remained quite certain that the authorities knew what had transpired, deciding to look the other way.

Sighting his prey on the seventh floor, Vinny marveled at the man's energy, apparently indefatigable. But suddenly, the Chief excused himself from his group of residents who were rounding with him and entered the lavatory. Here was his chance.

Chapter Fifty-Five

"Linda, I had a visit from an interesting fellow yesterday, not sure what to make of it," Conover began his phone conversation with Ferrante, employing his usual habit of launching into the point of his call, sans salutations of any sort.

"Good morning to you. I'm doing well, thank you."

Stacy ignored the snarky rejoinder. Not materially important. "A..." He looked down at his notes, "Stanislaw Brezinski, walked in here to warn me I think that two men that match the descriptions of our Dr. Cole and Mr. Orlander, were after our Dr. Marchetti. He used the words, 'harm' and 'trouble'. Seems as if he is a devoted patient of Marchetti's."

"And..."

"Well, you see, he is completely deaf and dumb..."

"Conover, the word 'dumb' is quite antiquated and not exactly PC," she upbraided the coarsely mannered detective.

"Sure, sure, consider myself 'woken up' counselor." He continued. "Somebody who accompanied him wrote the words for him as apparently he cannot read or write. That was the extent of it. Maybe something, maybe bupkis, hard to say. He had his name and address written out as well. I suggest you go call on him and bring a sign language expert. 25 Mark Twain Drive in Broadside."

Chapter Fifty-Six

In the bleakly lit courtroom Dr. Dan Marchetti, garbed in the dark-green and tan-striped jumpsuit issued by the county jail, sat escorted in the courtroom. From this angle, Linda could see part of his face, but he never turned to look at her. She noted how many DCH staff had joined his family to offer their unfettered support. According to Diane Werner, who was compiling a supporters' list for her daily 'Dan is Innocent' email, a number of Dan's former patients sat on the hard benches facing the judge.

Ferrante wasn't surprised to see how quickly the family had dropped everything to focus on helping their son and brother. She did, however, note the odd absence of Nikki Saxon, his girlfriend.

"The Commonwealth of Pennsylvania," a voice boomed now in the courtroom, "versus Dante Michael Marchetti."

Dante looked like a zombie, she thought, as she watched him rise as if the weight of the world was pushing his broad shoulders down.

"How do you plead Dr. Dante Marchetti?"

"Not guilty on all counts, Your Honor," Dan was saying now to the judge.

She sat woodenly, trying to listen, as the rest of the hearing unfolded.

Marchetti's lawyer, Eric Müeller, begin working to secure bail. Even after his speech about all the character support Dan had been offered and that he possessed a completely pristine record. Further reinforcement by spontaneous utterances from the audience, was quickly silenced by the gavel meeting the desk with loud whacks. Furthermore, Mueller asserted defiantly that the defendant posed neither a danger nor a flight risk, at which the lead DA bombastically objected that Dante's bail be extremely high and his passport should be surrendered. Negotiations began in earnest over the amount, which was finally lowered to $50K with Dan submitting to house arrest and wearing an ankle bracelet. It would be a pyrrhic victory but Dan would remain free until trial nevertheless.

Then Müeller moved for a speedy trial. Linda had learned that Dan had emphasized his wish to have this over as quickly as possible, so that he could get back to his life before his budding career was irreversibly damaged. Apparently, the thought had never occurred to him that he may never return to his once promising career because he would be spending the best years of his life behind bars.

Now she stared at the defendant's table where Eric Müeller—a stout blond man nearing forty, who was well-dressed, well-groomed, and well-spoken—wrapped up his pitch for a speedy trial. The swaggering DA, Bradden, wasted a lot of words on making no objections. He seemed as eager as the defendant to bring the case to trial, though of course, not for the same reasons.

At last, it ended. Müeller had secured both the financially manageable bail and the speedy trial, vowing to do his best to get that trial started much sooner than the summer. But Dan couldn't be released until the bail paperwork was actually processed. An officer came to escort him back to his cell.

There were a few brief moments at the railing in which he was allowed contact with his family. Gloria and Sal hugged him together, and Jerry gripped his arm, seemingly refusing to let go.

Finally, he was escorted back to jail to await his bail being posted. In the next moment, the inconsolable Gloria sat down again and wept uncontrollably, now embraced by the other two Marchetti men. Finally helped to her feet as the courtroom cleared for the next case, the family moved toward the doors with relatives shepherding them along the courthouse hallway. Friends and colleagues waved or nodded, smiled or gave a thumbs-up to the departing family. Before long, the crowd had exited the building and headed for the parking lot.

For some inexplicable reason, Linda, still gathering papers from the prosecutors table, found her thoughts drifting to how it would have been for Trey at the end. Potassium chloride was a perfect choice for euthanasia. Now someone or plural are employing methods that made it appear that at the very least, carelessness was at stake. Anotherwords, 'shit happens' or put more ominously, the providers themselves were using their knowledge to "hurry things along."

How easy it would be for any staffer to mix up a cocktail, open a valve, dislodge a tube, fiddle with the wiring of an EKG, and so forth. *Easy peasy when you have access.*

Once outside, Linda loved breathing in the fresh air as she walked the three blocks toward her car on the well-shaded streets. There were birds to listen to and squirrels to watch and neighborhood cats to pet, pretending they were her own. In the thicket of bushes bordering the sidewalk, she caught the unmistakable flash of orange and white as her favorite feral cat angled toward her. "Hey, Ginger!" she called in greeting. She didn't know the big, striped tomcat's real name, but what else would you call a cat that color?

Pulling a plastic baggie from her pocket, she fished out the single cheese stick she'd saved from her lunch. For her part, Ginger slipped out of the greenery and trotted to her with her own gift in her mouth: a captured bird. She dropped it at her feet and gazed up proudly, waiting for praise. *No!* Linda didn't blame Ginger, but even knowing that cats do this often couldn't keep her heart from ripping just a bit as she looked at the broken creature.

Squatting down, Linda studied the speckled-brown sparrow and realized, it wasn't dead after all. With one unblinking eye, it stared up at her, obviously terrified, but unable to move, wings pressed close against the crushed body leaking blood; its beak was open as it gasped.

Linda sat and took the bird gently into her hands. As soon as she felt it in her cupped palms, she knew the truth…it was dying. It was suffering, helpless, and scared. Linda wondered what that felt like.

****

Vinny entered the bathroom stall right behind the seventy-year-old physician, muffling any sound with his left hand and bending the man's right arm behind his back. Ballard's glasses, the old fashioned wire rimmed ones whose earpieces wrapped around his ears, now swung back and forth, the right one swinging in place. Suddenly, this hugely powerful assailant lifted the slightly built man upside down and into the toilet, violently kicking the door closed at the same time. Ballard fruitlessly tried to squirm free but began to suffocate from the water invading his nose and mouth. Within a very short time, he began to turn blue and simultaneously lose consciousness. Suddenly, Vinny heard the outside door open while a male nurse whistling Lady Gaga's *Shallow* entered but whose beeper went off concurrently.

"Room thirty-two stat."

"Shit," he muttered under his breath and exited immediately. "Can't even take a fuckin' leak."

Vinny let out a deep sigh and noticed that his victim wasn't moving. No pulse, nothing. Without wasting a second, he pulled the dead man upright by his collar, pulled his pants and underwear down and sat him on the toilet, propping his lifeless torso against the back wall. *A heart attack while on the crapper. That works.* Moments later, Orlander gathered his push cart and made for the service elevator.

Chapter Fifty-Seven

Dan couldn't fathom his text's tragic news that he imagined the entire hospital was now aware. Their Chief of Medicine had been found pulseless in the men's bathroom an hour before. Sitting on a toilet, how undignified for such a heralded and accomplished man! Must have been a cardiac event. Of course a man his age, no real surprise but he was always so spry, so incandescent, so lively. Even though on that fateful morning when Ballard relieved him of his duties, Dan knew deep down that the man had no choice but to do so under the circumstances. Now this horrific news. Dan's world was quickly unraveling. Pouring himself a scotch, he sat down on his living room carpet and cried unrepentantly.

****

Ferrante moved quickly to enlist the help of a professional sign language expert from an online company that would help her interview Stanislaw Brezinski, Marchetti's patient. Perhaps he could shed some light on the Deerwood Community Hospital 'situation'.

Sitting across from Stan in his meagerly furnished apartment in a seedier side of town that he paid for by working for the Easter Seals organization, she began.

"Mr. Brezinski, I need your help in understanding what you lip read that day in Deerwood Community Hospital's Emergency Room, but first, are these the men you saw that day?" The lawyer held up pictures of Cole and Orlander in front of her witness who shook his head affirmatively and without any hesitation, even before the translation.

"Okay, now. I understand Dr. Dan Marchetti is your doctor. How do you feel about the care you have received from him?"

Stan made a definitive and fervent 'thumbs up' motion with his right hand. Then he folded his arms around himself, an interesting gesture to say the least. The translator added,

"he makes him feel like he is a human being, not an oddity to be made fun of."

Linda stared at this kindly but homely man's face and couldn't help feeling a surge of overwhelming empathy well up inside her.

"That's wonderful. It can be a rather cruel world out there." She instinctively reached to pat his folded hands, now resting on his lap. A smile rapidly appeared on his innocent looking face. He began to sign rapidly now.

"The men ignored me completely as though I was invisible but I wasn't. They talked about doing things that I didn't understand to his patients but would lead to trouble for Dr. Dan. Since I saw him on the TV being arrested, I thought maybe they were responsible. He couldn't have done anything wrong, he is too good a person." The translator signed rapidly in order to keep up. Within moments, tears began to flow from the corners of Stan's eyes. Undeterred, Ferrante continued questioning the man for another thirty minutes before leaving. On one hand, he is very believable but on another, Bradden could and would try to destroy him on the witness stand! She would have to proceed cautiously but with some haste. Mr. Brezinski could hold the key to Marchetti's exoneration.

Chapter Fifty-Eight

"Nikki, can I ask you something?" Dan clicked the remote and soon there was quiet. Nikki had been reading a magazine at the end of the sofa, and he couldn't help feeling a gaping separation both physical and emotional. "Okay, I am going to get right to the point. Since my arrest, I have felt you pull away from me, and I am hurt beyond words. Do you think I am guilty of those insane charges?"

Dan stared accusingly at her almond-shaped eyes that lost the magical twinkle he had been accustomed to admiring. Eyes, indeed, were windows to her soul and hers had always managed to make him feel loved and, above all, safe. Eyes that registered full-throated acceptance and a burgeoning pride for being attached at the hip to him.

"No, I don't think so, Dan." Nikki's denial didn't match her body language, though, which looked defensive and closed. The truth, however, was inextricably tied to all the trauma she'd sustained in her youth and her inherent distrust of everyone she encountered, which now included Dan. Except for the children. They were too young to develop those unflattering traits.

"You don't *think* so? What kind of fucked-up answer is that? You don't think so. You know what *I* think?" He paused in order to contain his surging anger and betrayal. "I think..." Dan couldn't finish, suddenly overwhelmed with a sense of indescribable loneliness and of being on a tiny island with no friends, no career, and no future.

The brokenhearted intern grabbed his Pirates windbreaker, a gift from Trey. "Going for a walk. Right now I can't imagine how you would even consider myself capable of murder, Nikki." She watched him leave, her mouth agape, although in reality, the man she'd been convinced could do no wrong was probably nothing more than a fantasy now. Doubts were worsening everyday rather than lessening as she had hoped. Her migraines the past few days began to rear their ugly head, a phenomenon that always followed when her mind was deeply troubled.

Chapter Fifty-Nine

"So Nikki, how can I help?" Susan Kaputkin began, reciting her usual opening question whenever she began seeing a new patient in her now burgeoning practice. A licensed social worker and therapist for five years, word of mouth referrals from current and past patients had proved far superior to all the social media pronouncements one could muster.

"My life feels like it is unraveling before my very eyes and I stand helpless to do anything about it." Just then Nikki broke down, this despite promising herself that she would not allow herself to do so. How she despised women who couldn't keep their shit together when times were tough.

"How so Nikki?" Kaputkin responded, now pointing to her ever present tissue box on the small coffee table box separating the two. Nikki hesitantly reached for it, trying desperately to suppress her torment from bubbling forth just then, not wishing to appear weak or frail.

Dabbing gently at her eyes, she began to describe her relationship with Dan Marchetti, her miserable childhood, her distrust of male figures, her failed marriage and lastly her deep-seated instincts to run. One topic after another, only taking a brief pause to access a water bottle she carried everywhere she travelled. Nikki, normally reticent to divulge much about her past to others, least of all complete strangers, surprised herself with her candor at that moment. *Choosing a female therapist had a lot to do with it she surmised.*

"Basically, I am afraid to deal with problems head-on." Nikki straightened her back at that moment, her eyes fixated on her therapist, expecting a rebuke that never came.

Kaputkin interjected. "We're afraid of the outcome that confronting a problem might mean. Or perhaps, we are afraid of going through what it would take to solve the problem."

"I guess it comes down to finding it too hard to face my fears."

"What are your fears?" Nikki froze, the question posed creating the same look in her as a deer confronting an onrushing headlight.

"That…that Dan's trial will result in a conviction and place everyone around him in a world of shame and ostracism. My life has been lonely enough."

"I see." Kaputkin paused to thoughtfully contemplate her next question.

"How would you describe such a 'lonely' world?"

"I suppose," Nikki's voice began to crack,

"A lack of companionship, feeling left out, not in tune with people around me, having no one to turn to." Nikki's soft voice began to trail off, producing an awkward silence but catching herself, the troubled nurse exclaimed forcefully, "I cannot face that prospect again. I would rather be dead."

Chapter Sixty

"I'm bothered by something, Stacy blurted bout." Linda tilted her head at the sudden chink in the PI's certitude about Marchetti's guilt.

Flossing his teeth while he talked, a habit Linda found disgusting, "The Chair of Medicine was found dead on the crapper the other day."

"I heard. So, he must have had a cardiac event, it happens." Ferrante didn't know where he was going with this.

"He was found sitting on the toilet bowl itself, not with the seat down first. Who does that?"

"Maybe his heart gave out just after he pulled his underwear and pants down but before he was able to put the seat down," Linda offered, a quizzical look on her face.

"Maybe. Maybe. However, I dare to say that most people put the seat down first before undressing. Also, his tie was found pulled to the right, off center according to eyewitnesses at the code which had been called. His eyeglasses, the old style wraparounds, were dangling from his right ear, his hair was soaking wet as were the collars of his shirt and jacket. Needless to say, when discovered, the good doctor had been long gone so trying to revive him proved fruitless. Does make you wonder though."

"Wonder what?"

Just then, he put his floss down and rested his arms on his desk, his stare resolute. "Whether Ballard met with foul play. If I didn't know any better, you would think he was drowned in the toilet."

Chapter Sixty-One

Dan tried to sit still in the leather upholstered chair in his lawyer's office but he couldn't help shifting his position every minute or so. His thoughts drifted off to movies such as *Inherit the Wind*, where Spencer Tracy stood in court behind a large mahogany desk—and the one in *To Kill a Mockingbird,* where Gregory Peck spoke so eloquently to no avail as Judge Taylor announced that Tom Robinson had been found guilty of assaulting and raping Mayella Ewell. He loved those older movies but little did he know…

The four months since his arrest had been one long continuous nightmare. He would never forget those first few days in jail or the first time he talked to his brother after Nikki had contacted him.

"Jesus, Dan, how…?" his brother blurted in shock.

Dan, who had been able to keep his composure on the front lines of hundreds of bizarre and terrifying medical emergencies, lost it, and pleaded, "Jer, get me out of here, man. Please. Get me out of here."

At that, Jerry's voice also broke. They had been raised to be strong, proud Marchetti men, but now one of the greatest fears may happen: they could lose each other. "Hang tight, Danny."

" I will."

Dan shuddered as he remembered hanging up the receiver and being quickly ushered into a holding cell in an adjoining building, where he would remain until Jerry could fulfill his promise…if he could. It was a narrow, drafty, noisy cell with a cement floor, utilitarian steel sink and toilet, hard cot, and no window. Dan's belongings had been taken, and he had been issued standard jail garb, which was too big and hardly any warmer than the tailored shirt and pants he had ironed so proudly that morning.

For one of the rare times in Dan's twenty-eight years, he felt utterly powerless. Dan was not a selfish person but as the hours of pacing, staring, and worrying had worn on, he could no longer think about anything else but being found innocent. No innocent human being should ever have to endure such torture.

Of course, Jerry had come through, and so had his mom and pop and distant relatives whose names he had forgotten. Early in the day after Dan's arrest, his lawyer was secured, and he was freed on the bail money scraped together from every aunt, uncle, and cousin who saw the travesty as a personal attack on the whole family. Later, when Dan had asked, Jerry had cut him off with, "Don't worry about it. We Marchettis do what we have to do for our own."

So here he sat accused of being a murderer.

It was incredible. Dan had spent days with Eric Müeller going over hundreds of details, dealing with every possible fact that might undercut what his loyal friends saw as Bradden's political gambit. Eric began the conversation one morning. "The DA's accusations are based on circumstantial evidence and the conclusions of a fertile imagination, I'm afraid. He possesses a pathologic craving for publicity. The case was blatantly contrived, yet it has gone forward, and now we must convince the jury of the flimsiness of his assertions and conclusions." Dan appeared dazed. "Dan, we'll pick this up tomorrow. You look spent."

Dan and his lawyer exited through the red bricked office building and then through the underground parking facility that allowed them to bypass the media that had swarmed the building, hoping to get a glance at the "Intern Killer," as he had been termed by the tabloids. In them, he read that he was a sex-starved sociopath who had gotten rid of the two men who he feared would 'steal his woman' and responsible for euthanizing ailing patients who were "no longer viable."

Reaching their cars, angled near each other in the dimly lit space, they shook hands and parted ways for the day.

Dan headed home, just wanting to forget his chaotic life for a few hours.

Back at the apartment, in his accumulated postal mail, he saw a blue greeting card envelope with a familiar postmark and handwriting that had gotten just a bit shakier over the decades. This one he had to read.

Carefully, he extracted it from the pile, opened the envelope and withdrew a card with 'Thinking of You' on the front. Inside, his godmother had written:

My Dearest Dante,

After all of these years, you know that during difficult times, I like to once again rely on my faith in God to sustain me. Let me pose a question to you, dear boy. Do you know why your parents named you so? Well, in Latin 'Dante' means 'an enduring man, everlasting'. In Dante's *Inferno*, a wonderful poem and one of my favorites, we see a mortal man who was guided through the many circles of hell and the deepest depravity, only to have God demonstrate those divine qualities to which human beings can aspire. How? By simply putting him on a journey like the one you are on now. You will survive these ordeals, my sweet Dante, and mark my words, you will see the face of God. I am as certain of this as I am of anything in this life of ours.

Danny, I know in my heart who the real Dante Michael Sebastian Marchetti is. Stand tall and proud before the world, humble before God. You will prevail. Love always, Aunt Carmela.

P.S. And in the end, Dante comes upon his beloved Beatrice who is waiting in heaven for him.

These few simple sentences were enough to move Dan to tears. They came from a woman he had known all his life, who had loved him as an aunt and as a godmother should. Her story was one of the ones that Dan had told Trey to give the ballplayer hope, one that he recalled every time he was tempted to regard a patient as just a body, a diagnosis, or a case number. She had shown him that. Her influence, he was sure, had made him a better doctor, and it was a factor in his absolute revulsion that anyone could believe he would take a life. *But who could explain all the mishaps? What a euphemistic word. How about the word 'carnage'.*

Chapter Sixty-Two

Bradden gazed at the CNN broadcast on the 55 inch flat screen on his wall, contemplating the evidence against Dr. Dante Marchetti. Discovering a debate performance in medical school advocating for legalizing euthanasia for patients suffering from terminal conditions or exceptionally poor quality of life, was valuable. Placing Marchetti in proximity to every patient where medical mishaps occurred (four definite, one maybe) leading to medical harm or death, could not be simply ascribed to 'business as usual'. Sure, they appear as sentinel events elsewhere in the country but too many in such a short time. Nevertheless, it left room for pleading down to lesser charge on the part of the defense should he determine it the pragmatic thing to do to get a conviction. After all, conviction is the goal!

But Hartmann's death by a lethal dose of potassium chloride indicated an escalation of sorts where a targeted patient was a young, fit individual, albeit recently diagnosed with Multiple Sclerosis. Serious for sure but certainly not an immediate death sentence at all and very treatable he understood it to be. Euthanize him nevertheless? Marchetti may be a zealot but there was no evidence he was sociopathic or deranged.

Then there was Conover's suspicion regarding Ballard's death. A drowning? *You have to be shitting me!* If the suspicion was strong, he could have sought an autopsy but that would have been a difficult one to secure. In Pennsylvania, an autopsy can be authorized only when a sudden death cannot be recognized by a readily recognizable disease (Ballard had known cardiac disease as it turned out) or deaths occurring under suspicious circumstances, (wet hair and a disturbed collar and tie, hardly a slam dunk). Additionally, death from violence or trauma (such an act would require extraordinary strength to drown him in the bathroom stall amidst a struggle while no facial bruises were noted) and so forth. Lastly, Ballard was an Orthodox Jew (his real surname had been 'Baginski' which was changed when his grandparents came through Ellis Island). His family would most certainly object based on religious reasons and without a compelling belief that foul play was committed, judges usually accede to the family's wishes. Consequently, no autopsy was requested and therefore he was buried straight away. The truth was that Marchetti could have been in the wrong place at the wrong times or was made to look like the culprit. The odds that any charge that his District Attorney's office failed to pursue possible exculpatory evidence by extending his investigation in another direction were slim to none. Being charged with prosecutorial misconduct should it come to pass that other(s) were involved would never happen. Sure, in his time he had seen his fair share of unsavory behavior but statistics bore out that rarely were any prosecutors held liable. Besides, the bungling efforts by the detectives obfuscated the entire picture and left him no choice but to go after Marchetti, he would contend. Inefficient and sloppy were they and that is why a former member of the force, Stacy Conover, remained so critical to his prosecutorial work.

****

Orlander sat in Ferrante's office for a second meeting, now accompanied by his lawyer, a young defense attorney assigned him by legal aid.

"Mr. Orlander, do you recall a fellow who happened to be totally deaf who was present in the Emergency Room many weeks ago when you were engaged in a conversation with Dr. Cole one afternoon?" Ferrante inquired rather matter-of-factly.

"What deaf person?" he blurted out, taken aback by this question that seemingly appeared out of nowhere.

"Well, his name is not important right now but his testimony is. You see, he couldn't hear you but he reads lips very well. In fact, so well that he was able to tell us through a sign language service that you two had performed some activities to cause 'trouble' and 'harm' to Dr. Marchetti, and those words are a direct quote."

She paused to gauge his body language and any forthcoming response. Orlander spoke no word at all but his squirming and worried expression clearly indicated that he had become unnerved.

"Do you want to unburden yourself now and tell us what you two may have meant by these words?" *Approach this with care counselor for he looks primed to crack.*

"Don't answer that," cracked his attorney.

"I...I have no comment at all."

"No comment? So you're acknowledging that you guys did indeed discuss Dr. Marchetti using these words?" Vinny turned to his counselor for advice.

"Oh, Mr. Orlander, no lawyer can keep the truth from coming out."

Chapter Sixty-Three

Linda Ferrante entered the Motor Vehicle Department soon after it opened to renew her driver's license quickly before the crowds gathered, but with no such luck. There were already ten people in front of her, including Dan Marchetti, who stood a few feet away. He looked thinner than she'd remembered but surprisingly resolute. Just then he looked up from his phone and caught her gaze, eliciting a weak smile. After all, they were on opposite sides so she suddenly pretended to be searching her purse for her soon-to-be outdated license. It did not deter the young physician.

"Ms. Ferrante, I'm sorry to bother you but when I saw you here, just had to tell you that I could never do any of the things I am accused of, not in a million years." Dan's spoke calmly and earnestly. She'd always believed that eyes were indeed the window to one's soul and his spoke volumes. No question that he unnerved her.

"Doctor Marchetti, I cannot engage in any conversation with you, I'm so sorry but I'm certain you understand." Linda turned on her heels and exited the door, now sprinting the fifty feet or so to her car. Once inside, she began to weep as the last few minutes awakened a tsunami of frustration, guilt, and shame. *I really believe him.* Marchetti was no more guilty than she was of perpetrating these crimes. She knew it deep down to her bones, but yet there she was, playing her part in this peculiar chess match, so close to checkmating this noble knight. Her worse thought. Had she become bereft of empathy?

This last thought was the most frightening because she had become convinced that it was true. Except maybe for now. She felt distressed down to her very core about Dr. Dante Marchetti and Bradden's rush to judgement. That feeling was empathy, real, and yes, she did indeed feel something. A lot of something.

****

Vinny stared at the small bottle's label, *Paraquat,* an extensively used herbicide that gained fame in the 1970s when marijuana from Mexico was discovered to be covered with the poison, inflicting death and severe illness to many hoping to simply enjoy a little reefer.

In fact, he treated a young man a few years back who intentionally drank half of a bottle in order to commit suicide and exactly at the same time the next day suffered an excruciating death by asphyxiation. Linda Ferrante deserved no less of a fate after her little performance interrogating him the other day. *She was on to him.*

Ducking behind a large display of Coke Zero at the Weis Supermarket on Front Street, the resourceful healthcare worker bided his time waiting for just the right opportunity to exact his plan. Ferrante had just grabbed two six packs of bottled water when she suddenly remembered that she needed bathroom tissue paper two aisles down from there. Rather than pushing the now heavily laden cart, she chose to leave it there and quickly retrieve the paper goods.

Without wasting a second, Vinny had managed to twist off the top of one of the plastic bottles and pour a few milliliters of the toxic herbicide into one of the sodas before once again securing the top. *A real time bomb. She will feel fine for the day she drinks it, then all hell will break loose. Best part-there is no remedy and if you give her oxygen, it hastens her death!*

Chapter Sixty-Four

Mueller wasted no time in summing up where the legal issues facing his young client stood, staring directly across the mahogany table from Dan Marchetti in the Davis, Fromm, and Mueller law firm's conference room.

"Dan, you are being accused of expediting the deaths of Jane Salter and Joanne Cleary by altering their 'Positive End-Expiratory-Pressures' to dangerous levels, resulting in cardiopulmonary arrests."

"Wait just a minute…"

"Dan, let me finish, take notes, and I'll let you speak until your heart's content, afterward." Mueller took a sip from his coffee mug which read, "World's Greatest Lawyer." *Dan prayed that that designation was indeed true!*

"Second, you are being charged with expediting the demise of a Roscoe Delmar who after having been diagnosed with a Dissecting Abdominal Aneurysm, you addressed his shock-like blood pressure with MAST Trousers amongst other treatments. The trousers were subsequently found to be deflated by an emergency room nurse soon after the patient was pronounced dead from his ruptured aneurysm."

Dan could feel the heat in his neck surge as he was forced to listen to this crap.

"Third, your placement of a," by now Mueller dismissed any attempt to remember or pronounce correctly these medical terms, simply reading directly from his notes, "Sengstaken-Blakemore Tube directly lead to the rupture of a patient's esophagus, again resulting in his death soon thereafter from overwhelming sepsis." Mueller stopped for a moment to remove his eyeglasses to rub his tired, smallish hazel colored eyes.

"Now, an erroneous interpretation by yourself of an electrocardiogram whose machine was later found to be defective, possibly tampered with, will not be filed by the prosecution but may be slyly mentioned nevertheless…"

"Can I speak now?" Marchetti's face registered total disgust.

"What motive would I have to do these horrible things?"

"They claim you were obsessed with medical ethics, the 'status quo' if you will, and endorsed euthanasia as a lawful and justifiable action."

"What? I categorically deny that. Where do they get that from?"

"They cite an incident in the ICU after the death of a Sarah Damen where you vehemently criticized attendings and residents alike for and I paraphrase, 'making a mockery of a human life'."

"I did say that but not for the reason you allude. I had just lost a patient who I may add died a heart wrenching death, only to emerge from the room with a husband who threw himself on the bed next to his beloved wife, to find the others discussing the pathophysiology of a 'Saddle Embolus right outside the room. Heartless and inappropriate for sure." Mueller busied himself taking notes but then continued. There is also the matter of a debate as a student where you argued for the sanctity of euthanasia. Your word 'sanctity'. What did you mean by that word, a little unusual.

"Lastly, there are active investigations into the deaths of a Matt Saxon, Trey Hartmann, and Dr. Hugh Ballard that may result in additional charges levied against you."

Dan sat back in his chair and just crumpled, "Oh My God, me? Were they all murdered and if so, why in the name of God, would I do such anything? What motive would…" At once, he couldn't finish the sentence, instead taking that moment to crash his right arm down against the hard wood. The noise startled Mueller though he chose not to interrupt his besieged client just then.

"Why, because Dr. Ballard let me go? And Saxon and Hartmann, because I was jealous of Nikki's attraction to them?" Mueller remained quiet.

"That is preposterous!"

"You mentioned possible motives, I didn't say a word. Did such thoughts exist in you?" Dan just glared at his lawyer.

"Dan, the prosecution would jump on such voluntary observations."

Dan just brushed aside such advice, asking, "isn't it obvious what they are thinking? What phony proof do they say they have?"

"Ballard they believe was drowned though no autopsy was performed. Exhuming the body is a possibility so the lungs can be studied." Mueller hesitated briefly before continuing to let that fact register. "Trey Hartmann received a lethal dose of Potassium chloride in his steroid infusion with you one of the last persons to see him before he succumbed."

Lastly, Mueller sighed, "Matt Saxon, was injected with a paralyzing agent, and an empty ampule so marked with letters P-A-V-U-L-O-N was found in one of your coat pockets in the house staff's sleeping quarters."

"I am being set up!" Marchetti rose violently from his chair, his hellacious scream could be heard throughout the sedate offices of the firm.

"Please sit down Dan. At this point, we may need a change of strategy, and you might want to reconsider a plea bargain, if the prosecution would even go for it."

"No," Dan said without hesitation. "I am not guilty of any of this, and I will not consent to anything saying I am."

"You want your life back, don't you?" Müeller asked. "Dan, if you plead to a lesser charge, we may be able to escape a lifelong jail sentence and quite possibly a death sentence. I believe Trey's case is based on hearsay and simply will not hold up when exposed to the light of day. As for the hospital's inquiry that suspects Orlander responsible for the missing Pavulon ampules from the Anesthesiology carts, we just need to introduce this fact to create enough suspicion of others to handcuff the negligent homicide cases, showing the evidence to be circumstantial and contrived. Additionally, he had access to Hartmann and a propensity to inject medicines in victims' bodies. As for Ballard, it would take a man of considerable stature and strength to invert the victim and hold his head in the water sufficiently to suffocate him. Orlander is capable of just that. However, I would be remiss as your attorney if I didn't advise you of all the possibilities. Now, the district attorney has not approached me yet about a plea, but I suspect that that will happen as we proceed."

"What makes you think Bradden would go for it if I did want to plea bargain?" Dan asked dejectedly in a weak, almost defeated voice.

"A loss would greatly damage his political aspirations, but a lesser sentence would be viewed as a win-win for him, in my opinion," Müeller acknowledged.

"A win-win? For me, who would hire me and who will give me back my reputation, Eric?" Dan beseeched his attorney. "This is already breaking my family's hearts. You do anything legal you need to do to win this, all right? I intend to fight all the way."

"All right, Dan," Müeller said. "All right."

Chapter Sixty-Five

Vinny followed Ferrante every day that week to see if she would lead him to her star witness, using all of his sick time from work in order to do so. So far nothing. Though he had a fairly good recollection of what the deaf fellow looked like, he was certain that up until now she had stayed away from him. Today was another day. He had followed her car to an apartment complex in a poorer section of town, quite possibly today would yield some results.

After about an hour, the attractive lawyer emerged from the building accompanied by a man and a woman, the two strangers busy signing to each other. Squinting substantially now, he was now able to recognize the man as the patient in the emergency room. The two women waved goodbye and entered the lawyer's car while the witness walked in the other direction. Here was his chance. Vinny readied the Pavulon-loaded syringe and needle, crossed the street, and began to follow his prey.

Fifty feet became thirty, then twenty, and ten, Brezinski obviously unable to hear any footsteps. Removing the syringe from his jacket pocket, he looked around hastily to see if he had any company. Almost upon his prey by now, he readied his right arm to instill the paralyzing agent into his subject's neck when suddenly two police cars cut off the sidewalk in front of him. The officers emerged with the Glocks pointed at him, screaming, "Halt, police, drop the syringe Orlander now!" Their faces were deadly serious, the three men crouched in a shooting posture. Vinny began to raise his arms when suddenly, he stabbed the needle in his arm while also kneeling to the ground.

When the police grabbed the now empty syringe, Orlander lay prone, arms seemingly frozen in place, a cyanotic hue beginning to emerge on his face and lips. "Call an ambulance," the nearest officer to the stricken man yelled while another searched his vehicle for an Ambu bag. When he had finally returned with one, the respiratory therapist had become pulseless and in the throes of a respiratory arrest, the muscles needed for breathing motionless. Ferrante, now on the scene after surreptitiously having driven into a side street, hugged Brezinski while the signer busily communicated encouraging words to the frightened man.

"He says he never was so frightened in his life."

"Tell him he is a hero who has saved many lives. May God continue to bless him." Ferrante began to sob openly, the tension of the moment now dissipated and tremendous relief overtook her.

Chapter Sixty-Six

Dan stood on his apartment balcony, the sliding door opened to usher in some fresh air. The sparseness of his furnishings and the cheap, hideous green throw rug reminded him of how little effort he had undertaken to really make his place feel like a real home. Almost as if he knew that he wouldn't be staying long there, perhaps to be replaced by prison bars. The thought, though fleeting, of turning around and hurling himself off the balcony danced through his troubled mind.

Cooking always relaxed him. *I'll make some chili with some real heat and burn these goddamned thoughts from my mind.* In fact, he remembered, Alex had a chili powder that he purchased online from Texas that he raved about. Alex had recently returned from his extended leave after his suicide attempt and was on call tonight, but Dan knew he wouldn't mind him using the spare key he'd once used to save his friend's life.

Dan grabbed the keys and crossed over to Alex's apartment. Once inside, he made a beeline to his fellow intern's kitchen cabinet and found it after wading through so much crap. "I thought I was a pig. Jeez, his place is a worse wreck every time I come over," he murmured to himself.

After turning to exit, Dan noticed what appeared to be an open letter on the kitchen table, partially hidden by dirty dishes and a dirty coffee mug. He couldn't help recognizing the unmistakable Deerwood Community Hospital stationery and envelope. Dan reached for it but thought better of it. After all, reading other people's mail was wrong, but something made him grab for it a second time. He began to read:

Dr. Cole,

Welcome back. As you know, I followed through on your suggestions and arranged for a few early 'departures' for Marchetti's patients. After all, he needed to be taken down a few pegs, and they were terminal patients anyway. Certainly, the actions dimmed our illustrious doctor's star and made him appear more like the rest of us. His arrest I suppose was what the military deem, "collateral damage." However, I must confess that the act of taking a person's life can get addictive and even I daresay, intoxicating. Hence, Trey Hartman, Dr. Ballard, and even Matt Saxon. I believe you will cut me some slack here. As my grandmother often remarked, (translated to English), "we're cut from the same cloth."

Your friend,

Vinny

Suddenly appearing in the doorway, Alex Cole.

"I was in no shape to handle sick patients so I got 'Shoes' to cover for me. Dan, what are you..." he stopped midsentence, noting the memo in Dan's hand.

"Alex, is this what I think it is?"

"Yes. Your ticket to freedom, you lucky guy!" He then suddenly moved and retrieved a 9mm Springfield XD-M Elite model handgun from behind a large, empty deep-blue vase on the bookshelf. Pointing at the side of his head, he continued, "and my reason to exit this wonderful world we live in. Oh yes, Alex Cole has so much to be proud of and thankful for," he uttered mockingly.

"It was in my mailbox yesterday," pointing at the letter, he added, "Another sick fuck, huh?"

"I posted a copy of the letter to the prosecutor's office earlier today along with my own part in this whole mess. You will be completely exonerated." He paused just a moment and added, "I'm the one who caused all your problems. As you can see, I told that shmuck Vinny Orlander we should take you down a peg or so. It was my idea for him to fix it so some of your patients checked out a little early." Alex stared at the ground, girding himself for the outrage, the condemnation. "The fucker ran with it..."

"What? For what reason?"

"Isn't it obvious. I am so fuckin' envious of you. All the accolades from the attendings and all the attention. Jeez, you would think you walk on fuckin' water. Orlander fiddled with ventilator settings, Sengstaken-Blakemore tubes, damaged a lead wire on an EKG, released mast trouser valves...all those patients were gonna die anyway, but he, *we*, helped them along. As you can see, though, he did the baseball player on his own, Ballard, and even Matt Saxon. And the poor bastard, Lloyd Smith, wrong place, wrong time."

"Lloyd Smith? The Nitrous Oxide overdose?" He hesitated to make sense of it all. "Why in God's name would envy lead you to such heinous acts? You were well on your way. Wasn't that enough?"

"You know, I have asked myself that same question so many times. I've worked so hard to succeed, but *not* because I wanted to be the best doctor for my patients. Not at all. I worked so fuckin' hard because I wanted all the kudos, the esteem, the 'God-complex, all of it. You see, I have been in it for all the wrong reasons!" Cole's face was a crimson red by now from embarrassment and utter shame.

By making me look bad, thought Dan. *Depraved.*

Alex regained his composure. "I tried to end this pitiful life once before, but you saved me. Dante to the rescue once again," he chided sarcastically. He took a small cassette recorder from his jacket, turned it off, and placed it on the coffee table next to him. Without hesitating at all, he placed the barrel inside his mouth and discharged it.

Blood, skull fragments, and brain matter flew onto the wall, a hanging lithograph, and the carpet. The bullet ricocheted and struck Dan in the side, although he strangely felt no pain and merely noticed some blood trickling through his T-shirt. Lifting his shirt, he saw that the bullet had only grazed his side. He sat down on a kitchen chair for what seemed an interminable amount of time, trying desperately to fathom what had just taken place, though in reality it was only a few minutes. *I have to call the police.*

Chapter Sixty-Seven

Beep, beep. "Dr. Marchetti, stat call 7100, 7100..." There was no slow testing of the waters after the charges had been summarily dropped; Dan went right back into the belly of the beast. He dialed the numbers for the emergency room.

"Dr. Marchetti, a twenty-year old respiratory arrest," a voice said.

"Be right down." Dan hurried down the three flights of stairs, his heart pumping madly. His mind worked fast en route, thinking of all the possibilities: drug overdose, status epilepticus, motor vehicle trauma, bronchospasm...

Once inside the crash room, Dan saw a blue-tinged young man with baggy jeans, a snake tattoo on his torso, and two circular earrings in his right ear. His chest was being repeatedly pounded on by an EMT, while the respiratory therapist on duty alternately squeezed the Ambu bag and allowed it to fill for the best breath.

Vinny's fate had been sealed even before the arrest warrant had been served when he had removed his lab coat to attend to a slight stain on his scrub shirt that a doctor had mistakenly put on, thinking it his own. Finding the stolen ampules of paralytic drugs in the inner pockets had led to an internal investigation and then a theft charge, pending loss of his license. Add to that four patient homicides and one failed attempt, and Vinny would never have seen the light of day again if he had not ended his life.

A nurse Dan didn't recognize began informing him of the patient's vitals: "BP 60 systolic; pulse 40 and thready; IV in and normal saline wide open. Was partying, probably alcohol, narcs, maybe cocaine."

"Endotracheal tube," Dan replied, making his way to the head of the stretcher, all the while keeping his eyes on the monitor. "One amp atropine, one amp Narcan. How's the IV running?"

"We'll need a central line," the EMT replied.

"Okay, after I tube him." Dan was handed a laryngoscope and endotracheal tube. Taking the patient's head in his hands, Dan extended the neck and pinned the tongue back, with the blade of the scope to expose the vocal cords. He inserted the long tube through the opening in the cords, moving quickly, every moment precious.

"Got it!"

The nurse took her stethoscope and listened for breath sounds. "You're in," she stated emphatically. The patient's color was now pink thanks to the new supply of oxygen. "BP 100/60, pulse 120 and regular."

"Sinus tach. We may not need the central line after all," he said to the EMT. "A foley catheter, please." The EMT nodded. "Once you're in, let's send some urine for a drug screen. What blood work has been sent?" he continued.

"CBC, comprehensive metabolic panel, ABG," the young nurse replied quickly.

"Perfect." At that moment, the patient began to thrash in response to seeing strange people hovering over him; the tube in his throat intensified his madness.

"Great stuff, that Narcan," Dan quipped. "I'll be out talking to the family. Let me know when the lab work is back or if there's a change. I'll get an ICU bed ready."

Only then did he realize that his hands were shaking uncontrollably. He quickly hid them in the pockets of his white lab coat. Although he had been reinstated at the hospital, he remained more than five months behind his original cohort and had to make up the rotations as his friends rapidly moved through their second year of residency.

In a perfect world, and God knows no such thing exists, Dan would have preferred to keep up with them, but he knew he was lucky that this was the only impact of his ordeal on his employment; his future career trajectory had survived essentially intact. Dan would always be grateful for the intervention and steadfast support of Dr. Ballard, who held open Dan's residency slot long enough for him to return.

Personally, he was glad he'd been able to get back to work quickly rather than sitting at home with too much time to think. Not that he'd wanted to go back there, so he quickly made arrangements to move into a different building.

While the patient deaths were quickly moved to a closed status while other tragic outcomes were now under investigation, it was a while before the DA office would officially drop any further investigations.

Just that morning, Linda Ferrante had called to inform Dan that he was officially free and clear. She also asked to meet him for lunch.

Chapter Sixty-Eight

At 1:00 p.m. Dan headed for the lobby to meet Linda. He spotted her in a purple armchair reading a magazine. It struck him that she looked different, not at all like the lawyer he had dreaded during the court proceedings. In her jeans and sandals, she looked younger and surprisingly unimposing.

Linda looked up and caught sight of him approaching. She, too, was struck by Dan's appearance, distinctly more robust than their previous encounters. His face, once drawn and with deep, dark circles obscuring his brown eyes, now seemed to have awoken from a long sleep. His eyes sparkled and seemed to radiate a reborn zest for life.

"Hey," she greeted him as he reached her. "How are you holding up?"

"It's tough," he said, "but I'm happy to be alive and free. Still with many unanswered questions, insecurities, disbelief…"

"What about you? Got any cool legitimate cases at the DA's?" anxious to change the subject.

"Long story. I'm no longer working for the DA's office, actually. I officially 'resigned' as of the end of next week."

Dan raised an eyebrow. "Why?"

"Wasn't feeling it," she quipped, a twinkle of amusement in her eyes. "Besides, to be honest, the Braddens of this world are proliferating I'm afraid. What an asshole. He wants to be the next state attorney general and then governor; he'll go to any length to get there. *Any* length. District attorneys nationwide are out of control Dan." She shook her head back and forth. They went down to the cafeteria for sandwiches and sodas and, spotting a free table, they claimed it.

"Will it help to talk Dan?" Linda asked, sipping her soda. "I have always been a good listener."

Dan picked up his sandwich, a strange half smile appearing on his face. "You know, for a time there, I didn't think that I could ever trust myself to take care of sick patients again. I really didn't."

"Why not? You did nothing wrong. Those were fabricated charges, a concerted effort to set you up. You're no more responsible for anyone's death than I am."

Dan arched his face toward his lunch companion. "Listen, before those deaths, I felt myself sinking deeper and deeper into this pit…"

Linda tilted her head slightly. "What do you mean?"

Dan continued, "We see a lot of bad shit. It's a motherlode to take in." He ran both hands through his now closely cropped hair. "Most people are insulated from what goes on here. At times, I envy that…that protection, even freedom."

Linda began, "I guess you have to…" but he interrupted her in mid-sentence.

"I know; we have to detach ourselves from their problems, but at what cost?"

Linda found herself taken aback by this response.

"Dan, how about this? You represent hope, reassurance, strength, and courage to a patient. No small feat. Dan, you become a true "healer." That's a gift." She paused.

"That which comes from the heart goes to the heart."

Dan struggled for the right words.

"That which comes from the heart. I like that."

"Why Medicine Dan? What convinced you to go into such a demanding field?"

"When I was thirteen, my mother drove me over to the Cerebral Palsy Center and had me sign up to volunteer in their summer camp. But from day one, I felt right at home, helping each camper into their bathing suits, taking them in the water. Anything they asked of us, we did. Felt so useful, vital."

"So Medicine was a natural choice I guess from that experience."

"I guess, how about you, any experience or anyone inspire you?"

Linda shook her head. "Not a one and that's the problem. I kind of picked it as a fallback since I needed to make a living. Not for any love or attraction to it unfortunately. I envy you. I don't know if your mother intended it to happen, but she did a wonderful favor for you by volunteering you when she did."

"I believe you are right."

Placing her right hand on top of his, "Another thing, when we graduate from school, medical or even law, we are told we are 'doctors' or in my case, a 'lawyer'. But they are just titles really, the practical learning begins when we fly solo. That is when we learn how to manage…" Linda's voice began to trail off;

"You ok?"

Linda quickly gathered herself. "Only then you get blindsided by two very disturbed individuals!" she lamented, hunching up her shoulders, palms to the ceiling.

Linda sat back in the booth and offered sardonically, "as if your work wasn't difficult enough, my God without …" She just shook her head.

"These guys, all they wanted was to be recognized which I get. Hell, I wanted the kudos as well but when does such desperately yearning for something give way to crazy thinking, harmful thinking?"

"You just said it, *desperation*."

"All of these images flash through my mind." Dan stopped to take a deep breath while shaking his head in disbelief. "I'm still surprised people so unbalanced could get that far without anyone noticing. Vinny…even Alex Cole… Why Alex Cole was ever allowed to return so quickly to the program after he tried to hurt himself?" Ferrante shook her head in disbelief.

"Let me let you in on a little secret." Leaning forward, "health care professionals do not do a particularly thorough or honest job of policing themselves," Linda observed quietly.

"Besides, today we emphasize so very much what others think of us, our accomplishments or lack thereof…Cole and Orlander cases in point."

"One thing that puzzles me. In Orlander's pockets were two empty vials."

"Pavulon," offered quickly.

"One was Pavulon, the other methyl viologen, the herbicide 'paraquat'."

"Paraquat? That stuff is toxic as all get out." Dan appeared confused.

"When taken orally, it has a delayed effect but can cause death in up to 90% of cases. The lung effects are the worst I read."

"I saw one patient kill himself with it. Sought medical help after ingesting it, I guess had second thoughts. I knew from my research on it that this totally conversant human being, who now desperately wanting to live, would be dead in 24 hours." Dan just shook his head but all at once, blurted out. "Orlander killed the Chief presumably because he was on to him. Didn't you say you interviewed him as well and became suspicious?"

"Yes. What are you getting at Dan?"

"Maybe it sounds crazy but could be he planned on poisoning you? In fact, Vinny was the respiratory therapist involved in the care of that tragic overdose patient. He knew about its effects because he saw it happened." Dan looked shaken.

"Did he have access to your condo?"

"Double alarm system. No way."

"Did you do any grocery or beverage shopping recently?"

"Yesterday but what are you implying?" Linda looked perplexed, her head tilted to the right.

"This guy may have been whacked but was incredibly devious in carrying out his 'agenda' for lack of a better word. Were any of your groceries disturbed or look tampered with?"

"Come to think of it. The plastic casing for the Coke Zero six pack had a slight rip at the corner of it though I thought it occurred while carrying it to the car."

"Did you drink any of the individual bottles?" Dan asked quickly, his ardent concern now obvious on his troubled face.

" I was about to at dinner but thought the caffeine would keep me up since I was going to bed early for me... Oh my God," she exclaimed, tears welling up now in her almond shaped eyes.

"How about for dinner? Did you eat any of the groceries?"

"I brought sushi takeout home."

"Good. We need to get the stuff analyzed, especially the drinks."

"Of course."

Dan leaned back in his seat. "Brutal stuff, just fuckin' brutal." Just then, Dan's face contorted in a vain attempt to keep from crying.

"Then there is the matter of ... being alone. Just wanting to be loved by someone." Dan looked around, anywhere but straight ahead. *So embarrassing to admit he was lonely and needy.*

"Yeah, loneliness can suck. But you know what is even worse?"

"What?"

"Being with the wrong person and deep down, knowing it. Convincing yourself otherwise because the idea of having someone is better than not, we think. Not true though. Believe me I know. Same thing with career choices."

"I always felt this wall between Nikki and I, so hard to penetrate." Linda just nodded. *When you love someone, you don't run away when they are in trouble.*

Dan winced, his tired eyes groping for answers. Changing the painful subject, "the suffering I see does allow me the opportunity to feel and sometimes cry though. It's probably priceless." He paused. "Does that make sense?" He paused to formulate his next words. "My godmother believes its God's plan."

Linda listened intently and added, "Honestly, I don't believe there is a God, at least not a personal one anyway, Dan."

"Yeah, a lot of people don't. You are definitely not alone." He stared straight ahead. "You know, most of the patients I took care of this year taught me something; each life I touched was special." He looked directly into her eyes now. "You like poetry?"

Linda nodded. "Some. Not much." She tilted her head, her face registering confusion.

His voice lowered, "Read William Blake's *Auguries of Innocence.* It's about the small moments in one's life that are truly significant, magnificent, or painful. Each person's story and their struggles are gifts from God." He paused, his face reddened. "Jeez, listen to me citing poetry," his voice trailed off.

Linda shook her head. "I like that. There is so much to like about you…" her voice trailed off. Suddenly, she wished she could get to know him better but was embarrassed to display too obviously her blatant attraction to the young doctor. "Guess what I did yesterday?" she said, quickly changing the subject with her impish smile prompted by a random thought that suddenly danced into her head.

"What?" Dan inquired. He couldn't help noting how childlike, yet womanly, this lawyer could be.

"I decided to go online and check out what courses I would need to take to apply to veterinary school."

"You want to be a vet?"

"I think I might. I much prefer critters; they are always loving, nonjudgmental, no real agendas, and they don't feel the need to run marathons."

They both laughed and he said, "I get your point. Go for it! It's very competitive, you know. Harder than getting into med school, I think."

"I'm sure. But Dan, I am coming to realize that if I were to fast-forward my life to, let's say, one week before I die, what would I like to conclude from my days on this Earth? I realize that I, too, can feel something inside and help the world to be a better place…volunteering at the hospital helps…and believing in you." Linda blushed.

"You see, I have wrestled with poor self-esteem issues all of my adult life."

"Really. Why would that be? You are intelligent, perceptive and a very attractive woman." In his haste to boost her confidence, he had inadvertently stated how appealing he had found her. The timing couldn't have been worse, considering the trauma he had just survived. Too needy.

Linda covered his hand with both of her own.

"You're so sweet. The truth is I struggle with feelings of incompetence, inadequacy and at times, feeling unlovable. Mostly, I fear making mistakes and especially letting other people down. There you have it. The unvarnished truth."

"Being left by the proverbial side of the road by Nikki didn't do my feelings of self-worth any favors."

"Where is she now? Do you know?"

"Moved out of state I'm told. Starting over again. Surprisingly, I don't feel any anger toward her. I do believe she truly loved me. If the tables had been turned, I…"

Just then, a woman with the face of Ireland written all over it, approached Dan's table.

"Excuse me, aren't you Dr. Marchetti?" said another voice.

Dan looked up at the woman who had just spoken. "Yes, I am. We've met before?"

"Yes. I'm Rory Maguire's mother, Erin."

Dan recognized the name and her face immediately now, the vision of her son's mangled body quickly coming to mind. The last memories of Rory were tragic ones, his ravaged body lying in a near vegetative state while Dan lay prone on the ICU floor, courtesy of Rory's brother's flailing fist.

"I…I never got to apologize to you for what my son did to you, Doctor."

Dan held his hand up "Not necessary." He winced at the reminder of the incident; he'd rather not think about it. "It wasn't a total waste," he said to Mrs. Maguire. "I learned how much I loved a well-done steak after going a few weeks on Jell-O and yogurt."

Dan cringed at his thoughtless remark, as Erin Maguire shifted her feet uncomfortably. "I'm sorry. I was trying to be funny. You must really miss him."

"Yes, I do." She departed but not after she planted a gentle kiss on Dan's cheek.

Dante whispered just loud enough for Linda to hear, "To see the world in a grain of sand and heaven in a wild flower. Hold infinity in the palm of your hand and eternity in an hour…"

Epilogue

"Dan Marchetti, I mean 'Doctor' Dante Marchetti, in the flesh. What a treat, making a house call? I thought they were a thing of the past." Linda tried to act cool while totally floored by the unannounced visit.

Dan laughed nervously. "Thought I would bring you over the materials you will need, that is, if you are still amped up about going to veterinary school. GRE study materials," he stammered, embarrassed by his transparent cover story to see her again.

"Come on in. Yes, I'm serious like a heart attack. Bad joke huh considering what you do all day?"

"No, I like it. By the way, there was paraquat in one of the soda bottles you gave me to be analyzed." Linda just put her hand to her mouth.

"I owe you Dan." Dan just waved it off with his hand and entered her well-appointed condominium. The large collection of animal figurines and a menagerie of framed photos of animals taken on some African Safari Dan surmised, adorned one entire wall of her abode.

"You took these?"

"Yes I did. Two years ago in the Serengeti. You like?"

"They are amazing. Maybe someday…"

"You'll get there, no doubt at all Dan. Sit, can I get you something to drink? Some wine? Please excuse the mess but…" Linda blurted out, somewhat flummoxed by the sudden appearance of her surprise visitor. *Usually unflappable, her nervousness a sure sign of her real interest in this guy.*

"Some wine, some wine," croaked the multi-colored macaw in his cage in the corner of the living room. Dan giggled, "That's hysterical." Linda looked up from extracting the cork from the pricey *Magari* bottle in the kitchen, now peering underneath her white cabinets at Marchetti. A perfect choice as the name means 'If only' in Italian.

"Darlene convinced me that he would be a great companion …" her voice trailed off, thinking twice about sounding like such a *poverina* to a guy she felt so strongly about, maybe even falling in love with. Exactly the words she used to describe to her best friend, Debbie, the night before last.

"You look like you are having a little trouble with the cork, let me help." With that, Dan rose up and joined Ferrante in the kitchen; standing beside her, he began to deftly maneuver the latest sensation for wine drinkers, the 'Cork Dork'.

"Should have studied the directions," Linda commented, her cheeks now turning red with embarrassment.

"No problem."

"I think I am falling in love with him, Jill, I think I am falling in love with him, Jill," croaked Casey.

With that, Linda's face was now the color of a burgundy exposed to the light.

"Who is Jill?"

"A good friend. That stupid bird, he's a nut. Must have heard something on TV."

Dan just smiled and decided to respond.

"These birds, they have no filter, no filter at all." Just then, Dan took her face in his hands and kissed her gently.